Moving on, he turned down the street where Victoria lived. Her house was dark. A thought took him to her bedroom window. The sound of her breathing, low and even, told him that she, too, was asleep. He felt the prick of his fangs against his tongue as he listened to the steady beat of her heart, the thrum of blood moving through her veins. It aroused a hunger in him like none he had ever known before.

The affairs of the world no longer held any importance for him. His whole world had narrowed to only two things—the need for blood and the necessity of keeping this true identity a secret from mankind. Which reminded him that there was a vampire hunter in town . . .

GREAT BOOKS, GREAT SAVINGS!

When You Visit Our Website:
www.kensingtonbooks.com

You Can Save 30% Off The Retail Price
Of Any Book You Purchase!

- **All Your Favorite Kensington Authors**
- **New Releases & Timeless Classics**
- **Overnight Shipping Available**
- **All Major Credit Cards Accepted**

Visit Us Today To Start Saving!
www.kensingtonbooks.com

All Orders Are Subject To Availability.
Shipping and Handling Charges Apply.

DESIRE
AFTER
DARK

AMANDA ASHLEY

ZEBRA BOOKS
KENSINGTON PUBLISHING CORP.
www.kensingtonbooks.com

ZEBRA BOOKS are published by

Kensington Publishing Corp.
850 Third Avenue
New York, NY 10022

All Kensington titles, imprints, and distributed lines are available at special quantity discounts for bulk purchases for sales
promotion, premiums, fund-raising, educational, or institu-
tional use.

Special book excerpts or customized printings can also be
created to fit specific needs. For details, write or phone the
office of the Kensington Special Sales Manager: Attn. Special
Sales Department. Kensington Publishing Corp., 850 Third
Avenue, New York, NY 10022. Phone: 1-800-221-2647.

Zebra and the Z logo Reg. U.S. Pat. & TM Off.

ISBN 0-8217-7683-5

First Printing: February 2006
10 9 8 7 6 5 4 3 2 1

Printed in the United States of America

For the real Vicki,
because she didn't get the hero
the last time.

Chapter 1

It wasn't easy, destroying a vampire. Even when you found one tucked into his coffin at high noon, he didn't always go down without a fight.

Tom Duncan stared down at the body laid out in the satin-lined coffin. Edward Ramsey's body. Once, Ramsey had not only been Duncan's best friend, but he had also been the best vampire hunter in the business. Fearless. Relentless. But now Edward Ramsey was one of the Undead. And as such, he was filth, an aberration.

As such, he had to be destroyed.

Murmuring, "Sorry, old buddy," Duncan placed the sharp point of a hawthorn stake over Ramsey's heart.

He lifted the hammer, prepared to strike the blow that would destroy the monster his friend had become, when Ramsey's eyes flew open. Hissing, his eyes blazing like the fires of hell, Ramsey exploded out of the coffin, his fangs bared, his bony fingers curved like claws.

Duncan howled with outrage as Ramsey wrestled

him to the ground, screaming with terror as Ramsey's fangs pierced his skin, sinking deep into his throat . . . .

Tom Duncan bolted upright in bed, the sound of his own cries echoing in his ears.

Dammit! Sometimes it just didn't pay to go to bed at night.

Rising, he padded barefooted into the hotel room's tiny kitchen, switched on the light, and pulled a bottle of water from the fridge. After uncapping the container, he took a long drink.

Damn, he hated that dream.

Returning to the bedroom, he pulled on a pair of gray sweatpants and a black T-shirt, slipped his feet into a pair of sandals, grabbed a jacket, and left the hotel.

Outside, he took several deep breaths, chasing the last vestiges of the nightmare from his mind. Feeling somewhat better, he strolled down the street, enjoying the quiet of the night. It was peaceful, so peaceful. In spite of the chill in the air, he passed a number of people on the street and nodded at a group of teenagers gathered in front of a bowling alley. He waved to an elderly couple sitting side by side on a swing in their front yard. They looked to be in their late sixties or early seventies, and he wondered how long they had been married and how many kids and grandkids they had.

With a shake of his head, he rounded the corner. What the devil was the matter with him, wondering about such mundane things? Once he had decided to be a vampire hunter, he had put all thought of marriage and kids out of his mind. Few vampire hunters had families. A wife and children could too easily be taken hostage or used for revenge by an angry vampire. He had made his decision to remain single and he had never regretted it. He didn't know why he was thinking of it now. Maybe he was just getting maudlin in his old age.

He grunted softly. Thirty-five wasn't usually considered old, but in his line of work, it was ancient. But he didn't want to think of that, not now. He was taking a much-needed vacation and the last thing he wanted to think about was vampires. But he couldn't help it, not after the last hunt. Not after learning that the man he had once hunted with, a man he had considered to be his closest friend, was now a vampire himself.

Duncan shook his head. Out of all the people he knew, Edward Ramsey was the last person Duncan would ever have suspected of being a vampire. Of course, accepting the Dark Gift hadn't been Edward's choice. It had been thrust upon him by one of the Undead. But Edward had finally found a way to live with his new lifestyle and now he was married to another vampire and they seemed very happy together.

Duncan grunted softly. Maybe that was what had him feeling so lost, so alone. Ramsey had been his only close friend. Surprisingly, they were still friends but with vastly different lifestyles. It was still hard to believe that he had a friend who was a vampire. Several friends, if he counted Grigori and Marisa Chiavari and Ramsey's wife, Kelly. The five of them had survived an incredible battle against one of the most powerful vampires that had ever lived. After the battle, Duncan had shared his blood with Ramsey. Looking back, he still couldn't believe he had done such a thing, but how could he have refused Marisa? She had still been a mortal then and he had just finished congratulating her because, when all was said and done, it had been Marisa who destroyed Khira.

"You did it," he'd said, grinning. "By damn, you did it!"

"We all did it," Marisa had murmured. "And now I need you to do something."

"Sure, kid. I'll dispose of all this carrion, trust me." His gesture had included the twisted bodies.

"Not that," Marisa said.

"Just tell me what you want," Duncan had said. "And consider it done."

"Ramsey needs to feed."

Duncan had stared at her. *"What?"*

"He needs blood to replace what he's giving Kelly. He's not strong enough to hunt."

"You want me to . . ." Duncan had looked at Ramsey, then back at Marisa. *"This is carrying friendship a little too far, don't you think?"*

"No," Marisa had said, her voice calm.

"Why can't you do it?" Duncan had glanced at Grigori. *"You're used to it."*

"Yes," she had agreed calmly. *"I am. But Grigori needs to feed, too. You have no idea what it cost him to hold Khira at bay until I could . . . could . . ."*

"Okay, okay, you convinced me," Duncan had grumbled. He had picked up a vial of holy water as he moved toward the couch.

Ramsey had opened his eyes as Duncan approached. Edward's eyes had darkened with alarm and Grigori had tensed, ready to spring to Edward's defense if necessary.

"Relax," Duncan had said. *"A little insurance, that's all. Friend or no friend, you aren't turning me into a damned bloodsucker."*

Looking back, he remembered sitting down on the sofa and wondering if he was making the worst mistake of his life. In spite of all they had shared, in spite of the years they had hunted together, it made Duncan a little sad to realize there would always be that little part of himself that no longer trusted his best friend.

A few weeks after they had dispatched Khira, Edward and Kelly had approached him. Duncan had listened to their plan with wry amusement. Incredible as it seemed, Edward had decided to open a school to train vampire hunters and he wanted Duncan to be in charge. Duncan had given it some serious consideration but, in the end, he had turned the offer down. He didn't want to teach a bunch of green kids how to hunt vampires, he wanted to hunt them himself. He had helped Edward find another hunter, one who had been thinking about retiring from the hunt. John Randolph was a good man and Duncan knew he'd do a good job. Randolph had told Duncan that when he tired of the hunt, he would be welcome at the school.

With a sigh, Duncan went back to the hotel and packed his gear, then checked out of the hotel. Opening the trunk, he took a quick inventory of his kit: hammer and stakes, a mirror, a few strings of garlic, a half a dozen bottles of holy water, a saw and a crowbar, a flashlight, and a snub-nosed .38. He closed the trunk, then unlocked the door of his beat-up old Chevy Camaro and slid behind the wheel.

"Heigh-ho, Silver, away," he muttered with a wry grin. The bad guy, or *bad gal* in this case, had been defeated and destroyed. Good had once again triumphed over evil.

It was time to move on.

Chapter 2

Pear Blossom Creek was just a small Midwestern town, hardly more than a wide spot in the road. No one famous had ever been born there, or even spent the night. They had one fire truck and four policemen, two for the day shift and two who worked nights. Most of the residents were farmers, and everybody in town knew everybody else. It was a place where nothing out of the ordinary ever happened. Nothing, that is, until the stranger came to town.

He arrived on a dark and decidedly stormy Friday night in early-October. The storm was a real gully washer, the old-timers were quick to say, the likes of which hadn't been seen in more than a hundred years. A bad omen, some predicted.

Victoria Lynn Cavendish didn't put much stock in anything the over-seventy-five crowd had to say but she had to admit that in all her twenty-two years, she had never seen or heard a storm like the one pounding on the hammered tin roof of Ozzie's Diner. Nor had she ever seen a man quite like the one sitting at the booth in the far corner, she thought as she approached him.

He was dark, he was, and it wasn't just his clothing or his coloring. It was like *he* was a part of the darkness itself, a feeling that was reinforced when she looked into his eyes. Deep blue eyes that seemed as fathomless as Hellfire Hollow, as endless as eternity. His hair was long and straight and black as a raven's wing, the perfect complement to his straight black brows and long, thick eyelashes that would have looked feminine on any other man. But not on this man. His countenance was darkly beautiful and without blemish, in the way that Satan might appear beautiful as he carefully seduced you down the paths of sin. Looking at the stranger, she thought it might be worth the journey, perilous though it would undoubtedly be to both body and soul.

He remained unmoving under her perusal, a knowing smile curving his perfectly sculpted, sensuous lips.

With an effort, Vicki drew her gaze from his. "What can I get you, mister?" she asked, her pencil poised over her pad.

"What would you recommend?" His voice was low, almost mesmerizing, and strangely intimate, as if he knew her innermost secrets. As if he alone possessed the power to grant her every wish, fulfill her every desire.

She shook off her fanciful notions. He wasn't the devil. He was just a man. "The meat loaf's not bad." It wasn't really good, either, but she couldn't tell a customer that.

"Very well, I will have the meat loaf."

"You want mashed potatoes and gravy with that, or French fries?"

"Either one will be fine."

"And to drink?"

"Would you by chance have any red wine?"

Victoria stared at him. She had worked at the diner for almost four years and in all that time, no one had ever asked for wine, red or white or any other kind. "No, I'm sorry."

"No matter."

"So, what would you like to drink?"

His fathomless gaze rested on the hollow of her throat for a moment before he said, "Just coffee."

"Gotcha."

She could feel those wintry blue eyes on her back as she turned and walked away. Knowing he was watching her sent a shiver down her spine.

"That guy at booth six is . . ." Bobbie Sue Banks, one of the diner's other waitresses, shook her head. "I don't know who he is, but he's kind of spooky, don't you think?"

Spooky was just the right word. There was something just the slightest bit off about him. If she didn't know better, she might have thought he was some kind of alien. She remembered an old *Twilight Zone* episode in which the aliens had looked just like everyone else, except one hid a third eye under his hat and the other one hid the fact that he had more than two arms under his coat.

"Well, let's hope he's a big tipper." Vicki glanced over her shoulder at the booth in the back only to find that the mysterious stranger was no longer sitting there.

Frowning, she looked around the diner and then she saw him through the front window, walking down the rain-swept street with Sharlene Tilden, who had been sitting at table two. Sharlene was a cashier at Perry's Market. She came in for dinner every night at the same time. Sharlene was divorced and it was rumored that, since her divorce, she slept around, but that was none of Vicki's business. Anyway, she didn't believe it for a minute. Sharlene had never been the type to indulge in casual sex.

With a shrug, Vicki tore up the stranger's order and went to clear Sharlene's table.

The stranger was back again the following night, sitting at the same booth in the back corner of the diner, one arm flung over the back. Once again, he wore black jeans, a black T-shirt, and a long black coat. Once again, it was as if all the darkness in the world had gathered around him.

Taking a deep breath, Vicki pulled a pencil out of her pocket and went to take his order. "What'll it be?"

He lifted one shoulder and let it fall in a negligent shrug. "The special will be fine."

"Are you gonna stick around long enough to eat it tonight?" she asked, jotting his order down on her pad.

A wry grin lifted one corner of his mouth. "I might."

"Do you want coffee again?"

His gaze held hers for a long moment. Something flickered in the depths of his eyes, something primal and sensual that made her heart skip a beat and sent a rush of sexual awareness to every nerve and cell in her body.

"Sure." His voice was soft and low, and far too intimate.

With a nod, she dragged her gaze from his and went to turn in his order. Standing near the counter, she glanced around the room, noticing for the first time that Sharlene wasn't there. Vicki checked her watch, then shrugged. It was always possible that Sharlene had decided to eat dinner at home. She did that once in a while, though not often. She had told Vicki once that she wasn't crazy about cooking and she hated to eat alone.

Vicki noted the other regulars. There was old Bert Summers, who owned the local newspaper, and Judy West, who worked over at the Pear Blossom Creek Curl and Dye Beauty Salon. Judy was always trying out "a new look." Tonight, her shoulder-length hair was pink and teased into a beehive that made it look just like cotton candy. Jovial Rex Curtis, who owned and operated the car repair shop across town, was avidly reading the sports page; Maddy Malone, who was a teller at the Pear Blossom Creek Bank and Trust Company, had her nose buried in a book. Vicki had always thought Rex and Maddy were made for each other.

A pretty redhead sat alone at table five. Vicki didn't remember seeing the woman in the diner before, but that wasn't unusual. A lot of their customers were travelers passing through town who stopped in at the diner just long enough for a quick cup of coffee or a bite to eat.

Vicki turned away when Gus called her name to tell her that her order was up. As she carried the tray to the far side of the room, she noticed that the stranger was gone. Tonight, he had left a twenty dollar bill under his water glass.

Biting down on her lower lip, Vicki looked over her shoulder.

Somehow, she wasn't the least bit surprised to discover that the pretty redhead was gone, too.

Chapter 3

Victoria slept late Sunday morning. Looking at the clock through one bleary eye, she saw that she had missed early Mass. With a groan and a sense of guilt, she threw back the covers and swung her legs over the edge of the bed.

Yawning, she slid her feet into her slippers, pulled on her fuzzy pink robe, and padded into the kitchen. She turned the fire on under the old-fashioned coffeepot that had belonged to her grandmother, opened the curtains over the window, then went out front to pick up the paper, glad to see that it had finally stopped raining. She stood there a minute, enjoying the beauty of a crisp fall morning. After a good rain, everything always looked fresh, as if the earth had been reborn. The grass looked greener and brighter, the sky more blue. Even the birds seemed happier as they flitted from tree to tree singing their early-morning hymns to another new day.

Returning to the kitchen, Vicki poured herself a cup

of coffee, added a splash of milk and a spoonful of sugar, then sat down to read the paper.

She read the headline, blinked, and read it again.

BODIES OF TWO YOUNG WOMEN FOUND
NEAR HELLFIRE HOLLOW
FOUL PLAY SUSPECTED

Her coffee forgotten, she quickly read the story. The women had been found by a couple of teenage boys who had been out hunting squirrels in the dense woods near the Hollow. Both women had been fully clothed. There had been no signs of sexual molestation, and no outward signs of violence.

"Except for the two dead bodies," Vicki muttered.

The article went on to say that a large chunk of hair had been taken from the head of each woman, which led the police to believe the murders might be the work of a serial killer since they often collected trophies or souvenirs from their victims.

The story went on in detail about the reaction of the teenagers, both of whom Vicki saw in the diner from time to time. She gasped when she read the names of the deceased. Sharlene Tilden and Leslie Ann Lewis.

Vicki shook her head in disbelief. She had gone to school with Sharlene and her younger sister, Donna Jean. The Tilden family lived down the street from Vicki. If something so horrible could happen to Sharlene, it could happen to anyone. She frowned as she read the next paragraph, which stated that both bodies had been completely drained of blood.

A cold shiver ran down Vicki's spine. The article stated that as far as the police could ascertain, both

Sharlene and the other woman had last been seen at Ozzie's Diner.

The article went on to say that Lewis's next of kin had been notified and then, almost as an afterthought, mentioned that both of the deceased women had been redheads.

Vicki lifted a hand to her own red hair. Surely the fact that both of the victims had been redheads was mere coincidence.

If the story hadn't been so lurid, if it hadn't been reported by the police, she might have suspected it was just another one of the high school pranks that were so prevalent in Pear Blossom Creek in the weeks before Halloween. But the body found near Hellfire Hollow last year had been made out of newspaper, a couple rolls of duct tape, and a wig one of the kids had stolen from the Curl and Dye.

Vicki sat back in her chair. This was no high school prank. Two women had been murdered in two days. What on earth was going on?

Last seen at Ozzie's Diner, the paper said. She could have added that the last time she had seen the two women, they had been in the company of a tall, dark man who was a stranger in town.

She dressed hurriedly after a quick breakfast and went to Mass, where she lit a candle for Sharlene's soul and then, after a moment's reflection, she lit a candle for the other woman who had been killed.

Vicki stayed close to home the rest of the day. Feeling like she needed to connect with her family, she called her sister. Karen lived in St. Louis with her husband, Richard, and their four kids. Richard was an accountant for an insurance company. Most of their conversation was about Karen's kids and how fast they were growing. Richie was six, Lucy was five, Carolyn was three and a half, and the baby, Lori, was already five months old.

After about twenty minutes, Karen said, "Listen, I've got to go, the baby's crying. But you've got to come for a visit real soon, okay? Here's Mom."

Vicki spent the next hour chatting with her mother. As usual, most of the conversation was about Vicki's lack of a prospective husband.

"If you'd get out of that small town, maybe you'd find someone," Mona said.

Thinking of the recent murders, Vicki wondered if that wasn't a good idea, especially since the murderer seemed to have a fondness for redheads.

"I've got to go, Mom."

"You might give that nice Arnie Hall another chance."

"Mom, we've been through all that before."

"All right, dear. Tell Gus hello for me."

"I will. Talk to you soon, Mom. I love you."

"I love you, too, dear. Bye now."

Vicki was in the midst of doing her laundry later that afternoon when Bobbie Sue called.

"Hey, Vicki, any chance you could work for me tomorrow night? Steve's fixin' to take me to the Toby Keith concert over in Pine Grove."

"I don't know, Bobbie Sue . . ."

"Sakes alive, Vicki, it's *Toby Keith*! How often does he come here? How often does *anyone* come here? Please, Vicki?"

"But it's my night off. I was thinking of going to a movie."

"If you do this for me, I'll be your best friend."

Vickie had to laugh at that. It was something they

had said since they were children whenever they wanted something really bad. "You're already my best friend."

"Vicki Cavendish, I'm down on my knees here."

Vicki sighed. She was off on Monday nights, but how could she refuse? Bobbie Sue was obsessed with Toby Keith. She had all his CDs and she played them constantly. "Oh, all right, but you owe me big time."

"Anything," Bobbie Sue promised. "All you have to do is ask."

The murders were all anyone talked about on Monday morning. At the bank, at the post office, when she went to drop off her clothes at the cleaners, it was the main topic of conversation. The police were asking the townspeople to come forward if they had seen or heard anything suspicious, no matter how insignificant it might seem, and to let them know if they had seen any strangers loitering around town.

She had seen a stranger, Vicki thought as she drove to work later that evening, although she wasn't sure that sitting in Ozzie's Diner could be construed as loitering.

She felt a shiver of unease when that same stranger entered the diner a couple of hours later and again sat at the booth in the far corner. She hesitated before moving toward him, wondering if he had killed Sharlene and the Lewis woman. She glanced around the diner, noting that there were no single women, redheaded or otherwise, sitting at any of the tables tonight.

He smiled as she approached the booth. "Good evening."

He had a very sexy smile.

"Is there any point in my taking your order?" she asked, pulling her pad from the pocket of her apron.

His smile widened, revealing even white teeth that looked like they belonged in a toothpaste commercial. "Perhaps not."

"Why do you come in here every night?" she asked, slipping her pad back into her apron pocket. "You never eat anything."

His gaze moved over her in a way that made her blush from the top of her head to the soles of her feet. "Perhaps it is your company that draws me."

She crossed her arms over her breasts, her expression skeptical. It didn't happen often, but every now and then a stranger tried to pick her up. "Uh-huh."

"You do not believe me?"

"Listen, we're really busy tonight. Do you want anything or not?"

His gaze moved over her again, lingering on the hollow of her throat. It made her uncomfortable in a way she couldn't quite comprehend. If he told her she looked good enough to eat, she was going to slug him. "Well?"

He glanced quickly around the room, then shook his head. "No, I want nothing but to spend some time with you."

"Excuse me, but I'm working here."

She was about to turn away when his voice, deliciously soft and sinfully seductive, stayed her.

"Come out with me, Victoria. I will not hurt you, I promise."

She stared at him, thinking what an odd thing that was for a man to say to a woman. "I can't, sorry."

"Perhaps you will change your mind."

The thought of going out with him made her mouth go dry. "I don't think so."

She moved away from the table as quickly as she could without running. When she risked a glance at the booth a short time later, he was gone. Again, he had left her a generous tip.

She was too busy the rest of the night to spend much time thinking about the stranger, but later that night, when she was at home soaking in a hot bubble bath, his image rose up in her mind—dark blue eyes, long black hair, a fine blade of a nose, a strong jaw, sensual lips, cheekbones that were high and prominent, skin that looked a trifle pale. But then, maybe he didn't spend much time in the sun. Lots of people avoided it these days, what with all the worry about the dangers of too much sun and skin cancer.

Still later, while lying in bed watching a late movie, she found herself thinking of the stranger again, wondering if he would show up at the diner tomorrow night, wondering what would happen if she went out with him. She quickly put that idea right out of her mind. She had seen two women leave the diner with him, two redheaded women, and now they were both dead, their bodies dumped out near the Hollow, both drained of blood. There was no proof that the stranger had killed them. But then, there was no proof that he hadn't.

Still, she spent a few moments thinking how good it would make her feel if she could call her mother and her sister and tell them that she'd had a date with a really hot-looking guy. But she wasn't brave enough, or foolish enough, to go out with a total stranger, no matter how hunky he was, not when that stranger had been seen with two women who had been murdered.

Switching off the TV, she settled down under the covers. She should have gone to the police when she first read about the murders, she thought with a twinge of guilt. Of course, someone else might have already reported that there was a stranger in town. But that didn't excuse her. What if the stranger *was* the killer? How would she feel if he killed again because she hadn't gone to the police, because she had been reluctant to get involved? Would she have gone to the police sooner if the stranger weren't so darkly handsome and didn't have such a deep, sexy voice?

Not liking the answer than came to mind, she resolved to call the police first thing in the morning.

Tuesday night, Officers Ned Williams and Arnie Hall sat at table three, each working on his third cup of coffee. Vicki had called the police department earlier that day and told Chief Neil Ryan about the stranger who had been coming into the diner at about the same time each evening, and that she had seen him with both of the victims. Ryan had told her that he would send Ned and Arnie over to the diner later that night. And now they were here.

"I thought you said he came in every night," Ned Williams said, looking around. "I don't see him."

Vicki shrugged. "Well, he was **here Friday, Saturday**, and Monday nights about this time." **The diner w**as closed on Sundays. "Maybe he was just passing through."

Arnie Hall pulled a small black notebook from his shirt pocket and scribbled a few lines. He was a nice-looking guy, with curly blond hair and blue eyes and a deep cleft in his chin.

"Why didn't you call us sooner?" Ned asked.

Vicki shrugged. "I don't know. I guess I should have, but . . ."

"It doesn't matter," Arnie said. "Did you see him talk to Sharlene or the Lewis woman?"

"No, but I saw him leave with Sharlene."

"Did he make any overtures toward them at all?" Ned asked.

Vicki shook her head. "I don't think so, at least none that I'm aware of."

"Did he act like he knew them?" Arnie asked.

She shook her head again, thinking that she wasn't being much help. But then, she didn't really know anything about the man.

Arnie drummed his fingers on the table. "So, what makes you think this guy might have killed Sharlene and the Lewis woman?"

"I . . ." She lifted one hand and let it fall. "I never said that. I read in the paper that the police were asking for help and, well, I saw him leave with both of them and, well, I don't know, I thought he might have some information that would be useful."

"You did the right thing in calling us," Arnie said. He drained his coffee cup and reached for his hat. "If you see him again, let us know."

"I will. Are you two going to Sharlene's funeral? It's tomorrow morning at eleven."

Arnie nodded. "We'll be there."

"Yeah," Ned said. "You never know who might turn up."

"What do you mean?" Vicki asked.

"Killers have been known to show up at these things," Arnie explained.

"You're kidding!"

Ned shrugged. "It happens."

"Why would he take a chance like that?" Vickie asked.

"Who knows? To thumb his nose at the cops? To hear what people are saying? Like I said, who knows what goes through a killer's mind." He dropped a couple of dollars on the table, then rose. "Take it easy, girl."

"As always," Vicki replied.

"Give my best to your mom when you talk to her again," Arnie said.

"I will."

She watched Ned and Arnie leave the diner. They were both nice guys. She had dated Arnie a couple of times. He was a wonderful man and she had tried hard to fall in love with him but there just hadn't been any spark between them, at least on her part. Now, they were just good friends. Ned was married and the father of twin boys.

Scooping the greenbacks from the table, Vicki dropped them into her pocket, then carried the cups into the kitchen.

"You should give Arnie another chance," Gus said, winking at her.

"You sound just like my mother, you old goat," Vicki replied with an affectionate grin.

"Hey, since your papa passed on and your mama moved away, you are my business."

"I know, I know." Gus Jacobson had been her father's best friend. Since her father had passed away and her mother had gone to St. Louis to help Karen with the kids, Gus had adopted Vicki. Not that she minded. It was nice to know that, even though she was all grown up, she still had someone in town to look after her.

"Tell Bobbie Sue her order's up, will ya?" Gus asked.

"Sure."

Leaving the kitchen, Vicki came to an abrupt halt when she saw that the stranger had arrived and was sitting in his usual place in the back booth. Strange, how that particular booth was always empty when he arrived.

As though drawn by an invisible cord, Victoria walked toward him. As usual, he was all in black from the top of his head to the boots on his feet. Not for the first time, she noted how well the color suited him.

He lifted one dark brow as she neared his table. "The police were here." It wasn't a question, but a statement of fact.

"Yes." She wondered how he knew Ned and Arnie had been there. Had he been lurking outside in the shadows, peeking in the window?

"Did you call them?"

She hesitated a moment before replying. "Yes."

"Why?"

She had no intention of telling him what she suspected. Indeed, she was trying to come up with a good lie when his gaze locked with hers and she found herself telling him the truth.

"Because I saw you leave here with Sharlene and that other woman, and now they're both dead."

"Ah. And you think I killed them?"

"Did you?" It was a foolish question. As soon as the words were out of her mouth, she wanted to call them back. What if he said yes? What would she do then? What would he do?

She stared at him. Was he capable of committing such a heinous crime not once, but twice? Would he keep coming to the diner if he had? Would he be at the funeral?

His eyes narrowed, his gaze boring deep into hers. "You would not believe me if I said no, would you?"

"I . . . I don't know."

With a nod, he slid gracefully from the booth. It was

the first time she had stood next to him. Only now did she realize just how tall and broad he was. Power emanated from him, making the hair raise along her arms and her nape, sending a prickle of fear down her spine.

His gaze moved over her one last time and then he left the diner without a word.

Vicki stared after him, wondering who and what he was and if she would ever feel safe again.

Chapter 4

Tom Duncan picked up the three-day-old newspaper, his eyes narrowing as he perused the headlines:

BODIES OF TWO YOUNG WOMEN FOUND
POLICE FEAR SERIAL KILLER ON THE LOOSE
IN PEAR BLOSSOM CREEK

He quickly read the account, noting that there had been no sign of rape or physical abuse, no signs of a struggle. One of the women had been a resident of Pear Blossom Creek, the other a transient. Both had been single, both had been redheads, both in their early twenties. According to the newspaper account, the police suspected a serial killer, but Duncan knew better. It wasn't the work of a serial killer, but a vampire. And he had a sneaking suspicion he knew just which of the Undead was responsible.

After checking the time, he picked up the phone next to his bed and put in a call to Edward Ramsey.

Ramsey answered on the second ring. "Yeah?"

"Hey, Edward, it's me."

"Duncan! It's good to hear from you. How is everything?"

"Same as always. Listen, have you heard anything about Falco lately?"

"You mean Dimitri Falco, slayer of innocent women and children?"

"Yeah."

"He was one of Kristov's, as I recall? Hunted only redheads, right? Always took a lock of their hair for a souvenir."

"That's him."

"I haven't heard a word about him since he gave us the slip four years ago."

Duncan grunted softly. He and Ramsey had spent six months hunting for Dimitri Falco. They had scoured Russia, but the wily vampire had managed to stay one jump ahead of them the whole time, and then it seemed like he had vanished from the face of the earth.

"Wait a minute," Ramsey said. "Didn't Adams claim he destroyed Falco in South America last year?"

"Well, if he did, there's another vampire out there following the same M.O., and he's turned up in a little nowhere town in the Midwest called Pear Blossom Creek."

"Are you there now?"

"No, but I'm headed in that direction." Duncan paused. "So, how's life, or death, treating you these days?"

"It gets easier every night."

Duncan remembered talking to Ramsey after they had destroyed Khira. He had asked Edward what he missed most now that he was a vampire. Ramsey had replied that he missed his humanity, the warmth of the sun on his face, the ability to have a son to carry on the

Ramsey name. He had said the worst of it was the aloneness he felt sometimes, the sense of being separated from the rest of the world. And then he had smiled. It wasn't all bad, Ramsey had said. His senses were sharper, he didn't have to worry about catching the flu or growing old, he could read minds and control thoughts, move from one place to another almost before he knew he wanted to.

Duncan thought of that now as he asked, "Do you ever miss the hunt?"

"All the time."

"How's Randolph working out?"

"He's doing all right. You would have done better. Oh, Kelly says hi."

Duncan grinned. "Hi to Kelly. What do you hear from Marisa and Grigori?"

"Not much. Last I heard, they were in New York. Listen, Tom, call me if you need me."

"I will. So long."

Hanging up the phone, Duncan packed his gear and checked out of the hotel.

Twenty minutes later, he was on the highway headed for Pear Blossom Creek.

Chapter 5

Vicki had never liked funerals and counted herself blessed that she hadn't had to attend many of them. The last one had been three years ago for her great-grandmother. It hadn't really been a sad occasion. Great-grandmother Althea Neff had enjoyed good health all her life, lived to be eighty-nine years old, and died peacefully in her sleep. But this . . . Vicki glanced at Sharlene's family. Sharlene's younger sister, Donna Jean, sat between her mother and father trying not to cry. Sharlene's fiancé, Ron Garcia, sat beside Mrs. Tilden.

The chapel was full, the pews crowded with Sharlene's friends from high school and just about everyone else in town. Dozens of bouquets and wreaths made bright splashes of color in the front of the church. Sunlight filtered through a stained-glass window, washing over the closed casket in streams of variegated colors.

Drawing her gaze from the coffin, Vicki glanced discreetly around the chapel. Was the killer here? She saw Ned and Arnie across the aisle, looking somehow out of place in dark suits instead of their uniforms. Gus was there, along with Bobbie Sue and the other wait-resses from the diner. She saw Maddy Malone and Rex Curtis and Judy West. Bert Summers was standing in the back. He was writing something in a small note-book and she wondered if he was there as a friend of the family or in his professional capacity as owner and reporter of the newspaper.

Vicki turned her attention to the front again as the organ stopped playing and the minister stepped up to the pulpit. After offering a prayer, he read the eulogy, and then he offered words of comfort and assurance to Sharlene's family and friends.

Vicki was glad when the service was over. Stepping out of the church into the sunshine, she thought how good it was to be alive on such a glorious day and then felt a rush of guilt for thinking such a thing when Shar-lene was gone and her family was grieving.

Sobering, Vicki got into her car and followed the procession to the cemetery.

The atmosphere in the diner was subdued that night. Most of Ozzie's regular customers had been at the fu-neral that morning. She overheard people talking about the service, expressing sorrow for Sharlene's family, speculating on who the murderer might be, wondering if, and when, he might strike again and if, heaven for-bid, it could be someone they knew.

Vicki looked around the diner, then shook her head. She couldn't believe that any of the people she knew, people she had grown up with, could have committed such a horrendous crime not once, but twice.

A little voice in the back of her head reminded her that there was a man in town whom she didn't know anything about, a man who had been seen with both of the murdered women.

She shook the thought from her mind and then, for the third time in thirty minutes, she looked at the clock and the empty booth in the back. It was obvious that he wasn't coming in tonight. She should have been relieved, so why wasn't she?

"Vicki? Hey, Vicki!" Bobbie Sue shook her arm. "Gus has been calling you for the last five minutes. Your order for table two is up."

"Oh, thanks."

Gus frowned at her when she picked up the tray. "You okay?" he asked. "You seem a little distracted tonight."

"Stop worrying, I'm fine."

"Funeral got you down, didn't it? Well, that's understandable. She was a nice girl."

Vicki nodded, but didn't say anything. No need to tell Gus it wasn't Sharlene she was thinking about, but the man who might have killed her.

When another hour passed with no sign of the stranger, she put him out of her mind. No doubt he'd been just passing through, like everyone else. And it was probably just a coincidence that he had left the diner with Sharlene and the other woman.

When her shift was over, she grabbed her jacket and her handbag, gave Gus a quick hug good night, and went out the back door, only then remembering that she had left her car at home and walked to work that evening.

Slinging her handbag over her shoulder, she pulled the rubber band from her ponytail and shook out her hair, then crossed the parking lot toward the sidewalk.

Her steps slowed when she reached the corner. The

night seemed quieter than usual, ominous, somehow. A slight breeze rattled through the leaves in the trees along the sidewalk.

Resisting the urge to glance over her shoulder, she quickened her steps, gasping when a dark shape materialized out of the shadows to her right and a deep voice said,

"Good evening, Victoria Cavendish."

She pressed a hand to her pounding heart. "Lord, you scared me! What are you doing lurking out here in the bushes at this time of night?"

"Waiting for you, of course."

His words pleased her, but only for a moment. Pleasure quickly turned to fright when she remembered that, as far as she knew, this stranger had been the last man to see Sharlene and the Lewis woman alive.

She came to an abrupt halt under a streetlight, grateful for the illumination, weak as it was. "Why . . . why were you waiting for . . . for me?"

"I thought I would walk you home. There is a killer on the loose and in spite of what you think, it is not me."

"How did you know I walked to work?"

He shrugged. "Does it matter?"

"Yes. I think it does." She glanced up and down the sidewalk, dismayed to see that the streets were deserted. Would anyone hear her if she screamed? She did a quick mental search of her handbag, wondering if there was anything in there that she could use as a weapon.

He shoved his hands into his pants pockets. "I was watching your house."

"Watching? My house?"

He nodded.

"Why?"

Taking his hand out of his pocket, he wrapped a lock of her hair around his forefinger. "Because you have red hair."

She stared up at him, puzzled, and then felt a sliver of ice slide down her spine. Sharlene had had red hair. So had the other woman who had been killed.

She swallowed past the lump in her throat. "You don't think he'll . . . ?"

"That is exactly what I think."

Feeling suddenly light-headed, she swayed on her feet. "It is a serial killer, then, isn't it?" She had overheard Ned and Arnie discussing the possibility earlier that night.

"In a manner of speaking."

"You sound like you know him."

"Indeed."

"You do know him? Why haven't you told someone? You've got to go to the police, right away, tonight."

"I doubt if they would believe me."

"Why not?"

He took her arm, gently urging her along. "Let us not talk about that now."

"But . . . It's important."

"The police will never catch him."

"You sound very sure of that."

He nodded. "Surer than you can imagine." His hand slid down her arm, his fingers entwining with hers. His skin was cool, yet at the touch of his hand, frissons of sexual awareness sizzled up her arm.

Nothing like that had ever happened to her before. Feeling suddenly breathless, she looked up at him. Had she imagined that unexpected jolt of sensual heat, or had he felt it, too?

He was watching her in return, his eyes dark and hot.

It took her a moment to realize they had stopped walking, and another moment to realize that he was going to kiss her. Before she could decide whether she wanted him to or not, his mouth was on hers. His skin might have been cool, but there was nothing cool about his kiss! At the first touch of his lips on hers, heat engulfed her, a conflagration that threatened to consume her. His arms imprisoned her, drawing her body up against his. She shivered as she felt his hand slide up the back of her neck to delve into her hair.

He deepened the kiss, his tongue plundering her mouth, his arms tightening around her until she could scarcely move, scarcely breathe. Her heart was beating rapidly, pounding in her ears so loudly she wondered that he didn't hear it, too.

Or perhaps he did. He drew back, his gaze lingering on the pulse beating in the hollow of her throat. He placed his forefinger there, ever so lightly, and her heart beat even faster.

He lowered his head to her neck and took a deep breath, giving her the oddest impression that he was inhaling the scent of her blood.

The thought, though far-fetched, made her uncomfortable and she stepped away from him. "I think we'd better go."

"Yes," he said quietly. "I think that would be wise."

He took her by the hand and they resumed walking. She had to hurry to keep up with him, making her wonder if he was suddenly anxious to get her home and be rid of her.

They reached her house a short time later. It was a large two-story clapboard house with a tall chimney and a wraparound porch. During the spring and summer, roses and daisies grew in wild profusion behind the white picket fence. An enormous pepper tree shaded one side of the front yard.

Vicki opened the gate and he followed her up the red brick path to the porch. She opened the front door, then turned to face him.

"Thank you for walking me home," she said.

He nodded. "Keep your doors locked, Victoria Cavendish."

She frowned. She never locked her front door, or the back one either, for that matter.

"Humor me in this," he said. "At least for a time."

"On one condition," she said.

He lifted one dark brow in question. It reminded her of a bat taking flight.

"Tell me your name."

"Ah." What might have passed for an amused smile tugged at his lips.

"You do have a name, don't you?"

"Of course. Even the devil has a name."

The tone of his voice sent a shiver of unease down her spine. "And do you know it?" she asked hoarsely. "The devil's name?"

His expression turned hard and cold. "I do, indeed. It is a name you do not wish to know." He made a graceful, old-fashioned bow. "But my name is Antonio Battista."

She took a step backward, one hand clutching the edge of the door. "Good night, Mr. Battista."

"Buona notte."

Vicki glanced over her shoulder. The inside of the house was dark and quiet. She had entered that same dark house after work countless times before. Why was she afraid now?

"Would you do me a favor?" she asked.

"If I can."

"Would you wait here while I check the house?"

He nodded.

Taking a step back, she motioned him inside.

He glanced at the threshold that separated them. "Are you inviting me in?"

"Yes, of course. Come on."

With a nod, he crossed the threshold and stepped into the small entryway. "Do you often invite strangers into your home?"

"No. I'll just be a minute." Hurrying through the house, she turned on all the lights, then returned to the front door.

"Thank you." She grinned self-consciously. "I'm not usually such a 'fraidy cat, but the murders . . ."

"You are right to be cautious," he replied. "Remember what I said. Lock your doors. And bid no stranger to enter."

He was a stranger. Even as the thought crossed her mind, he had descended the stairs and disappeared into the night.

Vicki stared into the darkness. How could he have vanished so quickly? And how could he walk on the brick pathway without making a sound?

She closed the door and turned the lock, then hurried into the kitchen to lock the back door as well. Filled with a sudden anxiety, she moved through the house again, closing and locking all the windows and drawing the curtains, both upstairs and down.

She paused in the middle of her room, one hand pressed to her heart. What was she doing? Why had she let him frighten her like that? She had lived in Pear Blossom Creek her whole life and never worried about locking her doors.

But there had never been a murder before, either.

The thought sobered her. She would be foolish indeed not to take precautions, at least until the murderer was caught.

And what if Antonio Battista is the murderer?

The words moved through her mind. She didn't know a thing about him, yet she had let him walk her home. Of course, there was no harm in that. He already knew where she lived. Hadn't he said he had been watching her house? Still, he was a stranger. It had no doubt been the height of stupidity to let him into the house. She pressed a hand to her breast. She wouldn't make that mistake again! Although if he had intended to do her harm, he had just passed up the perfect opportunity.

Shaking off her worrisome thoughts, she went into the kitchen in search of her favorite comfort food. Something deep and dark and rich. It took her a moment to decide between a bowl of chocolate ice cream or a candy bar. Thinking of Sharlene, she decided life was too short not to indulge herself once in a while and with that in mind, she ate a big bowl of ice cream topped with hot fudge and whipped cream, with a Milky Way on the side, and went up to bed.

Later, when she was snuggled under the covers in the big old four-poster bed that had belonged to her grandmother, it was hard to believe that there was anything to be afraid of. She had always felt safe within these walls. Sometimes she thought she could feel her grandmother's spirit nearby, watching out for her.

With that comforting thought in mind, Vicki closed her eyes and drifted off to sleep, and in sleeping, began to dream.

She was walking through a dark wood. A brilliant silver moon hung low in the heavens, yet it did not penetrate the darkness beneath the trees. A voice warned her not to enter the woods but something deep within her compelled her to continue, and so she moved deeper and deeper into the forest. Deeper and deeper into the darkness. And then, far ahead, she saw a faint light that grew brighter as she moved toward it. As she drew closer, she saw that the light came from a single candle burning in the window of a small wooden cottage. The door opened of its own volition. She hesitated at the threshold, knowing that if she crossed it her life would be forever changed. And then she saw Battista. He was standing in front of an enormous fireplace. The flames rose behind him, casting eerie red and orange shadows on the walls and the floor, touching his long black hair with streaks of crimson. He held a goblet made of hammered gold in his hands. He offered it to her, but she backed away, afraid to look at the contents, afraid to look at him. Frightened now, she turned to leave, but the door was no longer open. She glanced over her shoulder, looking for another way out. But there was none. She looked at Battista, an appeal for help rising in her throat, but one look at his face told her he would not help her. Eyes burning like fire, he tossed the goblet aside and moved toward her. His long black duster flared behind him like some ominous shadow. She tried to run, but her legs refused to move. And then he was there, bending over her, his fangs bared. She cried out in fear as he lowered his head toward her neck, screamed in terror when she felt the sharp sting of his fangs at her throat . . .

Battista prowled the shadows around Victoria's house, his preternatural senses probing the night. He had no proof that Dimitri Falco was in the area, or even in the country, but there was obviously a vampire hunting in the area and some deep, preternatural instinct told him that it was either Falco or another like him.

There were two types of vampires in the world: those who had shed all of their humanity and those who clung to an illusion of their old life. The first type no longer considered themselves to be a part of the human race. Seeing themselves as superior beings, they preyed on humans the way any predator preyed on the weak and the helpless, killing without mercy. The second type held on to the illusion of their old life, their old ways. They took blood because there was no life without it, because the pain of abstaining was beyond bearing.

Dimitri Falco was the first type. Strong, powerful, arrogant. He had been made by Khira, who had been made by Alexi Kristov, an ancient vampire who had been one of the most powerful of their kind. Battista could hardly credit the fact that Khira had been destroyed. She had been defeated, not by another vampire, not by a hunter, but by a mortal woman. It was something worth remembering and only proved that no matter how old or how strong a vampire might be, they were all vulnerable. To the amusement of the Undead around the world, Edward Ramsey had been turned the night Khira was destroyed. The hunter had become the hunted.

Battista was about to find a place to settle down for the night when he heard Victoria scream.

He was in the house and at her bedside almost before the thought crossed his mind.

Vicki woke with the sound of her own cries ringing in her ears, screamed again as a dark shape materialized out of the shadows in a corner of her room.

"Do not be afraid," admonished a deep voice. "It is only me."

Hoping she was still dreaming, Vicki bolted upright, the blankets clutched to her chest. "What are you doing in my bedroom?"

"I heard you scream."

She peered into the darkness. "You heard me? How?"

"I was outside."

Her panic ratcheted up a notch. "What were you doing outside my house at this time of night?" With a hand that trembled, she turned on the lamp on her bedside table.

"Perhaps I was just passing by."

"I don't believe you."

He shrugged, as if it didn't matter whether she believed him or not.

"I think you'd better leave."

"You screamed. What was it that frightened you? Did you see someone?"

She drew the covers up to her chin. "I had a bad dream, that's all." *And you were in it,* she thought, but didn't say so out loud.

He cocked his head to one side, his dark gaze intent upon her face, almost as if he was trying to read her mind. Fortunately, that was impossible.

"It must have been rather a frightening nightmare," he remarked. "To have you screaming so."

He looked like the stuff of nightmares, she thought, with his stark good looks and dark penetrating gaze. Add to that the fact that he wore a black shirt and pants beneath a long black duster and he was dressed for the part as well.

Her heart skipped a beat as he took a step toward the bed. She glanced wildly at the door, but Battista blocked that escape. Her gaze darted to the window, but that way out held dangers of its own, since her bedroom was on the second floor.

"Victoria, do not be afraid. I mean you no harm."

She wanted to believe him, but something in his tone, the heated look in his eyes, warned her that she would be wise to be afraid, though she had no idea what good that would do her. She had no defense against him. He was bigger than she was and certainly stronger.

She shook her head as he drew closer, her hand reaching for the crucifix she wore on a silver chain. Battista came to an abrupt halt as a ray of moonlight filtered through the window, its light seeming to illuminate the cross at her throat until it burned with a silver fire all its own.

"I did not mean to frighten you," he said, his gaze locked on the crucifix.

"You didn't." It was a lie, and a bold one.

He inclined his head. "May your faith keep you safe this night," he murmured.

And then, to her surprise, he turned and vanished out the window.

Chapter 6

In the morning, Vicki was certain she had imagined it all, or that it had been just another dream. Surely she had only imagined that Antonio Battista had been lurking in the shadowy corner of her bedroom last night. And only in a dream could he simply vanish out the window like Count Dracula!

Thinking of Dracula reminded her of her nightmare and she lifted a hand to her throat, then laughed self-consciously. Did she really expect to find two little puncture wounds in the side of her neck?

A wave of sweet relief left her feeling weak when her exploring fingers found nothing out of the ordinary. She must be losing her mind, she thought, dreaming of vampires, imagining Antonio in her room in the middle of the night, expecting to find bites in her neck.

The nightmare troubled her all that day, though she wasn't sure why. She had never believed in visions, didn't believe that dreams could foretell the future, didn't believe in paranormal creatures lurking in the night, so why did this particular dream continue to haunt her?

She left for work a little before six. In spite of the fact that it was a lovely, warm evening, she decided not to walk.

She was getting into the car when she felt a sudden coldness sweep over her. Pausing, she glanced around. There was no wind, no hint of a breeze, but the coldness persisted. It took her a moment to realize that the cold wasn't caused by anything physical; it was more like a sense of evil surrounding her, a sense of impending doom.

Like the feeling she'd had the first time she had seen Antonio Battista.

With a shiver, she got into the car and quickly closed and locked the door.

She felt better when she reached the diner. She nodded at Bobbie Sue, then went into the back room. She stashed her handbag in her locker, pulled on a clean apron, and grabbed a fresh pad and a pencil.

She stopped in the kitchen to say hello to Gus, then went out to start her shift.

The diner was busier than usual for a Thursday night, though the atmosphere was still somewhat subdued. Ned and Arnie sat at one of the tables by the front door where they could keep an eye on everyone who came into the diner. Ned was reading the sports pages, Arnie was working the crossword puzzle. Maddy Malone was sharing a table with Rex and judging from the looks on their faces, there was more going on than just dinner. Vicki grinned inwardly. It was about time. The two had been dancing around each other for over a year. In addition to the regulars, there were several people she hadn't seen at Ozzie's before.

"Hey, Vicki."

Hearing Ned's voice, she went to see what he wanted.

"Has that guy been in here again?" he asked.

She hesitated, then nodded. "Yes, he came in after you left on Tuesday night. He knew you'd been here."

Ned grunted softly. "Did he say anything that struck you as suspicious?"

"No."

"I don't suppose he told you where he's staying?" Arnie asked. "We've checked the hotel and he's not staying there, or anywhere else in town as far as we can tell."

"I don't know. He didn't say."

"You be careful, Vicki," Ned said, his voice and expression sober. "There was another killing last night."

A coldness swept through Vicki. She had been with Antonio last night. Did that mean he was innocent? Or that he had walked her home and then committed another murder? "Who was it?"

"No one from around here," Arnie said. "According to her driver's license, she lived in Nashville. We're trying to locate her next of kin. You make sure and have Gus walk you out to your car until we catch this guy."

"Was she . . . ?" She couldn't bring herself to ask if she had been drained of blood.

"Yeah, same M.O." Arnie's gaze moved over her. "Be careful, Vicki. This guy only targets young single women with red hair and green eyes."

She nodded, the knot of fear in her stomach growing tighter.

"Be sure and keep your car doors locked," Ned said.

"And be sure to lock up at home, too," Arnie warned. "Don't open the door for anyone you don't know."

Vicki nodded. "Don't worry, I'll be careful."

The next two hours passed quickly and it wasn't until about eight-thirty that things slowed down. Vicki used the lull to refill the salt and pepper shakers and the sugar bowls, then she went into the kitchen for a cup of coffee.

When she returned to the dining area, Antonio was sitting at his usual booth in the back. Was he the murderer? But no, she thought, he, too, had warned her to keep her doors locked and to refuse entry to anyone she didn't know. But then, maybe that was just to throw her off the scent. Still, if he'd wanted to kill her, he'd had plenty of opportunity the night before.

He smiled as she approached the booth.

"The police are still looking for you."

"Indeed?"

"There's been another murder."

He swore under his breath. "Was it someone you knew?"

"No." She started to offer him a menu, then hesitated. "I don't suppose you need this?"

"No."

She tilted her head to one side. "Why do you come here every night?"

"You asked me that before," he reminded her with a faint grin. "Do you remember what I said?"

A faint flush climbed up her neck and into her cheeks. "You said it was to see me, but that's ridiculous. We don't even know each other."

"I know you." His voice was as dark as midnight, as deep as eternity.

She had to swallow before she could find her voice again. "Shall I bring you anything?"

"No need."

She laughed softly. "I'm beginning to think you're

some kind of eccentric character who likes to sit in diners and leave big tips."

"You have found me out, Victoria Cavendish." He glanced past her. "I think the chef is trying to get your attention."

"What? Oh, I'd better go." She turned to wave at Gus. When she looked back to where Antonio had been sitting, she saw a twenty dollar bill under the water glass, but he was gone.

Vicki frowned. How had he gotten past her without her noticing? She had only glanced away for a few seconds.

It was near closing time when another stranger entered the diner. He was a big man. Not just tall, but big, and built like a pro football player. He wore a pair of gray trousers and a white sports shirt open at the throat. But it wasn't his size that caused her to notice him. There was something about him besides his size, something in the way his gaze moved over everyone in the place. She had the feeling he didn't miss a thing.

Pasting a smile on her face, she offered him a menu. "Can I bring you a cup of coffee?"

"Black, thanks." He wore his dark brown hair short. His eyes, also brown, were wary and old beyond his years. His hands were big and capable looking. A heavy gold cross on a thick gold chain hung from his neck. Turning away from the table, she found herself wondering what he did for a living. Something that required a lot of strength, she guessed.

She returned with his coffee a few moments later. "So, what can I get you?"

"Steak and fries."

She jotted it down on her pad. "How would you like your steak?"

"Well done."

"Can I get you a salad to go with that?"

"No, thanks."

"Gotcha." She smiled at him again, a real smile this time, because he looked like he could use one. He smiled back and she realized that he wasn't bad looking.

"You've got pretty hair," he remarked. "Is it natural?"

She nodded, a sudden jolt of fear coursing through her. The murderer liked women with red hair.

"I'd better turn your order in," she said, and hurried away from the table.

What should she do? Should she call Ned and Arnie? Maybe she was overreacting. Lots of men had remarked on the color of her hair. But there was a killer on the loose now, a killer whose victims had all been women with red hair and green eyes.

When his order came up, Vicki took Bobbie Sue aside. "Remember that favor you owe me? Well, take this order to table four and finish my shift, will you, and we'll call it square."

"Sure, girlfriend. Something wrong?"

"No." Vicki thrust the tray into Bobbie Sue's hands. "I'll see you tomorrow night."

Going into the back room, Vicki grabbed her coat, then opened the kitchen door. "Gus, I'm going home."

"You sick?"

"No. Bobbie Sue's going to cover for me for until closing. I'll see you tomorrow night."

"You sure everything's okay?" he asked, his brow furrowed with concern.

"I'm sure. Night, Gus."

"G'night, kid."

Slipping into her coat, Vicki ducked out the back door into the parking lot.

She was about to get into her car when a tingling down her spine warned her that she was no longer alone.

"You should park out front," a deep voice remarked. "Under a light."

She whirled around, her mind racing. Her keys. She could use them for a weapon if she had to. Or she could just scream. Someone in the diner would surely hear her. She wished that she had remembered to take Arnie's advice and asked Gus to walk her out to her car.

"No need to cause a scene," the man said. "I just want to ask you a couple of questions."

It was the man from the diner. She clutched her keys tightly in one hand. "Questions about what?"

"My name is Tom Duncan. I'm looking for someone. A man about five foot ten. Looks to be in his late thirties. Blond hair. Yellow eyes."

"Yellow eyes?"

"Have you seen him?"

"No. And believe me, I'd remember someone with yellow eyes. Are you a cop?"

"No."

"Why are you looking for this guy?"

"It's personal."

"Well, I haven't seen him. Good night, Mr. Duncan."

"Good night, ma'am. You'd best be more careful in the future. Try to park under a light, and keep your doors . . ."

"Yes, I know. Keep my doors locked and don't invite any strangers into the house."

The man's gaze grew sharp. "Who told you that?"

"Practically everybody. You, the police . . . an acquaintance of mine."

"Have any strangers approached you?"

"Just you. Like I said, it's not likely I'd forget someone with yellow eyes."

"What's the name of this acquaintance? Is it someone you've just met?"

For a man who claimed he wasn't a cop, he sure sounded like one. "Yes, his name is . . ." She paused, suddenly reluctant to give out Antonio Battista's name. She didn't know this man. Of course, she didn't really know Antonio, either. "I'm sorry, Mr. Duncan, I don't think I should give out that information."

"It might be very important, Vicki."

"How did you know my name?"

He gestured at her uniform.

Of course, she thought, feeling foolish, it was on her name tag. "Who are you, anyway?"

"I'm a bounty hunter."

"A bounty hunter!" she repeated skeptically. "Didn't they die out along with the cowboy and the buffalo?"

"No, ma'am. We're still doing our job."

"So, you're looking for Yellow Eyes to collect a bounty? What did he do?"

"He's wanted for murder."

"Murder! Is he the one who killed Sharlene and the others?"

"It's very likely. Are you sure you haven't seen him?"

She nodded, overcome by a wave of relief. Antonio wasn't the killer.

"Thank you for your help, Vicki. If you see him, run like hell." He scribbled something on the back of a card and handed it to her. "That's my cell phone. Call me if you need me."

She tucked the card into her skirt pocket. She could feel him watching her as she slid behind the wheel. She locked her door, switched on the engine, turned on the lights.

She glanced out the rearview mirror as she drove

out of the parking lot. He was still standing there, watching her, his hands jammed into his pants pockets.

She shook her head. First Antonio, then the murders, and now this bounty hunter looking for some guy with yellow eyes. If she didn't know better, she'd think she was in the middle of a nightmare that refused to end.

She drove home faster than she should have and felt an overwhelming sense of relief when she pulled into the driveway. She stopped in front of the garage and stared at the door. Call her a coward, but there was no way she was driving into that dark garage tonight.

Shutting off the engine, she took the key from the ignition. She was about to open the car door when she happened to glance up at the front porch.

And saw a pair of glowing yellow eyes staring back at her.

Chapter 7

Frozen in terror, Vicki stared at the unblinking yellow eyes. He was here. The murderer was here, waiting for her on the front porch.

She made a stab at putting the key back into the ignition so she could restart the car and get the hell out of there before it was too late, but her hand was shaking so badly she couldn't manage it.

He was here!

She was still trying to put the key in the ignition when the yellow eyes blinked at her. Laughter bordering on hysteria rose in Vicki's throat as her neighbor's black cat jumped off the railing and disappeared into the hedge that separated her property from his.

Vicki sat in the car for a minute, taking deep breaths while she waited for her heart to stop pounding. When her breathing had returned to normal, she opened the car door.

Feeling foolish and relieved, she grabbed her handbag and got out of the car. Shaking her head, she climbed the stairs and reached for the doorknob. She frowned when the door didn't open and then blew out a breath of exasperation when she remembered she had locked it. She fumbled in the dark as she tried to insert the key into the lock. If she was going to start locking the front door, she was going to have to remember to leave the porch light on so she could see what she was doing.

She had just turned the key in the lock when she sensed she was no longer alone. Still a little on edge from seeing those yellow eyes staring at her, she whirled around.

"Forgive me," Battista said. "I did not mean to startle you."

"Oh," she breathed, one hand covering her pounding heart. "It's you."

"You were expecting someone else?"

"No, it's just that . . . Oh, never mind." She felt foolish enough. She didn't need to have him laughing at her for her inane behavior.

She pushed the door open and stepped inside, then glanced at Antonio over her shoulder. "Would you like to come in?" It was rather late to be entertaining company, but at the moment she didn't feel like being alone.

With a nod, he followed her into the house.

Vicki closed and locked the door. She dropped her handbag on a chair in the living room, shrugged out of her coat, and tossed it over her bag.

"You left in a hurry again tonight," she remarked. She waited for him to answer, but he didn't seem inclined to offer any explanation. Okay, so it was none of her business. "Do you want something to drink? Iced tea? Coffee?"

"No, thank you."

"Well, I need some." She went into the kitchen and put on a fresh pot of coffee.

When she turned around, Antonio was standing in the doorway regarding her through fathomless blue eyes.

"What are you doing here so late?" she asked.

"I wanted to be sure you made it safely home."

"So, you've just been waiting around outside?"

"No. I followed you here from the diner."

She frowned. "How did you do that? There wasn't anyone behind me."

A faint smile tugged at his lips. "Are you certain of that?"

"I am unless you were driving with your headlights off."

His smile widened. "There are other forms of transportation, my sweet one."

"Like what? A bicycle?"

He laughed softly. She had never heard him laugh before. It was a surprisingly sensual sound. It did odd things in the pit of her stomach.

She stood frozen in place as he moved toward her, felt her heart skip a beat as he stroked her hair, then cupped her cheek in his palm.

"You are beautiful, my sweet. Your hair is like a silken flame, your skin as soft as that of a newborn babe. And your eyes . . . Ah, they are as green as the meadows I played in as a child."

She stared up him, lost in the heat of his eyes, the husky resonance of his voice. He was beautiful, too, she thought, from his finely chiseled lips and patrician nose to his fine straight brows and sculpted jaw. She tried to visualize him as a child and couldn't. It was impossible to imagine that he had ever been young or vulnerable, or that he had once played childish games.

"Victoria . . ."

The hunger in his voice aroused an answering

hunger deep within her. Without conscious thought, she swayed toward him, went up on her tiptoes as he lowered his head. She closed her eyes as his lips found hers, their touch burning away every other thought, every other need, but the need to be in his arms, to feel the hardness of his body pressed intimately against her own. It was a most remarkable kiss, infusing her with warmth and a heretofore unknown sense of belonging.

Her arms slid around his waist and she clung to him, certain she would expire if he took his mouth from hers, if he deprived her of the touch of his hand, the nearness of his body.

She moaned softly when he lifted his head. "Don't stop." She looked up at him, then stared in disbelief at what she saw. Yet even as she told herself she could not be seeing what she was seeing, the faint red glow faded from his eyes and they were again a deep dark blue.

"Ah, Victoria," he murmured, his voice ragged. "I knew you would be sweet, but . . ." He shook his head as if to clear it and then took a deep breath. "I think perhaps I should go."

She was still too astonished by what she thought she had seen in his eyes to argue.

He gazed down at her a moment more, then turned and left the room.

Only after he was gone did she realize his footsteps had made no sound on the tile floor.

Vicki woke in the morning after a restless night. Her dreams had been filled with mysterious visions of figures swathed in black cloaks moving through dark shadows, of wolves howling beneath a bloodred moon, of a hooded man, his fangs glistening as he bent over her throat, of a blue-eyed cat and a yellow-eyed cat engaged in a brutal, bloody fight to the death.

She tried to shake off the disturbing images while she showered but to no avail, until she thought of Antonio's kiss the night before. That memory drove everything else from her mind. Where on earth had the man learned to kiss like that? It was like no kiss she had ever known before, dark and wild and filled with a deep hunger that had frightened and aroused her at the same time. Just thinking about it now sent a rush of heat through her, made her yearn to be in his arms again, to feel his mouth moving over hers . . .

Jerking her thoughts away from where they were headed, she turned off the water and stepped out of the shower.

It was Friday and she had things to do before she went to work. She dressed quickly in a pair of jeans and a T-shirt. Going into the kitchen, she whipped up some French toast and ate it while she read the morning paper, relieved to see that there had been no killings the night before, at least not in this part of the county.

After breakfast, she brushed her teeth, then slipped on a pair of sandals, grabbed her handbag and her keys, and drove into town. She had always loved Pear Blossom Creek, with its wide, tree-lined streets. She loved it that she knew just about everyone in town. She waved at Ned, who was coming out of 31 Flavors with his sons. Vicki smiled, looking forward to the day when she would have kids of her own. Of course, she needed to find a husband first. Maybe she needed to put an ad in the paper. She laughed at that as she imagined what people would say.

She picked up her cleaning, filled the car with gas,

returned her books to the library, and then stopped to chat with old Mrs. Heath, who was outside watering her garden.

Ramona Heath was ninety if she was a day and as spry as a teenager. She lived alone in a small red brick house on the corner of Fifth and Main. Gardening was her hobby and her passion and her gardens were the talk not only of Pear Blossom Creek but also of all the surrounding counties. Aside from a veritable jungle of flowers, Mrs. Heath grew the largest squash and pumpkins in the county. She also grew enough garlic to stock every store in the state. She had the plants growing under all her windows and in pots on either side of the front and back doors of the house.

Mrs. Heath also claimed to have the power of sight. Vicki didn't believe in such things, yet Mrs. Heath had predicted far too many events that had come to pass far too often for her predictions to be mere coincidence. Mrs. Heath also believed in ghosts and spirits and claimed to have spoken to her deceased husband during a séance. Her other quirk was that she never went outside alone after sundown. Ever.

Mrs. Heath turned off the hose and invited Vicki inside. As always, Vicki was amazed by the amount of clutter in the older woman's house. There were magazines and newspapers everywhere. Vicki thought Mrs. Heath must be the most well-informed woman in Pear Blossom Creek. She subscribed to newspapers from just about every major city this side of the Missouri. In addition to the papers, there were plants and knick-knacks and books on every available surface. A large crucifix hung over the fireplace.

Vicki followed Ramona into the kitchen and sat down at the table.

"Did you see the moon last night?" Mrs. Heath asked as she poured Vicki a glass of lemonade. "It was red."

"Red?"

Mrs. Heath nodded as she cleared a chair of a pile of newspapers and sat down. "As blood. And I heard a wolf howl."

Vicki shivered. "A wolf? Are you sure?"

Mrs. Heath nodded again.

Vicki knew there were wolves out in the country near Hellfire Hollow, but she had never heard of one coming into town. "It was probably just a dog howling."

"No, dear. It was a wolf. I'm going to call Neddie later and let him know."

Vicki grinned. Mrs. Heath was the only one who could call Ned Williams by his childhood nickname and get away with it.

"So, dear," Mrs. Heath said, "have you found yourself a young man yet?"

"Not yet, but I'm still looking." It had long been Vicki's dream to marry and settle down. She wanted to have the same sort of happy marriage that her parents had enjoyed, to raise some kids, to live out her life with a man who would love her as long as they lived.

"You should give Arnie another chance," Mrs. Heath said, patting her hand. "He's a fine young man."

Vicki rolled her eyes. Was everyone in town determined to see her married to Arnie Hall?

"You'll never find a better man."

"Maybe not," Vicki said, thinking of Antonio. "Then again, I might."

"Why, Victoria Lynn," Mrs. Heath said, her eyes twinkling, "have you found a beau you're not telling anyone about?"

"Now, Mrs. Heath, you know if that were true, you'd be the first one to know."

Mrs. Heath beamed at her. "You're such a sweet girl. You should have a family and a man to take care of you."

Sharlene had deserved to have a family, too, Vicki thought with a sigh. She had seen Ron at the gas station earlier. He had forced a smile when he waved at her. When she went to pay for her gas, Fred Black had told her that Ron had quit his job and was moving to Amarillo. She couldn't blame him. There were too many bad memories for him here. She seemed to recall that he had some family in Texas.

"Can I get your some more lemonade, dear?"

"No, thank you."

They chatted for a few more minutes and then Vicki gave Mrs. Heath a quick hug and took her leave.

Vicki spent the rest of the day dusting and vacuuming and doing her laundry, her mind filled with thoughts of the bounty hunter and Antonio and unblinking yellow eyes.

She was glad when it was finally time to get ready for work. Hopefully, the diner would have a crowd tonight and she would be too busy to think of grieving parents or howling wolves or dynamite kisses.

The bounty hunter was having dinner when she arrived. Steak again, she noted in passing. He was a real meat-and-potatoes kind of guy, she thought with a grin. Not bad looking, either. She wondered how long he was going to be in town and who the mysterious man with the yellow eyes was and if the hunter was any closer to finding him. It was still hard to believe that there was a killer on the loose in their sleepy little town.

She approached Tom Duncan's table when he pushed his plate away. "Can I get you anything else?"

He looked up, seeming surprised to see her. "Hi. What happened to Gladys?"

"Her shift ends at six. Can I get you some dessert?"

"I don't know. You got any apple pie?"

"Best in town."

"How about bringing me a big slice and a cup of coffee?"

"Sure. You want ice cream with that?"

"Why not? You only live once, right? Might as well enjoy the good things while you can."

Vicki thought about how true that was as she cut him an extra-large slice of pie and added a double scoop of ice cream. Picking up the coffeepot and the plate, she carried both back to table number four.

He murmured his thanks as she placed the plate in front of him, then refilled his coffee cup.

He took a bite of pie and smiled his approval. "You're right, it is good."

With a nod, she moved away from the table.

Tom Duncan glanced around the diner, noting that he was the only one eating alone. Everywhere he looked there were couples on dates or families enjoying a night out together. Even Ramsey had found a mate.

Well, he was tired of being alone, he thought irritably. Even vampire hunters deserved a night off.

His gaze settled on Vicki as she cleared a nearby table. She was a pretty thing. He'd checked earlier, noting that she didn't wear any rings.

While waiting for her to bring him his bill, he looked around the diner again. It looked like something out of the fifties, with its black and white tile floor. There was a long counter lined with stools cov-

ered in red vinyl. There was a jukebox in one corner
that played all the old fifties hits. He'd noted that Elvis
was a big favorite. There were old movie posters on the
walls. Again, Elvis was prominently featured. There
were booths along two of the walls; round tables covered with red-checked cloths stood in the center of the
floor.

When she returned to see if there was anything else
he wanted, Duncan took his courage in hand and blurted,
"I don't suppose there's any chance you'd like to go out
with me one of these nights?"

Vicki started to say no, then thought how nice it
would be if she could tell Mrs. Heath that she'd had a
date. "I might. What did you have in mind?"

"Dinner and a movie? Just dinner? Just a movie?
I'm easy."

"I'm off on Sundays and Mondays." She slid his bill
under the salt shaker.

"How about Sunday night? I could pick you up
about what, five? Six?"

"Six is good." Tearing a page out of her pad, she
wrote her address and phone number on the back and
handed it to him.

He looked at it briefly, then folded the paper in half
and put it in his shirt pocket. "Sunday at six," he said
with a smile. "Of course, I'll probably see you before
then."

With a nod, she went to clear table two.

Duncan whistled softly as he left the diner. It was
too nice an evening to go back to the hotel. Instead, he
took a walk about the town. It wasn't a big place but it
seemed prosperous enough. The people were friendly.
They nodded to him or called a greeting as he passed

by. It was the kind of place that reminded him of the old days, when most towns and cities were small and people didn't bother to lock their doors and everybody knew everybody else's business. A nice town where people expected to die of old age surrounded by friends and family, not dragged into the woods to be dinner for a hungry fiend.

He clenched his hands into tight fists as he felt his anger and his hatred rise within him. Vampires. They had been the bane of mankind since time began. The Undead could be found in every civilization known to man as far back as recorded time. Every culture had its own account of vampires, whether they were the tales of the *vukodlak* in Croatia or the *lupi manari* of Italy.

And just as there had always been vampires, there had always been vampire hunters. For centuries, all the firstborn males in Duncan's family had been hunters. Duncan knew his family was something of a rarity. Most hunters never married. Wives and children could all too easily become victims, pawns in a never-ending war between good and evil. He knew that being a hunter wasn't something that was passed from father to son in other parts of the world. Being a vampire hunter wasn't inherited. Rather, it was a calling that might come to anyone, like being a priest.

Edward Ramsey was the only hunter Duncan had ever known who had been turned into the very thing he had once hated and hunted. He tried to imagine what it would be like if he, himself, were suddenly turned. How had Ramsey reconciled what he had been to what he had become? What was it like to hunt mortals instead of vampires? Did it have the same kick?

He thrust the thought away and concentrated on his reason for being in Pear Blossom Creek. Three women had been killed and drained of blood. All had been redheads. All had been young and single and lived alone. It sounded like the work of Dimitri Falco, yet Henry Adams claimed that he had destroyed Falco in South America. Of course, it was always possible that Falco was dead and it was just a coincidence that the three murdered women had all been young with red hair.

Tom grunted softly. He had never believed in coincidence, which meant that either Falco was still alive or another vampire was copying his M.O. Either way, Vicki Cavendish was in danger. And she wasn't the only woman in town who fit the description of the vampire's victims. There were Suzie Collins, who worked at the post office, and Rhonda McGee, a nurse who worked the night shift at the hospital.

Stretching his arms and shoulders, Duncan decided it was time to call it a night. He had done all he could do tonight. Tomorrow, he would continue his search for Dimitri Falco.

Chapter 8

Antonio Battista roamed the dark streets, his preternatural senses probing the drifting shadows of the evening for some sense of the other. Lifting his head, he sniffed the wind, his nostrils taking in the scent of cool damp earth and the underlying stink of decay, the wood smoke rising from a chimney, trees and flowers and the myriad other smells and odors associated with mankind, but nothing out of the ordinary. He listened to the sounds of the night—crickets and tree frogs, the rustle of the wind through the leaves, the barking of a dog and, farther away, the faint howl of a wolf.

He turned toward the sound. Was it a wolf? Or one of the Undead?

With preternatural speed, he moved through the town, pausing in front of the houses where the other redheaded women lived, his vampire senses telling him that both were safely asleep inside.

Moving on, he turned down the street where Victoria lived. Her house was dark. A thought took him to her bedroom window. The sound of her breathing, low and even, told him that she, too, was asleep. He felt the prick of his fangs against his tongue as he listened to the steady beat of her heart, the thrum of blood moving through her veins. It aroused a hunger in him like none he had ever known before. Even the hunger he had felt that first night when he awoke as a newly made vampire paled in comparison. How many centuries ago had that been? Five? Six? After the first century or two, time had lost its meaning. He had no need for clocks or calendars. He woke with the setting of the sun, slept when it rose in the morning. The affairs of the world no longer held any importance for him. His whole world had narrowed to only two things—the need for blood and the necessity of keeping his true identity a secret from mankind. Which reminded him that there was a vampire hunter in town. Whether by coincidence or design, he didn't know. He had seen the man, Duncan, in the diner earlier that night and had felt a rare stab of jealousy when he saw the hunter and Victoria laughing together. It had taken all his considerable self-restraint to keep from storming into the diner and ripping the man's heart out.

He grinned in wry amusement. He hadn't been plagued by a foolish human emotion like jealousy in centuries. But now it rose in him again as he imagined Victoria with another man, and not just any man, but his sworn enemy. He should have killed the man long ago. To this day, he didn't understand why he had not dispatched the vampire hunter when he had the chance, but there had been something about Tom Duncan, some innate trace of courage and honor that Battista had found himself admiring in spite of himself. And now Duncan was here, on the hunt. The question was, who was he hunting?

Battista settled down outside Victoria's bedroom

window, prepared to keep watch until sunrise. Sitting there, his back to the wall, he gazed into the darkness, remembering . . .

He had been born in Italy. The memory of those long-ago carefree days was sweet indeed. He had been born the youngest son and little had been expected of him. His oldest brother, Joseph, had been given to the church. His other brother, James, would inherit the family vineyards. His five sisters were expected to marry well, but Battista had no expectations to fulfill. He spent his youth in the pursuit of reckless pleasure and he found it in abundance in the fruit of the vine and the arms of gorgeous women. Indeed, he might have spent the rest of his life in sweet decadence had it not been for a woman who had not been a woman at all. Mara. Mara, with hair like thick black silk and mesmerizing blue eyes. Mara, whose lips had promised an eternity of sensual pleasure but whose bite had damned him to an eternity of darkness. He had not seen her since the night she brought him across.

He had not realized how final the changes were that she bestowed upon him, or what the cost would be. In spite of his mother's pleas, his father had cast him out, calling him a soulless monster, the spawn of the devil. His sisters had looked on him in horror, his brothers had tried to kill him. Angry and confused, he had left home and never returned.

Since then, he had wandered the earth, selfishly taking what he required without regard for anyone's needs but his own. He had made love to countless women throughout the centuries but he had loved none of them. They had satisfied his hunger but found no place in his heart.

He turned his thoughts from his past to the present and the vampire who was preying on the people of Pear

Blossom Creek. No real vampire had ever been as cruel and vicious as Count Vlad Dracula Tepes. Known as the Impaler, he'd had a fondness for having people skewered on long stakes, an excruciating death that often took days.

It was said that he once invited all the poor, sick, and aged to a banquet where he provided them with a lavish feast. When it was over, he asked if there was anything else they desired. Sated for the moment, they said no, at which point Count Dracula left the banquet hall, locked the doors, and set the hall on fire, killing all who were within. It was this infamous count on whom Bram Stoker had based his fictional Dracula.

But it wasn't a fictional vampire terrorizing Pear Blossom Creek. The community of vampires was small, the number who still killed their prey smaller still now that both Alexi and Khira had been destroyed. He could count them on one hand—Andrew Bullivant, who liked to prowl Dracula's castle and never left Romania; Eric Franciscus, who was among the youngest of their kind; Carl Matheson, who killed any and all who crossed his path; and Dimitri Falco, whose victims were always young red-haired women.

Like Victoria. A sound from within the house had Battista on his feet in an instant, ready to defend her to the death if necessary, but she was only sighing in her sleep. He watched her through the window for a moment, wondering what it was she dreamed of. Judging from the smile on her face, it was pleasant indeed.

Dissolving into a fine silver mist, he slipped through the narrow crack under the window, then materialized at her side. He looked down at her, the urge to walk in her dreams almost overpowering. To do so would be an invasion of her mind, a betrayal of what little trust she had in him.

His gaze moved over her. How beautiful she was! Her hair was the red of autumn leaves, tempting his touch though he dared not succumb. Her skin was smooth and clear, her lashes thick where they rested on her cheeks. He watched the rise and fall of her breasts beneath the thin blanket and again felt the urge to reach out and touch her. Again, he restrained himself. He would not violate her while she slept.

He felt his heart, that cold dead organ in his chest, beat for the first time in centuries when, with a sigh, she smiled and murmured his name.

Vicki woke feeling embarrassed without quite knowing why, and then she remembered her dream. The one she'd had Wednesday night had been awful, the worst sort of nightmare, but this one had been wonderful. She had been walking on the beach at night. Moonlight had glistened like streaks of liquid silver on the water. The sand had been warm and soft beneath her bare feet. The song of the ocean had been like a lullaby. She had walked for what seemed like miles with only the moon and the sea for company when suddenly he had been there. He had been dressed in black, as always, his hair gilded by the moonlight, his eyes as blue and deep as the depths of the ocean. He had waited for her to draw near. As she approached, he had removed his cloak and spread it on the shore, then offered her his hand. She had taken it without fear, offered no resistance as he drew her down on his cloak. She had welcomed his kiss, her eyes closing in surrender, her body pliable in his knowing hands. He had made love to her all through the night, his hands caressing her, his voice joining with the lyrical ebb and flow of the waves, blending into a symphony that seduced her in both mind and body. She had given herself to him without restraint, became a part of him, wedded to him as the sea was bound to the sand and the moon to the tide, forever joined together, never to be parted . . .

Smiling, Vicki sat up and took a deep breath and in so doing, she breathed in his scent. But it was no dream. Antonio had been here, in her bedroom, while she slept.

The thought sent a jolt of fear through her, chasing away the pleasant afterglow of her dream. How had he gotten into her room? All the doors and windows had been locked when she went to bed. She knew, because she had checked them all twice.

Rising, she checked them all again, starting with the window in her room. All were locked. None had been tampered with as far as she could see.

Maybe she was imagining things. But no, she could still smell his scent in her room. She was fully awake now. She wasn't imagining anything. It gave her a decidedly uneasy feeling to know that someone had been in her house, in her bedroom, while she slept.

She was going to have a serious talk with Mr. Antonio Battista when she saw him again!

The opportunity came sooner than she expected. She was about to leave for work when he appeared on her doorstep. Dressed in black, as always. She wondered what kind of statement he was trying to make under all that black leather and cloth.

"Good evening, Victoria."

Such a formal greeting, she thought. Sometimes he sounded like some old-world count. "What brings you here?"

He lifted one shoulder in an elegant shrug. "I came to accompany you to work."

"Oh. Well, I'm glad you're here. We need to talk."

She took a step backward and opened the screen door. "Come in."

He paused a moment, then stepped across the threshold and into the living room.

"What do you wish to talk about?" he asked.

"Last night." She dropped her handbag and coat on a chair, then turned to face him, her arms crossed over her breasts.

"What about last night?"

"You were in my room while I was sleeping." It wasn't a question, but a statement of fact.

"Yes."

"Oh, you admit it! What were you doing there? How did you get in? All the doors and windows were locked."

"I meant you no harm, my sweet one, I only wanted to make sure you were all right."

"Why wouldn't I be all right?" she asked, then realized how stupid that sounded. There was a murderer running loose, a murderer who preyed on redheads. Maybe it wasn't such a stupid question, she thought. After all, none of the women had been killed in their homes.

"Do you wish me to apologize for worrying about you?" he asked with a wry smile.

"Yes. No. I don't know, but I want your promise that you won't come into my house again unless I invite you."

He bowed his head in acquiescence. "As you wish."

"You never told me how you got in."

"A trick of the trade, you might say."

She raised one brow. "What trade is that? Don't tell me you're a cat burglar."

He laughed softly. "No."

"What do you do?"

"Perhaps I shall tell you sometime."

"There's something else I'd like to know."

"You are full of questions this evening."

"Yeah, well . . ." She hesitated. Maybe asking wasn't such a good idea, but she had to know.

He crossed his arms over his chest, waiting.

"I saw you with Sharlene and that other woman, and . . . Did you know them?"

"That is not what you want to ask," he chided softly. "You want to know why I was with them."

"Yes."

"I walked them home, nothing more."

"Why?"

"You still think I might have killed them?"

"No, but . . ."

"I knew they were in danger. I walked them home and warned them against opening their doors to strangers."

"You were a stranger."

He smiled faintly. "A stranger, yes, but not a murderer of young women."

She glanced at the clock over the mantel. "I've got to go. I'm going to be late for work."

She was picking up her handbag when Antonio said, "Tom Duncan."

"What?"

"The man you were with last night. What did he want?"

"I don't see as how that's any of your concern."

He took a step forward. Though his expression didn't change, he seemed suddenly menacing. "What did he want?"

"Dinner, of course," she retorted. "Why else do people come into a diner? Well, except for you."

He clenched his hands at his sides. "There is more, something you are not telling me."

"He asked me for a date, not that it's any of your business."

He stared at her.

"What's the matter? Is it so hard to believe that someone would want to date me?"

Battista shook his head. "No, of course not." He didn't think the man ever thought of anything but destroying the Undead, but the vampire hunter had actually asked Victoria for a date. Battista knew hunters rarely married. It had never occurred to him that they might date from time to time. "Are you going out with him?"

"I've really got to go."

"Yes, of course." His face a hard mask, he turned and stalked out the door.

Grabbing her coat, she followed him out of the house, locking the door behind her.

She could feel him watching her as she unlocked her car door, tossed her coat into the backseat, and then slid behind the wheel.

She stared at him for a moment before she started the car and pulled out of the driveway.

He waited until she was out of sight, then dissolved into mist and followed her to the diner.

Chapter 9

Vicki couldn't help it. She kept glancing over her shoulder as she walked from her car to the diner. She had the oddest feeling that she was being followed but there was no one behind her, at least no one she could see.

She frowned, remembering how Antonio seemed to walk without making a sound. But he wasn't invisible, even if his footsteps didn't make any noise.

With a shake of her head, she went in the back door. She left her coat and her handbag in her locker, put on a clean apron, grabbed her pad, and went to relieve Gladys.

She nodded at Bobbie Sue, noting that there were only a few customers in the diner. But that was normal for this time of night.

Things picked up as the night wore on. It was about eight o'clock when Tom Duncan sat down at table four.

"Hi," she said. "Steak again?"

He shook his head. "No, I think I'll try something else. What do you recommend?"

"The shrimp looks good."

He tapped one finger on the table. "How about the meat loaf?"

"I'd stick with the shrimp if I were you."

"All right, shrimp it is."

"Do you want rice or fries with that?"

"Fries."

She jotted it down. "Coffee?"

"Sure."

"Be right back."

She brought him a cup of coffee but she didn't have time to stay and chat. Saturday nights were always busy. She saw Maddy and Rex sharing a hot fudge sundae and smiled. Two dates in less than a week. Perhaps there would be a wedding soon.

She was clearing table two when she happened to glance out the window. She was startled to see Antonio looking back at her through the glass. At least she thought it was Antonio. Before she could be sure, he was gone.

With a shake of her head, she went back to clearing the table.

Tom left a few minutes later, but only after reaffirming their date for Sunday night.

The rest of the evening passed quickly. It was half an hour before closing time when Vicki saw Antonio enter the diner. All the booths and tables in her section were full. But then a strange thing happened. She saw Antonio stare at Bert Summers, who was sitting at a booth in the back. Bert hadn't even finished his pie and coffee when he dropped a ten dollar bill on the table and headed for the door. Looking faintly smug, Antonio took the booth Bert had vacated.

Curious and strangely annoyed, she went to his table. "What did you do?"

"Do?"

She gestured at Bert, who was just walking out the door, then pointed at his barely touched plate. "Why did he leave so abruptly?"

"Maybe he remembered an appointment."

"You did something to him. I saw you."

"What did you see?"

"I don't know. You looked at him and all of a sudden he just got up and left without even finishing his order."

"Perhaps he was no longer hungry?" Antonio replied, his face inscrutable.

"Why didn't you just take one of the empty tables?"

He lifted one brow. "Why do you think?"

She pursed her lips, her brow furrowed in thought. Something wasn't right here, but what? "Was that you outside the window earlier tonight?"

He nodded.

"What were you doing out there?"

"Nothing, why? Is there something else you wish to accuse me of?"

"No, of course not," she said, feeling properly chastised. "I'm sorry." Looking up, she saw Gus watching her. "You'll have to order something."

"Coffee."

With a nod, she left the table.

At closing time, the diner was empty save for Antonio, who continued to sit at the booth in the back corner, his coffee untouched.

"What's with him?" Bobbie Sue asked, coming up beside Vicki. "He comes in here practically every night and never eats anything."

"I'm not sure."

"I think he's kind of creepy, you know?"

Vicki shrugged. "He seems nice enough."

"If you say so." Bobbie Sue removed her apron and

wadded it into a ball. "I'm going over to the Blue Horse for a while. I told Steve I'd meet him there. Do you want to come along?"

Vicki considered that for a moment. The Blue Horse Tavern was a dive located on the outskirts of town. They catered mostly to the young crowd who wanted to dance and drink a few beers but didn't want to make the trip into one of the bigger cities. She had received her first kiss on the dance floor at the Blue Horse.

"Sure," Vicki said.

"No sense taking two cars," Bobbie Sue said. "Why don't you go with me?"

"All right." Vicki glanced at Antonio, not surprised to find that he was watching her. "Just let me finish cleaning up."

As she approached his booth, Battista stood and dropped a twenty dollar bill on the table.

"You're a very generous tipper," Vicki remarked as she cleared the table.

"I like the service."

"Thank you. Good night."

With a nod, he turned and left the diner.

The Blue Horse was in full swing when Vicki followed Bobbie Sue inside. The lights were low, the music loud, the air thick with the combined smells of perfume and perspiration, lust and alcohol.

They made their way to the bar, where Bobbie Sue ordered a cosmopolitan and Vicki ordered a strawberry margarita. As she sipped her drink, Vicki nodded at several people that she recognized.

"Look, there's Linda Fay," Bobbie Sue said, pointing at a brunette who, unfortunately, had a long face that resembled a horse's. "She always was a homely thing, bless her heart."

Vicki nodded sympathetically. A few minutes later, Bobbie Sue went to dance with Steve Mitchell. Steve was a handsome young man who'd had a crush on Bobbie Sue ever since high school. Unfortunately, Bobbie Sue didn't see him as anything but a good friend.

A moment later, a good-looking guy strolled up to the bar and asked Vicki if she wanted to dance. They were making the usual small talk when Vicki felt a sudden chill. She glanced over her shoulder, her gaze drawn to a man standing at the end of the bar. He was tall and slender, with slicked-back blond hair. He wore a black turtleneck sweater and black slacks with a sharp crease.

Her heart skipped a beat when he pushed away from the wall. *No,* she thought, *please don't let him ask me to dance.* But even as the thought rose in her mind he was skirting the dance floor, walking toward her.

Her partner let her go with a smile and a murmured, "see you later," and then the stranger was taking her in his arms. He held her tightly, his hands cold on hers. This close, she could see that his eyes were a rusty yellow, like the color of dead leaves.

"So," he said, "do you come here often?"

The sound of his voice sent a shiver of unease down her spine. "No," she lied. "Do you?"

"From time to time." Releasing her hand, he reached out to stroke her hair. "Lovely," he said. "Is it your natural shade?"

She stared at him, remembering that Duncan had asked her that very same question. "No," she lied. "No, it's dyed."

Lifting a lock of her hair, he sniffed it. "I think not."

"I have to go." She twisted out of his grasp and hurried toward the bar where Bobbie Sue was chatting with Steve.

"Hey, girlfriend," Bobbie Sue said, smiling.

"Bobbie Sue, we need to go. Now."

"Why?"

"Please, Bobbie Sue, take me home."

"Sure, hon." Bobbie Sue kissed Steve's cheek. "Catch ya later, sugar."

"Come on!" Vicki grabbed Bobbie Sue's hand and practically dragged her out of the tavern.

"Vicki, slow down! What's with you?"

"That man in there. The one I was dancing with. The blond . . . I . . . He gave me the creeps."

"Is that all?"

"No! I think"—she glanced nervously over her shoulder as Bobbie Sue unlocked the car doors—"I think he might be the murderer."

"What? Are you serious?"

"Yes. Quick, get us out of here!"

"Don't tell me twice!" Bobbie Sue gunned the engine to life and drove out of the parking lot, tires squealing.

Vicki looked out the back window, her heart pounding. "Drive around for a few minutes. I want to make sure he's not following us."

"Vicki, you're scaring me."

"Good, cause I'm plenty scared myself!"

Bobbie Sue glanced in the rearview mirror. "Do you see anyone?"

"No." Vicki sank back in her seat, suddenly wishing that Antonio were there. She wouldn't be afraid if he was with her. The thought surprised her but it was true. In spite of everything, she felt safe with Antonio. She glanced over her shoulder again, but there were no lights following from behind.

"So, how's it going with Steve?"

Bobbie Sue shook her head. "It isn't."

"You know he's crazy about you. Do you think it's fair to keep leading him on?"

"I'm not leading him on. He knows how I feel. I mean, he's just as sweet as can be and fun to be with, but it's like dating my brother. I mean, I love him, but I'm not *in* love with him. It's like you and Arnie. There's just no spark. You know what I mean?"

"Only too well." Vicki glanced out the back window again.

"Sometimes I don't think we'll ever get married. Maybe we should move to greener pastures."

"Yeah, that's what my mother says."

"Is anyone following us?"

"I don't think so."

Bobbie Sue drove around for ten minutes, then headed for the diner. It was closed when they got there, the parking lot dark, when Bobbie Sue pulled up beside Vicki's car.

"Do you want me to follow you home?" Bobbie Sue asked.

Vicki considered that a moment, then shook her head. "I don't think so." She laughed self-consciously. "Maybe I was just overreacting."

"Well, you know what my mama always says, better safe than sorry. Have a good weekend. I'll see you Monday."

"Night, Bobbie Sue."

Vicki unlocked her car and got behind the wheel, quickly locking the door behind her. In spite of what she'd told Bobbie Sue, she couldn't shake the feeling that someone was watching her as she pulled out of the parking lot and made her way down the dark, deserted streets toward home. A shiver skittered down her spine when she drove past Sharlene's house. She needed to visit Sharlene's folks, but she just couldn't. What could she say? What kind of comfort could you offer someone whose daughter had died such a horrible death? How did a family ever get past the tragedy and move on?

Vicki slowed as her house came into view. Until now, she had always loved the fact that her house was the last on the block and that the woods started where the street ended. Now, she felt suddenly vulnerable and alone.

As she had the night before, she opted to park in front of the house instead of in the garage. Shutting off the ignition, she wished she had remembered to leave the porch light on.

Grabbing her handbag, she got out of the car and ran up the stairs to the front door. Her hand was shaking so badly, she couldn't get the key in the lock.

"Here," said a deep, familiar voice, "let me."

"Antonio." She wondered if he heard the relief in her voice.

Taking the key from her hand, he unlocked the door, then handed it to her.

She pushed the door open and stepped inside. When she turned to thank him, she saw that he was still outside. "Well, don't just stand there, come on in."

He followed her into the house, his presence putting all her fears to flight.

"What has you so upset this evening?" he asked, though he knew very well why she was upset.

Vicki dropped her handbag on the sofa and ran a hand through her hair. "I . . . It's probably nothing, but . . ." She sank down in the chair across from the sofa, her hands folded in her lap. "I went out to the Blue Horse with Bobbie Sue. It's a dive a few miles from town. There was a man there . . . He, I don't know, he just seemed spooky somehow, and he asked about my hair."

"Go on."

She looked at him, her brow furrowed. "He asked me if it was natural. There was something about the way he said it." She shivered. "I guess I let my imagination get the best of me. Anyway, I made Bobbie Sue drive me back to my car. And even though I didn't see anyone following me home . . ." Her frown deepened. "I was sure there was someone behind me." The way she had been sure the other night, only to find that it had been Antonio following her. "Maybe he was using some other means of transportation, too," she murmured, remembering what he had said the other night.

"Do not assume that I am like him," Battista said.

"Were you following me?" she asked, hoping he would say yes.

He nodded.

"Who was that man?" she asked. "Who are you? What are you doing in Pear Blossom Creek?"

"He is a murderer," Battista replied calmly. "A man without conscience or rectitude."

"That doesn't tell me who you are."

"Perhaps I shall tell you one day."

"Why not now?"

"You would not believe me."

"Why are you here?" She frowned. "Did you come here to find him?"

"No. The fact that we are both here is mere coincidence."

"So, what is it you do for a living?"

He shrugged. "I have no employment at the moment."

"Really?" She looked thoughtful for a moment. "Do you live around here?"

He resisted the urge to say he did not live at all. "No."

"Well, since you don't work, you can't be on vacation, so what brings you here?"

His gaze moved over her, lingering on her lips. "Fate, perhaps?"

Warmth spread through her, pooling deep within her being. "You're not married or anything, are you?"

"No, my sweet one. I would not be here with you if I were."

She nodded, then covered a yawn with her hand. "Sorry."

He glanced toward the window. "It grows late. I should let you get your rest."

She nodded, but he saw the fear in her eyes, fear of spending the night alone.

"I can stay, if you wish."

"Would you?"

He nodded. "I will keep watch outside."

"No! I mean, shouldn't you stay in here? I mean, wouldn't you rather stay in here? You'll be more comfortable."

"As you wish."

"I'll get you a blanket," she said. "And a pillow, and you can bed down on the sofa. Or you can watch TV for a while if you're not tired . . ." She closed her mouth. She was babbling, but she couldn't help it. His offer to spend the night had seemed like a godsend at first. But now, she wasn't so sure. Earlier, she had convinced herself she felt safe with him. Now that he was here, she was suddenly nervous at the thought of being alone with him, of having him spend the night in her house. After all, what did she really know about him?

He was watching her, his expression impassive, yet

she had the uncanny feeling that he knew exactly what she was thinking.

He brushed a strand of hair from her cheek. "Have you changed your mind?"

Had she? Did she want to be alone tonight? "No, no." She smiled. "I'll just be a minute."

She hurried out of the room and down the hall to the linen closet. There, she paused, one hand over her pounding heart. *Please, Lord, let me be doing the right thing.*

She pulled a sheet and a blanket out of the closet, along with an extra pillow and a clean pillowcase. Then, taking a deep, calming breath, she returned to the living room.

He was standing where she had left him.

Discomfited by the silence, she switched on the TV. The familiar voices of the cast of *Friends* filled the silence as she set about making up the couch and fluffing the pillow, all too aware of Antonio's nearness. She knew he was watching her every move. His gaze was almost tangible, like invisible fingers stroking her back, caressing her nape.

"There." She turned to face him. "I hope you'll be comfortable."

"Do not worry about me," he said.

She wondered if anyone had ever worried about him. He was tall and broad-shouldered. Strength and confidence fairly oozed from every pore. She had no doubt that he could look out for himself, and yet, far below the surface, she sensed a vulnerability. Or maybe she was just imagining it because it made him seem more human . . . She frowned, wondering where that thought had come from. Perhaps she was more tired than she thought!

"Well." She lifted her shoulders and let them fall. "Good night."

"*Buona notte.*"

Battista watched her leave the room, his gaze resting on the sweet sway of her hips, and then he shook his head. He was not here to admire her beauty or to seduce her. He was here to protect her, nothing more. But her image danced in his mind, the womanly scent of her hair and skin lingered in his nostrils.

To distract himself, he switched off the television, then strolled through the house, noting that she was a tidy housekeeper and that she favored the color mauve and had a fondness for candles and clocks. The living room was rectangular. Aside from the TV set, there were a high-backed sofa and a chair. A table held a lamp with a mauve shade. The furniture was mismatched but somehow blended together to create a homey atmosphere. A pair of tall bookcases were crammed with books, everything from cookbooks and dictionaries to literary fiction and murder mysteries.

The kitchen was small and neat and contained all the usual appliances. Two chairs flanked a round table covered with a mauve cloth. He peeked into the bathroom, then opened the door into what was meant to be a second bedroom, only there was no bed. A computer desk took up most of one wall. Two racks framed the single window, one filled with CDs, the other with DVDs. A large aquarium sat on a wrought-iron stand. Several pictures hung on the walls, including an autographed black-and-white photo of a man dressed as the Phantom of the Opera, and one of Victoria standing between a man and a woman that Antonio assumed were her parents.

Moving silently up the stairs, he paused outside Victoria's bedroom door. Closing his eyes, he listened to the even sound of her breathing, the steady beat of her heart, the quiet hum of blood flowing through her veins. His fangs pricked his tongue as his thirst roared to life, aroused by the scent of the crimson river beyond the door, the nearness of prey.

Needing to put some distance between them, he left the house. Standing below her bedroom window, he wondered what Victoria would think if she could see him now, with the lust for blood burning in his eyes. He closed his eyes, imagining what it would be like to take Victoria into his arms, to inhale her scent, to taste the salty sweetness of her skin, hear the accelerated beat of her heart as he took his first taste . . .

With a low growl, he thrust the image aside. He needed to feed and soon, but it would have to wait. He couldn't take a chance on leaving her alone, not with Falco out there. Hands clenched into tight fists, he took several deep breaths, willing his hunger into submission.

He was about to go back into the house when an instinct born of hundreds of years told him he was no longer alone. Lifting his head, he sniffed the wind, sorting through the myriad smells of the night—damp grass, trees, earth, rotting vegetation, the stink of human waste common to civilization.

He turned slowly, his preternatural senses filtering through the mundane until he pinpointed the inhuman scent of one of his own kind.

"Falco." The name whispered past his lips.

Mocking laughter echoed on the heels of the night wind. "I am here, Battista. Come, meet with me, brother. Let us speak of the delectable damsel who lies sleeping within the house."

"Be gone, Falco. She will never be yours."

"Women throughout the ages have been mine." Again,

the sound of mocking laughter rose on the wind. "No woman I desired has ever escaped me, brother."

"You will not have her!"

"You cannot stop me, Battista."

Antonio started forward, then paused. Haring off into the darkness and leaving Victoria unprotected was exactly what Falco wanted.

Muttering an oath, Battista dissolved into mist. In less than a heartbeat, he was inside Victoria's bedroom.

He materialized beside her bed, once again fighting the almost overpowering urge to surrender to the need that burned within him, to take her in his embrace, to taste her and touch her until he knew every delicious curve and contour of her body, every unexpressed hope, every unspoken dream.

Turning away from the bed, he sat on the floor as far away from her as he could get. He would not leave her room until the sunrise was upon him. He had never met Dimitri Falco, but he knew the creature's reputation. Falco was relentless in his pursuit of prey.

But he would not have Victoria.

Not this night, or any other.

Chapter 10

Dimitri Falco ghosted through the night. Leaving Pear Blossom Creek behind, he stalked the dark streets of the neighboring town. At this time of night, the only people out and about were those who enforced the law and those endeavoring to break it.

He found what he was looking for on a street corner.

He smoothed his hair and put on his most winning smile as he approached her.

Her gaze moved over him in a quick assessment, noting the cut of his clothes, his expensive shoes. "Hi, honey," she purred. "What's a handsome guy like you doing out so late?"

"What do you think?"

She tilted her head to one side. "You tell me."

He grinned at her. "I'm not the law, if that's what you're thinking."

She laughed softly. "Oh, honey, I know that."

He lifted a handful of her hair, let the silky strands slide through his fingers. "Beautiful," he murmured. "Is it dyed?"

"Dyed?" She looked insulted, and then she smiled. It was a blatantly seductive smile. "For fifty dollars, I can prove it's natural."

"Sounds like a bargain to me."

"I'll take the money first."

With a nod, he reached into his pocket and pulled out a hundred dollar bill.

Her eyes widened as he placed it in her hand. "I can't break that."

"Keep it." He reached for her hand, his fingers curling around hers in a grip that made her wince as he began to walk, dragging her behind him.

She tried to wrest her hand from his. "My house is the other way."

"My house is this way."

"But . . ."

"You don't want me to change my mind about that extra fifty, do you?"

She considered that a moment, then nodded. "All right, honey, as long as you're not into anything kinky."

"Kinky," he murmured. "We shall see."

Chapter 11

Tom Duncan swore under his breath as he read the morning paper. A woman had been murdered and drained of blood in the next town. Had Falco tired of hunting in a small town like Pear Blossom Creek and decided to move on to a bigger place, or was he just expanding his hunting grounds?

With a shake of his head, Duncan tossed the paper aside. He had searched Pear Blossom Creek from east to west and north to south. He had explored every inch of Hellfire Hollow, poked into every abandoned building, looked into every cave and crevice, but he hadn't found a thing. Zip, zilch, nada. Not a trace of Falco.

Finishing his coffee, he dropped a couple of dollars on the table to pay for his meal and left the café.

Outside, he took a deep breath. "Okay, vampire hunter," he muttered to himself. "Hunt."

* * *

The sound of church bells woke Vicki. Bolting upright, she glanced at the clock, then bounded out of bed. She was going to be late for early Mass. Again.

After dressing quickly, she skipped breakfast and left the house. Jumping into her car, she put the pedal to the metal, only to be pulled over when she was three blocks away from the church.

August "Augie" Ryan was shaking his head as he approached her car. "Vicki, where in tarnation are you going in such a rush on a quiet Sunday morning?"

Vicki looked up at him through the window. Augie was the oldest policeman in town. Augie was a big teddy bear of a man, with twinkling blue eyes and a winning smile. By rights, he should have retired years ago, but the people of Pear Blossom Creek wouldn't hear of it, and since his youngest son was the mayor and his oldest son was the chief of police, it was pretty much a given that Augie would be around until he was ready to retire.

Vicki summoned her sweetest smile. "I was on my way to Mass, of course. Where else would I be going on a quiet Sunday morning?" Where else, indeed, since everything was closed except the corner café and the hospital.

"Now, honey, you're just lucky it is Sunday and there's no one else on the road. Girl, you might have caused an accident a'speeding along that way."

"But I didn't, and I'm really late, so can I go?"

"I should write you up this time, you know that, don't you? It would serve you right."

"But you won't, will you?"

He rocked back on his heels. "I reckon not. But you slow down, girl, hear?"

"I will, Augie. Thanks!"

She pulled away from the curb at a sedate speed,

then glanced in the rearview mirror. Augie was still standing beside his police car, watching her.

With a sigh of exasperation, she kept to the speed limit the rest of the way to church.

She was driving home an hour later when she saw Tom Duncan walking down the street. She had a date with him tonight. How could she have forgotten?

Pulling over to the curb, she honked her horn.

He looked her way, frowning, then smiled when he recognized her.

Vicki rolled the window down. "Hi."

He nodded. "Hi yourself. What are you doing out and about so early?"

"Church."

"Ah."

"And why weren't you at Mass this fine morning?" she asked, then blushed. Just because be wore a cross didn't necessarily mean he was Catholic, and even if he was Catholic, that didn't mean he was in the habit of going to church. "I'm sorry, it's none of my business."

Duncan laughed. "Don't worry. My soul's in pretty good shape. I've relied on heavenly intervention far too often to turn my back on the church."

"Really?"

"Faith comes in handy in my line of work."

"I never thought of that, but I'll bet it does. Is there good money in bounty hunting?"

"Sometimes. Depends on who you're hunting and how bad your client wants him caught."

"You mean someone is paying you to hunt for Sharlene's murderer?"

"No. This time it's on me." He glanced at his watch. "Listen, I've got some business to take care of. Are we still on for tonight?"

Vicki nodded. "Sure. See you at six."

With a wave, he continued on down the street.

Vicki was on her way home when she saw Mrs. Heath outside watering her lawn.

After parking the car, Vicki got out and walked up the narrow path. "Morning, Mrs. Heath."

"Victoria, dear," the older woman said, looking up from beneath the brim of a wide straw hat. "How nice to see you in one piece."

Vicki frowned. "I beg your pardon?"

"I saw you earlier. You were driving your machine way too fast."

"Yes," Vicki said with a wry grin. "Augie thought so, too."

"Oh, dear, I hope that old fool didn't give you a ticket."

"Not this time."

"Well, that's good, though you really should slow down. So, how are you, dear?"

"I'm fine. And guess what?" Vicki could hardly wait to see the expression on Mrs. Heath's face when she told her about Duncan. "I have a date tonight!"

Mrs. Heath stared at her in what could only be described as alarm. "He doesn't have rusty yellow eyes, does he?"

In spite of the warmth of the sun, Vicki felt a sudden chill crawl over her skin. "Yellow eyes?"

Mrs. Heath placed her hand on Vicki's arm. "I saw him in a dream, dear. A horrid man with yellow eyes. He was knocking at your door." Her hand tightened on Vicki's arm. "Whatever you do, you must not let him in."

Vicki shivered. "No. No, I won't."

With a smile, Mrs. Heath released her hold on Vicki's arm, then turned off the water. "Have a good time, dear. And tell me, who's the lucky young man? Is it someone I know?"

"No, he's new in town. I met him at the diner a few days ago. His name is Tom Duncan."

Mrs. Heath's eyes widened. "Duncan? Did you say Tom Duncan?"

"Yes. Do you know him?"

Pressing one hand to her heart, Mrs. Heath sat down on the wrought-iron bench located in the midst of her garden. "Forgive me, dear, the name just took me by surprise, that's all."

"Do you know Mr. Duncan?"

"I dated a man by the name of Thomas Duncan years ago, before I met Mr. Heath. I might have married him, if he didn't have such a dreadful occupation."

"Dreadful in what way?" Vicki asked. The only dreadful occupation she could think of was being a mortician.

"He was a vampire hunter."

Feeling as though the earth had suddenly stopped spinning, Vicki stared at Mrs. Heath, and then she laughed. "You really had me going for a minute there."

"It's no laughing matter, dear. It's hard to believe that they exist in this day and age, but they do."

Vicki stared at the elderly woman.

"I know what you're thinking," Mrs. Heath said. "I didn't believe my Thomas when he told me, either, but then one night I saw one." She stared into the distance. "He tried to kill me. I'll never forget the sight of that creature, his eyes glowing like a wildcat's, his fangs coming toward me. It was Thomas who saved my life. I was young back then and easily frightened. When Thomas asked me to marry him, I ran away. Sometimes I wonder . . . No matter. What does your Mr. Duncan do?"

"He's a bounty hunter. People," she clarified, "not vampires."

Mrs. Heath patted Vicki's hand in motherly fashion. "Run along and have a good time, dear. It's time for my nap."

With a nod, Vicki returned to her car. Maybe Mrs. Heath was losing it. Vampires, indeed. They were the stuff of myth and legend.

After parking the car, she picked up the newspaper and carried it into the house. Dropping it on the kitchen table, she fixed herself a bowl of cereal and some toast and then sat down to read the paper.

One look at the headlines and she forgot all about eating.

FOURTH WOMAN FOUND DEAD
BODY DRAINED OF BLOOD

She quickly read the story. The body had been found in a vacant lot in Woods Hollow by a late-night jogger. There was no evidence of foul play. The police were certain that the murderer was the same person who had killed the three women in Pear Blossom Creek.

Bodies drained of blood . . . She shook her head, dismayed by the turn of her thoughts. There was no such thing as vampires. She repeated the words aloud, hoping that it would somehow reassure her, but it didn't. Vampires or not, someone was killing women and draining them of blood. Perhaps a Satanic cult was behind the murders. Didn't they use blood in their rituals? But good Lord, how much blood did one cult need?

She poured her breakfast down the garbage disposal, changed into a pair of jeans and a T-shirt, and went into the den to clean the aquarium. And all the while she thought about Tom Duncan and vampires. Of course, she knew there were stories and legends from ancient times, when anything that could not be explained logically was ascribed to something mystical or magical, like vampires or witches. In olden times, people believed that a moved or fallen tombstone, horses shying away from a grave, or footprints leading away from a grave were indications of a vampire's resting place. People with pale skin and long nails, or those who had no appetite and an aversion to bright lights, were also suspected of being vampires.

Others who might be accused of being vampires were those who were never seen during the day or who were reluctant to enter a house without an invitation. Vicki frowned. She had never seen Antonio during the day. He always waited to be invited into her house. She had never seen him eat . . .

Vicki shook her head in exasperation. She was becoming obsessed with the Undead. Vampires, indeed. Serial killers often behaved in ghoulish ways. That didn't mean this one was a vampire. Serial killers often killed their victims in bizarre ways, or kept body parts for souvenirs, or collected personal items. This particular killer liked to drain his victims of blood and take a lock of their hair. That didn't mean he drank the blood, but what did he do with it?

She remembered watching a special about vampires and those suspected of being vampires back when she viewed the existence of such things as an interesting myth and not a possible reality. One such, Elizabeth Bathory, had murdered hundreds of young girls and bathed in their blood, believing it would keep her young and beautiful. Eventually, the truth of what she was doing became known and she was walled up in her bedroom, where she died four years later.

"Stop it!" Going outside, Vicki lifted her face to the sun, letting its warmth wash over her. She took several deep breaths, clearing her mind of all her ghastly thoughts. Even if there were vampires, and she wasn't ready to admit such a thing, she was safe now.

She spent the next hour and a half working in the yard. She raked the leaves from the lawn, both front and back, pulled some weeds, and watered the grass, thinking she would have to mow it soon. Thinking how nice it would be to have a husband and children to help with the yard work. For a moment, she imagined her husband teaching their son how to mow the grass while she and their daughter worked in the garden. Later, they would sit in the shade and drink lemonade and then go for a walk in the woods, or go down to the lake for a swim . . . It came as no surprise that the husband of her dreams looked a lot like Antonio Battista.

Returning to the house, she put an Elvis CD in the stereo, made a cake and put it in the oven, and then fixed a quick sandwich for lunch. When she finished eating, she rolled up her sleeves and mopped the floors in the kitchen and bathroom.

And still, thoughts of vampires and bloodred moons crept into her thoughts. She recalled what Mrs. Heath had said and wondered if Tom Duncan was related to the Duncan that Mrs. Heath had known.

She would have to ask Tom about it when she saw him tonight.

She took the cake out of the oven, changed the sheets on her bed, then frosted the cake, and before she knew it, it was time to get ready for her date.

* * *

Standing on Vicki Cavendish's front porch, Tom Duncan straightened his tie, brushed a piece of lint off his trousers, and blew out a deep breath. He couldn't remember the last time he had been out with a woman. Hell, he wasn't sure he even remembered how to act on a date! He spent most of his life prowling around dilapidated houses or crawling around in caves and cemeteries. Hardly the kinds of places where a man was likely to meet a woman he'd want to take out. Then, too, he rarely stayed in one place long enough to get acquainted with very many women, let alone establish any kind of relationship. Of course, he might be here in Pear Blossom Creek for quite some time, since he hadn't found a single clue as to where his prey was hiding.

Running a hand over his hair, he summoned his nerve and rang the doorbell, all the while reminding himself that this was just one date, nothing more.

He couldn't help staring when the door opened. "Wow."

She smiled at him. "Thank you."

"You're welcome." He didn't know what Vicki had done differently, but she was a knockout in a pair of black pants and a short-sleeved, vee-neck green sweater that was the perfect foil for her red hair and made her eyes seem even darker and greener than he recalled.

"Are you ready to go?" he asked.

"Sure. Just let me grab my handbag."

He stood on the porch feeling like a teenager on his first date. "So," he said when she reappeared. "Where would you like to go for dinner?"

"The Sea Crest is nice."

"Great. Let's go."

"Do you know where it is?"

"No."

She smiled and took his hand. "That's okay, I do."

He opened the car door for her, closed it behind her. Walking around to the driver's side, he suddenly wished he was driving a new convertible instead of a beat-up black Camaro.

They talked about the weather and the possibility of rain on the ride to the restaurant. Duncan had the feeling she was holding something back, that she was dying to ask him something but didn't know how.

The Sea Crest was a nice place. The tables were covered in crisp white cloths. The lighting was soft enough to encourage lovers but not so dark as to discourage families. There were paintings of seascapes and tall-masted ships on the walls.

The hostess, apparently pegging them as lovers, showed them to a small table in a corner. She handed them each a menu, smiled, and left the table.

Duncan looked around. "Do you come here often?"

Vicki shook her head. "I've only been here once before."

"A special occasion?"

"A good friend of mine from high school had her wedding supper here two years ago. She reserved the whole place. Must have cost a fortune, but her family could afford it."

"Does she still live in Pear Blossom Creek?"

"No, they moved to Los Angeles. I keep thinking I'll go there for a visit one of these days, but . . ." She sighed. "You know how that goes."

"Do you ever think about leaving here?" he asked.

"Oh, sure, all the time, but . . ." She shrugged. "I guess I'm just a small-town girl. All I really want is to get married and settle down. What about you?"

"I've been giving that some thought myself."

"You say that like you're confessing to some horrible crime."

"Yeah, well, let's just say it's not something I ever really planned on."

Wanting to change the subject, he glanced at the menu. For a restaurant in a town that was only a speck on the map, the Sea Crest had big-city prices. But money was only money, and when he ate, he liked to have the best.

"Steak and lobster for me," he said. "How about you?"

"Shrimp and rice," Vicki said, closing her menu. "And a Diet Coke."

The waitress appeared a few minutes later and Duncan placed their orders.

As soon as the waitress left, Vicki leaned forward, her arms crossed on the table. "Can I ask you something?"

"Sure, anything."

"Are you really a bounty hunter?"

"Yes, why?"

"So you hunt escaped criminals, right?"

He hesitated a moment, debating the wisdom of telling her the truth.

"Tom?"

"Is there some reason you don't believe me?"

"No, of course not." She grinned, thinking what a good laugh they would have when she told him what Mrs. Heath had said. "I can't believe I'm telling you this, but a friend of mine thinks she knew a relative of yours who claimed to be a vampire hunter. Isn't that the silliest thing you've ever heard?"

She looked at him expectantly, waiting for him to

laugh. When he didn't, a cold chill ran up her spine. "Tom?"

He drummed his fingers on the tabletop, wondering how she would react to the truth. As much as he'd like to tell her a nice lie, she needed to be armed with the truth, to realize that her life was in danger. "Listen, Vicki . . ."

"Oh, Lord, it's true! You believe in vampires, too, don't you? You're as loopy as Mrs. Heath."

"Ramona Heath?"

Vicki nodded.

Looking dumbfounded, Tom sat back in his chair. "My great-grandfather used to talk about her." He shook his head. "I thought the name of the town sounded familiar. I can't believe she's still alive. She must be, what, over ninety?"

"You're a vampire hunter, aren't you?"

He didn't deny it. "'Do you want me to take you home?" She wouldn't be the first person to shun his company once they found out what he really did for a living.

"Yes. No. I don't know."

She stared at him. He didn't look like someone who went around staking vampires or cutting off their heads. He was an ordinary-looking man with broad shoulders and a craggy face and eyes . . . She looked deep into his eyes and knew that he was telling her the truth. Or at least the truth as he perceived it. He truly believed he was hunting vampires.

"That's why you're here, isn't it?" she asked. "You think a vampire killed Sharlene and those other women."

He nodded, his expression somber.

"I think I saw him. The killer. He didn't look like a vampire, though."

Duncan's whole demeanor changed. She had taken him for a nice, easygoing guy but now she saw the steel beneath his laid-back exterior. His eyes narrowed. A muscle worked in his jaw. "Where? When?"

"At the Blue Horse Tavern on Saturday night."

"What did he look like?"

"He was a little taller than I am, kind of slim, with blond hair. And yellow eyes."

Duncan swore under his breath. "Falco. Listen to me, Vicki, whether you want to believe it or not, he's a vampire. A very old vampire."

Vicki sat back, her mind reeling, not only because of what he was telling her, but because she believed him. In that instant her whole world and much of what she had believed in turned upside down.

"But . . . What's he doing here, in Pear Blossom Creek?"

Duncan shrugged. "Happenstance, maybe. Who the hell knows what a vampire thinks? But he's dangerous, I can tell you that."

"What does he have against redheads?"

"I couldn't say for sure. The story goes that when he was a mortal man, he was engaged to a red-haired woman. It's said that while they were engaged, she had several lovers and when he found out about it, he killed her and cut off a lock of her hair. Soon after that, there was a string of murders. All the victims had red hair. Soon after that, he was turned."

"Turned?"

"Into a vampire."

"How long ago was that?"

"I'm not sure. A thousand years ago, give or take a century or two."

"And he's been killing women all that time?"

"That's why he's got to be stopped. Now."

She was only vaguely aware of the arrival of the waitress with their dinner.

"You might as well eat," Duncan said with a wry grin.

Vicki stared at her plate. Eat? How could he think of food when there was a vampire loose in Pear Blossom Creek? One who had a fondness for killing redheaded women?

She watched Duncan cut into his steak. Juice oozed in the wake of the knife, reminding her of blood.

Feeling suddenly nauseous, she glanced out the window, felt her insides go cold when she saw a pair of glowing yellow eyes staring back at her.

Chapter 12

Vicki gasped, one hand flying to her throat. He was here!

"What is it?" Duncan asked, his gaze darting around the room.

"Out there! He's here!"

"Who's here?" Duncan asked. And then he knew. Swiveling around in his chair, he stared out the window. "I don't see anyone."

"He was there. I saw him."

Duncan reached for her hand. "It's all right, Vicki. Take a deep breath. That's right. You're safe in here with me."

She took several deep breaths, her gaze constantly darting to the window. She wanted to believe she had imagined it, but she hadn't. Those horrible yellow eyes had been watching her.

Duncan handed her a glass of water. "Here, drink this."

She didn't know what good drinking a glass of water

would do, but she was too upset to argue. Surprisingly, doing something so ordinary calmed her a little.

"Are you going to . . . to . . ." She couldn't say the words.

"Just as soon as I find him."

"Well, that shouldn't be too hard. He's right out there!"

"He's probably long gone by now. Besides, hunting vampires after dark is a risky business. I prefer to do it when the sun's up."

"Do you know where he stays during the day?"

"No, but I'll find him. It's just a matter of time."

"Yes, time," she murmured, and hoped that Tom found the vampire before the vampire found her.

"Don't worry. I'll get him." Duncan squeezed her hand. "Do you want to leave?"

Was he crazy? The way she felt right now, she wasn't leaving this place until the sun was up. "No."

Tom regarded her for a moment, then picked up his knife and fork and began to eat his dinner.

Blowing out a breath, Vicki speared one of the shrimp on her plate, thinking that if this was going to be her last meal, at least it would be a good one.

When they finished dinner, Tom asked if she would like to take a walk, but Vicki shook her head. She was never going to feel safe out on the streets after dark again, not as long as that fiend was somewhere out there.

"Let's go back to my place for dessert," she suggested. "I made a cake today."

"Sounds good to me."

Unable to help herself, she kept looking over her shoulder on the drive home.

"Relax," Duncan said. "No one's going to hurt you while I'm around."

She nodded, but all the while a little voice in her head wondered who was going to protect her when he wasn't around. The thought had barely formed when Battista's image rose in her mind.

They reached her house a few minutes later. She unlocked the door and turned on the lights. Maybe vampires couldn't cross a threshold uninvited, but she was still glad that she didn't have to go into the house alone.

She gestured at the sofa. "Make yourself at home. Would you like a cup of coffee with your cake?"

"I'd rather have milk, if you've got some."

"Sure."

Going into the kitchen, she pulled a couple of dessert plates and two glasses from the cupboard. She cut a generous slice of cake for Tom, a smaller one for herself, filled two glasses with milk, and put everything on a tray.

She had just opened the silverware drawer to get a couple of forks when the hair prickled along the back of her neck. Her heart pounded heavily in her chest as she tried to resist the urge to look out the window in the top half of the back door. Knowing what she would see and yet unable to resist, she slowly turned her head.

He was there, staring back at her, his yellow eyes glowing like a cat's in the dark. His lips moved and even though she couldn't hear the words, she knew he was calling to her. Her feet felt like lead as she took a step toward the back door, and then another.

He smiled, displaying even white teeth.

The sight jerked her out of whatever spell he had cast upon her. With a cry, she whirled around and ran into the living room.

Duncan sprang to his feet as she burst into the room. "What is it?"

She pointed a shaky finger over her shoulder. "There! He's out there!"

Tom didn't have to ask who she was talking about. "Stay here," he said curtly. "Lock the door behind me."

"Don't go!"

His gaze met hers. "It's what I do," he said, and then he was gone.

Vicki locked the door behind him, then ran through the house, making sure all the doors and windows were locked, the curtains drawn.

What was Tom doing out there? Hadn't he told her not an hour ago that he didn't hunt vampires at night?

Turning on the back porch light, she looked out the window, eyes and ears straining to see or hear something that would tell her what was going on. Was the vampire still out there? At first, she heard nothing, then the sound of running footsteps, a crash, a curse, and then silence.

She pressed her hand to her heart. Oh, Lord, had the vampire killed Tom?

She jumped when she heard a knock at the front door. "Who . . . Who is it?"

"Open the door, my sweet one."

"Antonio?" Switching on the porch light, she peered through the narrow window beside the door, murmured, "Oh, my," when she saw him standing there holding Tom in his arms.

"Come in!" She quickly unlocked the door and just as quickly locked it behind him. "What happened?"

"This idiot went after Falco."

Vicki stared up at Battista. "You know Falco? Are you a hunter, too?"

"A hunter?"

"You know, a vampire hunter. That's what Tom is." Only after she'd said the words aloud did she realize how foolish they sounded. No doubt Battista would think her mad. She waited for him to laugh at her, to tell her how foolish she was to believe in such things.

But he didn't laugh. "No," he said. "I am not a hunter."

"You don't think I'm crazy? For believing in vampires?"

"No."

"So . . . You believe in them, too?"

He nodded, his expression grim.

Vicki stared at him, speechless.

Battista looked down at Duncan. "Where shall I put him?"

"What? Oh, on the sofa, I guess."

With a nod, he relieved himself of his burden.

"Is he badly hurt?"

Antonio shrugged. "Hurt? He is lucky to be alive."

Vicki studied Battista for a moment. He was dressed impeccably in black, as usual. His hair was windblown, his deep blue eyes almost luminous. "What are you doing here, anyway?"

His gaze caught and held hers. Heat flowed between them like a thread of invisible fire. She pressed a hand to her heart, wondering why it was suddenly hard to breathe. Though no words were spoken, she knew in the deepest part of her being that he was there to protect her, that he would be there to defend her until the monster who was stalking her was captured or killed.

"That's very gallant of you," she murmured, and then realized he probably had no idea what she was talking about. Thinking of Antonio as her knight in shining armor was no more than wishful thinking on her part.

A slow smile curved his lips. "I will not let you down, my sweet one."

She blinked at him. Was he reading her mind? Had she read his?

A low groan from the direction of the sofa drew her attention. Looking past Battista, she saw Tom sitting up, his head cradled in his hands.

She hurried to his side. "Are you all right?"

"Yeah. I almost had him."

Sitting beside Duncan on the sofa, she combed her fingers lightly through his hair. He let out a yelp when her hand brushed against the large bump on the back of his head.

"You're bleeding!" she exclaimed as her fingertips came away bloody.

"I'm not surprised. I don't know what the devil he hit me with, but it felt like a sledgehammer."

"It was a rather large rock," Antonio said.

Tom looked up, frowning. "Who the hell are you?"

"No one of importance. I suggest you go to a doctor."

"I'm all right." Tom stared at the other man, his eyes narrowing. "You look familiar."

"Do I?" Antonio replied.

Tom lifted a hand to his head. "I'm sure we've met."

"You can figure it out later," Vicki said, taking a closer look at his injury. "I think Antonio's right. I think you might need some stitches."

Duncan lifted one hand to his head, wincing when his fingers hit the bump.

"You might have a concussion," Vicki said. "I'll . . ." She took a deep breath. "I'll drive you." She could think of a hundred things she would rather do than go out in the dark knowing a killer was out there, but what else could she do? She couldn't let Tom sit here and bleed to death on her sofa.

"No." The two men spoke simultaneously.

"I can drive myself," Tom said.

"I don't think that's a good idea," Vicki said. "I'll take you."

"We will both take him," Battista said. The tone of his voice indicated there would be no further discussion.

Vicki turned on the porch light, left lights burning in the living room, the kitchen, and her bedroom, and grabbed her purse.

By unspoken agreement, the two men put Vicki between them as they descended the porch stairs and made their way to where Tom had parked his car.

"I will drive," Battista said.

Tom climbed into the backseat, Vicki slid into the front seat. No one spoke on the drive to the hospital.

As had become her habit, Vicki kept looking over her shoulder, expecting and dreading what she might see. But there were no glowing yellow eyes staring back at her this time.

Battista pulled into the hospital parking lot a few minutes later. Exiting the car, he pulled the front seat forward and helped Duncan out of the backseat.

For a small town, Pear Blossom Creek boasted a modern hospital with all the latest equipment. A nurse in a crisp white uniform took one look at Tom Duncan's face, called for a wheelchair, and whisked him into an examination room.

Vicki crossed her arms over her breasts. "I hate hospitals," she muttered.

Battista nodded, his senses inundated by the myriad odors of drugs and antibiotics, of sickness and death. And blood. Rich red blood pumping in the hearts of patients and doctors alike, plasma stored in neat plastic bags. A veritable smorgasbord for a thirsty vampire. He turned away from Victoria lest she see the hunger he knew must be burning in his eyes.

Vicki paced up and down the corridor. She had a decided aversion to doctors and hospitals. Both reminded her of the days and nights she had sat at her grandfather's bedside during the last days of his life.

The soft shush-shush of leather-soled shoes heralded the return of the nurse.

"How is he?" Vicki asked.

"His condition is good, but the doctor wants to keep him overnight to make sure he doesn't have a concussion. He can go home in the morning."

"Can I see him?"

"Yes, if you like, but he's asleep."

"Oh." Vicki glanced at Battista, then looked back at the nurse. "Well, just tell him I'll call him in the morning, then."

"I will. And don't worry, he'll be fine."

"Thank you."

Turning away, Vicki headed for the door. She glanced over her shoulder to see if Antonio was behind her, surprised to find him right on her heels. It was a mystery how he moved so noiselessly in those boots when a nurse wearing soft-soled shoes could be heard walking in the corridor.

She stopped at the door, her gaze darting right and left through the glass.

Antonio opened the door and stepped out into the night, then turned and offered her his hand. She took it, grateful for his presence.

Antonio opened the car door for her. She checked the backseat before getting inside.

"He is not here," Battista said, getting behind the wheel.

"How do you know?"

He put the key in the ignition and started the engine. "I know."

She stared at him a moment, then locked her door. She hated being afraid like this. She had never thought of herself as a coward before, but she felt like one now, afraid of the dark, afraid of staying home alone after the sun went down.

She slid a glance at Antonio. He looked relaxed and confident, sitting there with one hand on the wheel. But then she noticed the taut muscle along his jaw, the way his gaze was constantly moving as he checked the road ahead and behind, peering into the darkness on both sides of the street.

"There was another murder." The words erupted from her throat, unbidden.

Battista nodded.

"He did it, didn't he? That thing with the yellow eyes?"

Battista nodded again.

"I guess he's going to stick around until there aren't any redheads left in town," she remarked, hoping he would deny it.

"I will not let him hurt you."

"What about Suzie Collins and Rhonda McGee? Can you defend them, too? And what about the women in nearby towns like Woods Hollow, and Pine Crest? There's bound to be some redheads in those places. And in all the other towns hereabouts. Can you protect them all?"

"I cannot save the world, Victoria."

"Can't you make him stop?"

"There is only one way to stop him."

"Can you do it?"

"I can try."

"You told me you weren't a vampire hunter," she said accusingly. "But you are, aren't you? Like Tom?"

"I am not." Battista made a sound of disgust in his throat. "I had heard he was one of the best, but from what I saw tonight, I am surprised he has lived as long as he has."

"He was trying to protect me."

"He cannot protect you from a hospital bed," Battista said gruffly, then added, in a softer tone, "I am all the protection you need."

Vicki stared at him. If she didn't know better, she would have sworn he sounded a trifle jealous.

She was still toying with that surprising thought when Battista pulled into the driveway and killed the engine. He exited the car, then made a slow circle around the vehicle, reminding her of a wild animal testing the wind for danger.

She rolled down the window. "Is he here?"

"No."

She wanted to ask him how he knew that with such certainty, but she was suddenly afraid of the answer.

Antonio opened the door for her and helped her out of the car. She hurried up the stairs, rummaging in her purse for her keys as she went. She was glad she had left lights burning on the porch and inside the house.

She was aware of Battista standing behind her as she unlocked the door, following her into the house, closing and locking the door behind them.

His presence filled the room as well as her senses. He smelled of cologne and musk and raw masculinity.

She dropped her keys and her handbag amidst the clutter on the coffee table, blew out a deep breath, and turned to face him. "Would you mind . . . Will you stay the night again?"

"If you wish."

"Thanks." She fidgeted with a lock of her hair. "I'll make up the couch for you."

"No need. I will not sleep."

"You didn't sleep the other night, either, did you?"

"Go to bed, my sweet one."

"Yes, I think I will." But she didn't move, and neither did he.

"You wish something?" he asked.

She shook her head. "No. Good night."

She started past him only to be stayed by the light touch of his hand on her shoulder. She could have walked on by. He wasn't holding her, but she stopped, her heart rate accelerating when she looked up and met his gaze.

Time slowed, could have ceased to exist for all she knew or cared. She was aware of nothing but the man standing beside her. His dark blue gaze melded with hers, igniting a flame that started deep within her and spread with all the rapidity of a wildfire fanned by a high wind.

Heart pounding, she looked at him, and waited.

He didn't make her wait too long.

He murmured to her softly in a language she didn't understand, then swept her into his arms and kissed her, a long searing kiss that burned away the memory of every other man she had ever known, until she knew only him, saw only him. Wanted only him.

He deepened the kiss, his tongue teasing her lips, sending flames along every nerve, igniting a need so primal, so volatile, she thought she might explode. She pressed her body to his, hating the layers of cloth that separated his flesh from hers. She had never reacted to a man's kisses like this before, never felt such an overwhelming need to touch and be touched. A distant part of her mind questioned her ill-conceived desire for a man she hardly knew, but she paid no heed. Nothing mattered now but his arms holding her close, his mouth on hers.

Battista groaned low in his throat. He had to stop this now, while he could, before his lust for blood overcame his desire for her sweet flesh. The two were closely interwoven, the one fueling the other. He knew he should let her go before it was too late, before his hunger overcame his good sense, before he succumbed to the need burning through him. He could scarcely remember the last time he had embraced a woman he had not regarded as prey. But this woman was more than mere sustenance. Her body fit his perfectly, her voice sang to his soul, her gaze warmed the cold dark places in his heart, shone like the sun in the depths of his hell-bound spirit.

He felt his fangs lengthen, his body tense as the hunger surged through him, a relentless thirst that would not long be denied.

Battista tore his mouth from hers. Turning his head away, he took several slow, deep breaths until he had regained control of the beast that dwelled within him.

"Antonio?" Vicki asked breathlessly. "Is something wrong?"

He took another deep breath before he replied, "No, my sweet." Summoning every ounce of willpower he possessed, he put her away from him. "It has been a long night. You should get some sleep."

She looked up at him, her eyes filled with confusion. He expected her to sleep, now?

He forced a smile. "Go to bed, my sweet one."

Vicki stared at him a moment; then, with a nod, she left the room. That was the second time he had kissed her and then backed away. Was there something wrong with the way she kissed? But no, he had been as caught up in the moment as she. She couldn't have been mistaken about that.

She closed the bedroom door behind her, then stood there, trying to sort out her feelings. She knew very little about Mr. Antonio Battista. She had no idea where he came from, who he was, if he had family or friends, or what he did for a living. But one thing she did know: no other man had ever affected her the way he did, intrigued her the way he did, made her want him the way he did.

Tomorrow morning, she thought. Tomorrow morning she would find out more about the mysterious Mr. Battista.

Chapter 13

He was gone in the morning. As she walked through the house, it was as though Antonio had never been there. Going into the kitchen, Vicki saw that he hadn't had so much as a cup of coffee to help him stay awake.

Frowning, she put some bread in the toaster and poured herself a cup of orange juice. He was an odd duck. He showed up at the diner every night and ordered food he didn't eat. She remembered asking him why he came to Ozzie's and his reply, something about it being her presence that drew him. It had been a flattering, romantic thing for him to say, even if it was a lot of poppycock.

Or was it?

Of course it was. She had known the man for less than two weeks. And shared two of the most potent, heady, amazing kisses she'd ever had.

After buttering her toast, she sat down at the table to eat, her mind trying to unravel the puzzle that was Antonio Battista.

She hadn't solved a thing when the phone rang.

It was Tom Duncan.

"Hi," she said. "How are you feeling?"

"Like a damn fool. Can you come and pick me up?"

"Sure. What time?"

"Whenever you can get here."

Vicki glanced at the clock. "Twenty minutes?"

"See you then."

She hung up the receiver, finished her orange juice, and went into the bedroom to get dressed.

Duncan was sitting on the edge of the bed when she entered his room. He looked up, his expression sheepish when he saw her. "Hi."

"Hi. You ready to go?"

"Yeah. The nurse went to get a wheelchair. I told her I could walk, but she said it was hospital policy, yadda yadda yadda."

Vicki grinned. "How's your head?"

"It hurts." He shook his head, then winced. "I can't believe I ran out after him like that. If anybody else had pulled a stupid stunt like that, I'd have given him a tongue-lashing he wouldn't soon forget."

"Would it make you feel any better if I bawled you out?"

"You're too late."

"Mr. Duncan? Are you ready to go?"

Vicki glanced over her shoulder to see a nurse standing in the doorway, a wheelchair behind her.

"Yeah."

Duncan settled himself in the wheelchair, his expression sullen. Vicki followed the nurse down the hallway and out the front door to where Vicki had parked Duncan's Camaro.

She pulled his keys out of the pocket of her jeans. "Do you want to drive?" she asked, "or would you rather I did?"

"Maybe you should."

"All right." She unlocked the passenger-side door. "Are you staying at the hotel?"

He grunted an affirmative as he eased down on the seat and closed the door.

Vicki turned the key in the ignition, looked over her shoulder, and pulled away from the curb. The Camaro might be old and beat up, but it ran like a dream.

"So," Duncan said, "tell me about Battista."

"What do you want to know?"

"Where did you meet him?"

"At the diner." She looked at Duncan and smiled. "It's where I meet everybody."

He grunted. "Is he from around here?"

"I have no idea. I really don't know anything about him."

"Yet he was prowling around your house late last night."

"It's a good thing for you that he was!" Vicki retorted.

"You're mighty quick to jump to his defense, considering you don't know anything about him."

She slid a glance in his direction. "What are you implying?"

"How do you know he didn't attack me?"

"Antonio? Why on earth would he do that?"

"He's new in town. I did some checking around. You told the police you saw him leave the diner with two of the murdered women. You do the math."

"He doesn't have yellow eyes."

"That could be a trick of the light, or he might wear contacts."

"Yellow contacts?" she asked skeptically.

Duncan shrugged. "I've seen stranger things."

"Are you suggesting that Antonio is a murderer

who . . ." She forced the words past her lips. "Who kills women and drains them of their blood?" She stared at him in shock when he didn't answer. "You don't think he's a vampire? You do, don't you?" she demanded when he didn't deny it. She thought of Antonio's potent kisses and her reaction to them and shook her head vigorously. "That's impossible! He was at my house the same night as Falco."

"They could be the same man," Duncan remarked, his voice thoughtful.

Vicki shook her head again. "Antonio doesn't have blond hair."

"Vampires can change their appearance."

"But they were both here at the same time," she reminded him. "Antonio chased Falco away and saved your life."

"I didn't see who hit me. It could have been Battista."

"Then why did he pretend to save you? It doesn't make any sense."

"You're right." Duncan rested his head against the back of the seat and closed his eyes. The hit on the head must have affected his thinking. If Battista were the killer, Vicki would be dead by now, Tom thought, and so would he. Unless Battista was playing some sort of insane game, but that didn't make sense, either. All of the vampire's kills had been quick and clean. He had stalked his prey, taken their blood and a lock of hair, and vanished.

But what if Falco had changed his M.O.? What if he was looking for a diversion from his usual method of killing? Thinking himself smarter than any mere mortal, the vampire could have decided to change the rules, make things a little more exciting . . .

Tom scrubbed his hands over his face. He hadn't

gotten much sleep last night. Now, with his head throbbing, he couldn't think straight, couldn't shake off the feeling that he had seen Battista somewhere before.

He opened his eyes when Vicki switched off the engine. She glanced at the hotel, then looked over at him. "Are you going to be all right here?"

"Sure."

"If you need anything, call me. I'll be home most of the day."

"I will, thanks." He frowned when she handed him the keys. "How are you going to get home?"

"I can walk. It's not that far."

"Are you sure? I can drive you, if you want."

"No, I can use the exercise. Take care of yourself."

On the sidewalk, she waved good-bye to Tom, then started down the street. She waved at old Mrs. Kent, who was sweeping the walkway in front of her son's florist shop, smiled at Toby Benjamin, who was mowing the grass in front of the library. Ordinary people doing ordinary things.

She paused in front of every shop to look at the displays. She told herself she was window-shopping, but she was really hoping to run across Antonio. She had quite a few questions she wanted to ask him, like what he was doing in town and where he came from, and what he did for a living, and why he never seemed to eat or drink anything and why she only saw him at night . . . .

Vicki frowned, annoyed with Tom for planting the ridiculous notion that Antonio might be a vampire in her mind. Antonio was no more a vampire than she was!

Crossing the street, she paused to look in the window of Cliff's Department Store, thinking it was time she bought herself some new jeans and sweatshirts, and maybe a dress or two, like the pretty green and white dress in the window.

Her mind made up, she went inside. There was nothing like shopping to take a woman's mind off her troubles.

Half an hour later, she emerged from the store carrying two large shopping bags. Inside were three pairs of jeans, two sweaters, two sweatshirts, a long black wool skirt, the green and white dress, a pair of black heels, and a matching handbag.

She hadn't bought any new clothes in, well, in forever. She told herself that the fact that she was doing so now had nothing whatsoever to do with Antonio Battista, though she had to admit she couldn't wait for him to see her in the other new dress she had bought, a slinky black jersey with a low back and a come-hither slit up one side. Of course, she had no idea when she'd have an excuse to wear such a thing but, as her mother always said, it was a smart girl who was prepared for any occasion.

She was about to turn down Fifth Street toward home when Mrs. Heath waved at her. Smiling, Vicki crossed the street.

"Good morning, Mrs. Heath," Vicki said. "Isn't it a lovely day?"

"Yes, indeed." Mrs. Heath turned the hose on her flower bed. "How was your date with your young man?"

"It was very nice. And you know what? He is related to the Thomas Duncan that you knew."

"You must be careful, dear. I'm sure your Mr. Duncan told you there's a vampire in town. I don't want him to get you."

"The man with yellow eyes," Vicki said.

"Yes, I should have told you before, but I didn't

want to frighten you." Mrs. Heath made a tsking sound. "That was foolish of me."

"How do you know about him?"

"Why, he's the one who tried to kill me all those years ago," Mrs. Heath said, her voice as calm as if they were discussing the color of her daisies. She patted her hair. "It's white now, but it used to be as red as yours."

Vicki stared at Mrs. Heath, unable to believe she could talk about it so calmly.

"Are you all right, dear?" the older woman asked. "You look a little pale."

Vicki shook her head, certain she would never be all right again.

Chapter 14

When she got home, Vicki hung her new jeans, skirt and dress on hangers and put them in the closet, along with her heels and handbag. She folded the sweaters and sweatshirts and put them in her dresser drawer, carefully concentrating on each task so she wouldn't have to think about what Ramona Heath had told her.

In the kitchen, she opened a can of soda, then sat down to read. After the first few pages, she put the book aside. She thumbed through a magazine, then went into the kitchen to get an apple. She washed it, then put it back in the fridge. Too restless to sit still, she went outside and started raking the leaves in the front yard.

It was a beautiful afternoon. The sun was shining. The birds were singing. The air was cool and crisp but not cold. The autumn leaves rustled beneath her feet as she raked them into a pile.

But all she could think of was yellow eyes and bodies drained of blood.

She shivered, suddenly chilled as she glanced over her shoulder. There was no one there, of course. It was broad daylight. Everyone knew vampires were active only after dark . . .

Tossing the rake aside, she went into the den and fired up her computer. She brought up Google in her browser, then typed "vampires" in the search window. The first page that came up read, "Web results 1-10 of about 2,310,000 for vampires."

It was going to be a long day.

Settling back in her chair, she began to read. She found a wealth of information in the first ten sites alone!

One site claimed that everyone knew about vampires and also knew that there were no such things, at least not as portrayed in Hollywood. But there were vampires; however, they didn't suck the blood of humans, instead, they drained them of energy. According to one site, those who were thought to be vampires could have been merely people suffering from a variety of diseases, including acute anemia, which would leave a person looking pale, and catalepsy, which caused temporary paralysis so that the sufferer appeared dead. A person with catalepsy could see and hear but couldn't move. Vicki shuddered, imagining the horror of a relative who laid a loved one suffering from this condition in a coffin for burial, thinking they were dead, and then saw that loved one trying to rise from the coffin.

Another site suggested that many things that could not be explained in any other way were attributed to vampires. One of the most astonishing was the fact that some unlearned people believed that in the 1300s, vampires had caused the Black Death, which was, of course, bubonic fever.

In ancient times, it was believed that a baby born with a caul, teeth, or a tail was doomed to become a vampire, as was the seventh son of a seventh son, and anyone unfortunate enough to be bitten by a vampire. It was also believed that a child born out of wedlock would become one of the Undead. She had to laugh at that. If every child born out of wedlock in this day and age became a vampire, the world would be crawling with them.

She could only shake her head as she read about the various ways people had used to destroy vampires. Some believed in burying the body face down so that if it tried to escape, it would only dig itself deeper into the earth. Sometimes wooden stakes were placed above the grave so that if the vampire tried to leave, it would stab itself, hopefully through the heart. Other methods of ensuring that a vampire did not rise again were wrapping the body in cloth or a carpet, or tying its arms and legs together.

Another site, which she found fascinating, stated that vampires were not supernatural or immortal, but that the vampire trait was part of their DNA, and this trait was likened to a viral imperfection. Some believed this trait could be passed on, some said it could only be inherited. There was another theory that vampires were beings who could not accept their own death, and when their body died, their soul invaded the body of an infant at birth, thereby providing the vampire with a new body and a new life. It was believed that these vampires went through many bodies, and for this reason they thought of themselves as old souls. It was believed that these creatures were hardier than humans, healed faster when hurt or sick, had heightened senses, and were extremely sensitive to sunlight.

By the time she reached the third page, her mind was swimming with so much conflicting information that she didn't know what to believe.

After shutting down her computer, she went into the

kitchen, surprised to see that the sun was setting. Amazing, how quickly one lost track of time while cruising the Web.

Standing in front of the refrigerator, trying to decide what to have for dinner, she happened to glance out the window. There was nothing there, but she went over and drew the curtains anyway, and then she went through the rest of the house, locking the doors, making sure all the windows were closed and locked, drawing all the curtains and drapes.

Feeling much better, she went back into the kitchen to fix dinner.

Feeling weary and utterly discouraged, Tom Duncan entered Ozzie's Diner. He took a seat at a table in the far corner, one hand idly exploring the bandage on the back of his head. In spite of his injury, he had spent the afternoon scouring the town for Dimitri Falco's resting place. Unfortunately, he hadn't found what he was looking for. Tomorrow, he planned to widen his search, perhaps take in Woods Hollow and Cottonwood. Of course, as swiftly as vampires could travel, Falco's hideout could be hundreds of miles away from Pear Blossom Creek.

With a sigh, Duncan picked up the menu.

He was still trying to decide what to have for dinner when the waitress approached his table.

"Hey there," she said brightly. "Have you decided yet, or do you need another few minutes?"

Tom looked up into a pair of sparkling brown eyes and wondered why he hadn't noticed her before. "How's the trout?"

The waitress, Bobbie Sue, according to her name tag, shook her head. "Not tonight."

"What do you recommend?"

"The fried chicken is looking really good."

"All right, I'll have that."

"Soup or salad?"

"Whichever one looks best."

"Soup," she said, and jotted it down on her pad. "Can I bring you a cup of coffee?"

He nodded. "Thanks."

He watched her walk away, admiring the sway of her hips, surprised by the rush of desire that infused him.

She returned a few minutes later with his coffee. "Here you go."

"Thanks. Say, I don't suppose you'd like to go to dinner and a movie some night?"

"I thought you were going out with Vicki?"

He shrugged. "It wasn't anything serious. Just dinner. What do you say?"

"Sure, I'd like that, as long as we don't have dinner here."

He laughed. "We'll go anywhere you like."

"Really?"

"Sure, why not?"

"My favorite restaurant's the Wayside Grill over in Woods Hollow. They have a new movie theater there, too."

"Sounds good to me. Just say when."

"I'm off tomorrow night."

"Tomorrow night it is."

Too nervous to relax, Vicki wandered through the house. She fed the fish, straightened a picture here, a figurine there. She glanced at the windows again and again, wondering if the vampire was out there, waiting, watching.

Finally, unable to resist, she went to the front window and peered outside.

And he was there, a stark figure standing on the sidewalk, his yellow eyes glinting in the darkness.

Vicki, come out to me. His voice echoed deep within her mind. *You know you want to. Even now, you're wondering what it would be like to succumb to me.*

"No!"

You can lie to yourself, but you can't lie to me.

"Go away!" She screamed the words.

You will be mine, Vicki Cavendish. Sooner or later, you will be mine. That weak mortal hunter, Duncan, cannot save you.

She was trembling now. His voice mesmerized her, tempting her to go to him, even as her own morbid curiosity urged her toward the door. No! She willed herself to stay where she was. Antonio would come. He would save her.

The sound of Falco's laughter rang out in her mind. *Battista can't save you. He's no match for me.*

"He beat you the other night!"

The vampire's anger rolled over her in thick black waves until she felt like she was drowning in pitch. And then, to her horror, she saw him bending over Sharlene's lifeless body, his mouth stained with her blood, a lock of Sharlene's hair clutched in his hand. Gradually, the image altered, the scene shifted, and suddenly the body at his feet was no longer Sharlene's but her own, and she knew she was looking into the future as he saw it.

"No." The word emerged from Vicki's throat in a choked whisper. "No."

The eerie sound of his inhuman laughter engulfed her, beating against her ears, penetrating her whole being until she was shaking from the pain of it.

I would have made you my queen. His voice was filled with fury. *Now, you will beg me for death before it comes.*

She stood rooted to the spot, too terrified to move, unable to think. She was going to die at his hands, and there was nothing she could do about it. Why not go out and get it over with now?

She stared out the front window while the vampire's threat echoed like thunder in her mind. If she went to him now, maybe he would forgive her for her earlier insolence.

"Victoria!" A fist pounded on the door. "Victoria, let me in!"

The door, she thought. She should answer the door, but her feet refused to move.

"Victoria, I know you are in there." His voice was quieter now, moving over her like cool water on a hot day, washing away her fears. "Open the door, my sweet one."

Freed from her earlier enchantment, she moved toward the door and turned the lock.

Battista stood on the porch, his dark eyes filled with concern. "Are you all right?"

She shook her head, searching for the words to describe the awful terror that had engulfed her, and then she burst into tears.

Muttering an oath, Battista crossed the threshold. Lifting her into his arms, he carried her to the sofa.

Vicki heard the door close. A distant part of her mind wondered how he had closed the door, but it was too painful to think and then it didn't matter. He was sitting down, cradling her trembling body against his broad chest, whispering to her in a language she didn't understand but found comforting just the same.

Gradually, her tears slowed and stopped but she didn't

move, didn't ever want to move. His large hand lightly stroked her back. His breath fanned her cheek. She felt cherished, protected.

"How?" she murmured after a time. "How is it that you always show up when he's here?"

"Does it matter?"

With a sigh, she shook her head. "No." All that mattered was that he was there now. Lately, it was only in his arms that she felt safe.

It was only later, after Antonio had tucked her into bed, that she wondered if Duncan was right after all. Maybe the reason Antonio always turned up on the same nights as Falco was because they were one and the same.

But somehow she was just too tired to care.

Chapter 15

Dimitri Falco stalked the dark streets, his fury growing as he thought of the woman who had dared to defy him. She was a stubborn one, a fact she would soon regret. He had chosen her as his next victim, and he would not be denied. Try as she might, she would not be able to resist him indefinitely. Her defenses would weaken. In time, she would come to him when he called.

He spat an oath into the night. He could take her by force if need be, but the mere idea rankled. In a thousand years, he had never had to force any female to surrender to his will. He would not start now.

Returning to his lair, he ran his hands along his trophy wall, his fingers delving into the thick red strands of human hair. He remembered each kill, the delicious terror imprinted on each face, the sweet nectar of each throat, no two exactly the same, each unique in its ability to satisfy his insatiable thirst.

He licked his lips as the hunger rose up within him,

at first no more than a thought, then a desire, then a need that would not be denied.

Soon, he thought. Soon she would be his. When that time came, she would regret the pain she had caused him by making him wait.

Chapter 16

Vicki wasn't surprised to awaken the next morning and find herself alone in the house. Rolling onto her back, she stared up at the ceiling. Antonio had held her all through the night. He had been there when she woke in the dark, terrified by dreams of Falco hunting her down, his fangs savaging her throat even as his hand ripped out a handful of her hair. Antonio's voice had soothed her fears. His intoxicating kisses had chased all thought of the nightmare from her mind. Secure in his embrace, she had reveled in the touch of his hands and his lips, every nerve and cell in her body tingling with desire. She wished that he had stayed the night, that they had made love, that he was lying there beside her.

With a sigh, she pulled on her robe and padded into the kitchen. She opened the curtains on a morning that was gray and dreary. A rumble of thunder promised showers before the day was out.

She poured herself a cup of coffee, annoyed that another night had passed and she hadn't gotten around to asking Antonio anything about his past or his present. Tonight for sure, she promised herself, and wondered again what he did during the day. She knew it wasn't work that kept him occupied, so what was it?

The sound of rain drew her gaze to the window again. So much for working in the yard. Ordinarily, she loved the rain, but not today. She needed to be busy, needed something that would keep her from thinking about yellow eyes and vampires and bodies drained of blood.

Now, in the light of day, even a rainy day, it was hard to believe that beings like vampires existed. They were supposed to be creatures of myth and legend, the focus of scary stories told around campfires late at night.

With nothing better to do, she decided to clean out the fridge. But even that mundane task backfired on her when she dropped a bottle of ketchup on the floor. She stared at the red stain spreading over the tile and thought of Sharlene and the other women who had been killed. She hoped their deaths had come quickly, before they had time to be afraid.

Grabbing a rag, she wiped up the mess, then went into the bathroom. She filled the tub with hot water, added a generous amount of bubbles, and grabbed a book from the shelf. Settling back in the tub, she lost herself in the fantasy world of Frodo and Sam where good always triumphed over evil and the world of men prevailed in spite of overwhelming odds.

Tom Duncan glanced at his watch. Almost five. He'd have to hurry if he was going to make it back to Pear Blossom Creek in time to shower and change his clothes and make it to Bobbie Sue's house by six.

Bobbie Sue. She had been much on his mind this

day, making it difficult to concentrate on what he was about. The thought of going out with her remained the only bright spot in what had been a decidedly unprofitable day. He had found nothing, nothing at all to indicate where Dimitri Falco might take his rest during the hours of daylight. With a shake of his head, Duncan wondered if he'd lost whatever gift for hunting the Undead he had possessed. Perhaps it was time to give up hunting and take up a new line of work, something a little less intense, like flipping burgers at McDonald's.

He muttered an oath when the small dirt road he had hoped was a shortcut to the main highway narrowed even further and then came to an abrupt end. He was about to curse his bad luck when he saw the points of a white picket fence barely visible behind a mountain of weeds and shrubbery. Glancing to the left, he saw a weathered sign that read SHADY CORNERS CEMETERY.

Feeling a rush of anticipation, he cut the engine and climbed out of the car. He went around to the trunk, grabbed a few necessary items, and made his way to the gate. It opened with a loud squeal of rusty hinges.

His footsteps made no sound as he moved among the graves, the majority of them overgrown with weeds and briars. Not surprising, he supposed, since the dates on most of the tombstones dated back to the early 1880s. Some were so ancient that time had erased the markings.

And then he saw it, a faint disturbance in the dirt near a crypt made of aged gray stone. A white marble angel sat on the top, sightless eyes staring into eternity.

Going suddenly still, Duncan paused outside the door of the tomb, his senses testing the air. A vampire rested behind the door. He knew it as well as he knew the sun would rise in the east.

The door to the sepulcher opened with a whisper of

stone against stone. Peering inside, he saw a single coffin on a raised dais.

Duncan took a step inside, his nostrils filling with the lingering stink of death and decay.

Holding stake and hammer at the ready in one hand, he lifted the lid of the coffin.

The body inside rested on a bed of white satin, its skin almost as pale as the cloth that lined the casket. A bit of dried blood was caught in the corner of its mouth, the red standing out in stark contrast against the wan complexion.

Taking a deep breath, Duncan placed the sharp tip of the hawthorn stake over the vampire's heart and raised the hammer.

Muttering, "Die, you bloodsucker," he drove the stake home.

The creature within the coffin shrieked as the stake penetrated its heart. Blood sprayed from the wound, splattering over Duncan, the vampire, and the walls of the tomb.

The vampire writhed in agony for several minutes and then, with a last hiss, the creature's body just aged away until there was nothing left but the vague outline of a body against the silk.

When it was done, Duncan turned away and wiped his face on his sleeve.

After days of searching, he had found a vampire.

Unfortunately, it wasn't the vampire he had been searching for.

Vicki hummed softly as she dressed for work that night. She was looking forward to getting out of the house. Anything was better than sitting at home thinking about vampires and listening to the rain pounding on the roof. She was anxious to see Gus and the other regulars, to hear people talking about mundane things like the weather and the price of gas. Here, at home alone, she had too much time to think about things she didn't want to think about.

Slipping into her coat, she grabbed her keys and her handbag and headed for the front door, only to pause with her hand on the latch.

Moving to the window beside the door, she drew back the curtain and peered out into the night. Was Falco out there, waiting for her in the darkness? She leaned forward, her eyes narrowing as she tried to see through the heavy curtain of rain.

A knock at the door caused her heart to leap into her throat.

"Victoria?"

"Antonio!" With a sigh of relief, she opened the door.

And looked into a pair of glowing yellow eyes.

Vicki stared at the vampire, her handbag and keys falling from fingers suddenly numb. His was a face she remembered all too well. Now, knowing what he was, it surprised her that his countenance was fair to look upon. A creature such as this, one who did such unspeakable things to the innocent, should be as ugly as the atrocities he committed.

He held out his hand and smiled. "Come to me, Victoria. It is your destiny."

His voice, which should have been as cold as the grave, beckoned her softly.

She took one step forward, and then another. One more step and she would be at his mercy.

His breathing quickened. His lips parted in a parody

of a smile. "Yes, yes," he murmured. "Come to me." His eyes blazed with anticipation as the toe of her shoe touched the threshold.

"No! Victoria, stop!"

Vicki shook her head as a wild cry, louder than the thunder that rolled across the heavens, reached her ears, breaking the vampire's enchantment.

Fangs bared, Dimitri Falco whirled around and hurled himself at the man standing at the bottom of the porch steps.

After slamming the door, Vicki ran to the window, but she could make out little of what was happening. Both Antonio and Falco were clad in black, making it difficult to separate one from the other. The rain blurred her vision. Thunder shook the earth. Lightning ripped through the lowering clouds. A short distance away, a tree went up in flames.

Needing to see what was happening, Vicki ran out onto the porch. She stopped at the edge, one hand wrapping around the post as she watched the battle below.

It was a strangely silent and graceful battle. Fangs flashed in the darkness, as blindingly white as the lightning that rent the skies.

Vicki pressed a hand to her heart, wishing she could see what was going on, praying that Antonio would emerge victorious, though she knew the odds were slim that he would survive a battle against an angry vampire. As the battle raged, they moved away from the porch toward the street, making it more difficult for her to see what was happening.

She shuddered, remembering bits and pieces of what she had read on-line—that vampires had the strength of twenty men, that they could change shape, that they could only be destroyed by driving a stake through their heart, burning them to ash, or cutting off their head.

Somehow, she doubted Antonio had a wooden stake or a hatchet stuck in his back pocket, so unless Falco was struck by lightning, there seemed little hope that Antonio would destroy him.

Her fingernails dug into the post as the battle grew more intense. There was a sudden silence as the rain stopped. The thunder grew quiet in the skies, and it was as if the whole earth were holding its breath.

Into the stillness came a high-pitched keening cry more horrible than anything Vicki had ever heard in her life.

There was a flurry of indiscernible motion near the street, and then, in the blink of an eye, the fight was over and only one man remained, indistinct in the darkness. He stood there a moment, his back toward her, staring into the distance, and then slowly sank to the ground, his body sprawled on the walkway, his head and face covered by the folds of a long black coat.

Holding her breath, Vicki backed toward the door. She stepped over the threshold and into the safety of her house, her gaze never leaving the dark shape sprawled on the sidewalk at the foot of the steps.

Was it Falco? Or Antonio?

She watched for what seemed like an eternity before the man on the pavement moved. Overhead, the moon pushed its way through the clouds.

On the street, the man sat up, brushing his coat aside, revealing a head of thick black hair. With a sigh of relief, Vicki ran out the front door and down the stairs.

"Antonio!" Grabbing him by the arm, she pulled him to his feet, her gaze darting right and left. "Hurry, before he comes back."

Staggering, he followed her up the stairs and into the warm haven of her home.

She quickly closed and locked the door, then turned to help him out of his wet coat.

"You're bleeding!" she exclaimed. In the light cast by the lamps, she could see that there was blood on the front of his shirt. He had a wicked-looking cut on his left forearm, another on his cheek, and still another on his neck. And he looked pale, so very pale. "You're not going to faint, are you? Here, sit down. Maybe we should go to the hospital. That gash on your arm looks like it needs stitching."

With a shake of his head, he sank down on her sofa. "No need."

"No need? It's almost to the bone. Did he have a knife?"

A faint smile tugged at Antonio's lips. "No, just his teeth."

Frowning, Vicki went into the kitchen. She filled a bowl with warm, salted water, pulled a couple of clean dish towels from a drawer, then went into the bathroom for a tube of first aid cream before returning to the living room.

Antonio was sitting where she had left him, his head resting against the back of the sofa, his eyes closed. For one horrible moment, she thought he was dead. From where she stood, it didn't look like he was breathing.

"Antonio?" She hurried to the couch and sat beside him. "Oh, Lord, Antonio, please don't be dead."

His eyelids fluttered open. "Undead," he murmured with a wry grin.

"What?"

"Nothing. Do not worry about me, my sweet one."

"But, you're hurt, bleeding." She placed the bowl, towels, and cream on the table beside the sofa. "Let me help you out of your . . ." She stared at his arm. It had stopped bleeding. What had been a nasty gash almost to the bone only moments ago was now no more than a wide scratch on his arm. The cut on his cheek had disappeared. The one on his neck was closing, fading, gone.

Vicki looked up to find him watching her, his expression impassive.

She sat back on her heels while her mind tried to make sense of what she was seeing. She tried to tell herself it was nothing out of the ordinary, that some people just healed faster than others. But cuts as deep as the one in his forearm didn't heal in a matter of minutes.

She clasped her hands in her lap, willing them to stop trembling. "What?" she asked in a voice that sounded nothing like her own. "What are you?"

Chapter 17

"I'm a vampire hunter."

Bobbie Sue stared at Tom Duncan, then rolled her eyes. "If you don't want to tell me what you do for a living, that's fine," she said coolly. "You don't have to make up some outrageous lie."

"It's not a lie," Duncan said.

"But there's no such thing as vampires," Bobbie Sue said. "Everyone knows that."

"Are you sure?"

"Of course. They're just make believe, like Franken-stein's monster and werewolves and aliens from outer space."

Duncan lifted his wineglass and took a long drink, wondering if he had just ruined his chances of seeing Bobbie Sue again. They were sitting at a cozy table in a dark corner of the Wayside Grill, getting to know each other over dinner. Bobbie Sue had told him about her life. She was twenty-two, the youngest of three children. She had been born and raised in Pear Blossom Creek. After graduation, she had moved to Nashville, where she had fallen in love with a Marine. When he was killed in a plane crash, she had returned home. She worked at Ozzie's Diner at night and went to beauty school during the day.

She stared at him over the rim of her glass. "Aren't they? Just make believe?"

"I wish they were."

Her eyes widened. "Is that why you're here? You're looking for a vampire?"

He nodded.

"I don't believe you."

Putting his glass aside, he leaned across the table. "I'm telling you the truth."

"No. No, there's no such thing."

He reached for her hand when he saw the panic rising in her eyes. If she couldn't handle the truth, he would only tell her a part of it, for now.

"Bobbie Sue, listen, I'm after the man who killed those women and drained them of blood. He thinks he's a vampire." His hand tightened on hers. "You're not in any danger. He only kills women with red hair—"

Her eyes widened in alarm. "Vicki has red hair."

"I've warned her to be on the lookout for a man with yellow eyes—"

"Yellow eyes! She saw him. At the Blue Horse!"

"I know. She told me." He regarded her thoughtfully. "Are you all right? You're not gonna run screaming into the night, are you?"

"No, silly."

"Do you still feel like a movie?"

"Are you sure Vicki's all right? Shouldn't you be watching her house or something?"

"I've been keeping an eye on her."

"But not tonight." She glanced out the window at the rain. If there really were vampires, this looked like the kind of night when they would be out. "I think we should go and check on her."

"All right."

Duncan finished his wine and paid the check. Hand in hand, they dashed across the parking lot to his car. He unlocked the door and helped her in, slid behind the wheel, and thrust the key into the ignition.

Bobbie Sue's nervousness transmitted itself to him and he gunned the engine. He had no business being out on a date when Dimitri Falco was on the loose and there were three redheaded women in town, anyone of whom could be Falco's next victim. Still, they all seemed like smart women. He had warned them there was a serial killer on the loose, admonished them to keep their doors and windows locked, not to go out alone after dark, not to invite any strangers, however charming they might be, into their homes. There hadn't been any killings in the last few days and Tom couldn't help hoping that the bastard had left town.

They drove straight to the diner. Duncan found a parking place by the front door and hurried into the diner with Bobbie Sue on his heels.

"She's not here!" Bobbie Sue exclaimed.

Duncan grunted softly. "Maybe she called in sick."

"I'll ask Gus."

When questioned, Gus shook his head. "I haven't heard from her. I called a few minutes ago, but she didn't answer the phone. I was about to call Ned and ask him and Arnie to go out to her place and look around."

"My date and I will go," Bobbie Sue said.

"Call me when you get there and let me know what's going on. It isn't like her not to call if she isn't coming in."

With a nod, Bobbie Sue left the kitchen and went back into the diner.

"What did you find out?" Duncan asked.

"She didn't call. I told Gus we'd go check on her."

"Let's do it."

"She must be home," Bobbie Sue said when they pulled into Vicki's driveway a few minutes later. "Her car's here and the lights are on."

Duncan parked his car beside Vicki's and turned off the ignition and the lights. Rounding the car, he opened Bobbie Sue's door, and they ran up the stairs to the porch.

Duncan rang the doorbell once, twice.

He saw Vicki peering through the window beside the door, then the door swung open and she was standing there.

"Hey," he said. "Are you all right?"

"Yes, why?"

"Gus was worried about you," Bobbie Sue said. "You didn't call in."

"Oh. I guess I forgot."

Bobbie Sue tilted her head to one side. "You forgot?"

Vicki glanced over her shoulder, then looked back at Bobbie Sue. "I'll call Gus. Is there anything else?"

"Vicki, is something wrong?"

"Wrong? No, of course not. Why do you ask?"

"You're just acting kind of, you know, weird."

"Is there anything we can do?" Duncan asked.

"I don't think so. I—"

"I need to use the restroom," Bobbie Sue said, and before Vicki could stop her, she swept into the house. "Oh," she said, "I didn't know you had company."

Duncan looked at Vicki, wondering if he and Bobbie Sue had interrupted something best left uninterrupted. "Who's here?"

"Antonio stopped by," Vicki replied, her voice tight.

"And he's bleeding," Bobbie Sue said, her voice shrill. "What happened?"

Duncan moved past Vicki, admonishing her to close and lock the door. Going into the living room, he stood in front of the sofa, his gaze narrowing as he took in Battista's appearance.

Duncan swore under his breath, his hand reaching up to curl around the heavy gold cross at his throat.

"I should have known," he said, his voice hard. "You're one of them."

"One of what?" Bobbie Sue asked.

"He's a dirty, no-good, blood-sucking vampire."

Bobbie Sue looked at Duncan and shook her head. "You said there was no such thing."

"I lied."

"So he's really a . . . a . . ." She uttered a wordless cry, then her eyes rolled back in her head and she fainted.

Duncan caught her before she hit the floor, but his eyes remained locked on Antonio's. "I knew you looked familiar."

Antonio lifted one brow but said nothing.

Duncan's eyes narrowed. "It is you, isn't it?"

Vicki stared at Antonio in stunned disbelief. "Tell me it isn't true."

"I was going to tell you," he said, rising. "It is one of the reasons I came here tonight."

She covered her mouth with her fingertips, remembering the passionate kisses they had shared, horrified beyond words to think that she had kissed a man who wasn't even a man. A man who wasn't even alive, who drank blood to survive! Feeling suddenly light-headed, she thought that she, too, might faint. She sank down on the sofa, too stunned to speak, too numb to think.

Duncan stared at Battista over Bobbie Sue's inert

form, then swore a vile oath. Here he was, in the same room with a vampire, and all his gear was outside in the trunk of his car. Of course, even if it were close at hand he couldn't reach it, not with his arms full of soft feminine flesh.

Battista looked at Victoria. "Forgive me," he murmured, and then, to her astonishment, he vanished from her sight.

Muttering a curse, Duncan sat down on one of the chairs and cradled Bobbie Sue to his chest. "Dammit, I should have recognized him sooner."

Vicki crossed her arms over her breasts. This couldn't be real. She had to be dreaming again. "Where did you meet Antonio?"

"We didn't 'meet,' exactly. I was on my way back to my hotel one night, minding my own business, when I decided to take a shortcut through a vacant lot. He was there, bent over some poor kid. I pulled my .38 from my coat pocket and held it down at my side. I don't know why. I knew the gun wouldn't save me if he decided to attack. Something passed between us that night. I'm not sure what it was. I stood there, watching, while he finished drinking that kid's blood. When he was through, he whispered something to the boy and the boy walked away, looking none the worse for wear. Battista stared at me for what seemed like an eternity. I've no doubt he could have killed me that night. Instead, he bowed in my direction and then he vanished."

When he finished speaking, the silence in the room was complete save for the sound of the raindrops dripping from the eaves.

Vicki stared at the spot where Battista had stood only moments before. Duncan had told her that vampires were real, and she had believed him. She had read about the bodies being drained of blood. She had seen the creature with the yellow eyes. And still, in some deep corner of her mind, she had not truly believed such creatures existed.

She knew now why she had never seen Antonio during the day.

She knew now why she had never seen him eat or drink anything.

She knew now how he had followed her home and how he had gotten into her house when the doors and windows were locked. Oh, Lord, she had invited a vampire into her house! He could come in any time he wanted.

Stricken, she looked over at Tom. "I'll have to move."

"What?"

"I invited him in. He can come in whenever he wants."

"If you tell him to go, he'll have to go."

"Really? Just like that?"

"Just like that."

Bobbie Sue stirred in Tom's arms. Her eyelids fluttered open and she frowned. "What happened?" She glanced around, a blush rising in her cheeks when she saw Vicki.

"You fainted," Tom said, sitting her up in his lap. "Are you all right now?"

She looked confused a moment. "Fainted? Oh, I remember now . . ." She glanced at Tom and then at Vicki. "It was just a bad joke, right?"

"I wish it were," Vicki said.

Bobbie Sue slid off Tom's lap. "I think I want to go home."

Blowing out a sigh, Duncan stood. "All right."

Bobbie Sue started toward the front door, then paused. "Vicki, don't forget to call Gus."

"I won't."

"Are you going to be all right, here by yourself, hon? Maybe I should stay."

"Thanks, but I'd really like to be alone."

"But—"

"Don't worry about me, Bobbie. I'm going to turn on all the lights and the TV, and I'm not going to open the door for anyone, believe me!"

"Well, all right," Bobbie Sue said dubiously.

"I'll come by and look in on you later," Duncan said.

With a nod, Vicki followed them to the door. She closed and locked it behind them, then looked at the clock. It was still early. In spite of what she'd told Bobbie Sue, she should probably just go to work, but the thought of going out into the dark, alone, was just too daunting.

Going to the phone, she called Gus and told him she was sorry she hadn't called sooner, but she didn't feel up to working that night, which was certainly true enough.

After hanging up the receiver, she went from room to room, checking the doors and windows to make sure they were locked, though it seemed a waste of time now. Falco might not be able to cross the threshold, but there was nothing to keep Battista out.

And even as the thought crossed her mind, she heard him calling her name.

Slipping her hand inside the collar of her uniform, she touched her grandmother's crucifix, taking comfort in the feel of the silver in her hand.

She took a deep breath, then went to open the front door. Antonio stood on the porch in a pool of yellow lamplight.

"You can't come in," she said quickly. "I forbid it."

He lifted one brow in wry amusement but he made no move to cross the threshold. "You have nothing to fear from me, Victoria. I will not hurt you."

"Yeah, right."

"If I meant you harm, you would be dead by now."

The truth of the words chilled her to the marrow of her bones.

"Why did you come to Pear Blossom Creek? What are you doing here?"

"I was on my way to my house in Oregon when I stopped here to rest during the day. I sensed Falco's presence when I rose the next night. I decided to stay and see if he was also passing through to somewhere else."

"But he wasn't."

"No."

She made a soft sound in her throat. Maybe he was telling the truth. He had told her he had walked Sharlene and the other woman home to protect them, to warn them not to open their doors to strangers. If only they had listened! Or maybe they had. She recalled her own powerful urge to leave the safety of her house when Dimitri Falco had called to her.

"Why did you come back here tonight?" she asked.

"To tell you not to be afraid to go out after dark, that even though you do not see me, I will be watching you."

"That was some trick you pulled tonight, disappearing like that. How did you do it?"

"I did not disappear. I merely moved faster than your eyes could see."

"Where do you live?"

"I do not live anywhere," he replied, and she heard the hint of self-mockery in his voice.

"Where do you stay when you aren't here?"

"I have a house in Oregon, on the coast, and another in Maine, and one in Florida."

"Really?"

"I also have a villa in Italy and a castle in Spain."

"How long have you been a . . . a vampire?"

He thought a moment, then said, "Six hundred and twelve years."

"Six hundred and twelve years," she repeated, her voice tinged with awe. "That means . . ." She did some quick mental arithmetic. "You were alive in 1394."

He nodded.

It was mind-boggling, the things he must have seen. So many changes in six hundred years. What had it been like, to watch the world change so drastically? She looked up at him, noting that there was no sign of the injuries he had incurred earlier. His skin was smooth and clear again. He had changed clothes. Black again, she noticed, and wondered if his entire wardrobe consisted of black shirts and trousers and long black dusters.

"It must be hard to live so long and see everyone you know and love pass on."

"I have loved no one."

"No one in over six hundred years? Which are you, monk or eunuch?"

He laughed softly, bitterly. "Neither. I have had many women, but I have loved none of them."

She crossed her arms over her breasts as the wind picked up, driving the rain before it. "Why not?"

"Because I did not wish to see them look at me the way you looked at me earlier. You should go and sit by the fire," he said. "You are cold."

Since she was shivering, there was no point in denying it. "Are you all right?"

He nodded. "Good night, Victoria."

He turned to leave. She watched him walk down the stairs and she realized she didn't want him to go. Okay, he was a vampire, but he had also saved her life, comforted her when she was afraid, thrilled her with his kisses. Did she really want him to leave? What if she never saw him again?

It was that thought that made her call, "Wait!"

Pausing at the bottom of the stairs, he glanced over his shoulder, a question in the depths of his eyes.

"Please don't go."

"I am not going anywhere," he said quietly. "I will be nearby if you need me."

"Do you . . . Would you like to come in?"

"Is that what you want?"

"Yes, very much."

He regarded her a moment before climbing the stairs. He moved as quietly as a panther, and looked like one, too, she thought, with his black hair and dark attire.

She stepped back and he crossed the threshold into the living room. She didn't know what was different about him tonight but she felt it, a faint tremor in the air around her as he entered her home.

Taking a deep breath, she closed the door behind him, turned to find him watching her.

"Are you sure you want me here?"

"Why do you ask?"

"I can smell the fear on your skin, hear the rapid beat of your heart."

She stared up at him. "You're making that up."

With a shake of his head, he moved toward the door.

"Antonio, please don't go. I can't help being afraid." She sat down on the sofa, her hands clenched in her lap. "This is all so new to me."

Nodding, he sat in the chair across from the sofa.

Silence stretched between them. She tried not to stare at him, but she couldn't help it. She had seen him wounded and bleeding only a short time ago.

"Do all vampires heal so rapidly?"

"Yes."

"Must be nice. I mean, just think of all the money you save on doctor bills. And you'll never need a face lift. And since you don't eat, you must save a fortune on groceries, and—"

"Victoria."

"I'm sorry, I'm just . . . I don't know what to say."

"We never had trouble talking before."

"I know, but—"

"You did not know what I was before."

She nodded.

His gaze caressed her face, lingering on her lips. "I am sorry you had to find out like this, my sweet one. I had hoped . . ."

"Hoped what?"

"It does not matter now."

"Tell me."

"In six hundred years, I have not wanted a woman the way I want you. I had never thought to find a woman I could trust. A woman I could love, until now. I knew it was wrong of me to hold you, to kiss you, when you did not know the truth, and yet I could not help myself."

His voice wrapped around her, as warm as a blazing fire on a cold winter night, but it was nothing compared to the heat smoldering in his eyes. Eyes that weren't the yellow of a killer stalking her small town, or red like those portrayed in horror movies, but a deep dark blue. Eyes filled with aching desire, and eons of loneliness that she could not begin to imagine.

Vicki licked her lips, remembering the power of his kisses, the way her whole body had responded to his touch. Earlier that night, the memory of kissing a vampire had seemed repulsive but now, suddenly, she wanted to be in his arms again, to feel his body against hers.

"Antonio . . ."

"I should go."

"Please stay. I'm not afraid when you're here."

"It is best if we do not see each other again."

"What? Why?"

"Perhaps I should have said it will be easier for me if we do not see each other again."

"I don't understand."

"I am a vampire." He held up his hand, silencing her. "It is the curse of my kind to feel things more strongly than mortals. Love. Hate. Pain. Passion. All are intensified. I cannot go on being near you and not touch you." He paused, his gaze resting a moment on the pulse beating in the hollow of her throat. "Not taste you." His eyes burned into hers, leaving no doubt as to his meaning.

"So, you're saying it's all or nothing? Your way or the highway?"

He grinned, amused by her choice of words. "Something like that."

"I don't sleep around," she said, "so I guess you'd better go." But even as she said the words, she knew it was the last thing she wanted. In spite of everything, she was attracted to Antonio. No other man had ever appealed to her the way he did, made her feel the way he did.

"You misunderstand me," he said. "I am not asking for your virginity. I am only saying that I want to get to know you better, to spend time with you, to stay here, with you, for as long as you will let me. I want your companionship . . ." Again, his gaze lingered on her lips. "And your affection."

"You said for as long as I'll let you. What does that mean, exactly?"

"I think you will soon grow weary of me, and when that time comes, I will trouble you no more, though I will not leave this place until Falco is destroyed."

"What makes you think I'll get tired of you?"

"Because I am a vampire. Because I cannot be with you during the day. Because I will be possessive and demanding of the time that we can share. And because nothing can come of whatever feelings grow out of our relationship. Do you understand what I am saying?"

"I think you're warning me not to fall in love with you."

"Yes. Think carefully about what I have said. I will come for your answer tomorrow night."

"There's just one thing," she said. "What if you fall in love with me?"

"I am already in love with you, my sweet one," he replied, and for the second time that night, he disappeared from her sight.

Chapter 18

Bobbie Sue sat on the sofa, a blanket draped around her shoulders, a cup of hot tea cradled between her hands. "So, it's true, all of it? You're a vampire hunter and Antonio is a vampire?"

Duncan nodded.

"And Sharlene and those other women, they've all been killed by a vampire?"

"Yeah."

"It's just one vampire doing the killing, right? I mean, Antonio isn't . . ."

"Well, I can't be sure of that," Duncan admitted. And at the same time, he admitted something he had known but refused to acknowledge for years. Between the two of them, Ramsey had been the true hunter. Duncan had been the slayer. Not for the first time, he wondered if it was time to hang up his vampire kit and find another line of work. Maybe something here, in Pear Blossom Creek. Maybe it was time to settle down and get married, maybe to a pretty girl like Bobbie Sue, and raise a couple of kids.

"Are you going to . . . you know?"

"I'm sure as hell gonna try."

"Both of them?"

"That's the only way to be sure I've got the killer," Duncan said, and then he laughed softly. All vampires were killers. No matter how civilized and friendly they might seem, killing was in their nature. It was a fact he would be wise to remember. Now, in addition to looking for Falco's resting place, he would have to search for Battista's as well. Dammit, he wished Ramsey were siding him on this one.

"But what about Vicki? I think she really likes Antonio."

He grunted softly. "Believe me, the world will be better off without him, and so will she."

Bobbie Sue didn't argue, but she looked unconvinced.

Duncan sat down on the sofa and put his arm around her. "You'll just have to trust me on this."

Chapter 19

Vicki didn't get any sleep that night. She sat on the sofa in front of the fireplace thinking about Antonio, reliving every moment she had spent with him as she tried to decide what her answer would be when she saw him again. Had he been an ordinary man, the decision would have been easy, she thought, or would it? Maybe, subconsciously, part of his attraction was the fact that he wasn't an ordinary man.

One thing was certain, if he weren't a vampire, she would most likely be dead by now, and so would he. Only the fact that he was a vampire had enabled him to fight off Falco's attack. It was a sobering, disturbing thought.

So, what was she going to do? She thought of all the men she had known and dated. They had all been nice guys, but none of them had held her interest for long. There had been no excitement, no sparks, nothing beyond friendship. Their caresses hadn't excited her or made her long for more than kisses. She had never been tempted to surrender her virtue for a night of wild passion, at least not until Antonio entered her life. Since the night she had first seen him, she had thought of little else.

It wasn't fair. She had finally found a man who fascinated her, and he wasn't a man at all. As attracted to him as she was, there seemed little point in pursuing their relationship. He had made it quite clear that there couldn't be anything serious between them, and he was right. No matter how she felt about him, they were as different as day and night. She laughed bitterly. Day and night, indeed.

He had said he loved her.

And she was horribly afraid that she was dangerously close to falling in love with him.

With a sigh, she hugged one of the sofa pillows to her chest. It was obvious that no matter what decision she made, sooner or later she was going to end up with a broken heart.

She fell asleep on the sofa, her dreams disjointed and confusing. Sometimes Antonio was chasing her and sometimes she was chasing him and then, without warning, it would be Falco chasing her, his breath hot on the back of her neck. She woke feeling hungry and out of sorts with barely enough time to shower and dress and make it to work on time.

"Hey, Red, how are you feelin'?" Gus asked.

"Fine, thanks."

"I guess it was just a twenty-four-hour thing," Gus remarked.

She frowned and then remembered that she had called in sick the night before. "I guess so. How's the crowd tonight?"

"Same as always."

With a smile, she went out into the diner, wondering if Antonio would come in.

The first hour passed quickly, with the dinner crowd keeping her and Bobbie Sue busy. Vicki had the feeling Bobbie Sue wanted to talk to her, but there was no time until the dinner crowd dispersed.

As soon as the diner cleared, Bobbie Sue took her aside. "You don't mind my dating Tom, do you?"

"Mind? Of course not. Why should I mind?"

"Well, you went out with him first and I . . . Well, I just wanted to make sure I wasn't stepping on your toes."

"Don't worry about it. So tell me, are you going out with him again?"

"I want to, but I don't know. I mean, what he does for a living kind of creeps me out." Bobbie Sue lowered her voice. "Can you believe all this? Vampires in the twenty-first century? I still can't believe it."

"I know what you mean. Can you imagine what would happen if the word got out? People would either lock us up in the loony bin, or they'd panic and run amok."

Vicki glanced up, her pulse quickening in anticipation as the bell over the door rang, but it was just Rhonda McGee. She looked around and took a seat at one of Vicki's tables.

"So, what do you think I should do?" Bobbie Sue asked. "About Tom?"

"What does your heart tell you?"

"To see him again," Bobbie Sue said, smiling. "Thanks."

With a nod, Vicki went to take Rhonda's order. Not surprisingly, Rhonda brought up the recent murders and the fact that she and Vicki were both redheads.

"It's unsettling," Rhonda said. "I never used to be afraid to go out at night, you know? But now . . ." She shrugged. "I'm thinking of asking if I can work the day shift for a while."

"I don't blame you," Vicki said. "I've been thinking about that, too. You haven't seen a man with yellow eyes, have you?"

"Yellow eyes? No, I'm sure I'd remember that."

"Well, if you see him, run like the devil himself was after you."

"Vicki, you're scaring me."

"Good, because he's the killer."

Rhonda's eyes widened. "How do you know? Have you seen him? Oh my gosh, you have! When? Where?"

"At the Blue Horse the other night."

"Thanks for the warning. I was going over there later."

"Well, don't. And don't invite any strange men into your house."

"You're the second one to tell me that."

"Oh?"

Rhonda leaned forward, her voice low and intimate. "A really good-looking guy walked me home from the hospital one night and warned me about that. I don't know who he was, but I was really tempted to ask him in, stranger or not . . . Oh, there he is now."

Feeling as though a million butterflies had just taken flight in her stomach, Vicki glanced over her shoulder. And there he was, dressed all in black, as usual, his hair damp from the rain that had started to fall a short while ago.

His gaze found hers. The electricity that arced between them could have lit up the whole state.

As though drawn by an invisible string, Vicki followed him to the booth in the back.

"Hi," she said, hoping he wouldn't notice how breathless she sounded.

"Good evening, Victoria."

She laughed softly. "Good evening."

"You find that amusing?"

"No. Well, yes. Haven't you ever seen Dracula?"

He lifted one brow. "Excuse me?"

"You know, the movie, *Dracula*. He also says 'good evening.' "

"Ah. I saw you talking to Miss McGee. Is she a friend of yours?"

"In a town this small, everyone is either your friend or a relative. She said you warned her not to open her door for strangers."

He nodded.

"She also said she was tempted to ask *you* in."

Man or vampire, they all had egos. It was blatantly obvious that he was flattered.

"Do not let me keep you from your work," he said.

"All right." She cocked her head to one side. "So is it true that you never eat and that you never drink anything but . . . you know?"

He nodded, his gaze intent upon her face as he waited for her reaction.

She took a deep breath. "Well, I guess nothing on the menu will tempt you, then."

"Only you."

The look in his eyes, the husky longing in his voice, made her knees go weak. Reluctantly, she went to wait on her other customers.

He sat in the booth the rest of the evening, one arm across the back, toying with a cup of coffee that he never drank.

Gus grumbled a bit about that until Vicki told him that Antonio was there to see her safely home.

When Bobbie Sue heard that, she took Vicki aside and asked her if she had lost her mind.

"He's a vampire," Bobbie Sue said, glancing around to make sure no one overheard her. "A vampire, Vicki. And Tom, well, he hunts them, you know, and . . ."

"And what?"

"He's going to kill him or destroy him or whatever it is he does."

"What? Why? Antonio hasn't done anything to anyone."

"Vicki, read my lips. He's a vampire. They kill people and drink their blood."

"No." Vicki looked over at the booth where Antonio was sitting. In spite of what she had just said, she couldn't dismiss the truth of Bobbie Sue's words. Hadn't Antonio himself told her just that night that he drank blood? Where else was he going to get it, if not from . . . from people he killed? So he wasn't responsible for killing Sharlene and the others. That didn't mean he hadn't killed others, only that he hadn't been caught.

It was all she could think about during the remainder of her shift. She served platters of steak and shrimp and bowls of soup and all she could think about was Antonio and how many people he must have killed to survive as long as he had.

He was waiting for her outside when the diner closed. Without a word, he walked her to her car, waited while she unlocked the door and got behind the wheel.

"Get in," she said. "We need to talk."

The ride home seemed longer than usual. His presence in the car was almost overwhelming. Never had she been so aware of how very male he was. He exuded strength and power and a sense of invincibility that was both reassuring and frightening.

When she pulled into the driveway, he got out of the car first. As he had before, he scanned the yard and the trees beyond before he opened the door for her.

Inside the house, she closed and locked the front door, then went into the living room and sat down. He followed her, still silent. He didn't sit down, simply stood there, waiting, as if he knew what was coming.

"You drink blood," she said. "Where do you get it?"

He grunted softly. "What you want to know is how many people I have killed."

"Yes."

Antonio paced the length of the room, then came to stand in front of her once again. "I am not like Dimitri Falco. I do not kill for pleasure. I have killed in the past. I do not deny it. I have killed to preserve my existence. I have killed to defend myself, but never without cause."

"But you have to kill to live, don't you? How often? Every night? Once a week?" Even if he only needed sustenance once a year, he would have killed over six hundred people.

"There is no need for me to take life, Victoria. I can take what I need without killing. I have been a vampire for a very long time. My need for blood grows less with each passing year, though my desire for it has not changed."

"Tom Duncan intends to kill you."

Battista lifted one brow. "Indeed?"

Vicki nodded. "Bobbie Sue told me."

He made a sound deep in his throat. It sounded almost like a growl.

"Can he? Kill you?"

"I am already dead, but he can destroy me, though he will have to find me first."

She didn't find that very comforting. Of course, Duncan hadn't been able to locate Falco thus far, though she prayed that would soon change. Hopefully, Duncan would never find Antonio's resting place, wherever that might be.

"Did you think about what I said last night?" Battista asked.

"Are you kidding? I haven't been able to think of anything else."

"What have you decided?"

"I want you in my life." She hadn't known what her answer was going to be until that moment. Now, hearing the words, they felt right. "So, I guess we're going steady." Using such an outdated term made her cheeks grow hot.

"Going steady." He repeated the words, his tone faintly amused, as he sat down beside her. "You are sure? You have no doubts?"

"Oh, I have a lot of doubts, but I'm not listening to them."

He smiled at her.

Was he pleased with her answer, she wondered, or just amused?

He leaned toward her and she knew he was going to kiss her. She put her hand against his chest, staying him.

"There's just one more thing. You're not planning to drink my blood, are you?"

He glanced briefly at her throat. "Only if you want me to."

"No worries, then," she said, confident that even if she lived to be a hundred, she would never ask him to do anything so inherently repugnant.

Chapter 20

Vicki woke with a smile the next morning. She was going steady. With a vampire.

A look at the clock showed that it was already past noon. She never slept this late. Clutching a pillow to her chest, she laughed out loud. She had only been going steady with Antonio for one night and already her life was changing, but she supposed that was to be expected. After all, it was obvious that if she wanted to spend time with Antonio, she was going to have to adjust her hours to his, since he couldn't adjust his to hers. The diner closed at midnight on Tuesday, Wednesday and Thursday, and at one A.M. on Friday and Saturday. That meant that she had from closing time until dawn to spend with Antonio on the nights she worked. Sundays and Mondays, when she was off, they would have more time together.

Filled with a rush of nervous energy, she dressed and ate a quick breakfast, then cleaned the house from top to bottom, excited at the prospect of seeing him again that evening. If Antonio had been a normal, mortal man, she would have planned an intimate candlelit dinner, baked a seven-layer chocolate cake, bought a bottle of vintage wine. But that was out of the question. Maybe she could find a bottle of blood somewhere . . . She grimaced at the thought, only then remembering that he had never really answered her question of where and how he fed. If he didn't kill to survive, did he just prey on unsuspecting women? She shook her head. If that were the case, the papers would be filled with stories of women who had been preyed upon, and the tabloids would be shrieking that there was a vampire running amok. Maybe there were people who offered to let him drink their blood, people like Goths who were really into the whole vampire scene.

She knew she shouldn't be wondering about such things, but she couldn't help it. There was so much she didn't know. Maybe he could give her a list of dos and don'ts for people dating the Undead.

Laughing at the thought, she went into the bathroom to take a shower and get dressed for work.

Antonio was waiting for her when she left the house that evening. The surge of pleasure she felt at seeing him again made her knees go weak. It wasn't fair for him to have such a devastating effect on her senses.

She smiled as she hurried down the stairs. "Hi."

"Hi."

She laughed out loud. "What? No 'good evening' a la Dracula?"

"I thought I would try to make my speech more contemporary."

"Oh."

Her heartbeat ramped into overdrive as he bent his

head to kiss her. When he would have let her go, she wrapped her arms around his neck and deepened the kiss.

His body responded instantly and before she knew what was happening, he had her backed up against the porch, his body pressed intimately against hers as his hands began a slow exploration of her body.

That quickly, she was on fire for him. Feeling as though she could never be close enough, she pressed herself against him. A soft moan rose in her throat as she ground her hips against his.

Lifting his head, he looked deep into her eyes. "Victoria . . ." Her name was a low groan on his lips.

"Wow."

"Wow?" He arched one brow, his dark eyes alight with amusement.

It was a good thing she had to go to work, she thought. It was the only thing that kept her from taking him by the hand and leading him back into the house and up the stairs into her bedroom. And into her bed.

"Maybe we can take up where we left off later?" she suggested.

"It would be my pleasure to do so."

She was smiling again. "And mine." She handed him the keys to her car. "Why don't you drive?"

"As you wish."

Ever the gentleman, he opened the door for her, then got into the car.

Vicki sat back in her seat, content to do nothing more than look at him. Every time he glanced her way, her insides turned to mush. She had never felt this way about a man. It amazed her that she felt so strongly about him after only a few weeks. In some ways, she felt as if she had known him forever. Forever, she thought.

He would live forever, while she would not. She shook the depressing thought from her mind. She wouldn't think about that now.

He glanced over at her. "Is something wrong?"

Knowing he had noticed her staring at him brought a rush of heat to her face. "No, why?"

"I find you very attractive also."

"Thank you."

"I feel you still have questions you would like to ask me."

"Well, maybe one or two. Like, why do always wear black and . . . Well, you never did tell me how you satisfy your hunger or your thirst or whatever you call it."

"When I feel the urge to feed, I call someone to me and take what I need."

"You mean you hypnotize them?"

"Yes. And when I have satisfied the craving, I wipe the memory from their mind. As for wearing black . . . It blends with the night." He looked at her and grinned. "And it looks good on me."

"It does that," she agreed. She fell silent for a moment and then lifted one hand to her neck. "Have you ever hypnotized me?"

"No."

"How can you drink . . . blood? Isn't it gross?"

He pulled into the diner's parking lot, found a space, and killed the engine. "It is normal for me to ingest blood, just as it is normal for you to eat and drink mortal food."

"Are there a lot of vampires running around?"

"More than you might think."

It was not a comforting thought.

Exiting the car, he opened the door for her, took her hand, and helped her out. He kept hold of her hand as he walked her to the back door.

"Will you be in later?" she asked.

"If you wish."

"I do."

"Then I shall be here." He kissed her hand, then turned it over and kissed her palm. The touch of his lips sent a shiver of pleasure rocketing up her arm. "Till later, my sweet one."

Antonio handed her the keys to the car, lifted a hand in farewell as she entered the building, then walked across the parking lot to the sidewalk. He had not fed in several days, and he dared not put it off any longer. Being with Victoria stirred more than his passion, and he had no wish to lose control in her presence and frighten her away, not now, when she was just beginning to trust him again.

With preternatural speed, he left Pear Blossom Creek. A short time later, he was strolling down Cottonwood's main thoroughfare. At this time of evening, the streets were crowded. He grinned inwardly, wondering what Victoria would say if she knew where he was and what he was doing. Wandering through the townspeople was like walking through a human buffet, trying to decide which dish to try. Most people thought all blood was the same and in some ways, perhaps it was. But to a vampire, no two mortals tasted alike.

He followed a pretty brunette for several blocks, inhaling her scent, whetting his appetite. When she reached an alleyway, he moved up beside her and drew her into the darkness, his mind easily overriding her objections. He took her in his arms, his mind speaking to hers, soothing her fears as he brushed the hair away from her neck, then lowered his head, his eyes closing in the sheer ecstasy of feeding.

With his hunger assuaged, he wiped his memory from her mind, then escorted the woman back to the sidewalk and vanished from her sight.

He walked until he found a bench under a tree in a small park. Sitting down, he gazed into the darkness. So many changes since he had been born. Once, people had walked or ridden beasts of burden wherever they wanted to go. Now they could go across the country in a matter of hours. Once, it had taken days for a letter to reach its destination. Now e-mail went across the world in a matter of moments. Machines now did many household tasks, giving women more free time than they had ever known. Books that had once been laboriously printed, one copy at a time by hand, were now turned out by the thousands.

Progress, he thought, it was a wonderful thing and yet, on occasion, he longed for the days of his youth, when every dawn had promised a new adventure.

With a shake of his head, he left the park. There was no point in thinking about the past. His parents, his brothers and sisters, everyone he had grown up with, the town where he was born, were long gone. It was a lonely life, being a vampire. To make friends with humans, to grow fond of them, meant that, inevitably, they went the way of all flesh, leaving you alone once again. If you kept yourself apart from humanity, the results were the same.

Which made him think of Victoria. For the first time in centuries, he had let himself care for a mortal. He was sorely afraid that this time, when the inevitable separation came, he would not be able to bear the loss, or the pain that was sure to follow.

He was nearing the end of the city limits when a faint cry of terror reached his ears, and with it the strong coppery scent of fresh blood.

Falco!

A thought took him to a deserted part of the city,

where the vampire was savaging the throat of a young woman with curly red hair.

"Let her go!"

Falco lifted his head. His lips were smeared with crimson, his eyes blazed with the lust for blood. He hissed when he saw Battista.

"You want her?" Falco said with a snarl. "Take her!" Ripping a lock of hair from the girl's head, he hurled her body toward Battista; then, with a wave of his hand, the vampire disappeared into the night.

Battista looked down at the girl in his arms. She was as limp and lifeless as a rag doll. Blood oozed from the hideous wound in her throat. She couldn't have been more than twenty years old.

A howl of anger rose in Battista's throat as he cradled her body to his chest.

And that was how Duncan found him a few moments later.

Tom came up short when he saw the two people in the shadows. It was pure luck that he was in town. He had come here earlier in the day, searching for Falco's lair, and been about to call it a night when he'd heard an ungodly howl that had sent shivers down his spine. He knew that sound. He'd heard it often enough in his line of work.

He touched the cross at his throat for luck, then pulled his .38 out of one coat pocket and a bottle of holy water from the other.

"Put the girl down, easy like," he demanded.

"Do not be a fool, Duncan."

"Battista!" Tom took a step forward, his eyes narrowed. "I knew it. Put her down."

"You know nothing."

"I know you've killed your last innocent woman."

"I did not kill her."

"Yeah, right."

"I am putting her down." Antonio laid the girl's body gently on the sidewalk.

And Duncan went into action. Springing forward, he dumped holy water over the vampire's head, then fired his pistol, hoping to bring the vampire to his knees so that he could take his head.

Battista hissed as holy water splashed across his face and trickled down his neck, every drop burning into his skin like acid. The bullet struck him in the chest, but he recovered quickly. With a roar of pain and rage, he backhanded Duncan across the face.

The hunter reeled backward, momentarily stunned.

And Battista vanished into the darkness.

Vicki checked the clock on the wall, counting the minutes until it was time to go home. She had waited all evening for Antonio to come into the diner, and when he didn't show up, her imagination went into overdrive, coming up with all sorts of reasons for his absence. He had forgotten. He had left town. He had changed his mind about wanting to spend time with her. He had met someone else . . .

She cleared the last table, helped Bobbie Sue refill the salt and pepper shakers and replace the packets of cream and sugar substitutes, still hoping that Antonio would appear, until Gus came out of the kitchen to lock the front door.

"See ya tomorrow night, Bobbie," he said cheerfully.

"Sure thing," Bobbie Sue said. "Night, Gussie."

He glowered at her.

"Come on, I'll walk the two of you out. Oh, don't

forget to come in costume tomorrow night," he reminded them. "It's Halloween."

Halloween, Vicki thought. How could she have forgotten that when every house in town was decorated with ghosts and goblins and jack-o'-lanterns, and the windows of every business, including the diner, wished the world a happy Halloween?

Outside, she bade Gus and Bobbie Sue good night, then glanced around the parking lot, expecting Battista to be there to meet her, but there was no sign of him.

Remembering that he wasn't the only vampire in town, she quickly unlocked her car, got behind the wheel, and locked the door.

So, she thought as she drove home, where was he? She told herself not to worry, he had promised to look after her. What was it he had said? *I will be there if you need me.* Did that mean he was somewhere nearby, even now?

Tom Duncan was waiting for her on the porch when she got home.

"Hi," she said. "Is something wrong?"

"Falco's not the only killer in town," he said brusquely. "I caught your boyfriend red-handed tonight."

"I don't believe you!"

"I saw him with my own eyes. He was holding the body in his arms."

Vicki shook her head. "No."

"Yes. She was just a kid, maybe eighteen or nineteen."

"He told me he didn't kill when he . . . that he didn't have to take life."

"Well, he sure as hell took this one. I took her body to the morgue myself. She didn't have enough blood left to fill a teacup."

The image made her sick to her stomach. Pressing

one hand to her mouth, she unlocked the front door and dashed into the bathroom. Bending over the toilet, she was violently ill.

Tom was there to hand her a damp towel when she got up. "Do you know where he is?"

Vicki wiped her face, then rinsed her mouth. "No," she said dully. "I haven't seen him since he drove me to work."

"I don't know what his game is," Duncan said, "but I don't have to tell you that you're in danger. Whatever you do, don't let him in."

"But if he meant to hurt me, he's had plenty of opportunities to do so."

Duncan shrugged. "Like I said, I don't know what his game is. Maybe he likes to pick one girl and string her along until he decides to leave town."

Vicki tossed the towel into the hamper. "Thanks for letting me know."

"I'm sorry," he said. "I know that you . . ." He made a vague gesture with one hand. "I know you liked him."

"It never would have worked anyway." She wanted to make Tom think it didn't matter, that Antonio hadn't meant that much to her. She failed miserably.

Tom gave her shoulder a squeeze. "Do you want me to stay?"

"No." All she wanted was to be alone with her broken heart.

"Are you sure? I don't like the idea of you being here alone."

"I'm sure."

"You've got my number. Call me if you need me."

"I will."

She walked him to the door, stood there while he

climbed into the Camaro and drove away. With a sigh, she closed and locked the door. If she didn't have the worst luck in the world with men, she didn't know who did. Not only was Antonio a vampire, he was a liar and a killer.

She was about to go to bed when she heard a knock at the back door. Alarm skittered through her. Should she answer? She clutched the crucifix at her throat. Was it Falco, trying to trick her again?

She called, "Who's there?" when the caller knocked a second time.

"Antonio."

"Go away. You're not welcome here."

"Victoria, I can explain."

"No." She shook her head, her hand tightening around the thick silver cross. "You lied to me! Tom told me everything. He saw you."

"Victoria, please listen to me. I did not kill her. It was Falco."

"I don't believe you!"

She waited a moment and when there was no reply, she pressed her ear to the door. Hearing nothing, she drew back the curtain. Antonio was standing near the door, bathed in a slender ray of moonlight, one hand pressed against his left cheek. His eyes were closed. Was he hurt?

She was about to turn away when she spied a dark figure moving stealthily toward the house. A figure with glowing yellow eyes.

With a wordless cry, she flung the door open, grabbed Antonio by the arm, and dragged him into the kitchen.

Heart pounding, she slammed the door in Dimitri Falco's face.

His scream of outrage rattled the windows. He stared at her through the glass, his eyes burning with hatred.

"You will be mine!" he screeched. "Though I kill a hundred women, nay a thousand before I take you, you will be mine!"

And so saying, he vanished from her sight.

Chapter 21

Turning away from the door, Vicki stared at Antonio's back. She was alone in the house with a vampire, a vampire who Duncan was convinced had just killed a young woman.

Maybe she should have let Antonio and Falco fight it out again. Maybe they would have killed each other this time. But even as that uncharitable thought crossed her mind, she knew she couldn't have let that happen, because deep in her heart, she didn't want to believe Antonio had lied to her.

Moving in front of him, she saw that his hand still covered his cheek.

"Are you all right? Can I—Oh my Lord!" she exclaimed when she saw his chest. "You're bleeding! What happened?"

"Duncan shot me."

"Here," she said, pulling a chair out from the kitchen table, "sit down."

"Do not fret, Victoria. I will be all right."

"Yes, yes, I know, supernatural healing and all that. Sit."

He dropped into the chair.

"Let me see," she said, reaching for his hand.

"No, Victoria."

"Let me see." She pulled his hand away from his cheek, and wished that she hadn't. The left side of his face was badly burned. In some places, it was black. The burns extended beyond his cheek. Blisters were scattered down the side of his neck, and when she eased his shirt away, she saw that they continued across his shoulder and down his arm. "What happened?"

"He threw holy water on me before he shot me."

She had read that holy water repelled vampires. She'd had no idea that it burned them so badly. She knew he had tremendous healing powers but this . . . She had never seen anything so ugly.

Unbuttoning his shirt, she slipped it off his shoulders, revealing a smattering of more burned flesh and a small, neat hole in his chest only a few inches away from his heart. It seemed odd that the bullet had done less damage. The bleeding had stopped. Even as she watched, the angry redness around the wound faded, the hole grew smaller and then just disappeared.

"Amazing," she murmured. "Simply amazing." She looked at his cheek again. "I've got some first aid cream. It might ease the pain."

He looked doubtful, but she had to feel like she was doing something to help, no matter how insignificant it might be.

He sat unmoving while she smeared the ointment on his cheek, down his neck, over his shoulder and down his arm.

And all the while Tom's warning voice echoed in the back of her head. *You're in danger. Don't let him in.*

Capping the jar, she put it on the counter. "You didn't kill that girl, did you? Tell me you didn't."

"I did not kill her." He looked up, his gaze searching hers. "I found Falco with her. She was already dead."

She folded her arms over her breasts. "Every woman he kills from now on will be my fault."

"No!" Rising, he reached for her, then dropped his arms to his sides. "You are not responsible for anything that madman does. You cannot blame yourself."

"You heard what he said! He said he didn't care if he had to kill thousands of girls before he got to me."

"Victoria, he will continue to kill until he is destroyed. It is what he does, what he has always done."

"Then why does he want me so badly? What makes me any different from any of the others?"

"Perhaps because I want you."

I want you. Three simple words spoken so fervently that, for a moment, she could think of nothing else but being in his arms, succumbing to the heat in his eyes, the longing so evident in his voice. A yearning that echoed her own unspoken longing.

Needing to touch him, she lifted a finger to his ravaged cheek. "Does it hurt very much?"

"Like hellfire."

"Are you sure it will heal?"

"In time." He took her hand in his, his thumb moving slowly back and forth over her knuckles. "Why did you let me in? I am sure Duncan warned you not to, yet you did not listen."

She stared at his hand holding hers. "I didn't want to believe him."

He lifted one brow. "So you brought me into your home to see whether or not I would rip out your throat?" he asked, amusement heavy in his voice.

She laughed, but there was no humor in it. "I saw

Falco coming after you and . . ." She shrugged. "I could tell you were hurt and I was afraid if the two of you got into another fight that . . ."

"You were worried about me?" He laughed. The soft, sexy sound moved over her like black velvet. "Ah, my sweet, you are like no other woman I have ever known."

She stared at the light dusting of curly black hair that covered his broad chest, at the finely sculpted muscles in his arms and shoulders, the ridge of muscle across his belly, and felt a sudden stirring of desire. She tamped it down. This was no time to be admiring his masculine beauty. He was badly hurt. There was a vampire out there who wanted to kill her, who had vowed to kill and kill again until she was his.

"What does he mean, exactly, when he says I'll be his?"

"You do not want to know. Just trust me when I say he will never have you."

He was right, she didn't want to know, but she couldn't let it go. "He wants to kill me," she said. "What could be worse than that?"

Battista resumed his seat at the table. After a moment, Victoria sat down across from him.

"There are many things worse than death," he said. "Falco wants to own you, body and soul. If that happens, you will be his slave, subject to his every whim, his every desire. You will have no will of your own, no mind of your own."

"You're talking about more than just hypnotism, aren't you?"

Antonio nodded. It was much more than a mere hypnotic spell. It was like stealing a mortal's identity and leaving nothing behind but an empty shell whose only thoughts were those fed into it by its master.

Zebra Contemporary Romance

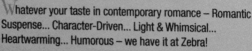

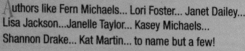

To start your membership, simply complete and return the Free Book Certificate. You'll receive your Introductory Shipment of FREE Zebra Contemporary Romances, you only pay $1.99 for shipping and handling. Then, each month you will receive the 4 newest Zebra Contemporary Romances. Each shipment will be yours to examine FREE for 10 days. If you decide to keep the books, you'll pay the preferred subscriber price (a savings of up to 30% off the cover price), plus shipping and handling. If you want us to stop sending books, just say the word... it's that simple.

FREE BOOK CERTIFICATE

Yes! Please send me FREE Zebra Contemporary romance novels. I only pay $1.99 for shipping and handling. I understand that each month thereafter I will be able to preview 4 brand-new Contemporary Romances FREE for 10 days. Then, if I should decide to keep them, I will pay the money-saving preferred subscriber's price (that's a savings of up to 30% off the retail price), plus shipping and handling. I understand I am under no obligation to purchase any books, as explained on this card.

NAME _____

ADDRESS _____ APT. ____

CITY _____ STATE _____ ZIP _____

TELEPHONE (_____) _____

E-MAIL _____

SIGNATURE _____

(If under 18, parent or guardian must sign)

Offer limited to one per household and not to current subscribers. Terms, offer and prices subject to change.
Orders subject to acceptance by Zebra Contemporary Book Club. Offer Valid in the U.S. only.

Thank You!

CN026A

THE BENEFITS OF BOOK CLUB MEMBERSHIP

• You'll get your books hot off the press, usually before they appear in bookstores.

• You'll ALWAYS save up to 30% off the cover price.

• You'll get our FREE monthly newsletter filled with author interviews, book previews, special offers and MORE!

• There's no obligation – you can cancel at any time and you have no minimum number of books to buy.

• And – if you decide you don't like the books you receive, you can return them. (You always have ten days to decide.)

lll..l..lll....ll.l.l.l.l...ll.l.l.l.l...lll.ll...ll...l

Zebra Contemporary Romance Book Club
Zebra Home Subscription Service, Inc.
P.O. Box 5214
Clifton NJ 07015-5214

PLACE
STAMP
HERE

Vicki looked at him thoughtfully for a moment. "Can you do that?"

He nodded again, his gaze hard on hers.

"How can you do it? I mean, how is it done?"

"Vampires have many supernatural powers."

She had come across some of them in her reading, but she had shrugged them aside. Even though she now knew vampires existed, she wasn't sure she believed that they could control the weather or turn into mist or wolves, or that they could manipulate people's minds. But then she remembered Antonio had said he called his prey to him. If he could do that, maybe he could also do all the other things the books claimed. If so, it meant he could also fly, control animals, and, worst of all, make other vampires. She wondered if he had done so.

It was a sobering thought.

His eyes narrowed under her scrutiny. "You are afraid of me again. Why?"

"What? Oh, no, nothing."

"Victoria, your face is as easy to read as print on a page."

"Have you ever made another vampire?"

"No. It is a responsibility I have never wanted."

"What do you mean?"

"It is a life against nature, to be a vampire. Not everyone can adjust to such a life. Some go mad, like Falco. I have enough deaths on my conscience. Had I brought someone like Falco across, I would have all his deaths on my conscience, as well."

It was too much to think of now. She glanced at the clock. It was almost two A.M. She needed to get some sleep.

"Maybe you should stay here tonight," she suggested.

"No."

"Why not?"

There were few things on earth he feared more than being found when he was at rest, vulnerable and nearly helpless. Though it pained him to admit it, he trusted no one to know where he took his rest, not even this woman he had come to love.

"Antonio? Why can't you stay here? You can sleep in my bedroom and shut the door and I'll sleep on the sofa."

"I wish I could stay," he said, "but . . ."

"You're probably right," she said. "Duncan was here earlier tonight. I'd hate for him to come back tomorrow and find you here."

Battista glanced out the window. It would be dawn in a few hours.

"Can I get you anything before you go?" Vicki asked, then bit down on her lip. She had nothing to offer him. *Nothing but blood.* The words tiptoed through the back of her mind.

As though reading her thoughts, Antonio stared at the pulse beating in her throat. Though he had fed earlier, he needed to feed again. Fresh blood would help him heal faster, ease the pain of his wounds which, even now, burned with all the fires of an unforgiving hell.

Vicki's eyes widened. One hand flew to her throat.

"You are safe from me, my sweet one," he said quietly. Rising, he reached for his bloodstained shirt and shrugged it on. He needed to feed before he sought his rest.

"Should you go out there now?" Victoria asked. "What if Falco's waiting? Or Duncan?"

"I must go."

"You're going out to . . . hunt, aren't you?"

He didn't deny it.

"Please don't go."

"Victoria, I appreciate your concern more than you know, but I need to feed to restore my strength. If I do not, I will grow weaker. I cannot afford that now." He needed to be strong if he was going to protect her. It had become his reason for existing. He had not realized how empty his existence had become until he met her. Knowing she would be there when he rose filled each night with new possibilities.

"Does it hurt?" she asked.

"Does what hurt?"

"When you bite them, does it hurt?"

"No. It can be most pleasurable, especially if one is willing."

"Pleasurable! How? I had a dog bite me once. Believe me, there was nothing pleasant about it."

"But I am not a dog, my sweet one. The bite of a vampire can be a sensual thing. There are those who are addicted to it."

Hardly aware of what she was doing, she lifted a hand to her throat.

Battista followed the movement, his gaze again settling on the hollow of her throat. He listened to the beat of her heart, his nostrils filling with the sweet scent of her life's blood. He smelled the heat of her skin. It mingled with the scent of toothpaste and shampoo, soap and deodorant. And woman. A woman who was in the prime of life, vibrant and untouched.

He felt the prick of his fangs against his tongue as his hunger thrummed within him. No man had ever touched her. No vampire had ever tasted her. It was a potent combination, and a powerful temptation. No wonder Falco wanted her.

He rose abruptly. "I must go."

"Wait." She looked up at him, her eyes wide, her breathing erratic. "Promise me you'll only take a little."

She heard the words and couldn't believe that she had said them. Only days ago she had been so sure she would never ask him to do such a thing.

Battista stared at her, unable to believe his ears, afraid to believe for fear she was playing some cruel joke. He clenched his hands at his sides to keep from pulling her into his arms. "You need not do this."

"No, I want to. If you're going out tonight, you need to be strong."

He held out his hand. "Come, then."

Putting her hand in his, she followed him into the living room. He sat down on the sofa, drawing her down beside him.

"Relax," he murmured. "I will not hurt you."

She swallowed hard, her gaze fixed on his.

"Close your eyes."

"Why?"

"Please."

She did as he asked, her body tensing as he drew her into his arms. His kiss was gentle, his lips warm. He kissed her for a long time until she relaxed in his arms. He stroked the line of her back, kissed her cheeks, the curve of her throat.

She moaned softly, lost in a mindless sea of pleasure. He nuzzled the soft skin behind her ear, laved it with his tongue. She felt a brief sting, like a mosquito bite, and then the heat of his mouth on her skin.

A distant part of her mind told her she should be afraid, she should push him away, what he was doing was horribly, terribly wrong, but she didn't care. Never had anything felt so wonderful.

She whimpered softly when he drew his mouth away. She looked up at him through a red haze, or was it that his eyes were red? She felt a tiny spark of fear push its way through the lassitude that suffused her. What if Duncan had been right? What if she was in danger? She tried to be concerned, but being afraid required too much energy.

With a sigh, she closed her eyes and drifted away.

Battista cradled Victoria in his arms. A drop of blood slid down her neck. He watched it a moment before licking it away. Never had he tasted anything so sweet. The heart he had thought long dead stirred within his breast as he gazed down at her. Never had he seen anything more beautiful, or more vulnerable.

He held her through what remained of the night, memorizing each feature, imprinting her face in his mind for that day in the future when he would have to let her go.

Sensing the coming of dawn, he carried Victoria to bed and tucked her under the covers, then brushed a kiss across her cheek.

"*Sogni dolci, il mio amore*," he murmured. Sweet dreams, my love.

Chapter 22

Bobbie Sue stood in the middle of her living room, trying to decide which costume to wear to work, when Duncan came to call.

"I didn't expect to see you today," she said.

"If you're busy, I can come back later."

"No, no, nothing like that. I'm just surprised to see you, that's all." She smiled at him. "Surprised, but pleased." She took a step back. "Come on in."

He followed her into the living room, noting the bright yellow walls, the white wicker furniture, the colorful throw pillows.

"What's all this?" He gestured at the sofa, which was covered with brightly colored dresses, hats, scarves, and a variety of wigs.

"Oh, that. I'm trying to decide whether to be a cheerleader, Cleopatra, or the bride of Frankenstein."

"Oh, right. It's Halloween."

"Gus likes us to wear costumes to work." She held up a slinky black dress and a long black wig. "I could go as Vampira . . . Oh, geez, that would be in really bad taste, wouldn't it?" She tossed the dress and the wig aside. "I suppose I could just go as a waitress."

She sat on the love seat and patted the cushion beside her. "Come, sit down and tell me what you're going to do tonight."

"Nothing much."

"You look a little blue. Is anything wrong?"

"I was hunting Falco last night and found Battista instead."

"Found him where?"

"With a dead girl in his arms."

"Oh, no! Poor Vicki. Does she know?"

"I told her about it last night. I just hope she takes my advice and stays away from him."

"I think she's in love with him."

Duncan grunted softly. What was it about vampires that women found so irresistible? He thought of Marisa and Kelly. Did they ever regret accepting the *Dark Trick* to be with their vampire lovers? He couldn't imagine giving up his humanity, or never again watching the sun rise on a new day. Nor did he want to give up the pleasure of eating a good steak, or enjoying a good cup of strong black coffee first thing in the morning, or an ice-cold beer on a hot summer day.

He grunted softly. "Do you think she knows where his lair is?"

"I don't know. I could ask her."

"Thanks." It was a slim hope. Even if Vicki knew where Battista took his rest during the day, he was pretty sure she wouldn't tell him. That was another thing about women who were infatuated with vampires. They were fiercely loyal. Still, asking Vicki couldn't hurt. He needed all the help he could get, because he sure wasn't having any luck on his own. "I haven't been able to find

Falco's resting place, either," he muttered glumly. "The man's as elusive as quicksilver."

"I guess you'll be leaving town after you find him."

"I was planning to, but now . . ." Duncan took a deep breath. He had never been at ease with women. Give him a stake and show him a vampire and he knew what to do, but put him in a room alone with a woman he was attracted to, and he behaved like a bumbling, tongue-tied idiot.

"But now?" Bobbie Sue coaxed.

He ran a finger around his shirt collar. "I've been thinking about settling down, you know, finding another line of work."

"Oh? Were you thinking of settling down in any place in particular?"

He cleared his throat. "This seems like a good place."

"Oh, it is." She leaned toward him. "Wouldn't you like to kiss me, Tom?"

"Very much."

"Well?"

Scooting closer, he slipped one arm around her waist. And still he hesitated.

With a soft laugh, Bobbie Sue slid her hand around his nape, pulled his head down, and kissed him. It was like touching a match to a flame. The sparks she had never felt with Steve shot through her like a bolt of electricity.

She was breathless when they parted.

"You were right," he said, his voice ragged. "This is a good place."

Chapter 23

"Trick or treat!"

Vicki opened the front door, smiling at the trio of children standing on the porch. Spiderman, Frodo, and Harry Potter looked up at her, all holding pillowcases that were already bulging with goodies.

She dropped a candy bar in each bag, waved to the mothers waiting patiently on the sidewalk, and closed the door.

For the next half hour, there was a steady stream of trick-or-treaters ringing her doorbell, from cute little angels and devils to teenagers wearing hideous masks. She had just picked up her handbag and keys and taken a last look in the mirror to make sure her Tinkerbell wings were straight when the doorbell rang again.

"Oh, I love your costumes," Vicki said, glancing from a very realistic-looking Darth Vader to an equally impressive R2-D2.

"Thank you," said the taller of the two in a high-pitched voice. "I hate to impose, but could we use your restroom? My little boy needs to go."

"Oh, sure, come in." Vicki held the screen door open for Darth Vader and her son.

Darth Vader gave R2-D2 a little push, then followed him inside.

"It's this way," Vicki said. She started down the hall, then stopped when she heard the front door close. Turning, she saw Darth Vader standing close behind her. There was no sign of R2-D2.

Fear snaked down Vicki's spine. She opened her mouth to ask what was going on, but no words came out.

And then Darth Vader removed her mask.

And Vicki found herself staring into Dimitri Falco's cold yellow eyes.

"Trick or treat," he said in that same high-pitched voice. And then he laughed. "And what a sweet treat you will be."

Stunned, Vicki stared at him. Pushing her fear aside, she tried to remember what Duncan had told her about making a vampire depart. But Falco was on her before she could form the words. His hand closed around her throat, squeezing, tighter, tighter, until all she could see were his eyes.

And then nothing at all.

Battista made his way down a street crowded with parents and kids, most of them in costume. Ballerinas, devils, elves, witches, warlocks, and vampires. On this one night, his dark clothing and long black coat fit right in. Knowing that Tom Duncan now considered him fair game, Battista kept his senses alert as he turned down the street toward Victoria's house. He glanced at the night sky, quietly cursing the need that had sent him in search of prey. He was late tonight. She had probably already left for the diner.

Pausing at the end of the walkway leading to her house, he lifted his head and sniffed the wind. "Falco." The man's foul stench polluted the air.

Hurrying up the stairs, Battista knocked on the door. There was no answer. The door opened at the touch of his hand. Her handbag and keys lay on the floor.

With preternatural speed, he hastened to the diner. Hoping against hope, he glanced in the window, his gaze sweeping the inside. There was no sign of Victoria.

Hurrying through the front door, he cornered Bobbie Sue. "Where is she?"

Her eyes grew wide. "I . . . I don't know."

"Did she come to work tonight?"

"N . . . No."

He swore a vile oath. "He's got her."

"Who . . . Who's got her?"

"Falco."

"Take your hands off her and step away, Battista."

Turning, Antonio came face-to-face with Tom Duncan. "Falco has taken Victoria," he said, unable to hide the desperation in his voice.

"And I'm taking you."

"Did you not hear what I said?" Battista demanded. "Victoria's life is in danger."

"First you," Duncan said resolutely, "and then him."

Battista snorted. "Are you going to stake me here, in front of all these people?"

Duncan glanced around. Though their conversation had been too low to be heard by others, the diner's customers were all looking in their direction, curious as to what was going on between the two men and the waitress. To onlookers, it no doubt looked like two men arguing over a woman.

"We are wasting time that we cannot afford to waste," Battista said. Dropping Bobbie Sue's arm, he left the diner.

"Dammit, wait a minute!" Duncan hurried after Battista, but when he reached the sidewalk, there was no sign of the vampire.

Cloaked in the shadows of the night, Battista closed his eyes and sought for the sound of Victoria's heartbeat amongst the hundreds of others in the town, thanking whatever Fates there were that she had allowed him to take her blood the night before. Doing so had forged a link between them that could not be broken so long as one of them survived.

It took only moments for him to separate hers from all the others. Like a wolf on the scent, he followed the beat of her heart. It led him out of Pear Blossom Creek, across the state highway and the weed-infested field beyond.

Her heartbeat grew louder as he climbed a hill and descended the other side. There, he found a small house built of weathered wood and stone. There were iron bars on the windows, iron-barred security doors at the front and the back. A chain-link fence surrounded the property. A padlock secured the gate. Two large Dobermans paced the length of the fence.

No lights shone in the house.

He cursed softly, wondering how he had missed finding this place before. It provided little consolation to know that Duncan hadn't found it, either, he thought, uttering a wordless sound of disdain. He

was surprised the hunter could find his way home
without a map.

Dissolving into mist, Battista floated over the fence,
then slipped under the back door. Once inside the cottage, he assumed his own shape. Standing in the dark,
he listened to the sounds of the house, then followed
the siren call of Victoria's heartbeat. It led him through
a small door in the kitchen and down a flight of stairs
that ended in the cellar.

The frantic beat of her heart came to him more
loudly now, as did the sound of her breathing, rapid
and afraid.

A second door led into a larger room swathed in
darkness.

He found Victoria chained to the wall across from
the door, her arms drawn over her head, held in place
by a pair of heavy silver manacles that gleamed even in
the dark. A second set of manacles bound her ankles.
For a moment, her appearance startled him, and then
he realized she was wearing a Tinkerbell costume and
the odd protrusions at her back were wings.

He moved quickly to her, wondering, fleetingly, how
Falco had managed to bind her with silver chains, but
his relief at seeing her alive and well overcame every
other thought.

She gasped when he placed his hand on her shoulder.

"Shh, my sweet one."

"Antonio! Oh, Antonio."

"Did he hurt you?"

"*Oh, Antonio.*" From the doorway, Dimitri Falco's
voice mimicked Victoria's.

Battista whirled around, quietly cursing as Falco's
familiar stink stung his nostrils.

"Kill him!" Falco's voice echoed off the stone walls.

Four hulking shapes moved past Falco. With his preternatural sight, Battista saw the vacant expression in their eyes, knew that Falco had bent their minds to his will. Two of the zombies carried long wooden stakes. The other two carried vials of holy water.

Falco screamed, "What are you waiting for? Kill him, you fools!"

The zombies carrying the holy water threw it in Battista's direction. He raised his arms to protect his face, swore as drops of water sprayed over his hands, face, and neck like acid rain.

The zombie nearest him lunged forward, the wooden stake clutched in his fist driving toward Battista's heart.

With a cry, Antonio dissolved into mist and fled the room.

Traveling on the wings of the night, he returned to the diner in search of Duncan.

He found the hunter seated at a back table devouring a steak.

Tom looked up, startled, when Battista suddenly appeared in the chair across from him. The vampire looked even worse than he had before. Fresh blisters spread like freckles across his cheeks.

"I need your help," Battista said urgently. "Now."

"Yeah, right."

"We have no time to waste. I know where Victoria is."

Duncan dropped his fork on the table. "Let's go."

Bobbie Sue hurried toward them. "Tom, where are you going?"

"To get Victoria. See ya later."

"Wait! I want to go."

"No! You stay here!" Duncan said, and followed Battista out into the night.

"My car's this way," Duncan said.

Moments later, they were at the house in the hollow.

Duncan killed the engine and turned off the light. "You think she's still here?"

"Yes," Battista said curtly. Getting out of the car, he started toward the house.

"Hold on a minute," Duncan called.

Battista grimaced as Duncan opened the trunk of the Camaro and pulled out a stake, a hammer, and a large bottle of holy water.

Duncan grinned. "Let's go."

He stopped grinning when two Dobermans materialized out of the darkness, barking frantically. "You got a plan for getting past the dogs?"

Taking hold of the padlock in one hand, Antonio gave a sharp jerk and it came away in his hand. "Wait here," he said, and slipped through the gate.

Growing, both dogs walked stiff-legged toward him. And then, as his gaze met theirs, they dropped to the ground, tails wagging.

Without waiting to see if Duncan was following, Antonio headed for the back door. As expected, the iron security door was locked. Grasping two of the bars, he gave a good hard yank. There was an unearthly screech as the bolts were torn out of the wood.

Tossing the iron grate aside, he kicked in the wooden door.

He had no sooner done so than the four zombies rushed toward him out of the darkness, illuminated by a faint shaft of moonlight.

He grabbed the first one and broke its neck.

Muttering an oath, Duncan drew his revolver and fired three quick shots. It dropped the remaining zombies in their tracks.

Grunting softly, Battista hurried down the stairs to the basement. The smell of fresh blood grew stronger as he neared the door.

Victoria's blood.

Opening the door, he rushed to her side, grief and rage welling from deep within him when he saw the gaping wound in the curve where her neck and shoulder met.

Throwing back his head, he howled his rage.

Duncan stood in the doorway, stake in one hand, .38 in the other. "Is she dead?"

"Not yet." Antonio reached for the manacle that spanned her right wrist, only to jerk his hand away, hissing with pain, as the silver blistered his flesh.

"I don't suppose there's a key?" Duncan asked.

Battista shook his head.

"Then we'll have to do it the hard way. I'll be right back."

Battista stroked Victoria's brow. "My sweet one, can you hear me?" He stroked her cheek with his uninjured hand. Her skin was cold beneath his fingertips, her breathing shallow. Ripping a strip of cloth from his shirttail, he wrapped it around the hideous wound in her throat.

He looked up as Duncan ran into the room, a pair of bolt cutters in his hand. In moments, he had cut through the chains. "Let's get out of here. We'll worry about the cuffs later."

With a nod, Battista put his arms around Victoria, holding her upright while Duncan cut the chains at her feet. As soon as she was free, Antonio swung her into his arms and carried her up the stairs and out of the house. The dogs whined softly when he went out of the gate.

He watched impassively as Duncan set fire to the house.

"He won't be coming back here, that's for damn sure." Duncan glanced at Victoria. "Is she . . . ?"

"She is alive."

"We'd better get her to a doctor. I think she's going to need a transfusion right quick."

Battista hesitated, reluctant to let anyone else look after her. His own blood was far stronger than the blood of mortals.

Looking up, he met Duncan's gaze.

"I know what you're thinking," the bounty hunter said. "Are you sure that's what she'd want?"

"No." He knew it wasn't what she wanted, but what he wanted. He carried Victoria to the car and got in, cradling her in his arms while Duncan drove to the hospital. The cuff on her left wrist burned even through his clothing where her arm rested against his chest, but it didn't matter. Nothing mattered now but saving her life.

The hunter's Camaro was old and beat up, but it hauled. Duncan pulled into the hospital emergency parking lot five minutes later. Leaving the motor running, he hopped out of the car and opened the door for Battista, then turned and ran into the building, hollering for help.

An orderly hurried out with a gurney.

Antonio was reluctant to surrender Victoria's care to anyone else, but he placed her gently on the gurney, then followed the orderly inside. Duncan was standing at the nurse's station, filling out the required paperwork, explaining that she'd had an accident on the highway out of town.

Slipping around a corner, Battista dissolved into

mist, then went into the examining room where they had taken Victoria. The doctors and nurses worked quickly, washing and stitching the raw wound in her neck while another nurse set up the necessary equipment to replace the blood Falco had taken. He wondered what the medics would think if they knew what had really happened to her.

Even in his incorporeal state hovering unseen near the ceiling, he was not immune to the scent of blood. It enveloped him, arousing his hunger, making it difficult to remain in his inhuman form.

He listened to the quiet conversation of the doctors and nurses as they worked. Between asking for instruments and calling out Victoria's vital signs, they speculated on how she had received the wound in her throat and why there were manacles on her wrists and ankles.

"Car accident indeed," the doctor said. "More like some sort of sex game that went wrong." Removing his gloves, he stepped away from the table. "I think you'd better call the police first thing in the morning. They'll want to talk to her when she wakes up. And see if you can get hold of a locksmith to come over and get those cuffs off her."

"Yes, Doctor."

Half an hour later, Victoria was tucked into a hospital bed between crisp white sheets. A locksmith had removed the shackles from her wrists and ankles, ointment had been applied to the abrasions they had left on her skin.

Battista stood beside her bed, his hand holding one of hers. Her color looked a little better, her breathing was less labored. Her hair framed her face like a fiery halo.

He vanished from sight each time a nurse came in to

check Victoria's blood pressure, reappeared the minute they left the room.

He remained by her side through the remaining hours of the night. As dawn threatened to chase the darkness from the sky, he brushed a kiss across her cheek, whispered that he loved her, and hastened to his resting place before the sun could find him.

Chapter 24

Vicki woke slowly, confused by the pungent aromas that flooded her nostrils. Her bed felt strange, her throat hurt, she couldn't move her left arm.

Opening her eyes, she stared at her surroundings—the pale green walls, the small TV sitting on a corner shelf, the bandages on her wrists, the IV dripping down a tube into her arm.

She frowned. What was she doing in a hospital?

It came back to her in a rush. She had admitted Falco into her home. He had drugged her and abducted her. Things were a little hazy after that. She remembered being locked in a cellar, her arms chained to a wall, remembered Falco's voice whispering in her ear, describing in dark detail precisely what he intended to do to her. She had seen it all vividly in her mind as he told her exactly how he would drink from her every night until she no longer had the strength or the will to resist him. It would be painful, he said, beyond any pain she had ever known. He would consume her blood and with it all her memories until she was nothing but an empty husk, and then he would flood her mind with his wants, his desires. She would be his slave, subject to his every whim, until she no longer pleased him, and then he would drain her dry and cast her aside.

"You've seen my minions," Falco had said, gesturing at the four creatures who did his bidding. "That's what you will become."

Vicki covered her mouth with her hand, stifling a cry of horror as she imagined herself as one of those pitiful creatures. She had to get out of here, had to leave town before Falco tricked her again. Next time she might not be so lucky . . .

She frowned. How had she gotten here? She didn't remember escaping from Falco.

She was still puzzling over the matter when Bobbie Sue and Duncan entered the room.

"You're awake," Bobbie Sue said brightly. "How are you feeling, hon?"

"Not good."

"I was so worried about you." Bobbie Sue thrust the bouquet in her hands into a pitcher of water. "Thank goodness they found you in time."

"They?"

"Don't you remember?"

"No."

Bobbie Sue dropped into the hard plastic chair beside the bed. "Tom and Antonio charged into Falco's hideaway like the Lone Ranger and Tonto and rescued you."

Vicki looked at Tom, a question in her eyes. "The two of you? Together?"

"Yeah. You should have seen us," he said, grinning. "We wiped out Falco's zombies, grabbed you, and then burned the place down. He won't be going back there any time soon."

"You killed them, the zombies?" Vicki asked. True, they had been under Falco's spell, but once they had been human, with all the same hopes and dreams as everyone else. "Wasn't there some way to save them?"

Duncan shook his head. "No. Believe me, they're better off dead."

"Where's Antonio? Is he all right?"

"He was fine, last I saw him," Duncan said. Moving up behind Bobbie Sue, he placed his hands on her shoulders. "We think you should come and stay with us when you get out of here."

"That's right," Bobbie Sue said, covering Duncan's hand with one of her own. "It isn't safe for you to be home alone as long as that monster is on the loose."

Vicki glanced from Tom to Bobbie Sue. "Stay with the two of you?"

A faint blush rose in Bobbie Sue's cheeks. "Yes, well, Tom's living with me now."

"Really?"

"I know, it's kind of sudden," Bobbie Sue said with a shrug, "but after what's been happening the last couple of weeks, I realized life's too short and uncertain not to grab what you want with both hands." Glancing over her shoulder, she looked up at Tom. "And he's what I want."

"I'm happy for you," Vicki murmured. "For both of you."

"So, can we bring you anything?" Bobbie Sue asked. "A nightgown? One of Gus's cheeseburgers? A chocolate shake?"

"That would be wonderful. Thanks."

"No problem, girlfriend. So, how soon will you be getting out of here?"

"I'm not sure. I'm waiting for the doctor to examine me. Is Gus terribly upset that I missed work again?"

"Well, he was until he found out what happened. Don't worry about your shift. Gladys and I will cover for you until you get back."

"Thanks."

"Well, we'd better be going so you can rest, hon. Oh, here." Delving into her bag, Bobbie Sue withdrew a paperback novel and dropped it on the tray. "I thought you might like something to read."

"Thanks."

Rising, Bobbie Sue kissed Vicki on the cheek. "I'll call you later."

"Let us know if you need anything," Tom said, squeezing her hand.

He turned to follow Bobbie Sue out the door, but Vicki called him back.

"What is it?" he asked.

"You're not still going to . . . to try and destroy Antonio, are you? Not now."

"He's a vampire, Vicki. Destroying them is what I do."

"But last night you were working together!"

"Yeah." Duncan ran a hand over his jaw. "I know." He had worked with vampires before, he thought, thinking about Grigori and Ramsey. Maybe it was just another sign that it was time for him to look for another line of work. Lately, he was spending more time with the Undead than the living. "Get some rest," he said gruffly, and left the room.

The doctor came in later that morning. He looked at her chart and asked a few questions, then examined her wound. He pronounced it healing nicely, but concluded that she should spend another night in the hospital.

With a sigh of resignation, Vicki thanked him, then closed her eyes and slept.

When she woke, her room was filled with dozens of

red roses. They filled every available space. She plucked the card from the nearest bouquet. It read, *All my love, A.*

No one had ever sent her flowers before. She was still smiling when a nurse came in to remove the IV.

A short time later, lunch arrived, along with a box of chocolates and another dozen roses. The card read, *I am dreaming of you. A.*

After lunch, she settled down with the book Bobbie Sue had left for her, but she couldn't concentrate on the words. She kept seeing Falco's fiendish yellow eyes, hearing his voice in her ear as he outlined his plans for her, watching the zombies obey his commands. She wondered who they had been before Falco enslaved them. Three had been in their thirties; the fourth no more than twenty. And now they were dead because of her.

She shivered with the memory, thinking how sad it was that their families would never know what had happened to them.

Hearing heavy footsteps, she looked up to find Ned and Arnie striding toward her.

"Afternoon, Vicki," Ned said.

"Hi."

Arnie nodded at her, then closed the door.

Vicki looked from one to the other. Neither was smiling. Arnie was holding a thick canvas bag. "Is something wrong?"

"We'll let you know," Ned said in a tone she had never heard before. "Why don't you tell us what happened to you last night."

Vicki's heart skipped a beat. "Oh, that. It was nothing, just an accident."

Reaching into the canvas bag, Arnie pulled out a set of heavy silver manacles and held them up. "Really? What kind of accident?"

She stared at him, her mind racing. What should she say? They would never believe the truth. But she didn't like them thinking what they were obviously thinking, either. She blew out a breath. "I have nothing to say."

"Like hell! Something went on last night," Ned said, "and I want to know what it was and who else was involved."

Vicki crossed her arms over her chest. "It wasn't anything for the police to get involved in. No one else was hurt." She swallowed hard, thinking of the four dead men. "I made a stupid mistake. If you want to arrest me for that, fine, go ahead."

Ned stared at her, his eyes narrowed. "The old house out at the Hollow burned to the ground last night. Would you be knowing anything about that?"

"No."

Ned swore.

Arnie gave her a hard look, then dropped the manacles back into the bag. "I don't know what happened," he said, his voice grim, "but you aren't doing yourself or anyone else a favor by refusing to talk to us."

"I'm sorry, but I've got nothing to say."

"If you change your mind," Ned said flatly, "give us a call."

"I will."

Vicki stared after them as they left the room. Maybe she should have told them the truth, she mused, then shook her head. If she started going on about vampires and vampire hunters, they'd think she was insane. Instead of lying in a hospital bed, she would probably find herself in a padded room. So, instead of them thinking she was insane, now they probably thought she was involved in some sort of kinky sex. She wasn't crazy about that idea either. Crazy, she thought, that was definitely the right word for the way her life had been going lately.

She frowned. Maybe she should tell Ned and Arnie the truth. They needed to know what they were up against. But even if they knew, what could they do about it? If a vampire hunter couldn't find Falco, what chance did Ned and Arnie have? She weighed the pros and cons until her head ached.

Eager to think of something else, she turned on the TV and lost herself in the antics of an old *I Love Lucy* rerun.

Her dinner tray arrived an hour later, and then one of the nurses came in to take her for a walk down the hall.

Bobbie Sue, Gus, and Mrs. Heath all called to see how she was doing. Bert Summers came by to talk to her, anxious for a scoop. She told him the story she had concocted, that she had fallen in the vacant lot outside of town and cut her neck on an old piece of barbed wire. She wasn't sure if he believed her or not, but she was certain he wouldn't believe the truth.

As soon as the sun set, Antonio strolled into her room carrying a huge bouquet of red roses with a red balloon heart in the center. Just seeing him made her spirits soar.

"I was hoping you'd come," she said.

"Where else would I go when you are here?" He glanced around the room. "Where should I put these?"

"Antonio, all these flowers must be costing you a fortune. Here, put them on the table by the phone. I'll ask the nurse to bring me another vase."

Pulling a chair up to the bed, he sat down, then reached for her hand. "Are you all right?"

"I am now." She studied his cheek, noting there were a lot of new blisters. The old burn looked ugly and painful but didn't look as bad as it had before. "Does it still hurt?"

He nodded. "When can you leave here?"

"Hopefully tomorrow. It's up to the doctor."

"I do not want you to go back to your house."

"That's what Bobbie Sue and Duncan said. They want me to stay at Bobbie's house with them."

"They are living together?" Antonio asked, a note of surprise in his voice.

"So it would seem."

"Is that what you wish to do, stay with your friend?"

"Not really, but I don't want to stay home alone, either, not now."

"You are welcome to come and stay with me."

Vicki stared at him. "Stay with you? Where?"

"At my house in Maine. I think you would like it there."

"I've never been to Maine. What's your house like?"

"It is a castle of sorts, though not as large as most. The house sits in the middle of several acres of land, most of it heavily wooded. A very wealthy man had it brought over from England for his bride some three hundred years ago. He thought it would please her, but the poor girl fell down a flight of stairs and broke her neck. Some say she fell because she was frightened by the ghost of the castle's former mistress. Some say it was because her husband pushed her."

"I've never believed in ghosts," Vicki mused. And then she looked at Antonio and smiled. "But then, I never used to believe in vampires, either."

Leaning forward, he touched the bandage at her neck. "I am sorry you had to learn of us in such a painful manner."

"Me, too. But then, if it weren't for Falco, I never would have met you, would I?"

"Perhaps not. Or perhaps fate would have managed to bring us together sooner or later."

"I'd like to think so. Is there really a ghost? Have you ever seen it?"

"Of course."

"You're kidding, aren't you?"

"No."

"Did she try to hurt you?"

"No. She is a lovely, lonely soul."

"And you really saw her? Did she speak to you?"

"Yes. We are kindred spirits, Lady Kathryn and I. We have spent many a lonely night keeping each other company."

Vicki stared at him, not knowing whether to believe him or not.

"Will you come with me to Maine, Victoria? I can protect you there until Duncan destroys Falco."

She shivered at the mention of the vampire's name. "What if he follows us?"

"My home is well protected. He will not be able to enter . . . " Antonio looked at her, one brow raised, "so long as no one invites him in."

"I suppose it was foolish of me, what I did. But it never occurred to me that he would come to my house disguised as Darth Vader, of all things."

"Now you know better. You will not make that mistake again."

"That's for sure!"

"You will come with me, then?"

"Yes, I'd love to see your castle. And your ghost." She blew out a sigh. Talking about ghosts made her think of the four men Falco had hypnotized.

Antonio squeezed her hand. "What is it that troubles you?"

"The police came to see me today."

"Indeed?"

"They wanted to know how I got hurt. They had the manacles Falco used. I didn't know what to tell them, so I didn't tell them anything. What should I do?"

"You did the right thing. Telling the police about Falco will only start a panic. Even though people claim that they do not believe we exist, given the right catalyst, they can soon turn into a mindless mob eager for blood. I have seen it happen before," he said. "Many times. When it happens, innocent people die. Sometimes, ignorance is best."

"I guess so."

"We will leave as soon as . . . " He glanced over his shoulder at the sound of footsteps.

Vicki followed his gaze, and a moment later Bobbie Sue and Duncan entered the room.

"Hey," Bobbie Sue said. "Saints be praised, you're looking a lot better tonight. How are you feeling, hon?"

"Better, thanks. Why aren't you at work?"

"Gus gave me an hour off so's I could come and visit you. He acts so tough, but he's just an old softie, you know that."

Vicki nodded. Everyone in town knew Gus was a soft touch. He contributed to every charity known to man, bought Girl Scout cookies by the case, supported the local Boy Scout troop, donated money to the hospital building fund and the PTA.

She looked at Duncan, who was staring at Antonio. Only then did she feel the tension in the room.

Apparently Bobbie Sue felt it, too. Tugging on Duncan's arm, she said, "Come on, Tom, I think we should go."

He grunted softly. "I'll wait for you outside."

Bobbie Sue bent down to give Vicki a hug. "Don't

worry about anything, hon," she said. "Everything will work out."

"Listen, Bobbie Sue, I'm going away with Antonio."

Bobbie Sue's eyes grew wide. "You are? When? Why?"

"As soon as I get out of here. Because I want to. I need you to tell Gus for me, okay? Just tell him I'm taking my vacation a few months early."

"Well, sure, but"—Bobbie Sue lowered her voice—"are you sure this is a good idea? I mean, I know you're attracted to Antonio and everything, but Vicki, he's a vampire."

"Yes, I know," Vicki replied dryly. "I'll call you, okay?"

"I hope you know what you're doing, hon."

"Me, too." Reaching up with her free arm, she gave Bobbie Sue a hug. "Just be sure *you* know what *you're* doing, you know, with Tom."

Bobbie Sue grinned. "We sure picked a pair, didn't we?"

"That we did."

"Night, Vicki. Antonio." With a wave and a smile, Bobbie Sue left the room.

When they were alone again, Antonio again took Victoria's hand in his. "So, you will come with me?"

She nodded. "How soon do you think we should leave?"

"Tomorrow night. Can you be ready by then?"

"I think so."

But later that night, alone in bed, when doubts and fears are the strongest, she couldn't help wondering if she was putting distance between herself and a killer or walking blindly into the lion's den.

* * *

The doctor okayed Vicki's release the next morning. As soon as she knew she could leave, she called Bobbie Sue and asked if she'd mind driving her home, and if she would please stop off at her house and bring her something to wear since all she had was her bloody Tinkerbell costume, which she intended to get rid of as soon as possible. Once she had a ride home, Vicki asked the nurse to distribute the roses Antonio had sent her to some of the patients who didn't have any friends or visitors, all except for the dozen he had given her personally.

Now she sat on the bed, waiting for a nurse to bring her a wheelchair. Bobbie Sue sat beside her, idly thumbing through an old magazine.

After a few minutes, Bobbie Sue tossed the magazine aside. "So, where are you and Antonio going?"

"He has a house somewhere in Maine. We're going there. Should be interesting," Vicki said with a grin. "It's supposed to be haunted."

Bobbie Sue stared at her. "You're going to a haunted house with a vampire? Have you lost your mind, hon?"

"I know what I'm doing," Vicki assured her.

"You don't sound all that convinced to me," Bobbie Sue retorted. "Are you sure you know what you're doing? He's a vampire, Vicki. It's not like he just thinks he's one, you know. He really is, and they kill people."

Vicki took Bobbie Sue's hands in hers. "I love him, Bobbie. What else can I do?"

"Sakes alive, hon, I can think of a lot of things that would be smarter!"

"I know, so can I."

"Where is this house of his?"

"I'm not sure. Somewhere on the coast. He said it's a castle."

"A haunted castle on the coast of Maine?" Bobbie

Sue asked incredulously. "How Stephen King can you get? Are you sure you won't change your mind and come and stay with me?"

"I'm sure. And no matter what Tom says, I'm sure he'd rather I didn't stay there."

Vicki stood as the nurse appeared in the doorway. "Let's go, Bobbie Sue. I've got a lot of packing to do when I get home."

Chapter 25

Vicki stood in the middle of the living-room floor. It seemed like years had passed since she had been home last. After putting the roses in a vase, she went through the house and opened all the curtains and the window in the kitchen.

She was going to miss this place. Even as the thought crossed her mind, she told herself she wasn't leaving Pear Blossom Creek forever—just for a few weeks, until Dimitri Falco was no longer a threat—but she couldn't shake the feeling that her life was about to undergo a major change, and that she would never live in this house or in this quiet town again.

Shaking off her feelings of doom and gloom, she went upstairs and took a long, hot shower, washing away the antiseptic smell of the hospital. She slipped into a pair of comfortable sweats, pulled her suitcase off the top shelf of the closet, and began to go through her clothes, trying to decide what to take and what to leave. Figuring a castle in Maine would probably be cold and drafty this time of year, she packed mostly

jeans and sweaters and long-sleeved shirts. She added
a few dresses, a warm nightgown and robe, slippers,
underwear, several pairs of shoes, and a pair of fur-
lined boots. She packed her toiletries in a small bag,
added her camera, a portable CD player and her favorite CDs, and the book Bobbie Sue had given her.
She called the utility company and left a message on
their answering machine, informing them she would be
going on vacation and to please turn off the gas, electricity, and phone until further notice starting the day
after tomorrow. She started to write a note to the mail-
man, but stopped when she realized she didn't have a
forwarding address. She would have to ask Antonio
about that later.

In spite of her repeated assurances to herself that
there was nothing to worry about, she grew increasingly nervous as the day wore on.

She spent an hour on the phone with her sister and
her mother, then drove over to see Mrs. Heath.

"Victoria, dear!" Mrs. Heath said, taking Vicki's
hands in hers. "I've been so worried about you."

"Worried? Why?"

"Well, dear, you know how rumors spread in a town
this size." Mrs. Heath placed a hand over her heart.
"Now, dear, I know it's none of my business how you
conduct your social life, but land sakes, child, what
were you thinking?"

Perplexed, Vicki said, "I'm afraid I don't know what
you're talking about."

Mrs. Heath cupped her hand to Vicki's ear and whispered, "Bondage."

"Bondage!" Vicki stared at the other woman. "I'm
not doing anything like that. Where on earth did you
hear such a thing?" she asked, but of course she knew.
You couldn't keep a secret in Pear Blossom Creek. The

fact that she'd been wearing manacles when she was admitted to the hospital must be all over town by now.

"At the market this morning. It was all anyone could talk about."

Vicki groaned softly. Before nightfall, her reputation would be in shreds. Bondage, indeed! "Mrs. Heath, you've got to believe me—"

"Now, dear, you don't have to explain anything to me, but, well, and this is none of my business, have you been to confession lately?"

"Mrs. Heath, I swear to you, there's nothing like that going on, honest. It's all a misunderstanding. It was Falco. He kidnapped me and imprisoned me in that old house down by the Hollow."

Mrs. Heath sat down on the stone bench, her face going pale. "Oh, my dear! Thank the good Lord that you're all right. You haven't told anyone about him, have you?"

"No, I didn't think anyone would believe me."

"You're so right." Mrs. Heath blew out a deep breath. "I tried to tell people what had happened to me. No one believed a word I said. I had no proof, of course. My father threatened to send me to a convent if I didn't stop telling such outrageous stories. My mother took to her bed. I knew right then that when the truth was ugly, people didn't want to hear it."

For a moment, Vicki was tempted to confide in Mrs. Heath, to tell her about Antonio, but she quickly decided against it. The woman would only worry more if she knew there were two vampires in town instead of one.

Vicki was about to take her leave when ten-year-old Jimmy Hernandez came running down the street, crying incoherently.

"Jimmy," Vicki called, "what's wrong?"

"Body!" Slowing, he stopped in front of her, panting hard. "My dad . . . We were fishing . . . He found a body . . . near the lake. He sent me . . . to find Officer Williams."

Vicki glanced at Mrs. Heath, then looked back at Jimmy. "Do you know who it . . . who it was?"

Jimmy nodded. "Miz Collins," he said, and ran down the street toward the police department.

"Victoria, dear, I think it's time you got out of town."

"Yes," Vicki said. "I think you're right."

Another murder. Another girl drained of blood, her body discarded in a ditch like an empty cup. It was all Vicki could think of while she paced the floor, waiting for the sun to go down. Waiting for Antonio.

She practically jumped out of her skin when the doorbell rang. "Victoria?"

"Antonio!" Remembering how Falco had imitated Antonio's voice, she peered out the window to find him looking back at her. *Vampires can change their shape.* She paused with her hand on the door knob. "How do I know it's you?"

"Search your senses. They will tell you."

"How do I do that?"

"Open your mind. Think of me, of the kisses we have shared."

She did as he said and knew without doubt that it was Antonio standing on her porch. She could feel his essence, unlike that of anyone else. Smiling, she opened the door.

"Are you ready?" he asked.

"Yes. Did you hear about . . . about Suzie Collins?"

"Yes." A muscle worked in his jaw.

"I feel like such a coward, running away like this."

Antonio drew her into his arms. "I am the coward," he said, his breath fanning her cheek. "I fear I cannot protect you here, and I cannot abide the thought of losing you." He gestured at the luggage she had stacked beside the door. "Is that everything?"

"Yes, except for my coat and pocketbook."

"Let us go, then." He gathered the bags under one arm, then held out his hand.

"Just let me get my keys."

"You will not need them."

"No?"

"No." He wrapped his arm around her waist and held her close against him.

"Relax."

"How can I relax when I don't know what you're going to do?"

"There's nothing to be afraid of. Close your eyes and trust me, my sweet one."

Taking a deep breath, she closed her eyes. She experienced a sense of movement, as if she were flying, a sudden queasiness in the pit of her stomach, followed by a feeling of weightlessness, as if she had left her body behind.

"Are you all right?" His voice sounded in her ear.

"I don't know. Am I?" Opening her eyes, she glanced at her surroundings, murmured, "Oh my," when she saw the castle. It sat on a verdant hill, looking almost iridescent in the moonlight. A long curving driveway stretched away from the front of the house. There were trees everywhere, all heavy with fall foliage. The air was thick with the scent of rain, damp earth, and moss.

"Welcome to my home," Antonio said.

Taking her by the hand, he led her up the stone steps. The door opened as if by magic. Candles sprang to life, lighting their way through a narrow foyer tiled in black and gray and into a large parlor with vaulted ceilings and tall, leaded windows. Tapestries hung on three of the walls, depicting a variety of hunting scenes. Other than that, there were no pictures or decorations in the room. The furniture was heavy and dark. A massive stone fireplace, the mantel higher than the top of her head, took up most of the fourth wall. A fire sprang to life in the hearth.

Startled, she took a step backward. "Another vampire talent, I suppose. Maybe you should make me a list."

He smiled at her, obviously amused.

"I'm serious," she said, frowning. "All these supernatural powers are disconcerting, you know."

"I am sorry," he said. "I will try to warn you in the future."

"How did we get here so fast? At least, it seemed fast." Still feeling a little queasy, she pressed a hand to her stomach. "Don't tell me," she said. "Just something you pulled out of your bag of tricks."

He dropped her bags on the floor. "Relax, my sweet one. I know you are nervous at being here, alone in a strange place with a vampire."

Nervous didn't begin to explain what she was feeling. Any why did the word *vampire* suddenly seem so ominous?

"Would you like to see the rest of the house?"

"Sure." Anything was better than standing there feeling like a bug under a microscope.

"The kitchen is this way."

He flicked a light switch, then led her down a flight of stone steps into a large room that was, for all intents and purposes, empty save for a rectangular table and a couple of chairs. A long counter ran the length of the room; there was a pantry at one end that was bigger than her bedroom at home. Like the kitchen, the pantry was empty. She was certain that if she opened the cupboards that lined one wall, she would find they were equally empty. Several large windows were located above the counter.

"I shall purchase a stove and a refrigerator." Antonio glanced around the room. She had a feeling he didn't come down here often but then, why would he? "And some food, of course."

"I'm surprised you have electricity," she remarked as they returned to the parlor.

"It is a recent addition."

He led her down a narrow hallway, showing her the rooms on either side. There was a large library stocked with books, an office that held little more than an antique rolltop desk, and three rooms that were empty.

There was a second parlor at the back of the house. She knew immediately that this was where Antonio spent most of his time when he was here, mainly because of the enormous television screen that took up a good portion of one wall. A black leather chair that could easily hold two and a large square end table were located in front of the TV. Several books were scattered across the table. There was a fireplace in the corner. A bearskin rug took up a good deal of floor space in front of the hearth.

She looked up at Antonio and grinned. "Now I know why you have electricity."

He grinned back at her. Moving toward a large oak cabinet, he opened the doors, revealing an expensive stereo system, hundreds of CDs, and what looked like a thousand DVDs.

"Wow! I had no idea you were a couch potato."

Going to stand beside him, she perused the DVD titles, pleased to see a few of her favorites, like *Pirates of the Caribbean, Doc Hollywood,* and *Gladiator,* on one shelf.

Another shelf must have held every vampire movie ever made, from the early black-and-white film *Nosferatu* to the more contemporary movie *The Lost Boys,* as well as every *Dracula* movie ever made, from the first black-and-white one starring Bela Lugosi to her all-time favorite starring Frank Langella. Antonio even had the Spanish version of *Dracula.* Vicki recalled reading in an old movie magazine that the Spanish version had been filmed on the same set as the Bela Lugosi movie and that many critics thought the Spanish version was a better film. Sandwiched in among the others were *Dracula's Daughter, Son of Dracula, The Return of Dracula, Horror of Dracula,* and one she had never heard of, *Billy the Kid Versus Dracula.* There were a number of Hammer Dracula films, too, along with the Gary Oldman version and Anne Rice's *Interview With the Vampire.*

Vicki looked up at Antonio. "Have you watched all of these?"

He shrugged. "The nights can be long and lonely."

"I wouldn't think a vampire would want to watch movies about vampires."

He grunted softly. "They are always good for a laugh."

"Really?" She wondered what he had found humorous in *Interview With the Vampire.* She had watched the movie on TV with Bobbie Sue. Even though she knew it wasn't real, she had closed her eyes during the bloody parts. And now she was alone in the house with a vampire. A real vampire.

Shivering, she crossed her arms over her chest.

A moment later, a fire crackled in the hearth in the corner.

"Come," he said, "I will show you to your room."

He led her up a winding staircase. Candles flickered in wrought-iron sconces along the wall. He led her down a wide corridor lined with a deep maroon carpet. The doors on either side of the corridor were open. All the rooms appeared to be bedrooms. Only one was furnished. The chair and table looked to be genuine antiques, as did the bed and the mirror, though it was hard to be sure in the flickering candlelight.

"That was Lady Kathryn's room," Antonio remarked, and then grinned. "I suppose it still is."

He stopped at the end of the corridor in front of the only closed door. Opening it, he stepped inside and switched on the lights, revealing a large square room with leaded windows and an old-fashioned four-poster bed flanked by a pair of rosewood nightstands. The walls were a pale yellow, and a deep gold carpet covered the floor. The comforter and curtains were white. An antique rosewood armoire stood across from the bed; there was a matching rocking chair in one corner, a small desk and matching chair in another.

"It's lovely," she murmured.

"I am pleased that you like it."

"Where do you sleep?"

"Nearby." He gestured at a closed door. "The bathroom is in there."

She opened the door, revealing a claw-footed bathtub, a marble sink, and, to her relief, a modern toilet.

"Do you think you will be comfortable here?" he asked.

"Are you kidding? It's beautiful, but . . ."

He looked at her, one eyebrow arched in question.

"What will I do here during the day when you're . . . sleeping?"

"Whatever you wish, so long as you are inside before sunset. My car is in the garage, the keys are in it. There is a small town a few miles down the road." His gaze caressed her; his hand stroked her cheek, then slid down her neck, his thumb resting in the hollow of her throat. "I must go out for a short time. Please, make my home yours."

"I'll need my bags."

The words were scarcely out of her mouth before he had vanished and reappeared, her luggage in hand. He dropped the bags on the bed. "Do you wish anything else before I go?"

"I don't think so. Well, maybe something to eat," she said when her stomach growled rather loudly.

He brushed a kiss across her cheek. "I will not be gone long."

She watched him leave the room. Needing something to do, she unpacked her bags and put her clothing away. Everything fit nicely in the armoire, including her shoes.

Going into the bathroom, she took a quick bath, then changed into her gown and robe. She brushed out her hair, then went down the stairs and into the back parlor. She was trying to decide which DVD to watch when there was a ripple in the air. Turning, she saw Antonio walking toward her, a takeout bag in one hand and a covered Styrofoam cup in the other.

The scent of French fries filled the air, making her stomach growl again.

He placed the sack and the cup on the table beside the chair, gestured for her to sit and eat.

She felt ill at ease sitting in his chair and eating in

front of him while he stood, watching her. Did he remember the taste of solid food after so many years of being a vampire? It was strange to think he had never tasted anything as common as a hamburger and fries or had a Coke. Did he miss eating? Drinking something other than blood? Dared she ask?

"Don't you ever?"—she picked up a French fry— "you know, miss eating and drinking? I don't mean grabbing a quick burger at the mall, but don't you ever miss enjoying a glass of wine with a leisurely meal?"

"We did not have time for many leisurely meals when I was growing up," he replied. "My father worked us hard from dawn till dark. As for wine, I am able to enjoy a sip or two from time to time. It reminds me of what I was," he said, his voice suddenly melancholy. "And what I have lost."

"I'm sorry, Antonio."

"It was a long time ago, my sweet one. I do not often think of the past."

Still, she regretted making him think of it now. A look into his eyes told him he was no longer thinking of food. And suddenly, neither was she.

Heat flowed between them. He whispered her name, and she went into his arms with no memory of leaving the chair. His mouth covered hers, his kisses hot and greedy, his tongue a flame that threatened to set her whole being on fire. She clung to him in breathless anticipation as he kissed her again and again, each kiss more potent that the last. Somehow, they were lying side by side on the rug in front of the hearth. His hands slid under her gown, hot against her skin as he stroked her foot, her ankle, her calf. Eager to touch him in return, she pulled his shirttail from his trousers and ran her hands up and down his back. His skin was cool be-

neath her fingertips. A distant part of her mind wondered how his skin could feel so cool when she felt as
though her whole body was about to go up in flames.

She teased his lips with her tongue, felt the sudden
tremor that ran through his body, thrilled at knowing
she could arouse him. His arms were like steel around
her, his body taut, quivering with desire.

He wanted her, there could be no doubt of that. And
she wanted him.

She kissed him boldly, her tongue dueling with his,
her mind and body yearning toward him, hungering for
more, until she felt the prick of his fangs against her
tongue.

With a wordless cry, she drew back. She opened her
eyes, a quick primal fear rising from the depths of her
being when she saw the hunger burning like a flame in
the depths of his eyes.

In an instant, he was on his feet, his back toward
her, his hands clenched at his sides.

Vicki stared at his back, one hand pressed to her
throat as she willed her heart to stop pounding as she
tried to figure out why she was upset. It wasn't as if she
hadn't known that he was a vampire.

Silence stretched between them. She wished he
would say something, anything. Wished she could think
of something to ease the tension that grew more strained
with every passing moment.

"I did not mean to frighten you," he said quietly. "I
am sorry."

She wanted to deny it, to tell him she hadn't been
afraid, but it was a lie and he would know it.

Several minutes passed before he turned to face her.
"Forgive me?"

"Of course."

When he offered her his hand, she hesitated a moment before taking it and letting him pull her to her feet.

That brief hesitation did not go unnoticed.

With a slight bow, he released her hand. "I will bid you good night," he said. "Please, stay up as long as you wish. My home is yours."

Before she could say ah, yes, or no, he was gone.

Vicki stared after him, her heart and mind in turmoil. Why had she reacted that way? She had known Antonio was a vampire, but it hadn't kept her from being afraid. Nor had it kept her from feeling stark fear for her life and her soul.

Curling up in the chair, she stared into the fire, wondering if she might not have been safer staying in her own home.

Chapter 26

Vicki woke with a yawn. She glanced at the high ceiling, the yellow walls, the rosewood armoire, and frowned. For a moment, she couldn't remember where she was, and then she recalled falling asleep in Antonio's easy chair the night before.

Throwing back the covers, she sat up. He must have carried her upstairs to bed, though she had no memory of that, either.

Rising, she went into the bathroom. After showering and brushing her teeth, she dressed and went downstairs.

The silence in the house was a bit unnerving. All the drapes were drawn and she went from room to room, opening the heavy draperies, until the rooms were flooded with sunlight.

When her stomach growled, she started to go downstairs to the kitchen, only then remembering that there wasn't any food in the house. She continued on anyway.

Opening the curtains, she was surprised to see sev-

eral cardboard boxes on the counter. Peeking inside the
boxes, she found everything she could possibly want,
from the basics, like sugar and salt and pepper, to several kinds of bread and a variety of canned fruits and
vegetables. She also found a box of apples, bananas,
and oranges. And several bottles of water.

The last box held pots and pans and a set of expensive silverware, as well as a couple of women's magazines, the local *TV Guide*, and a cookbook. She grinned.
Did he think that, because she was a waitress, she didn't
know how to cook?

It touched her that he had gone out shopping for her.
And not just for groceries. A new refrigerator and stove
gleamed in their respective spaces. She wondered how
on earth he had managed to get the appliances deliv-
ered in the middle of the night.

Curious, she opened the refrigerator. It was stocked
with milk, orange juice, grapefruit juice, butter, two
dozen eggs, bacon, four kinds of lunch meat, three kinds
of cheese, and a variety of fresh produce. There was
also a six-pack of root beer and another of 7UP.

Vicki shook her head. Her refrigerator at home had
never held this much food at one time.

Later, after a leisurely breakfast of bacon, French
toast, and orange juice, she put the groceries in the
pantry, washed and dried her few dishes, and then went
upstairs. She put a Tim McGraw CD in the player, then
went up to make her bed.

When that was done, she wandered through the
house from top to bottom, noting as she did so that
there were no mirrors in the house, and no telephones.
For the first time, she wished she had a cell phone, but
in a little town like Pear Blossom Creek, there was really
no need for one. Still, her mother had been after her to

get one, for emergencies. Of course, back in Pear Blossom Creek, if you needed help, all you had to do was stand on the corner and ask. And sometimes you didn't even have to ask!

In the kitchen again, she noticed a small door in the back of the pantry. It opened with a squeak and she peered down a narrow flight of stairs. A flick of a switch turned on a low-watt lightbulb hanging from a cord at the foot of the stairs. Keeping one hand on the wall, she went down the steps, several of which creaked under her weight. At the bottom, she found herself in a large cellar lined with shelves, all of which were empty.

She was about to go back upstairs when she saw the coffin. Looking at it sent an icy shiver down her spine. Was this where Antonio slept during the day? If she lifted the lid, would she find him inside?

She stood staring at it for several minutes, wondering if she dared open it. Would he know if she did so? Would he be angry?

She took a step toward the coffin, and then another. Did she dare?

Compelled by some morbid desire she didn't understand, she moved toward the coffin. She ran her hand over the wood. It was like no coffin she had ever seen before except in old monster movies. Long and rectangular, it was made of untreated wood.

Taking a deep breath, she lifted the lid and peeked inside.

It was empty.

Filled with a sudden, inexplicable fear, she dropped the lid back into place, ran up the stairs, and slammed the door behind her. Standing in the middle of the pantry, she took several deep, calming breaths, and then frowned. If the coffin was empty, where was Antonio?

She pondered that for several minutes, deciding that the coffin he slept in must be in another part of the house, no doubt behind a locked door.

Maybe she would ask him about it later. Then again, maybe not. He had refused to tell her the last time she had asked.

With a shake of her head, she grabbed a jacket and went outside. She walked around the grounds. There were trees everywhere, their leaves a riot of reds and golds and autumn brown.

She paused at a fountain. It wasn't working, of course, but it was lovely just the same. A mermaid made of blue stone reclined on a large shell in the center of the fountain. King Neptune stood behind her, trident in hand. Had the fountain been working, water would have poured out of the trident's tines and rained down upon the mermaid. Perhaps Antonio would turn it on for her.

She moved on, following an overgrown brick pathway that led to the rear of the house. Here, she found a number of topiary trees. Though they were in need of trimming, she could see that one was an elephant standing on its hind legs, another a whale, another a bear.

She looked up at the house, noting the turrets and towers, the arched windows, the narrow catwalk that went all the way around the castle. It really was a lovely place.

She stopped at the garage on the way back to the front of the house. It was an obvious addition, though it was built like a small castle, complete with turrets at all four corners. Curious to see what kind of car Antonio drove, she opened the door and stepped inside.

It was, she saw, a three-car garage. And there were three cars inside. A sleek black Corvette. A black Jaguar that looked ready to pounce. And a gleaming silver Lexus.

One thing was for certain. The man had expensive taste in automobiles!

It took her five minutes to make up her mind. In the end, she picked the Corvette. Just sitting behind the wheel was exhilarating. For some reason, it made her think of Tom Duncan and his beat-up Camaro. Grinning, she turned the key in the ignition and the engine roared to life.

Driving a Corvette was a heady experience for someone who had never driven a sports car. Comparing it to driving her Honda was like comparing a fine racehorse to a plow horse. Sure, both would get you where you wanted to, but there was a world of difference in the ride.

She drove past the town and just kept going, loving the feel of the car, the purr of the engine, the way it handled. With John Michael Montgomery on the radio singing about letters from home, she thought life was just about perfect.

After cruising for half an hour or so, she turned around and headed back to town. As Antonio had said, it wasn't very big. In fact, the town of Kay's Crossing didn't look much bigger than Pear Blossom Creek. Still, it had a Starbucks and a McDonald's and a number of department stores, including a Target and a Wal-Mart, as well as some smaller specialty stores. An old-fashioned movie theater was located across from an Applebee's restaurant. Surprisingly, they were showing two movies for the price of one, something she knew had been common years ago. She remembered hearing her parents talk about how theater admission prices had only been twenty-five cents, and for that, you got two movies, a bunch of cartoons, and a newsreel. Now producers and directors worried if their movie ran more than two hours, and ticket prices were pushing ten dollars.

Vicki parked the car, being careful to lock it, and then went window-shopping. Like most small towns, this one was friendly. The people she passed on the street smiled at her; most of them said hello.

She went into a quaint little café for lunch, and then went in search of a pay phone. Her first call was to her mother, but no one answered the phone. She left a message saying she was on a short vacation and that she would call back in a day or two. The second call was to Bobbie Sue.

"So, how are you and Duncan getting along?" Vicki asked.

"We're getting married."

"Married? When?"

"Well, we haven't set the date yet, but probably in the spring. He's going to give up hunting and become a teacher at some school that trains vampire hunters, if you can believe that. Anyway, I'm taking him home to meet my folks. We're leaving in a few minutes."

"That's great, Bobbie Sue. I'm happy for you?"

"Thanks. I'm pretty happy about it myself."

"How long will you be gone?"

"Not long. Gus would only give me a couple of days off. We'll be back Thursday night. I have to be at work Friday afternoon. Gladys is out with the flu. We could sure use your help at the diner. Do you think you'll be back soon?"

"I don't know. I hope so."

"So, how are things with you? He hasn't turned you into a vampire or anything, has he?"

Vicki lifted a hand to her throat. "Of course not."

"What's his place like?"

"It's a castle, and I mean a literal castle. You should see it, Bobbie Sue."

"Have you seen the ghost yet?"

"Not yet. How are things there? Have there been any more murders?"

"No, at least none that I've heard about. Tom thinks Falco must have left the area. I sure hope so. Oh, guess what? Maddy and Rex eloped! Can you believe that?"

"I think it's wonderful. How's Gus?"

"He's pissed off cause you're gone, of course. When are you coming home?"

"I don't know. I guess when Antonio thinks it's safe."

"Well, make it soon. I can't get married without you, you know."

Vicki smiled. "I'll call you soon."

Replacing the receiver, Vicki felt a slight twinge of jealousy. Bobbie Sue was getting married.

Out on the street again, Vicki spent a moment wondering what to do next. She wasn't ready to go back to the castle. Maybe she'd just go to the movies, even though she had already seen the movie that was playing. Still, you couldn't see Johnny Depp too often.

It was almost dusk when she left the theater. As the sky grew darker, she grew increasingly nervous. On the drive back to Antonio's, she kept looking over her shoulder. She told herself she was being foolish, that Falco couldn't possibly know where she was, but she couldn't help it.

She breathed a sigh of relief when she drove into the garage and parked the car, relieved to be home and more relieved that nothing had happened to the car while she was driving it.

She was walking up the stairs to the front door when she felt a sudden chill in the air that had nothing to do with the temperature and everything to do with the sense of being watched. Refusing to look over her shoulder for fear of what she might see, she unlocked the heavy wooden door and dashed inside, slamming the door behind her.

"Victoria, my sweet, what is wrong?"

"Nothing, I just . . . I felt like someone was watching me."

A muscle twitched in Antonio's cheek. "Did you see anyone?"

"No, but . . ." She took a deep breath. "It felt like Falco. Could he be here? Does he know where you live?"

"It would be easy for him to follow us," Antonio replied, "but as I said, you are safe within these walls." His gaze trapped hers. "You must not be out of the castle after the sun goes down, my sweet."

"I know, I didn't mean to be, but I went to the movies and I just forgot about the time."

He drew her into his arms. "You are safe now."

"And hungry." She smiled up at him, the expression dissolving when she saw the look in his eyes. He was hungry, too. But not for food.

"Do not worry, my sweet one, I do not intend to devour you, though I am sure you would be to my liking."

"Maybe."

"Something else troubles you."

"Well . . ." She shook her head. "It's just hard for me to think of you . . ."

"Drinking blood?"

"Yes. I'm sure I'll get used to it, in time."

"Perhaps." He drew his knuckles lightly across her cheek. "Go and have your dinner, Victoria, and I will have mine."

"Speaking of dinner, how'd you manage to get a stove and refrigerator here so soon?"

He grinned. "Have you not heard the expression *money talks*?"

"Bribery, eh?"

"Just the promise of a munificent gratuity. And now, I must go."

"Will you be gone very long?"

"No."

"All right."

Leaning down, he brushed a kiss across her lips. She tasted faintly of salt and butter. "Remember, do not answer the door for anyone, not even if it sounds like me."

"Don't worry, I won't."

He kissed her again and then he was gone. She thought about that kiss while she fixed dinner. She wasn't really all that hungry after the popcorn and Coke she'd had at the show, so she made do with an avocado and tomato sandwich and a glass of milk.

Sitting there, she glanced around the room. She was in a castle, a real castle, with a vampire. It was exciting and a little scary and she wouldn't have missed it for the world.

It took only a few minutes to clean up the kitchen and then she went back upstairs and into the back parlor.

Antonio was already there, waiting for her.

"That was quick," she remarked.

He nodded, then gestured for her to join him.

The overstuffed chair was easily big enough for the two of them and she found it was quite cozy, sitting there with his arm draped around her shoulders, her thigh pressed intimately against his.

"What did you do today?" he asked, "besides go to the movies?"

"Well, I drove your Corvette. It was almost like flying! It's a great car."

"If you like it, it is yours, although you may want to drive the Jaguar before you decide."

"You're going to give me one of your cars, just like that?"

"Of course."

"But—"

He put a finger over her lips. "It pleases me to do so, my sweet. Pick whichever one you wish. I have no particular attachment to any of them."

She kissed the tip of his finger. "That's very generous of you. Can I ask you something?"

"You may ask me anything," he said, grinning faintly. "Though I do not promise to answer."

"I saw a coffin in the basement. Is it yours?"

He nodded, his expression grim. "It is the one I was buried in after I was turned."

Vicki grimaced as she imagined him lying inside, dead but not dead.

"I bought a new one some years ago."

"Oh," she said, trying not to look horrified. "How nice."

"Shall I describe it to you?"

"No, that's all right."

"It is quite comfortable." His gaze moved to her throat. "And big enough for two."

"Please, can't we talk about something else?"

"Shall I tell you how beautiful you are? Or how much it pleases me to have you here, in my home? Shall I tell you that I dream of you when I am at my rest? Shall I tell you of what I dream?"

His voice was like rich black velvet sliding over her skin, warming her in ways and in places she had never felt before. "You dream of me?"

He nodded, his eyes hot as his gaze moved over her face to the pulse beating in her throat.

"Is that what you dream of?" she asked. "Biting me?"

"Yes, but it is so much more than that."

She had to agree with him there. His bite had been like nothing she had ever experienced in her life. It still astonished her that it hadn't repelled her; indeed, if she was honest with herself, she would admit that she wanted him to do it again.

And he knew it. She could see it in the way he was looking at her, as if he was just waiting for her to ask. But she couldn't. It wasn't natural to want such a thing.

"It is natural for my kind," he said quietly. "It is natural for me."

"You're reading my mind, aren't you?" she accused indignantly.

"I cannot help it. Your thoughts come to me clearly, especially when you are angry or frightened." His gaze lingered on her lips. "Or when you are aroused."

His words sent a rush of heat to her cheeks.

"One taste, my sweet? Would you refuse me one taste?"

"You've already had one."

"Would you deny me another?"

"Is that why you brought me here? For dessert?"

He laughed softly. "No, but it is a tempting idea."

She glared at him. "That's not funny!"

"One taste?" he entreated. "One sip? A few drops?"

"I don't know . . ."

"What is it that you crave above all else?" he asked.

"Chocolate," she replied quickly. "Rich, dark chocolate."

"How do you feel when you have not had it for several days?"

"I get cranky." She'd had a candy bar in the show that afternoon and stopped at a convenience store to buy several more on the way home.

He nodded. "For me, your blood is like rich, dark chocolate. No one else satisfies me as you do. No one ever will."

When he put it like that, how could she refuse?

"Just a little, you promise?"

With a nod, he drew her onto his lap. He teased her lips, each kiss growing longer and deeper until she was lost in a world of sensual pleasure. The room grew darker as night dropped her cloak across the land, increasing the sense of intimacy between them.

He kissed her again, his lips sliding down her neck. He licked the pulse in the hollow of her throat, then kissed his way to the soft, sensitive skin behind her earlobe.

She was breathless with wanting when she felt the sting of his fangs, followed by a rush of sensual pleasure. She moaned softly, one hand cupping the back of his head to hold him in place.

He made a strangled sound. His hands curled over her shoulders as the hunger reacted to her response.

The sound of her heartbeat filled his ears, growing faster.

With a low groan, he drew back and turned his head away lest she see the hellish glow in his eyes. Deep inside his mind, the hunger urged him to take her, both body and blood, and satisfy all his needs. It was tempting, so tempting. Her taste lingered on his tongue, his nostrils filled with the scent of her, warm and womanly and ripe for the taking . . .

She looked up at him, her expression slightly dazed, her lips swollen and slightly parted. "Antonio, don't stop."

He had no wish to do so, but he dared take no more.

Moving her off his lap onto the chair, he went downstairs to the kitchen and filled a glass with orange juice.

He stood there a moment, breathing heavily while he fought to restrain both his hunger and his desire.

When both were again under control, he returned to the parlor.

"Here." He handed her the glass. "Drink this."

She did as he asked, remembering that the Red Cross always gave her orange juice after she donated blood, too. She had a sudden urge to laugh.

"Vicki Cavendish," she murmured, "vampire blood bank."

"Victoria, you must never think of yourself like that!"

"Sorry," she said with a lopsided grin. "I may go back to the Red Cross. They always give me cookies with my orange juice."

Antonio stared down at her, not knowing whether to laugh or cry.

Instead, he lifted her into his arms and sat down. "Finish your juice, my sweet one, and the next time I ask you to indulge me, tell me no."

"Next time," she murmured, and fell asleep in his arms.

He caught the glass before it fell to the floor. For her own good, there could not be a next time.

Chapter 27

Dimitri Falco prowled the perimeter of the castle, his anger growing with every step. She was here. Her blood called to him as a Siren called a sailor to the sea. And he would have her. In spite of that thieving bastard, Battista, in spite of that accursed vampire hunter, he would have her!

But first he would have to dispose of Battista.

How best to do it? That was the question. It would have to be something slow and painful. Pondering the possibilities made him smile with anticipation.

They thought they were safe, the two of them locked inside the castle. It pleased him to let them think so, for now.

Chapter 28

For the second time in as many days, Vicki woke in bed with no recollection of how she'd gotten there. She lifted a hand to her neck. Little frissons of heat warmed her palm when she touched the place where Antonio's mouth had been. It puzzled her that something that sounded so repulsive could bring such pleasure.

Lying in bed, she wondered how things were going at the diner, how Duncan and Bobbie Sue were getting along, if Mrs. Heath had started making pumpkin pies and cakes for the fall social held at the church each year, if there had been any more murders. Though she had been in the castle only a couple of days, it seemed as though she had been cut off from the world.

A sudden rush of cool air had her sitting up and looking around to see if there was a window open. Seeing nothing amiss, she swung her legs over the side of the bed and went into the bathroom to take a shower. She lifted a hand to her neck, her fingertips exploring the stitches. No doubt she would have a nasty scar.

After dressing in a pair of jeans and a sweater, she went downstairs for a bowl of cereal. Sitting at the table in the kitchen, she again felt a sudden chill in the air. Was Antonio playing tricks on her? But no, he was resting in some secret hideaway.

Frowning, she washed her dishes and went upstairs. And the chill followed behind her.

At the top of the stairs, she whirled around, her gaze darting right and left as the chill grew stronger. She let out a shriek as what felt like a cold hand touched her cheek.

A peal of merry laughter filled the air and then, to Vicki's astonishment, the ethereal figure of a tall, slender woman in an old-fashioned peach-colored gown appeared before her.

"Good morrow," said the woman.

Vicki blinked and blinked again. It was Antonio's resident ghost, she was sure of it. "Lady Kathryn," she murmured.

"You've heard of me!" The ghost clapped her hands in delight. Vicki noticed that her feet didn't touch the ground.

"Yes."

"Welcome to my humble home," Lady Kathryn said. "It is so wonderful to have another woman in residence. Please, do come into the parlor and sit down so that we can have a nice, long chat."

With a nod, Vicki followed the ghost into the front parlor and sat on the sofa.

Lady Kathryn perched on the chair, her back perfectly straight, her hands folded in her lap. "What brings you to the castle? Did that handsome creature, Battista, invite you?"

"Yes," Vicki said.

"Is he not the most charming man you have ever

met?" Lady Kathryn asked, a dreamy look in her eye. "He is so tall and so handsome."

Vicki nodded, bemused that a ghost would still be interested in such things.

"Come now," Lady Kathryn said, "you must tell me all about yourself. Who are your people and where do you come from?"

"I'm from a little town called Pear Blossom Creek. My family is from Kentucky."

"Is that in the Colonies?"

"No," Vicki replied with a grin.

" 'Tis quite bold of you to come here without a chaperone," Lady Kathryn remarked. "Are you and Antonio betrothed?"

"No, we're just . . ." Vicki paused. Just what? Friends? No, they were certainly more than friends. Friends didn't drink your blood! Not just friends, not quite lovers.

Lady Kathryn nodded. "I see," she said, her dark eyes smiling. "I had a liaison like that before I married Lord Dunsmere. It was quite satisfying. Indeed, I might have married Thomas had his family not been so poor and my father not so insistent that I marry Dunsmere. Not that Dunsmere was a bad man, you understand, but . . ." She lifted one hand in an elegant gesture. "He was rather older than I was and quite boring. Both in bed and out."

Vicki burst out laughing, then quickly covered her mouth.

Lady Kathryn laughed, as well. "I know, 'tis quite wicked of me to speak so of the dead, but . . ." She shrugged. "I feel I can be honest with you. And speaking of being honest . . ." She leaned forward, her expression suddenly sober. "You do know that Antonio is, how shall I say this, different from other men?"

"Yes, I know."

Lady Kathryn reached forward and patted Vicki's hand. Her touch was cool but intangible. "I am so glad you are here. The poor man has been quite lonely these past few hundred years."

Vicki shook her head. For a few minutes, she had almost forgotten that she was talking to a ghost, or that there was anything unusual about Antonio. But talk of a few hundred years brought her swiftly back to reality. She laughed inwardly. Reality, indeed. Everything that had happened since the night Antonio first entered the diner seemed like some kind of fever-induced dream.

"Has he shown you the house?" Lady Kathryn asked. "It has been in my late husband's family for generations."

"Yes, Antonio gave me a tour. It's a fabulous place." Vicki wanted to ask if there were any other ghosts haunting the castle, but she was afraid she might offend Lady Kathryn, and surely if there were, Antonio would have mentioned it.

"Thank you." Lady Kathryn smiled, pleased, and then grew serious once more. "I saw a strange man wandering the grounds late last night. Are you expecting visitors?"

Vicki shook her head. "No."

"I do not recall seeing him in the area before. He had the most peculiar eyes."

Fear jolted down Vicki's spine, making it suddenly hard to breathe. "Peculiar?"

"Yes, they were yellow, almost like a cat's eyes. Very strange." Lady Kathryn frowned. "Is something amiss? You look quite pale."

Vicki took several deep breaths. She felt pale. And frightened. Only last night she had asked Antonio if

Falco could have followed them. Now she knew that he had.

She was fixing dinner when Antonio appeared in the kitchen. She felt a sudden rush of heat warm her cheeks when she turned and saw him standing there. His gaze met hers and her mind flooded with images of being in his arms, of his mouth on hers. And suddenly it wasn't the chicken baking in the oven she was hungry for, but the feel of his arms around her, his mouth crushing hers, his voice whispering in her ear.

"Ah, my sweet one," he murmured. "For me it is the same."

"Then why are you standing way over there?"

He lifted one brow, smiled a smug masculine smile when she pointed one finger at him and beckoned him to come to her.

He closed the distance between them in two strides and drew her into his arms. Lowering his head, he branded her lips with his.

She wrapped her arms around his neck and held on tight as he deepened the kiss, his mouth scorching hers, his tongue a flame that burned every other thought from her mind.

His hands moved over her back, slid down to cup her buttocks, drawing her more firmly against him, letting her feel the heat of his arousal.

She moaned, a raw animal-like cry of need, as she pressed herself against him, wanting to be closer, closer. Her hand delved under his shirt, her nails raking the cool skin of his back.

He breathed her name as he rained kisses on her face, her neck, the hollow of her throat. He might have taken her there, on the kitchen table, if a sudden rush of cool air hadn't filled the room, followed by a peal of merry laughter.

"Really, Antonio," Lady Kathryn said, "can you not wait until you have her under the sheets?"

Cheeks hot with embarrassment, Vicki looked over Antonio's shoulder to see the ghost standing in the kitchen doorway, her eyes sparkling with mischief.

Antonio muttered an oath as he loosened his hold on Victoria and turned to face the intruder. "I have not seen you for days and now you appear?" Though his voice was gruff, Vicki didn't miss the underlying note of affection. "Be gone with you, spirit!"

Lady Kathryn laughed again as she glided into the room. "Are you two so caught up in each other you would let the house burn down around you?" She gestured at the stove. "Yon dinner is aflame."

"Oh, no!" Vicki ran to the stove and opened the door. The chicken wasn't on fire, but it now resembled charcoal more than chicken. She pulled the roasting pan from the oven, uttering a wordless cry of pain as the hot metal burned her hand.

Antonio was beside her in an instant. Taking her injured hand in his, he bit his finger hard enough to draw several drops of blood, which he spread over the angry burn on her hand.

"What are you doing?" Vicki exclaimed, and then murmured, "Oh, my," as the throbbing pain receded to a dull ache and then disappeared.

She looked up at Antonio, shocked beyond words at what had just happened. She looked down at her hand, which was healing before her eyes, the raw, red patch fading until only healthy pink skin remained.

"That's . . . it's . . . " She stared up at him, stunned.

His gaze met hers, filled with the knowledge of what she was feeling, thinking. Gently, he lifted her hand and brushed a kiss across her palm. "I am sorry I ruined your dinner."

She nodded. Did all vampires possess this wondrous gift of healing? If so, he should be saving lives, healing children, fighting disease in every corner of the world.

"No," he said quietly. "It does not work like that."

"Why not? Why would it work for me and not for someone else?" She looked at his ravaged cheek. It looked better each time she saw him. In the places where it had healed completely, there was no sign of a scar. "Think of the lives you could save."

"No, my sweet one. It works for you because we have . . ." He hesitated to say the word.

"We have what?"

"We are bonded, heart to heart and soul to soul."

At his words, Vicki's heart began to pound. "We are? When did we do that?"

"When I first tasted you."

"But . . . Falco drank from me." Fear twisted in her gut, worse than anything she had ever known. "Does that mean that I'm bonded to him, too?"

"No."

"Why not?" She lifted a hand to the stitches in her neck. "He took far more blood than you did."

"Because I tasted you first," Antonio said. "But, more importantly, you gave yourself to me willingly."

"And if I hadn't?"

"There would be no bond between us."

"That's how he found us, isn't it? Because he took my blood?"

Antonio nodded. "But he has no power over you."

"Well, this has been most enlightening." Lady

Kathryn hopped down from the top of the refrigerator where she had been sitting and observing. "There's just nothing like young love, is there?"

"Young?" Antonio asked with a wry smile. He had not been young for over five hundred years.

"Perhaps I should have said new love," Lady Kathryn amended airily. "Behave yourself, Antonio. Do not bed the girl until you have wed the girl."

And with that bit of unexpected motherly advice, Lady Kathryn vanished from the room.

"She's quite a character," Vicki remarked.

"Indeed," Antonio said dryly.

Lady Kathryn's talk of marriage left Vicki feeling oddly nervous. As much as she cared for Antonio, as much as she loved him, if she was being honest, she knew they could never marry or have a normal life together. The thought saddened her. Not wanting to dwell on it, at least not while he was in the room, she pasted a bright smile on her face.

"Well," she said, going to the refrigerator and pulling out a large bowl, "it looks like I'll just be having salad for dinner."

"Victoria?"

"What?" She pulled a fork from the silverware drawer and placed it on the table, along with the salad bowl and a bottle of Italian dressing.

"Something has upset you."

"I'm not upset."

"You cannot lie to me, my sweet. What is it that troubles you? Was it Lady Kathryn's reference to marriage?"

"Why should that upset me?"

Moving up behind her, he placed his arms around her waist and drew her back against him. "I would like nothing more than to make you my wife."

"Would you?" she asked tremulously.

"You know I would." His breath warmed her cheek. "I can think of nothing that would give me more pleasure, but you would not be happy as the wife of a vampire."

When she started to protest, he turned her in his arms and silenced her with a kiss. "You would not mind at first, but in time you would come to resent the hours that I cannot be with you, just as you would come to resent the fact that the years had no claim on me."

She wanted to argue with him, to tell him that she loved him, that the differences between them didn't matter, but in her heart, she knew they did, knew that everything he said was true. In time, she would grow old and frail while he remained young and robust.

Breathing deeply, he buried his face in the wealth of her hair. "When Falco has been destroyed, I will take you home to your old life."

His words dropped like cold stones into the pit of her stomach.

"It is for the best, my sweetest one."

"Whose best?" she cried. "Not mine! If you loved me, you wouldn't want to leave me!"

"I do not want to leave you, but in time you would come to hate me, and that is something I cannot bear."

Whispering, "I don't want to live without you," she pulled his head down and kissed him, pouring all her love and all her desire into that one searing kiss.

Antonio moaned deep in his throat as hunger and desire warred within him. For a moment, he returned her kiss with all the passion and yearning in his heart and then, with a strangled cry of despair, he put Vicki away from him and fled the room before his hunger and his desire dragged them both down a path that could only lead to disaster.

Chapter 29

Fleeing the castle, Battista sought refuge in the dark of the night. Finally, after centuries, he had found a woman to love, a woman who accepted him for what he was. A woman who wanted him.

Lost in thought, he walked through the heavily wooded area that surrounded the outskirts of the land bordering the castle's perimeter. Maybe he was wrong to turn her away. There was no reason why they couldn't spend a few years together. He could give her pleasure for a little while, ease his own loneliness. And when she tired of living with him, she could return to her old life, find a husband, settle down, raise a family . . .

A low growl rumbled in his throat. Who was he kidding? Once he possessed her, body and soul, he would never let her go. He was a vampire, not a saint. What was his, he fought for and protected. What was his, he kept. He wasn't noble or kind. He couldn't love her for a year or two and then just let her go.

You could make her what you are.

The possibility had been in the back of his mind

since the first night he saw her, but this was the first time he had dared put it into words. With a savage cry, he thrust the thought from his mind. She would never agree to be as he was, and he loved her too much to force the Dark Gift upon her. And yet . . . It would do away with so many of the barriers now standing between them.

Then ask her, urged the same persuasive voice in the back of his mind. *All she can do is say no.*

Yes, perhaps that was the answer.

And if she says no, then you can force her to accept it.

No! Never that. But perhaps there was another way. If he gave her a little of his blood from time to time, it would prolong her life, keep her young.

But eventually she will grow old and die and you will be alone again.

But at least they could have a life together.

What kind of life would that be for either of you? Like must marry like for true happiness, true understanding.

Victoria, a vampire . . . He pictured it in his mind. She was lovely now. Touched with the Dark Gift, she would be even more beautiful, every feature enhanced and perfected. She would be a goddess . . . But would she still be Victoria?

Have you changed? the voice asked. *Are you not the same as you were before?*

And therein lay the answer. He had changed. He was a hunter now, a killer, and though he had not taken a human life in years, the urge to do so was always there. It had taken decades of self-denial and discipline to overcome the savage need to devour the blood and steal the life of his prey. Even when he knew he didn't have to kill to survive, the urge to do so remained strong within him. Almost, he had become like Falco, a creature without remorse, without compassion. A killing machine that took what it wanted with no regard for the hapless mortals it preyed upon, no thought for the pain and grief of loved ones left behind.

He remembered the night when he had made the decision to turn his back on killing. He had been a vampire for no more than seventy-five years at the time. He had been hunting the docks along the coast of Italy when he had come upon a woman and her child. Smiling in anticipation of an easy kill, he had pulled the woman into an alleyway. She had struggled in his arms, begging him to spare the life of her child. He had ignored her pleas as he bent her back over his arm and savaged her throat. There had been no tenderness in him, no effort spent to give her pleasure or ease her fears. Like a wild beast, he had no thought but to ease the pain of his hunger. The woman was limp in his arms, her heartbeat almost nonexistent, when he happened to look down into the face of the little girl still clinging to her mother's skirts. Brown eyes wide with fear had looked up at him.

"Mama! Mama!" Tears ran down the girl's dirty cheeks as she tugged on her mother's skirts. "Please, *signore*, do not hurt her."

The pain in the child's eyes, the note of tender pleading in her voice, had penetrated the hard shell he had erected around his heart. Until that moment, he had intended to dine on the child as well. Now, he saw himself through the eyes of that child. What he saw sickened him.

He looked at the woman in his arms. Her face was deathly pale, her breathing shallow. Biting his own wrist, he held it to the woman's mouth and commanded her to drink. A few drops brought the color back to her face. Her heart beat grew stronger, her breathing less erratic.

After lowering the woman to the ground, he had taken the child into his arms and looked deep into her eyes. "You will not remember this night," he said. "You will not remember me."

She nodded.

Reaching into his pocket, he withdrew what money he had and pressed it into the little girl's hand. "Take care of your mother, *ragazza*."

The child nodded again.

Antonio had looked at the woman and the little girl one last time, imprinting their memory and the memory of what he had almost done in his mind. And then he had fled the scene. He had never killed again save to preserve his own existence.

Lost in thought, for a moment he did not realize he was no longer alone. Thrusting the past from his mind, he lifted his head, his senses probing the night.

They were on him before he could defend himself. Heavy silver chains whistled through the air, wrapping around his neck, his chest, his arms and legs, until he was trussed like a turkey bound for market. The silver burned through his clothing, scorching his skin, rendering him helpless to resist.

Laughter rolled over him, filled with malevolent delight.

And then Dimitri Falco strutted into view, preening like a peacock. He circled Battista, rubbing his hands together like a miser about to count his gold.

"Well done," Falco said to the six hulking creatures standing in the shadows. "Well done. Perhaps, when I'm through with you, I will let you go."

Antonio stared at the zombies. They stood unmoving,

their faces expressionless, yet he detected a faint trace of comprehension in their eyes. Did they remember who they had been before Falco enthralled them? Were they aware of being under Falco's malevolent spell? Did some last bit of humanity cling desperately to the hope that he would free them from his spell? That he would grant them their freedom once again?

He fought the urge to give voice to his own pain as the silver burned deeper into his skin. It was the worst agony he had ever endured save for the one time he had not made it to his lair before sunrise. That had been a pain so intense, so excruciating, that he had never forgotten it. But this . . . He was panting now, unable to draw a deep breath. This was almost as bad. In time, it would be equally lethal.

"Bring him."

With one accord, the six zombies lifted Antonio and followed Falco into the deep woods.

Vicki wandered through the house, her emotions in turmoil. At first she was angry with him. How dare he arouse her again and then abandon her! If he didn't want her, why did he hold her and kiss her until she wanted him, needed him, more than breath itself, and then just walk away? It was cruel and thoughtless. And besides that, he did want her. She might not have had a lot of experience with men, but she knew desire when she saw it in a man's eyes, not to mention the obvious physical signs.

As the hours passed, anger turned to worry. Where was he? Surely he intended to return? Hadn't he sworn to protect her, no matter what? Was he outside, prowling around the perimeter of the house to make sure Falco wasn't there?

Standing by the front window, she peered out into the night, but it was too dark to see anything. Heavy clouds covered the moon and the stars.

"Antonio, are you out there?"

"He is not on the grounds."

Vicki glanced over her shoulder at the sound of Lady Kathryn's voice. "Do you know where he is?"

The ghost closed her eyes, her brow furrowed, and then she shook her head. "I have no sense of him being nearby."

"Maybe I should go look for him," Vicki said dubiously.

"No! There is evil afoot tonight."

Vicki shivered. In her mind, evil and Dimitri Falco would always be linked together. "Do you know where Antonio takes his rest?"

"Of course."

"And he's not there? You're sure?"

"Aye, quite sure. He never retires before dawn, you know. Poor man. I suppose if one can't move about during the day, then one doesn't waste a moment of the time one has." The ghost flitted around the room, zooming up to the ceiling, twirling around and around in midair. "Sleep," she said. "He curses it while I cannot find it."

"You can't sleep?"

"No. I have no need for it, you know, and yet I miss it dreadfully." She lighted on the top of the cabinet that held the stereo system. "I find it rather odd to miss something I no longer need. 'Tis like . . . " She frowned a moment. "Like missing one of last year's gowns," she decided. "Do you not find that strange?"

"I guess so," Vicki said absently. She looked out the window again. Where was he?

"Shall I go and look for him?" Lady Kathryn asked. "Would that ease your mind?"

"Can you leave the castle?"

"Of course, though I can't leave the grounds." The ghost smiled wanly. " 'Tis the fault of that horrid Molly MacTavish that I must stay here," she said, her eyes flashing.

"Who's Molly MacTavish?"

"She was a scullery maid. A more troublesome wench never lived. She hated it here, and she hated me because I refused to let her return to Scotland. She pushed me down the stairs, you know? And as I lay there, dying, she cursed me, saying I should never know peace in the next life until I had learned to be more charitable. Imagine that! Me, more charitable! If it had not been for me, she and her brat would have been begging on the streets. Ah, well, what's done is done. Wait now, while I go have a look and see if I can find that handsome lout."

It seemed like hours passed before Lady Kathryn returned.

"Did you find him?" Vicki asked anxiously.

"Aye, that I did."

"Is he all right?"

"Nay, I fear his life is in grave danger."

"Where is he? I've got to go to him!"

"Nay, you must not! He is guarded by six huge men who do the bidding of another. Any of them could break you in half."

"Where have they taken him?"

"There is an old lambing shed deep in the heart of the woods that lie west of the castle grounds. 'Tis there he's being held."

"Is he all right? Did he see you?"

Lady Kathryn shook her head, her expression woeful. "They have chained him to the floor with chains as thick as a man's wrist. The six beasts sit in a circle around him, like wolves around a carcass. From time to time they poke him with silver knives to make him bleed."

Vicki moaned softly as she imagined his agony. Wrapping her arms around her waist, she paced the floor. No ordinary men could have laid hold on Antonio. She remembered the creatures that had been enslaved by Falco. Had he created more of them? Oh, why wouldn't he leave them alone? She had done nothing to him!

"Tomorrow," she said, thinking aloud. "Falco will have to go to his lair, wherever that might be." She nodded. The zombies would also be at their weakest in daylight.

"You cannot mean to go after him alone?" Lady Kathryn exclaimed. "'Tis madness!"

The ghost was right, of course. She needed help. She needed Tom Duncan.

Chapter 30

Battista stared blankly at the ceiling of the shed, his hands knotted into tight fists, his breathing shallow and rapid, every muscle in his body taut with pain. It rolled over him and through him in never-ending waves, each more excruciating than the last. His skin was badly blistered where the silver touched his flesh. Each link burned into him, scorching him like the sun he had avoided for the last six hundred years.

He was only vaguely aware of the six zombies that surrounded him, relentlessly poking at him with slender daggers made of silver. The scent of his blood hung heavy in the air.

He tried to concentrate, tried to gather his waning strength, but the silver drained him of energy, and the pain . . . It was impossible to ignore.

He had seen Lady Kathryn hovering overhead earlier in the evening. He had tried to tell her to go and warn Victoria that Falco was nearby, but the heavy chain around his throat prevented him from speaking.

With what little strength he had left, he cursed himself for his carelessness. He had promised to protect Victoria, and now she was at the castle, defenseless and alone. Would Falco send his creatures after her? If he did, would the castle's threshold be strong enough to repel them?

He had to get out of here, had to get back to Victoria before it was too late, but he was too weak too move, too weak to do anything but lie there while the silver burned his flesh and Falco's creatures slowly drained him of blood.

Closing his eyes, he prayed for dawn and blessed oblivion.

Chapter 31

Vicki didn't get much sleep that night. She drank gallons of coffee, paced back and forth from one end of the castle to the other while her mind filled with vivid images of Antonio being tortured, bleeding. Lady Kathryn said he was bound with silver chains. She knew what that meant from the books she had read. Falco had had his creatures bind her with silver chains because he'd known it would keep Antonio from freeing her. She wanted to scream at Falco, demand that he leave them alone.

She was on the road to town as soon as dawn's first light brightened the sky. She stopped at the first business she came to and demanded to use the phone. She quickly punched in Bobbie Sue's number, only then remembering that Bobbie Sue and Duncan had gone to visit Bobbie Sue's parents.

On the verge of tears, she hung up the receiver. She had no one else to call, no where else to go for help.

So, she thought, driving home, she would have to rescue Antonio herself.

She went into the parlor and sat down on the sofa. Yawning, she glanced at the clock. It was only a little after eight. She would just close her eyes for a few minutes . . .

She was walking through the woods, the same dark wood she had seen in her dreams once before. She moaned softly, wanting to wake up, but she couldn't escape the dream. She frowned when she realized one thing had changed. The moon was no longer shining. Now the sun ruled the sky. But it was the same voice warning her not to enter the woods, a voiced she now recognized as Antonio's. Though she yearned to turn and flee, she was again compelled to continue on, and so she moved deeper and deeper into the forest. Deeper and deeper into the darkness that even the sun could not penetrate, until she saw the same small wooden cottage. As it had before, the door opened of its own volition. Once again, she hesitated at the threshold, knowing that if she crossed it, her life would be forever changed. And then she saw Antonio . . .

Vicki let out a scream when she saw Falco standing behind Antonio. There was no fireplace now, no flickering red and orange shadows on the walls. Instead, there was only blood. Antonio's blood, splattered on the floor and the walls. He cradled the same golden goblet between his hands. He held it out for her to see, and this time she looked inside. Bright red liquid swirled inside the cup. Horror rose from deep inside her. It wasn't his blood. It was hers. Eyes filled with anguish, he lifted the cup to his lips while Dimitri Falco's insane laughter rang out in the night.

Vicki woke with a scream on her lips. A glance at the clock showed it was almost noon.

Rising, she went downstairs. A cup of coffee and a couple of protein bars served as breakfast and lunch.

She glanced at the clock again. There were only five hours or so until dusk, and she had a lot to do before then.

Aware that the clock was ticking, Vicki gathered up several heavy blankets, grabbed her handbag and the keys to the Lexus, and headed for town again. Her first stop was a Catholic church. Hurrying inside, she filled an empty Coke bottle with holy water, murmured a quick prayer for forgiveness, and ran out of the church.

Her second stop was at a discount store, where she bought several yards of heavy black plastic sheeting, which she put in the trunk along with the blankets.

Her third stop was Naughton's Gun Shop. To her dismay, she learned that she couldn't just buy a gun and walk away. There were forms and papers to fill out, a waiting period. She begged and pleaded, but the man behind the counter was adamant.

Discouraged, Vicki murmured her thanks and walked toward the exit. She had to have a gun. There was no way she could overcome Falco's brutes with her bare hands.

"Hey, lady."

She glanced over her shoulder. "Are you talking to me?"

A young man standing beside a glass case displaying knives nodded. "I couldn't help overhearing your conversation. Sounds like you're in trouble."

"You have no idea."

The man lowered his voice. "I've got a Glock out in my truck that I'd be willing to sell ya."

"A Glock?"

"A gun. You don't know much about guns, do you?"

"Not a thing. Is it a good one?"

"Oh, yeah. It's reliable, durable, lightweight, and easy to use. I think you'll like it."

"How much do you want for it?"

He glanced over his shoulder to where the proprietor stood watching them. "Let's go outside."

She hesitated only a moment, wondering if she dared trust him. He was tall and lanky, with long blond hair and a scraggly beard. He wore a cut-off T-shirt and baggy jeans. His arms were covered with tattoos. But this was no time to be picky. He had a gun. She needed a gun.

Taking a deep breath, she followed him outside and around the corner to where his truck was parked. Unlocking the passenger side door, he opened the glove box and pulled out a rather nasty-looking weapon.

"How much?" she asked.

"I'll let you have it for three-fifty." He cocked his head to one side. "You don't know how to use it, do you?"

"No."

"So, why do you want a gun?"

"I'm not selling my life story, I just want to buy a gun. Do you want to sell that or don't you?"

He chuckled. "All right, lady, have it your way."

"Will you take a check?"

"Ordinarily I wouldn't, but I think I can trust you."

She pulled her checkbook out of her handbag and quickly filled in the amount. "Who should I make it out to?"

"Randy."

"Just Randy?"

He nodded. "If you want, I can show you how to fire it." He handed her the weapon, then tucked her check into his pants pocket.

"That would be great."

"There's a vacant lot a couple of blocks from here. The old man from Naughton's lets his customers go there to try out his guns. Why don't you follow me over and I'll give you a couple of quick lessons?"

Again she hesitated. And then she nodded. She had never fired a gun in her life. A little instruction might keep her from shooting herself in the foot. "All right."

She was apprehensive about being alone with a strange man in a vacant lot, but as it turned out, they weren't alone. Four boys were tossing a football back and forth in the center of the lot when they arrived.

The boys stopped what they were doing when they saw her get out of the car with a gun in her hand.

"Looks like you're going to have an audience," Randy said, coming up behind her.

She was afraid he was right. The teenagers had gathered into a tight knot and now they stood a short distance away, watching her, a bunch of long-haired boys in faded jeans, T-shirts, and black leather jackets.

"Ignore them," Randy said. During the next forty minutes, he showed her how to hold the pistol, how to aim, how to fire. "Okay," he said, pointing at a battered target several yards away, "squeeze off a few."

Holding the pistol the way Randy had taught her, she squeezed the trigger. She had expected the noise to be much louder, but it was nothing like in the movies. In reality, gunfire sounded more like a loud pop or a car backfiring than a big explosive bang.

"All right," Randy muttered. "This time try it with your eyes open."

He worked with her until she managed to hit the target three times out of seven. "Keep practicing," he said, patting her on the shoulder. "I think you're getting the hang of it."

"Thanks for your help."

"Remember, don't aim for the head," he said matter-of-factly. "It's a small target. Aim for the biggest part of whatever you're after. You've got a better chance of hitting something. And don't try any of that shoot-to-wound crap, either. If you need a gun to defend yourself, then whoever's after you is probably out for blood."

One of the boys left the others and swaggered toward her. He had shaggy blond hair and brown eyes. A scar zigzagged down his left cheek to the edge of his jaw.

"You going to war, lady?" he asked.

Vicki started to say, no, of course not, but then she nodded. "Yes," she said. "I am."

"All by yourself?"

Vicki nodded.

He jerked a thumb over his shoulder, indicating his friends. "You need some backup?"

She stared at him. "Are you kidding? I could use an army."

He sauntered toward her. "So, what happened?" He waved his friends over. "You catch your boyfriend in the sack with another broad?"

"I wish it were that easy. Listen, thanks for your offer, but I can't accept it. I can't be responsible for—"

He laughed. "Lady, no one's been responsible for me since I was fourteen."

"I believe you." She watched the other three boys saunter toward her. "But what about your friends?"

"No sweat. We can all take care of ourselves."

He introduced his companions as the Torch, Link, and the Hammer. "And I'm Twist."

Interesting names, she mused. "Pleased to meet you . . . gentlemen."

The Torch was tall and slender, with dark red hair and blue eyes. She wondered if he'd gotten his nickname from the color of his hair, but somehow, she doubted it. Link could only be described as average—

average height, average weight, light brown hair and eyes. The Hammer was short and a little overweight. He had black hair and dark brown eyes and looked like he could take on the world all by himself.

Vicki had thought they were kids in their early teens; now she could see that they were all around eighteen or nineteen years old. Seeing them up close, she didn't doubt for a minute that they could take care of themselves, or that they knew the score. They were the kind of guys mothers warned their daughters about.

"So, when's the rumble?" the Hammer asked.

Vicki glanced at her watch. "Right now."

"Then what are we waiting for?" Link asked. "Let's go!"

Her gang scrambled into a late-model Ford pickup, two in the front, two in the back, and then waited for Vicki to lead the way.

Her father was right, she thought as she pulled onto the road. The Lord did provide.

She felt a surge of gratitude for her escort when she pulled up in front of the ramshackle shed in the woods. Even in broad daylight, it was dark in this part of the forest. The shed itself seemed ominous somehow. There were no windows, only a narrow door. No sound came from within.

Was it possible that Falco's goons weren't there? Could she be that lucky?

Pulling her crucifix out from under her sweater, she held it in her hand and murmured a hurried prayer and then got out of the car.

Clutching the pistol in one hand and the bottle of holy water in the other, she walked toward the shed. A glance over her shoulder showed her that Twist and his gang were right behind her. She wasn't surprised to see that all four of them carried guns. The Hammer carried a knife in his free hand that looked to be a good twelve inches long. Link had a thick chain coiled around one fist.

If things hadn't been so serious, she would have laughed at the picture the five of them must have made marching across the clearing toward the lambing shed.

When they reached the door, the boys spread out around her, two on each side.

"I'll go in first," Twist said.

Vicki nodded.

Twist looked at his gang. Each of them nodded at him in turn.

"Let's do it," he said, and kicked in the door.

The other three boys swarmed in after him. Vicki brought up the rear.

Twist stood unmoving a few feet inside the door. Shifting to one side, Vicki stared at the scene in front of her. Antonio was spread-eagled on the warped wooden floor, held in place by thick silver chains. Someone had removed his shirt, his shoes and socks, and rolled up the cuffs on his trousers. Silver manacles that must have been at least two inches wide circled his wrists, ankles, and neck. Even in the dim light, she could see the ugly red streaks and blisters that rose on his skin wherever the silver touched him. His eyes were closed. As near as she could tell, he wasn't breathing, but maybe that was natural when he was . . . resting.

He looked . . . dead.

Six zombies surrounded him. They looked up, their expressions blank. All six looked like they had been kidnapped from a pro football team.

"What the hell?" Link muttered.

Twist looked at Vicki. "You weren't kidding about needing an army. What's our next move?"

"I want the man chained to the floor. To get him, we have to go through the others."

The Hammer swore a crude oath. "I was afraid you'd say that."

"Shouldn't be too hard," Link said. "They look like they're glued to the floor." He took a step forward. As soon as he was within a foot of the nearest zombie, the creature began to move toward him, its arms extended.

Link fired two shots in quick succession and the zombie sank to the floor without a sound.

Vicki stared in horror as the other five surged to their feet and lumbered toward them.

"This one's mine!" Torch hollered. He fired twice and the second zombie hit the floor with a thud. "Like shooting fish in a barrel!" he crowed.

Vicki turned away, her hands pressed over her ears as Twist and his gang took out the other zombies. Her gaze settled on Antonio. Was he still alive? A distant part of her mind chuckled at her choice of words. Vampires weren't alive. They were Undead. She wondered if Falco had destroyed him, if he was now truly dead.

The vampire twitched as the coppery scent of blood filled the air.

She hurried to his side when all the zombies had been taken care of. "Antonio? Antonio, can you hear me?"

He didn't move, didn't speak.

"We have to get him out of here," she said. "Hurry!"

"Who is this guy?" Twist asked.

"There's no time for that now." Bile rose in her throat when she saw the burns on Antonio's body. She frowned as she realized the chains were bolted to the floor.

Twist jerked his head toward the door and Link ran outside.

"I think we're too late," the Hammer remarked. "He looks dead."

Link reappeared a couple of minutes later and after a good deal of swearing, he managed to cut the manacles at Antonio's hands and feet and neck.

"Let's go," Vicki said. "Hurry!"

The Hammer hoisted Antonio onto one shoulder and headed for the door.

"Wait a minute!" Vicki cried.

"Something wrong?" Twist asked.

"Yes. Just stay here a minute. I'll be right back."

Hurrying out to the Lexus, she opened the trunk and pulled out the plastic sheeting. She ran back to the shed, aware that the sun was already setting. They had to get out of here before Falco returned.

Inside once more, she wrapped the black plastic around Antonio from head to foot. When she was finished, he looked like a mummy.

"What the hell?" Link asked. "Why'd you do that?"

"I don't have time to explain. A very bad man will be here soon, and believe me, you don't want to be anywhere around when he gets here."

"Worse than these guys?" the Torch asked, looking at the zombies that littered the floor.

"Much worse," she said. "He made them."

She had a feeling there wasn't much that scared Twist and his gang, but that did it.

The Hammer again hoisted Antonio onto his shoulder and headed for the door.

Following him, Vicki murmured a silent prayer of thanks for Twist and his gang. She had been so worried about Antonio, so anxious to find him, she hadn't stopped to wonder how she would get him out of the shed. On her own, she would never have been able to lift him, let alone carry him out of there.

"Where do you want him?" the Hammer asked.

"Here, in the trunk."

Twist and his gang exchanged looks that clearly wondered how they'd gotten mixed up with a woman who was insane.

"You want us to follow you?" Twist asked.

"No, that won't be necessary." She covered Antonio with the blankets and closed the trunk. "I don't know how I can ever thank you."

Twist shrugged. "We didn't have anything better to do today. So long, lady."

"Good-bye."

Aware that the sun was setting way too fast, she got into the Lexus, locked the door, and drove as though all the devils in hell were at her heels. The sun had set by the time she reached the road to the castle.

Once inside the garage, with the door closed, she switched off the ignition, then leaned forward and rested her forehead on the steering wheel.

She had him safely home. But had he survived the trip? After taking several deep breaths, she got out of the car, took several more deep breaths, and opened the trunk.

Chapter 32

"Antonio?" She tossed the blankets out of the trunk and removed the plastic sheeting that covered him. "Antonio!"

He lay as still as death. And he looked pale, so pale. The burns on his neck, wrists, and ankles were a dull ugly red. His cheeks looked hollow, the skin drawn tight across his cheekbones. His whole body was covered with burns that looked like tiny cuts. What had Falco done to him?

Biting down on her lower lip, she leaned forward and touched his shoulder. "Antonio?"

With a savage growl, his hand closed around her wrist, his fingers squeezing until she thought the bones might break.

His eyes opened, glowing red in the overhead light of the garage. He stared at her and there was no recognition in his gaze, only a burning hunger.

Fear seized her. Fighting down the urge to pull away, she said, quietly. "Antonio, it's me. Victoria. I've brought you home."

She looked down at his hand. His thumb stroked the inside of her wrist, back and forth, back and forth. He licked his lips and she caught a glimpse of his fangs, a telltale sign that he was hurting and weak from the blood he had lost.

She fought down a rising sense of panic. Did he know who she was? In his current state, would it make any difference?

"Antonio, listen to me. You're safe now. You're home. Falco can't hurt you anymore." His hand tightened on her wrist at the mention of Falco's name, his nails digging into her flesh. "Antonio, you're hurting me."

His eyes narrowed as his gaze focused on her face. "Victoria?" His voice was low and edged with pain.

"Yes. Yes, it's me."

He let go of her arm and his hand fell to his side. "Sorry . . . if I hurt you."

"We need to get inside, quickly."

He nodded and she helped him out of the trunk, her stomach churning with revulsion when she got a good look at him. The words *death warmed over* flitted through the back of her mind.

He moved as if every step caused him pain. She recalled that he had told her once that vampires felt things more intensely.

Combating a sense of urgency, she helped him up the stairs, constantly glancing over her shoulder for fear she would see Falco or more of his zombies advancing toward them. It was obvious that Dimitri Falco had no conscience, no sense of pity or compassion for those he so callously enslaved.

She breathed a sigh of relief when they were safely inside, the heavy front door closed and locked behind them.

She guided Antonio to the front parlor and then to the sofa. He sat down heavily. Resting his head against the back of the sofa, he closed his eyes.

She stood looking down at him, wondering what she should do, wondering how he could survive when he looked so ghastly pale. She moved toward him, needing to touch him.

"Go away from me, Victoria."

"No. You need help. What can I do?"

"Go away." He spoke between gritted teeth. "You cannot give me what I need."

"Why not? I've done it before?"

"I need more than a mere taste."

She swallowed hard.

"Go, my sweet, you are far too tempting and too near and I am too weak to long resist."

"You can't mean to go out," she said. "Not tonight."

"I must." A muscle worked in his jaw; she saw his hands clench into tight fists.

He was hurting beyond anything she could imagine. She backed slowly toward the staircase, wondering how safe she would be in her room if he changed his mind. It was his house, after all. There was no protection for her here, no threshold to keep him out.

Her heel hit the bottom step and she stopped. She couldn't let him go hunting tonight. Falco could be out there, waiting, knowing that Antonio would need blood to ease the pain, to heal his wounds. She didn't know how Falco had managed to catch Antonio off guard before, but she knew he would be an easy mark now.

She took a deep breath. She would be dead now if not for Antonio. He had warned her against Battista, rescued her from a fate worse than death. She could not abandon him now, when he needed her more than ever.

Squaring her shoulders, she went back into the living room and sat down on the sofa beside him.

His nostrils flared. He opened his eyes. Eyes that glowed with the lust for blood. "Go." The word sounded as if it had been torn from his throat. "Go. Now."

"Take what you need, Antonio. But please don't hurt me."

He shook his head. "I cannot promise that. Not now. Please, Victoria, sweeting, go while you can."

"I'm not leaving you."

His hands clenched at his sides. "This is madness. You do not know what you are saying."

She thought so, too, but she couldn't leave him, couldn't bear to see him suffering.

Battista closed his eyes again. He didn't trust himself to drink from her, not now, when his thirst was nearly out of control, when he was weak with pain. The burns from the silver throbbed relentlessly. They would not heal overnight. Without blood, they would not heal at all. Though it had been years since he had killed anyone, he knew that, should he hunt tonight, the poor unsuspecting mortal who crossed his path would not live to see the dawn of another day. When he drank tonight, he would take it all.

He opened his eyes, noting for the first time the silver crucifix on a chain around Victoria's throat. Perhaps there was a way to take what he needed without taking a life.

"Victoria, you cannot give me all I need."

"Why not?"

"Because I would have to take it all."

She stared at him, her eyes widening as his meaning sank in.

"But I want to take a little, enough to dull the pain."

"But you said that wouldn't be enough."

"If I can take some from you, I can take the rest from someone else." He would probably need to drink from at least two, perhaps three, but if he was in control, no one would die. "Do you understand?"

She nodded, her eyes shining with trust. He only hoped he could live up to it, that he would not spend the rest of his existence regretting his weakness.

"Hold on to your crucifix." He slipped his arm around her shoulders. "If you begin to feel light-headed, press it against my face."

"But . . ."

"It will make me stop."

"All right." She clutched the cross tightly in her hand.

"You are a very brave woman," he murmured as he lowered his head. "I can think of no other who would bare her throat to me at a time like this, when there is no one here to help you."

Vicki closed her eyes. She didn't feel very brave. Her hand tightened around the crucifix as she felt his breath on her neck, the sharp sting of his fangs, the mind-blowing pleasure as he drank from her. It always astonished her, the pure delight, the sense of blissful contentment . . .

Pleasure turned to fear as she felt suddenly dizzy. "Antonio? Antonio, stop!"

For a moment, she was afraid he was beyond hearing, beyond stopping. She lifted her hand, the cross bared on her palm. "Antonio, stop, please!" He was already hurting. She didn't want to cause him more pain.

With a low groan, he drew away.

For a moment, she saw him as he truly was, his eyes red, his fangs lowered. And then he was her Antonio again, his eyes dark with concern. "Victoria?"

"I'm all right. Are you?"

"Better now." Drawing her closer, he brushed a kiss across her lips. "I must go out for a while." He stroked her cheek, his eyes filled with such tenderness it made her heart ache. "Do not wait up for me," he said, and he was gone.

"Yeah, right," she muttered. "Like I'm gonna get any sleep until you get home." She sat there a moment, thinking that she must be getting used to being bitten, since she hadn't passed out this time. She was, however, famished.

But food could wait. She went through the house, turning on all the lights and making sure all the doors and windows were locked. She wished she had some of Mrs. Heath's garlic to spread around. Suddenly, the old lady's quirks all made sense. Well, if Mrs. Heath could outsmart Falco and live to be ninety, so could she!

In the kitchen, she fixed a huge ham and cheese sandwich and poured a big glass of milk. She added an apple, a banana, and a few cookies to the plate and carried everything upstairs to the back parlor. Sitting in Antonio's chair, she turned on the TV and flipped through the channels, settling on an old comedy starring Rock Hudson and Doris Day. No dark dramas tonight! No sci-fi movies about aliens. Tonight she needed laughter.

But she couldn't concentrate on the movie. Where was Antonio? Where had he gone to look for prey? How long did it take him to feed? Would he come back to the castle tonight? Did he rest here during the day? And most troubling of all, where was Falco? They had escaped him this time, but what about next time? Would they ever be free of him? Did he take his rest in that old shed? If so, she needed Tom Duncan's help. She would call Bobbie Sue tomorrow.

The end credits were running on the TV when Antonio returned. One minute she was alone in the room and the next he was there, beside her.

Sometime between the time he'd left the castle and his return, he had changed into a pair of black jeans and a black T-shirt. The burns at his throat, wrists, and ankles were still visible, still painful looking, though the burn on his cheek was nearly gone.

"Are you feeling better?" she asked.

He nodded.

She gestured at the burn mark on his neck. "Does it still hurt?"

"Like the very devil."

"Well, that's not surprising, since the devil did it."

Antonio looked at her, sadness reflected in his eyes. "We are the same, he and I."

"No!"

"We are both vampires, sweeting. Both killers who prey on others to survive."

"No! I refuse to accept that. You are nothing like him! Nothing, do you hear me?"

"Perhaps not now, but—"

"No buts. People make mistakes, but they can change. You've changed. You're not like him anymore and I won't have you saying you are! Do you hear me, Antonio Battista?"

He laughed softly. "What a warrior you would have made. You would not have stayed behind while your man went out to fight. No, you would have taken up a sword and ridden beside him."

"I don't know how to ride."

He laughed again. "Ah, Victoria, what will I do when you are gone?"

"I'm not going anywhere," she said, but in the back

of her mind she heard his voice telling her that, when it was safe, he would leave her so she could return to her old life. Well, he could think that for now if it made him feel better, but he was stuck with her whether he liked it or not. Life with Antonio. He made her feel wonderful, beautiful, and more desirable than any other woman on the planet . . . life with a vampire . . . What would it be like to never see him during the day, to eat all her meals alone, to sleep alone, to age while he did not? And what about children?

She looked at him, mute, and knew by his expression that he had divined her thoughts. "I'm sorry . . ."

"There is nothing to be sorry about, my sweet. You only want what every woman wants. I wish I could give you everything you want, everything you need, but I cannot."

She stared at him. How could he talk about it so lightly? He had come into her life like a whirlwind, made her love him, made her need him. Did it mean nothing to him? He was like no one else she had ever known. No man alive could compare to him.

His expression told her he knew what she was thinking.

"I can't believe you really mean to leave me when this is over."

"It is for—"

"Don't you dare tell me that it's for the best!" She wiped the tears from her eyes. "I thought you loved me. You said you loved me."

"Do not doubt it. If I did not love you, I would have seduced you long ago, Victoria Cavendish. I would have taken your love and your blood and left you with nothing."

Tears dampened her cheeks. She made no move to wipe them away, only stood there looking up at him, her expression filled with anguish. She was hurting, and it was his fault.

"Victoria . . ."

"Kiss me."

He yearned to take her in his arms, to feel her hands on his flesh, her body writhing in ecstasy beneath his. Had he thought he could stop with one kiss, he would gladly have obliged, but he was hurting and weak. Taking blood had eased the pain somewhat, but in his weakened state, he did not trust himself to make love to her without taking more of her blood as well. And if he tasted her again, he did not trust himself to stop.

"I cannot, sweeting. I must go."

"But it's still early."

"Yes, but I need to rest." Rising, he moved away from her, away from the temptation of warm flesh and pouting lips. "It will help me heal faster."

"You're not just saying that?"

"I would not lie to you."

"Good night, Antonio."

"If you do not see me tomorrow night, do not worry."

"Why won't I see you? Where are you going?"

"I may sleep through the night."

"Oh."

He murmured, *"Buono notte,* my sweet." And then, as though to remind her of what he was, he vanished from her sight.

"He loves you very much."

Vicki looked up to see Lady Kathryn sitting on the edge of the mantel, one leg crossed over the other. "I know."

"Like must marry like," Lady Kathryn said wistfully. "A lady cannot marry a commoner. A vampire cannot marry a mortal." She smiled faintly. "Or even a ghost, more's the pity. He is such a delectable creature."

"I guess you're right," Vicki said thoughtfully. "Like must marry like for there to be true togetherness, true happiness."

Chapter 33

Vicki slept late the next day. After rising, she showered and ate breakfast. She made her bed. She read a book. She watched a movie. She ate lunch. She took a nap. And still it seemed like an eternity until the sun went down.

She waited all that night for Antonio to appear. At midnight, she admitted that he wasn't coming. She couldn't blame him, not really. If sleep made him feel better and heal faster, then sleep was what he needed. But she missed him terribly just the same.

She rose early the following morning, dressed quickly, and drove to the nearest phone booth to call Bobbie Sue.

Bobbie Sue answered on the fifth ring. "Girl," she said, yawning, "do you know what time it is?"

"Eight-fifteen. Is Duncan there?"

"Eight-fifteen!" Bobbie Sue exclaimed. "I'm late for school! Talk to you later, Vicki. Duncan, telephone."

A moment later, Tom's voice came over the receiver. "Hi, Vicki. Is something wrong?"

"Yes. Falco is here."

Tom grunted. "I guess that explains why things have been so quiet here. Are you all right?"

"Yes, for now." She quickly explained everything that had happened since she had left Pear Blossom Creek. "We need to find him, and I need your help for that."

"I'll be there as soon as I can. Look for me sometime tomorrow afternoon."

"Thank you."

"Don't worry. Just stay inside." He paused. "Does Battista sleep in the house?"

"I don't know. Why?"

"Just curious."

"We're only hunting Falco," Vicki reminded him.

"Sure, sure."

"If you have any intention of hunting Antonio, then stay there."

"Listen, Vicki—"

"No, you listen. I'm in love with Antonio. If you're thinking of going after him, then I'll look for Falco on my own."

Tom cursed.

"I want your word, Tom."

"All right, you've got it. I won't hunt Battista."

"You swear?"

"I swear."

As soon as she hung up the receiver, she was beset by doubts, doubts that only grew stronger on the ride back home. What would Antonio say when he found out that not only had she called Tom for help, but she had given Battista's address to a vampire hunter?

Lady Kathryn swooped into the back parlor shortly after Vicki arrived home. "Ah, there you are," she said. "I was afraid you had left us."

"No." Vicki sat down, her fingers drumming on the arm of the chair.

"You seem worried," Lady Kathryn remarked. "Is something amiss?"

"I called on a friend of mine, Tom Duncan, for help. He'll be here sometime tomorrow."

"You mean, here, at the castle? Oh, my dear, what have you done?"

"We need help," Vicki exclaimed. "I can't find Falco on my own, and Antonio's in no condition to hunt for him. You know that."

"Are you sure you can trust this man, Tom?"

"I hope so. You've got to tell me, does Antonio take his rest here in the castle?"

Lady Kathryn floated around the room, looking much like one of the ghosts in Disneyland's Haunted Mansion as she flitted about.

After a moment, she settled on her usual perch on the stereo cabinet. "I'm afraid that is something you will have to ask Antonio."

Vicki blew out a sigh. She wasn't looking forward to telling Antonio what she had done.

Whenever she was troubled, Vicki cleaned house. That was what she did now. She mopped and dusted. She washed the windows. Since there was no washer or dryer in the castle, she filled the kitchen sink with soapy water and washed her underwear, then hung it over the kitchen chairs to dry.

She skipped lunch and indulged in a huge ice cream sundae, and then she took a nap.

It was dusk when she woke, and Antonio was sitting on the edge of the bed, watching her. For once, he wasn't wearing black. Instead, he wore a pair of faded gray sweatpants and a gray short-sleeved T-shirt that looked butter soft.

"Did you run out of black clothes?" she asked, though she suspected his change of clothing had more to do with comfort than anything else.

"Even I get tired of black occasionally," he replied with a wry grin.

She was glad to see that he looked a little better tonight. The burn across his throat didn't seem quite so red. His skin didn't look quite so pale.

"You have been busy," he remarked.

"Busy?" Dread coiled in the pit of her stomach. Had Lady Kathryn told him about her phone call to Duncan?

"The castle fairly sparkles. I doubt it has ever been quite so clean."

"Oh, that." She sat up, not meeting his gaze. "How are you feeling tonight?"

"Better." He studied her face, listened to the beat of her heart. "Something troubles you."

"Does the name Falco ring a bell? He troubles me."

"You may as well tell me what is bothering you."

"Or what? You'll read my mind?"

"If I must."

"Oh, all right, I called Tom Duncan today."

Antonio's eyes narrowed ominously. "Indeed?"

"I thought we needed help, someone who can hunt Falco during the day."

"Go on."

She slid her legs over the edge of the bed and gained her feet, putting some distance between them. "I asked him to come here."

"Here?" Antonio rose and stalked toward her. "What do you mean, *here*?"

She looked up at him. Rarely had he looked as menacing as he did now, his throat scarred, his eyes burning with barely suppressed anger. He reminded her of a panther about to pounce. And she was his prey.

"Tell me you did not invite him to my home," he said, his voice tight.

She took a step backward. "I . . . I'm sorry. I didn't know what else to do."

Antonio snorted. "Duncan could not find Falco in Pear Blossom Creek. What makes you think he will be able to find him here?"

"I don't know. I just know we need help, and—"

"I have fought my own battles for over six hundred years," he said quietly. "I have not always won, but—"

"Oh, please, don't give me any of that macho vampire crap. What about the other night? Should I have just left you chained to the floor in that shed? Should I have just waited here, twiddling my thumbs, hoping you'd find a way to free yourself?"

His anger melted in the face of hers and he laughed softly. "You are right. I needed help that night and my warrior woman came to my rescue."

"I'm sorry, I just didn't know what else to do."

"When will he be here?"

"Sometime tomorrow. He asked me if you slept here." She looked up at him. "Do you?"

"I did. I will find a new place to rest tomorrow."

"Why? He promised he wouldn't hunt you."

"You will forgive me if I place no faith in the word of a vampire hunter."

"I'm sorry. I guess I've made a mess of everything."

"No. I am too weak to hunt Falco. And you are too inexperienced. Perhaps Duncan can accomplish what we cannot, though I doubt it. And now, I must go out for a while."

"No! He could be out there."

"I must feed."

"You know you don't have to go out for that, not anymore."

"I cannot keep taking from you, sweeting. It is not good for you."

"But it's good for you, isn't it?"

He nodded. "More than you know."

"Then let's not waste time arguing about it, okay?"

"Victoria, what am I to do with you?"

Taking him by the hand, she led him to the easy chair and sat down on his lap. "Whatever you want, Antonio."

"You tempt me, woman, in more ways than you can imagine."

She smiled, pleased, as she tilted her head to the side, giving him access to her neck. She saw the hunger rise in his eyes as he lowered his head, the glint of his fangs. Hard to believe she had once found the thought of the vampire's kiss repulsive. Women the world over would be hunting for vampires if they knew what pleasure could be found in their arms.

She closed her eyes as wave after wave of sensual pleasure moved through her. She knew, without knowing how she knew, that every time he drank from her, it bound them more closely together. Hopefully, by the time they had destroyed Dimitri Falco, Antonio would find it impossible to exist without her. She was already certain she couldn't exist without him.

She moaned a soft protest when he drew away. "Can I ask you something?"

"Of course." His knuckles caressed her cheek. "How could I refuse you anything now?"

She took a deep breath. "Do you like being a vampire?"

"Yes, I do."

"All of it?"

He nodded. "All of it."

"And you don't miss the sun or food or anything else?"

"Not anymore. Although . . . I would like to have had a son."

"It's not too late," she said, thinking how wonderful it would be to have Antonio's son.

"It is eternally too late," he said.

"Why? Can't you have children?"

"No. Can you imagine how quickly we could flood the world with vampires if we could reproduce? I have existed over six hundred years. Think of the number of children I could have sired in that time."

She had no doubt that it would be a staggering number if she could do the math in her head. "Will you tell me something else?"

"Ask."

"What's it like, when you sleep? Do you dream?"

He smiled faintly. "I never dreamed until I met you."

"Really? What do you dream about now?"

"I am not sure you want to know."

"Oh, but I do."

"I dream of making you mine, of making love to you in every way that a man who is also a vampire can make love to a woman."

She contemplated his answer for several moments. How many ways were there for a vampire to make love? The question raised a number of interesting possibilities. She frowned. Did vampires make love differently than mortal men? It was a topic she decided not to pursue at the moment. "Can I ask you one more thing?"

"You want to know where I take my rest."

"Will you show me?"

"If you wish." There was no harm in it now. He

would never sleep there again. Setting her on her feet, he took her by the hand. "Come."

He led her out of the parlor and up the stairs. Like most old castles, this one had a number of hidden doors, passageways, and bolt-holes. About halfway up the staircase, he stopped and pressed his hand against the wall. A portion of the wall slid back, revealing a yawning maw of darkness.

"Do you still want to see it?" he asked.

She nodded.

He had to admire his warrior woman's courage. He knew she wasn't as calm as she appeared. Her palms were suddenly damp; he could hear the rapid beat of her heart.

Still holding her by the hand, he led her down a narrow, winding staircase into a darkness that was blacker than black.

Vickie didn't know how he did it, but suddenly a dozen candles sprang to life and she saw that she was in a small oval room. The floor and the walls were made of gray stone. There was nothing in the room save for the candles and an oversized coffin with the lid raised.

Antonio released her hand and stepped away, his face carefully impassive as he waited for her reaction.

Vicki stared at the sleek ebony wood, the pristine white silk that lined the inside. Try as she might, she couldn't hide the revulsion in her voice. She was sure it showed on her face, too, but she couldn't help it. "Do you like this part of it, too?"

"It is just a place to rest," he replied quietly. "Nothing more."

"Couldn't you rest just as well in a bed?"

He shrugged. "I have, in the past."

"Then why . . . ?" She gestured at the casket, unable

to believe anyone would willingly choose to sleep in such a thing.

"It serves to remind me of what I am."

She turned to face him. "Why on earth would you need reminding?"

"It is a quirk of mine, nothing more." He held out his hand. "Come, let us go."

He didn't have to ask her twice. She was more than willing to put this place behind her. Climbing the stairs, she wondered if he had agreed to show it to her in hopes of making her see why they could not have a life together.

"You must be hungry," he remarked when they returned to the parlor.

She was, now that he mentioned it.

"Go and fix yourself something to eat."

"Come with me?"

He shook his head.

"Why not? What are you going to do?"

"Nothing sinister, my sweet. I will wait for you in the back parlor."

"You won't go out, you promise?"

"Am I to be a prisoner in my own house?" he asked, a fine edge to his voice.

"No, of course not." She turned away, stung by his tone. She couldn't help it if she was worried about him. Couldn't he understand that?

"Victoria, I did not mean to offend you."

"Go on, go outside, do whatever you want. I don't care."

He laughed softly. One minute she was a warrior woman, fighting demons to save him, and the next she was like a child, her feelings easily hurt.

"I will not leave the house," he said. "I promise."

Keeping her back to him, she nodded.

His hands on her shoulders kept her from leaving the room. "Ah, Victoria," he murmured with a shake of his head. "What a treasure you are."

She blinked back sudden unexpected tears at the warmth and the wonder in his voice.

He chuckled softly as her stomach growled in a very unladylike way. "Go and eat. We will talk later."

With a nod, she left the room.

Antonio stared after her, admiring the sway of her hips, until she was out of sight. Feeling as though he were six thousand years old, he made his way to the back parlor, sat down, and closed his eyes. Pain. He was only free of it when the daylight sleep was upon him. It burned through him now like a living flame.

He had thought to leave Victoria when Falco had been destroyed. Now, he wondered how he was ever going to let her go. In six hundred years, he had never needed anyone the way he needed her. It wasn't just her blood he craved, sweet as it was; no, he craved her company, the sound of her laughter, the touch of her hand, the way she melted against him when she should have run away, screaming in fear. He still couldn't believe she had come to rescue him, didn't want to think what would have happened to her if she had failed. How could he let her go?

How could he not? He had seen the look of utter revulsion on her face when she saw where he slept. Though she might think she loved him, he knew that would soon change. No mortal woman could long endure sharing a vampire's life. No mortal woman should have to. It was a life against nature, beyond mortal endurance. Even vampires had been known to seek their own destruction when their existence became more than they could bear.

He thought of Edward Ramsey. The knowledge that

the world's most formidable vampire hunter had been turned had spread quickly through the vampire community. And there had been much rejoicing, he recalled with a faint grin. It was said that Ramsey had taken a vampire wife.

His Victoria, a vampire.

He frowned, unable to imagine her as such. Some souls were made for darkness and some for light, and she was a creature of light and laughter, a woman made to love one man, to bear his children, to grow old at his side.

He shook the thought from his mind. To think of her with another man would surely drive him mad. Until Falco was destroyed, she was his. For now, he would not think beyond that.

Her scent reached his nostrils. Moments later, she entered the room.

He knew she was standing in front of him before he opened his eyes, knew from the wary expression on her face that his hunger showed in his eyes.

"Do you need to . . . ?" She licked her lips nervously. "You know?"

He nodded, not trusting himself to speak. Frequent feeding would help his wounds to heal more quickly. But it wasn't only that. Her very nearness aroused his hunger. Already, his fangs were lengthening in response.

He clenched his hands to keep from reaching for her. "I can go out."

With a shake of her head, she sat down beside him, as trusting as a kitten.

His arm went around her shoulders. He brushed a lock of hair aside to expose her neck. So warm, so willing. He closed his eyes, fighting for control, thinking how easy it would be to take it all. If it was anyone but Victoria . . . He pushed the thought from his mind. In spite of his words to the contrary, he wasn't like Falco, had never been like Falco.

Lowering his head, he took what he needed, what he craved.

What he feared he would never be able to live without now that he'd had a taste of it.

Chapter 34

Tom Duncan arrived at the castle at two o'clock the following afternoon. He followed Vicki into the front parlor, sat down at her invitation.

"This is quite a place," he remarked, settling back on the sofa.

"Yes. Can I get you anything? Coffee? Soda?"

"Not right now. So, tell me everything that's happened since you got here." Taking a seat at the other end of the sofa, she started at the beginning and quickly brought him up to date.

He grinned when she told him about the four young men who had come to her aid. "You're damn lucky they turned out to be decent guys, or I might have been reading your obit in the paper."

"I know, but at the time it never crossed my mind to be afraid. I was too worried about Antonio to think about anything else."

"You've really got it bad for that bloodsucker, don't you?"

"Don't call him that."

"He's fed off you, hasn't he?"

"What if he has?"

"Hey, it's your life. I just hope you know what you're getting into. So, you ready to go hunting?"

"Me?"

"Why not?"

Why not indeed? It was as much to her benefit as anyone else's to find Falco. Maybe more.

Vicki grabbed her coat and they left the house. "Looks like rain," she remarked as she got into the Camaro.

"Yeah, I think it's following me."

She settled back in her seat and fastened her seat belt. "Do you have any idea where to look?"

"No. I just want to drive around, get the lay of the land. A friend of mine is coming in sometime tonight to give us a hand."

"Another vampire hunter?"

"He used to be."

"What is he now?"

"A vampire." Duncan slid the key into the ignition.

Vicki stared at him in disbelief. "You're kidding, right? Don't we have enough vampires already?"

"Ramsey was the best hunter in the business before he was turned. I don't know where else to go for help." Duncan shook his head. "I've never had this much trouble finding one of the Undead before. I don't know, maybe I've lost my touch. Maybe Falco's more than a vampire. Maybe he's a ghost, too."

"I know a ghost," Vicki remarked, smiling. "Maybe you'll get to meet her."

"Yeah, right." Putting the car in gear, he drove toward the front gate.

"Seriously. Her name is Lady Kathryn. She haunts

the castle, although I'm not sure *haunt* is the right word. She's not very scary."

"Just what we need."

"Well, she helped me find Antonio."

Duncan pulled over and put the car in Park. "Maybe we should go take a look at that shed where you found Battista before we do anything else."

"We'll have to go on foot from here," she said. "There's no road from the castle grounds."

"Okay by me." After killing the engine, Duncan grabbed a jacket from the backseat and got out of the car.

With a shrug, she unfastened her seat belt and headed toward the woods. "It's this way," she said, glancing over her shoulder to make sure he was behind her.

The clouds grew thicker and darker as they made their way through the trees.

"I can't see the sun," she said, glancing at the sky.

"So?"

"The sun is supposed to kill vampires, right? But the sun isn't shining today. So, could he be up and moving around?"

"Old ones can probably rise early on days like this," Duncan replied, frowning. "I really don't know if they can go outside. I sure as hell hope not."

Vicki shivered. Falco was an old vampire. What if he was at the shed, waiting for them?

"Did you bring your vampire-killing kit?" she asked.

Duncan patted his jacket pocket. "Holy water in here." He paused to pick up a narrow branch, then pulled a knife from one of his other pockets and began whittling the end of the branch to a sharp point.

That was it? A bottle of holy water and a makeshift stake? It didn't do much to ease her nerves or increase her confidence.

It was drizzling when they reached the shed.

"I'm not sure I can go in there again," Vicki said.

"That's all right. You stay here, I'll check it out."

"Do you think you should go alone?"

"I doubt if Falco would hang around now that he's been discovered here once."

Vicki nodded. She crossed her arms over her chest, shivering a little, while she watched Tom go into the lambing shed. She wondered if the bodies of the zombies were still inside. What if Tom was wrong? What if Falco was inside, waiting?

She took a step forward, ears straining for some sound that would tell her what was happening inside. Her mouth went dry as she imagined Duncan stepping into the shed and coming face-to-face with a vampire who was wide awake and ready to strike. A bottle of holy water and a wooden stake seemed like puny weapons against a vampire who was hundreds of years old.

She had worked herself into a fine state by the time Duncan returned.

"There's no sign of him," he said..

She glanced past Tom. "What about the zombies?"

"No sign of them, either. Some blood on the floor, but that's all." He shrugged. "Looks like he got away again."

They spent the rest of the day driving through the town, stopping whenever they saw what looked like an abandoned building. They saw a few vagrants, a couple of teenagers hitchhiking on the main road, but no sign of the Undead.

At dusk, they turned and headed for home.

And found Edward Ramsey waiting for them on the castle's front steps.

Vicki studied the vampire while Duncan made the introductions. Ramsey was tall and lean, with short blond hair and ice blue eyes. It was hard to judge his age but she guessed he had been somewhere between thirty-five and forty-five when he was turned. A thin scar ran along his right cheek. He wore a light blue turtleneck sweater and a pair of dark blue slacks. When he shook hands with Duncan, she noticed there was a cross tattooed on his right palm.

Vickie stood there while Duncan quickly brought Ramsey up to speed, wondering what she should do. She wasn't exactly sure just what vampire protocol dictated she do in a situation like this. Should she invite Ramsey inside? How would Antonio feel about having another vampire in the house?

She was still debating what to do when Antonio materialized at her side, attired in his ubiquitous black.

The conversation between Duncan and Ramsey stopped abruptly. Ramsey stepped away from Duncan, his gaze focused on Antonio. The two vampires regarded each other for several long moments, almost as if they were sizing each other up, Vicki thought, and perhaps they were. She looked from one to the other. Antonio was a little taller and a little broader through the shoulders. He had been younger than Ramsey when he was brought across, but Antonio had been a vampire hundreds of years longer than the former hunter.

Power arced between the two vampires, as though they were testing one another. It made her skin prickle and the hair raise at her nape.

"Antonio Battista," Ramsey said. "I've heard of you."

"And I have heard of you." Antonio glanced at Victoria, then back at Ramsey. "Why are you here?"

"I asked him here," Duncan said.

Antonio looked at Duncan. "What gave you the right to invite him to my home?"

"He's my friend. And the best vampire hunter in the business, as you well know. I thought we could use the help."

"And when Falco has been destroyed, what then?"

"Then we'll all go home," Duncan said. "Right, Edward?"

Ramsey nodded. "I have no quarrel with you, Battista. I'm only here because Duncan asked for my help. If you don't want it, I'm gone."

Battista considered Ramsey's words, then looked at Duncan. "Perhaps you are right." Turning, he opened the door and stepped inside. "Welcome to my home."

Vicki breathed a sigh of relief as she followed the men into the house. It looked like there was going to be a truce, at least for the time being.

She listened quietly as Duncan, Antonio, and Ramsey spent the next hour proposing and dismissing a dozen plans for destroying Dimitri Falco.

"If we want to trap him, we need bait. And we all know there's only one kind of bait he'll fall for."

Vicki went cold inside as all three men turned in her direction.

Antonio shook his head. "No."

"I think Edward's right," Duncan said. "I've spent weeks looking for Falco. So have you. We haven't had any luck. He kidnapped Vicki. You were almost killed. I don't see as how we have any other choice."

"I will not risk Victoria's life."

"In the meantime, he's killing another woman every

night," Duncan said. "How long do you intend to let that go on?"

"I said no."

Vicki laid her hand on Antonio's arm. "I think Tom's right. I should be all right with the three of you there to protect me."

"She can wear a thick silver collar around her throat," Ramsey said, "and bracelets on her wrists. I see that she already wears a crucifix. Even if he gets near her, he won't be able to touch her if she doesn't panic."

"I need to do this," Vicki said. "It's my fault all those other women are dying. Falco said it himself. He said he'd kill thousands if he had to."

"He will kill them regardless," Antonio said. "I will not risk your life."

Vicki lifted her chin defiantly. "You can't stop me. It's my life, and my decision."

Antonio glared at her.

"It's settled, then," Ramsey said.

Duncan grinned, amused that, in spite of being a vampire himself, Ramsey so easily fell into the role of vampire hunter.

"Victoria should go into town tomorrow afternoon and stay until dusk. Is there a road that isn't traveled often?"

"There's a back road that leads to the castle," Antonio said.

"Good. Victoria, you take that route. Drive slow. You need to be on that road . . ." He paused and looked at Antonio. "How soon can you rise?"

"As soon as the sun starts to go down."

"What about Falco? Do you have any idea when he rises?"

"He is an old vampire," Antonio said. "He probably

rises the same time that I do. Perhaps a little earlier. What about you?"

"I can rise as the sun sets, same as you."

"Such a thing is unusual in one so young," Antonio remarked, obviously impressed.

"I have good blood," Ramsey said, grinning.

Antonio lifted one brow.

"The blood of Alexi Kristov and Khira runs in my veins, as well as that of Grigori Chiavari."

"A potent combination," Antonio remarked.

"So I'm told," Ramsey said. "All right, we need to time this perfectly. Victoria, you need to be on that road twenty minutes after the sun goes down. Antonio, you and I will follow her. Duncan, you'll be in the backseat under a blanket. Victoria, I want you to get out of the car and pretend there's something wrong with it. If Falco's anywhere in the area, he'll find you. As soon as you see him, you'll throw holy water in his face." Ramsey looked at Duncan. "I'm assuming you've got some handy?"

"What do you think?" Duncan replied.

"Right. It should distract Falco long enough for Battista and me to take him down. We'll hold him. Duncan, you stake him and I'll take his head."

"Just like the good old days," Duncan remarked.

Ramsey nodded, his expression wistful. "Exactly."

"I do not like it," Antonio said. "Too many things can go wrong. If Falco finds Victoria before we get there, Duncan and Victoria could both end up dead, or worse."

"It's a chance we'll have to take," Duncan said, his eyes gleaming in anticipation of the hunt. "Right, Vicki?"

"Right."

"My warrior woman," Antonio murmured.

"I need a drink," Duncan said. "I don't suppose you've got any whiskey here?"

Vicki shook her head. "No, sorry. The strongest thing I've got is Coke."

"Then Coke it is."

"Do you want it in the can, or in a glass with ice?" Vicki asked, rising.

Duncan rose. "I need to stretch my legs. I'll go with you."

Antonio watched Victoria and the vampire hunter leave the room, aware that Ramsey was watching him.

Slowly, Antonio turned his gaze on the other vampire. Not counting his confrontations with Falco, it had been years since he had been in the company of another of his kind. Vampires did not normally associate with one another. They tended to be solitary creatures. Most were fiercely protective of their hunting grounds. Antonio knew little of Edward Ramsey other than that he had once been a relentless hunter who had been turned and was now married to a vampire. He had heard of Kristov and Khira, of course. And of Grigori Chiavari. Like Grigori, Ramsey had brought his mortal lover across.

"Your woman," Antonio said. "Has she fully accepted the Dark Trick? Does she regret being turned?"

"No. She seems content."

"And Grigori's woman?"

"It was her choice." Ramsey regarded him for several moments. "You're in love with Victoria, are you not?"

"If I am, it is not your concern."

"You're wondering what kind of vampire she'd make."

"Were you a mind reader as well as a hunter?"

Ramsey shook his head. "It doesn't take a genius to

know what you're thinking. You love her. She obviously loves you. It's the only way you can truly be together."

"I would not ask her to make such a sacrifice."

"It should be her choice, not yours."

"I am making it mine. I love her as she is. Warm, human. Filled with the frailties and foibles of mortality. I would not change her."

"I used to hunt vampires," Ramsey reminded him. "I thought they were the scum of the earth, not fit to live. In many cases, I was right. Kristov was a monster much like Falco. But then I met Grigori, a vampire with honor. Eventually I realized that becoming a vampire doesn't make a man evil. A good man will remain a good man no matter what form he takes, just as evil remains evil."

"Do you have a point to make?" Antonio asked impatiently. "If so, make it."

"The point is, she would still be the woman you're in love with, only more so."

"I would not rob her of the chance to marry and have a family. It is something she wants, something I can never give her. I have taken her blood. I have put her life in danger. I will not deny her the one thing she wants above all else."

Ramsey nodded. "As you said, it's your choice."

"What's your choice?" Vicki asked as she entered the room.

"Whether to allow Ramsey to spend the night in the castle," Antonio replied smoothly. "He has declined."

"Well, I hope you don't mind if I stay," Duncan said.

"Not at all," Antonio said, "so long as Victoria approves."

"It's all right with me. I'd welcome the company."

"Maybe I'll get to see the ghost," Duncan said.

"Ghost?" Ramsey said. "What ghost?"

"The castle's haunted by a lovely ghost," Vicki said. "You'd like her."

"Perhaps another night," Ramsey said, rising. "It's getting late and I've not yet had my dinner." He looked at Antonio. "Do you mind if I hunt in the town?"

Vicki glanced from one to the other, thinking that she must be watching vampire etiquette in action.

"So long as you only take the blood," Antonio said, "and not the life."

"As you wish. I'll see you all tomorrow night."

With a courtly bow, Ramsey left the house.

"If you'll tell me where to bed down, I think I'll turn in," Duncan said.

"I'll show you," Vicki said.

Leading the way, she went up the stairs, wondering if she should tell Duncan that he would be sleeping in Lady Kathryn's chambers. She doubted if a vampire hunter would be afraid of a spirit, but you never knew.

"Here we are," Vicki said. Opening the door, she felt a distinct chill as she stepped into the bedroom.

"It's customary to knock when one enters a lady's bedchamber," Lady Kathryn said imperiously.

"Oh, I didn't know you were here," Vicki said. She glanced at Duncan. He was staring at the ghost, who sat in front of a low dressing table, idly brushing her ghostly tresses. "Tom, this is Lady Kathryn. Lady Kathryn, this is Tom Duncan. He's a friend of mine."

Rising, Lady Kathryn glided toward them. "Sir Duncan, I'm pleased to meet you," she said, extending her hand.

Looking nonplussed, Duncan hesitated a moment, and then, to Vicki's surprise, he bowed over Lady Kathryn's hand.

"The pleasure is all mine, Lady Kathryn," he replied gallantly.

Looking pleased, Lady Kathryn rewarded him with a smile and then looked at Vicki. "What brings the two of you to my room at this late hour?"

"Tom needs a place to sleep," Vicki explained. "And since this is the only room with a bed besides mine . . ."

"It's all right," Tom interjected. "I can sleep on the sofa downstairs."

"I won't hear of such a thing," Lady Kathryn said. "What kind of hostess would I be to allow a guest to sleep on the couch? You may use my room, of course. I'll share Victoria's."

Tom glanced at Vicki. "Is that okay with you?"

"Sure." Since Lady Kathryn didn't really sleep, sharing a room didn't include sharing a bed. However, since the ghost no longer had any concept of time, Vicki figured she wouldn't have much use for the bed, either, since Lady Kathryn would probably want to spend the night chatting. "Good night, Tom."

"Yeah, good night," he said, trying not to stare at Lady Kathryn. The ghost was flitting around near the ceiling and then, in the blink of an eye, she was gone. Tom glanced around the room. "Where'd she go?"

"Who knows? See you tomorrow."

Vicki left the room and Tom closed the door behind her.

In the corridor, she heard him mutter, "I've seen a lot of things in my day, but a ghost! Man, now I've seen everything."

Grinning, she hurried downstairs to where Antonio was waiting for her.

Chapter 35

Antonio stood at the front window staring out into the night. It was amazing, how much his life had changed since he met Victoria. Not so long ago, his nights had been peaceful, almost monotonous. He had risen with the setting of the sun, sought his prey, then spent the rest of the dark hours in restful pursuits. He had enjoyed going to the theater or to the movies, or spending an evening reading a good book. He had taken long walks. He had spent time in each of his various abodes. The house in Oregon was the most modern. He probably should have taken Victoria there, but the castle was his favorite place, probably because of Lady Kathryn. They had spent many a night together, two lost and lonely souls who found comfort in each other's company.

And now Victoria was here. He turned at the sound of her footsteps coming down the stairs, his nostrils flaring as she entered the room. She smelled of soap and shampoo and woman. A woman ripe for the taking . . .

She smiled at him. "You're not too upset about Duncan staying here, are you?"

"No."

"I'm glad, especially since he's about to marry my best friend. Bobbie Sue took him home to meet her folks earlier this week." She sat down on the sofa, looking pensive. "Would you like to meet my mom and my sister?"

He lifted one brow in obvious amusement. "I think a better question would be, would they like to meet me?"

"Well, sure, why wouldn't they? We wouldn't have to tell them you're a vampire, you know."

"And if we stayed longer than an hour or two, how would you explain the fact that I do not eat or drink or cast an image in a mirror? And would they not think it odd that I could not be found during the day?"

"Yes, I suppose so."

If they went to St. Louis, her mother and Karen would assume Antonio was on vacation, so she wouldn't be able to excuse his absences during the day by telling them he was at work, although she might be able to come up with some plausible excuse, like he was the head of a big company that was looking to open an office in St. Louis. Of course, the fact that he didn't eat posed another problem. Her family would expect them to stay at the house. Antonio might be able to skip a meal or two, but not all three.

But the mirror thing would be the biggest obstacle. One wall in Karen's living room was mirrored from floor to ceiling, as was one of the walls in the dining room. The closet doors in the bedrooms were mirrored, as well. Her sister's house was small, and she believed that the mirrors made the rooms look larger.

"So, we won't go visit my folks," she said with a dismissive shrug. "It's no big deal."

But it was one more aspect of her life that he couldn't share.

Sitting down on the sofa, he put his arm around her waist and drew her close. With a little sigh, she rested her head on his shoulder. "This is nice," she murmured. "Just the two of us, alone in front of the fire."

He nodded, thinking how much he would miss her when she was gone.

Chapter 36

Vicki woke late again the next morning. Rising, she was filled with a mingled sense of anticipation and dread. If all went as planned, they would be rid of Falco by nightfall. It sounded so simple, but there were a hundred things that could go wrong, any one of which could get one or all of them killed.

While showering, she told herself there was nothing to worry about. Antonio would protect her. Ramsey and Duncan were both vampire hunters, and Ramsey was a vampire. They knew what they were doing.

"Everything will be all right." She repeated the words over and over again as she dried her hair.

A look out the window showed that it was drizzling, and she dressed accordingly in a pair of jeans and a bulky green sweater.

Tom Duncan was sitting at the kitchen table drinking a cup of coffee when she went downstairs. "Morning."

"Hi." She poured herself a cup of coffee and sat down across from him. "Are you hungry?"

"I could eat."

"What would you like?"

He shrugged. "Anything you feel like fixing is fine with me."

"Scrambled eggs and bacon sound okay?"

"Perfect."

She finished her coffee, then set about making breakfast. "Have you and Bobbie Sue set the date yet?"

"She wants to get married in February, on Valentine's Day."

Vicki smiled, thinking how romantic that sounded. If she were getting married in February, she would want her attendants to wear red and carry red and white flowers.

"She wants you to be her maid of honor, but that's probably no surprise."

"Not really." She opened a package of bacon and dropped several slices in a frying pan and put it on the stove. "She said you're going to give up hunting."

"Yeah, it's time."

Vicki scrambled some eggs and poured them into another pan. "Do you think you'll miss it, hunting, I mean?"

"Probably for a while. It's quite a high when you're closing in on your quarry. Adrenaline pumping, heart pounding in excitement when you find the vampire's lair and you know he's yours for the taking."

Vicki turned away from the stove, sickened by his description. She couldn't help imagining Duncan finding Antonio's resting place and . . .

"You look a little green," Tom remarked. "I guess what I do for a living doesn't make for very good breakfast conversation."

"Not really," she agreed with a weak smile.

She served breakfast a few minutes later. Sitting

there doing something as mundane as eating bacon and eggs made her think of Antonio again. He'd said he no longer missed solid food. How long would it take to adjust to a warm liquid diet? Would years have to pass before she got used to never seeing the sun again, or enjoying a cup of hot chocolate on a cold winter night, or pigging out on her favorite candy, or eating popcorn at the movies? What was it like to never see your reflection in a mirror again? How did female vampires put on their make-up?

"Vicki?"

She looked up at the sound of Tom's voice. "Did you say something?"

"Where were you just now?"

"Oh, just lost in thought."

"Want to tell me what you were thinking about?"

"Vampires, of course. Isn't that what we're all thinking about these days?"

"Vampires?" Tom asked. "Or one particular vampire?"

"Actually, I was wondering what it would be like to be one."

Duncan swore a vile oath, then immediately apologized.

"I guess you've never considered it," Vicki said.

"I can't imagine anyone in their right mind even thinking about it. They're all killers. Doesn't matter if they're handsome and charming or repulsive and meaner than hell, underneath, they're all killers. Sure, some have learned to survive without killing, but most don't want to. After they've been vampires for a while, they no longer consider themselves as human and they no longer give any thought to taking human life. We're food, prey, fodder, nothing more."

She stared at him, repulsed by the ugly picture he

had painted. "What about your friend, Ramsey? Is he like that?"

"Like I said, they're all like that."

"I don't believe it."

"You don't want to believe it because you're in love with Battista."

And that, she thought, said it all.

Vicki grew more anxious with each passing hour. She tried to read. She tried to watch television. She stared out the window at the rain. She played chess with Tom, but she couldn't concentrate on the game and finally gave up. She wondered if he was as cool and calm as he appeared. How could he be?

She fixed lunch, then tried to take a nap, but to no avail. She couldn't relax.

Where was Antonio? How soon would he be able to rise? She needed to see him, to touch him, hear the sound of his voice. Were they doing the right thing? Maybe they should just pack up and go to his villa in Italy. Maybe Falco wouldn't find them there. It was tempting, so tempting, but then she thought of Sharlene and Leslie Ann Lewis and all the other women Falco had killed in the last few weeks. The hundreds and thousands of women he would murder in the future because she was too chicken to do what had to be done. And running wouldn't accomplish anything. He had taken her blood. He would find her no matter where she tried to hide.

Staring into the flames blazing cheerfully in the fireplace, she took a deep breath. Antonio called her his warrior woman. The good Lord willing, that's what she would be.

She practically jumped out of her skin when Duncan announced it was time to go.

They decided to take the Lexus since it had the most room in the backseat.

"Have you got everything you need?" she asked.

"Yeah, don't worry."

Vicki's hand was shaking so badly she could hardly get the key in the ignition. She patted her jacket pockets, reassured when she felt the two bottles filled with holy water. She made sure her crucifix was on the outside of her jacket.

She drove to town and stopped at a jewelry store, where she bought a thick silver collar and two silver bracelets. She put them on while inside the store and immediately felt better.

They made one more stop at a toy store, where Duncan bought two squirt guns.

"What are they for?" Vicki asked as they walked back to the car.

"We'll fill them with holy water. That way you won't have to waste time opening the bottles, and your aim will be better."

She grinned. "Where on earth did you get an idea like that?"

"Saw it in a movie once," he said as he climbed into the back seat. "Try to relax. If you're too tense, Falco will suspect something."

"Relax? You're kidding, right?" She covered Tom with a heavy wool blanket, then climbed behind the steering wheel. She touched the squirt guns for reassurance, turned on the ignition, and drove toward the secondary road.

A glance outside showed that they had timed it perfectly.

Surprisingly, she grew calmer as the miles went by. She knew exactly when she reached the place where Antonio and Ramsey were waiting, though she wasn't sure how she knew.

She stopped the car in the middle of the road and left the engine running.

"Do you see anything?" Duncan whispered from the backseat.

"No." It was hard to see more than a few feet in any direction because of the rain.

"I'm going to get out of the car."

"Leave the door open so I can hear what's going on."

"All right."

Taking a deep breath, she opened the door and got out of the car. She stood there a moment, glancing up and down the road, and then lifted the hood and looked at the engine. With a shrug, as if she didn't know what the problem could be, she began walking back and forth alongside the car, as if she were hoping someone would stop and offer assistance.

Where was Antonio? Where was Ramsey?

Where was Falco?

She shoved her hands in her jacket pockets, her fingers caressing the squirt guns for reassurance once more.

She knew he was there before she saw him. A ripple in the air, a sudden sense of menace, she didn't know what warned her, but she turned abruptly and there he was, striding through the rain toward her, a malevolent grin on his face.

"So, we meet again."

She swallowed hard, her courage deserting her now that he was there.

"Nothing to say?" he asked. "No word of greeting?"

He was only a few steps away now, close enough that she could see his fangs, the red glow in his eyes.

"Go away!" she cried, loud enough so that Duncan would be sure to hear. "Go away or I'll scream!"

"And who will hear you?" Falco said, sneering.

He reached toward her.

Panicked at the mere thought of his touch on her skin, she jerked her hands out of her pockets.

He looked at the squirt guns, one a bright pink, the other neon green. Surprise and amusement were reflected in his eyes.

Until she squeezed the triggers.

A harsh cry of pain erupted from his throat as twin streams of holy water struck him full in the face. With a scream of rage, he lunged toward her, his hands like claws, his face contorted.

She reeled backward, desperate to avoid his touch. She squeezed the triggers again and again. And still he came toward her, a harsh wail on his lips.

She screamed as his hand closed over her arm.

And suddenly Antonio was there. He tackled Falco from the side, his momentum carrying them both to the ground.

Duncan scrambled out of the back of the car, a four-foot stake and a mallet in one hand, what looked like a machete in the other.

Ramsey streaked toward them. "More holy water!" he said. "Keep him too weak to change."

Vicki pulled one of the bottles from her pocket and dumped the contents over Falco's face and body. Bucking wildly, he screamed in rage and pain as he endeavored to free himself, but to no avail.

Vicki turned away as Duncan placed the sharp point of the stake over Falco's heart.

There was one last hideous scream, and it was over.

The scent of blood defiled the air and she knew that Ramsey had taken Falco's head. Moving away from the grisly scene, she dropped to her knees in a patch of wet grass and was violently ill.

"It is over," Antonio said, coming up behind her.

"Here." Duncan passed her his handkerchief.

Vicki wiped her mouth. She could hear Duncan and Ramsey congratulating each other. Antonio stood beside her, one hand lightly squeezing her shoulder.

"Come," he said. "Let us go home."

"What about the body?" she asked.

"Do not think of that now."

Taking her by the hand, he helped her to her feet.

Careful not to look at what was left of Dimitri Falco, Vicki climbed into the Lexus. Duncan got into the backseat. Antonio got behind the wheel.

They drove in silence until curiosity got the best of her. "Why did Ramsey stay behind?"

"He is going to dispose of the body," Antonio said.

"How?"

"He will take it deeper into the woods and stay with it until dawn. The sun will take care of the remains."

With a nod, Vicki stared out the window though there was nothing to see.

Antonio glanced at her from time to time. He had been worried that she would be hurt when it was time for him to leave her. Now, he thought she would most likely be glad to see the last of him. Considering all that she had been through since he entered her life, he couldn't blame her. He should have been relieved. Instead, he found himself wishing that things could be different between them. If he lived another six hundred years, he knew he would never forget her, never find another to take her place in his heart.

He pulled into the garage and killed the engine.

Moving like a robot, Vicki let herself out of the car.

Antonio followed her up the stairs and into the house. "Victoria?"

She didn't turn around. "I'm going to bed. Tell Duncan good night for me."

He said nothing, merely watched her climb the stairs.

Duncan entered the room a few minutes later.

Antonio slowly turned around, and they regarded each other warily for several moments, the vampire and the vampire hunter.

"Well," Duncan said briskly. "I guess I'll be going." He glanced around the room. "Where's Vicki?"

"She has gone to bed."

Duncan grunted softly. "She's a hell of a woman."

"Yes."

"Thanks for putting up with me. I'll just go up and get my things. Tell Vicki I'll see her at the wedding."

Antonio nodded. He waited until Duncan was out of the room, and then he vanished into the night.

Chapter 37

Vicki stood at her bedroom window, listening to the thunder that rolled across the sky. Now and then, lightning ripped through the clouds, illuminating the yard and the trees beyond. The sound of the rain was steady and soothing.

The nightmare was over. Dimitri Falco had been destroyed. Never again would he terrorize her or kill innocent women. A part of her was glad that she'd had a hand in defeating him. Another part was horrified by what had happened. She told herself he had been evil, beyond redemption, and yet she couldn't help feeling guilty that she had helped take a human life. Although, technically, he hadn't been a human man but a vampire. And he hadn't been alive, but Undead.

She pressed her hands to her throbbing temples. It was over and done. Dwelling on the ugliness of it wouldn't help.

She glanced at the door. She had expected Antonio to follow her to her room. Was he downstairs, waiting for her?

Going into the bathroom, she splashed cold water on her face, then took a couple of aspirin. She returned to her room, changed into her nightgown, and went to bed.

She left the light on, wondering if she would ever again feel comfortable sleeping in the dark now that she knew there were monsters prowling the night. But Falco was dead. Surely a little backwater town like Pear Blossom Creek wouldn't attract another one for a long time, if ever.

She was almost asleep when she realized she was no longer in bed alone. She would have run screaming out of the room if a strong arm hadn't circled her waist.

"Shh, my sweet one, it is only me."

"Antonio."

"Go to sleep, beloved. There is nothing for you to fear."

She snuggled against him, all her anxiety forgotten now that he was there, holding her in his arms.

"I love you," she murmured, and slid over the abyss into sleep.

There were no bad dreams that night.

Vicki woke with a smile on her face. Eyes still closed, she reached for Antonio, frowned when she realized she was alone in bed. Coming fully awake, she realized it was morning and he was gone.

Would he ever tell her where he rested during the day? After all they had been through together, did he honestly think she would betray his hiding place? Or was it that he didn't want her to see him when he was . . . what? Whatever it was, she preferred to think of it as sleeping.

Sitting up, she saw a note propped on the table beside the bed. She smiled when she recognized Antonio's handwriting.

Victoria—Duncan has gone back to Pear Blossom Creek. He said he would see you at the wedding. Gather your things and I will take you home tonight. Love, A.

Her smile faded as she reread his note. For all his talk about loving her, now that the danger was over, it seemed he couldn't wait to get rid of her.

Fighting tears, she made the bed, then packed her clothes. If he wanted her gone, then she would go.

Going downstairs, she went into the kitchen and fixed a cup of tea. She had no appetite for breakfast.

Lady Kathryn joined her at the breakfast table a few minutes later. "I do so miss a good cup of tea," she said wistfully, then frowned. "Are you crying?"

"No," Vicki said, sniffling, "of course not."

"What's wrong, dear?"

"I'm going home tonight."

Lady Kathryn smiled. "Ah, yes, I heard that that monstrous beast, Falco, had been destroyed. It was very brave, what you did."

"It didn't feel brave."

"Well, it was. I must say, I'm sorry to see you go. Perhaps you'll come back and visit again soon."

"I'd like to, but I'm afraid that won't be possible."

"What has that man done now?" Lady Kathryn asked indignantly.

"Nothing. He . . . He just doesn't want me."

"Why, of course he does! Any fool can see that. He's just afraid, don't you know, afraid of loving you, afraid of losing you."

"Losing me? Why should he lose me? I love him, too."

"Time has no meaning to a vampire," the ghost said. "But for a mortal . . . Well, think how hard it would be

for him to watch you grow old while he stayed the same.
And eventually . . . Well, he'd be alone again. Sometimes it's easier to do without something you love than
to have it for a short time and then lose it, don't you
see?"

"Yes, I guess so." *Like must marry like,* Vicki thought,
remembering what the ghost had told her before. It
might be true, but it didn't make the hurt go away.

Antonio appeared at sundown. He looked incredibly
sexy in a pair of tight black jeans and a black sweat-
shirt. Just looking at him make her heart race and her
insides tingle. She wanted nothing more than to spend
the rest of her life making him happy.

"Are you ready?" he asked.

She nodded, too close to tears to speak.

She closed her eyes when he put his arm around her.
Once again, she experienced that sense of flying swiftly
through the air, a sudden queasiness, like being sea-
sick, followed by a familiar feeling of weightlessness,
as if her soul had left her body behind.

The next thing she knew, she was standing in the
middle of her living room. "I guess you'll be going
now," she said, blinking rapidly to keep from crying.

"The danger is past."

"I don't want you to go."

"Victoria . . ."

"I want you to stay." The word *forever* hovered unspoken in the air between them. "Will you stay, at least
for a little while?"

He nodded. Dragging it out would not make it easier
for either of them, but he couldn't bear the sadness in
her eyes. Another week, perhaps two. What harm could
it do? She was young. Perhaps she would come to real-

ize that what she felt for him was no more than infatuation for a creature unlike anything she had ever known. Perhaps when she realized how little she had in common with a vampire, it would make leaving her easier. If he was lucky, maybe she would ask him to leave.

She smiled when he agreed to stay. It warmed the cold places in his heart. He would do anything she wished just to see that smile.

Vicki glanced around her house. Except for a fine layer of dust on everything, the house looked the same as always. Odd, that it no longer felt like home.

"Oh!" she exclaimed. "My fish!" How could she have forgotten about them?

They were dead, of course. Looking at them, she burst into tears.

"Victoria." Antonio had followed her into the den. Drawing her into his arms, he held her close. He knew she wasn't crying for the fish, at least not entirely. It was a natural reaction to everything she had been through in the past few weeks, a release of tension and fear and the horror of Falco's death.

He stroked her back, his whole body attuned to her every breath, her every heartbeat. The fragrance of her hair and skin teased his nostrils, the scent of her blood spoke to his hunger.

Gradually, her tears subsided and she stood, unmoving, in his arms, her cheek pillowed on his chest. Awareness sparked between them.

Antonio rested his chin on the top of her head. How long could he refuse to take what he so desperately wanted? How could he take her innocence knowing he was going to leave her?

He groaned low in his throat as his body warred with his conscience.

She leaned into him, her arms sliding up around his

neck. "You want me," she said, "I know you do." Drawing his head down, she pressed her lips to his.

He crushed her body to his, his mouth devouring hers as if he could never get enough, as if he would never let her go. She was every dream he had refused to acknowledge, every hope for a future he could never have.

His hands caressed her, memorizing every soft, sweet curve, the silky-smooth texture of her hair, the line of her back, the way her body so perfectly molded itself to his.

He closed his eyes, imprinting the way her hands felt on his body as she began a slow exploration of her own, the way her breath caught in her throat when she felt his arousal, the way her tongue dueled with his.

"Antonio, please . . ."

He looked into her eyes, eyes filled with love and trust and yearning, and knew he would never be able to forgive himself if he took what she was offering. Making love to her, stealing her virginity, would prove he was as much a monster as Dimitri Falco, but instead of taking Victoria's life, he would be taking her innocence, something he had no right to take and nothing to give in return.

"Victoria, listen to me—"

"No! I don't want to hear it. Not now. Not ever."

"There can be no future for us, sweeting. You must know that."

"I don't believe that!" But there it was again, Lady Kathryn's voice telling her that like must marry like.

She opened her mouth to argue, but found herself unable to speak when his gaze caught and held hers.

"You will hear me," he said. "I cannot be what you want or what you need. I cannot be a husband or a father. I cannot share your life, and you cannot share mine. In time you would come to hate me for the sacrifices you would have to make to stay with me. I told you before, a vampire's existence is a life against nature. I could not bear your hatred. I could not bear to watch you grow old, knowing I had cheated you of the chance to live a normal life, to have a family. I love you. You must never doubt that. I love you as I have never loved anyone else. I know I told you I would stay for a while, but I think it is best for both of us if I go now. Prolonging our good-bye will not make it easier for either of us."

He kissed her then, pouring all his love and his longing into that one soul-deep kiss.

"I love you, Victoria Cavendish," he said fervently. "Please forgive me."

Unable to speak or to move, she could only stand there while tears dripped down her cheeks.

"*Buono notte*, my sweet one," he whispered, and disappeared in a swirling gray mist.

Released from his spell, she sank down on the floor. Wrapping her arms around her waist, she rocked back and forth while silent tears rained down her cheeks.

He was gone, and she would never fall in love again.

She grieved for a week and then she pulled herself together and went back to work. Gus welcomed her with a bear hug and a smile, and after the first hour or so, it was as if she had never been away.

When people asked where she had been for so long, she shrugged and said she had been on a much-needed vacation.

Bobbie Sue was glowing with happiness, eager to show Vicki her engagement ring, properly outraged at the way Antonio had behaved.

"I can't believe he would just leave you like that!" Bobbie Sue said during one of their breaks. "I mean, really, after all you did for him! Why, you saved his life, the ungrateful . . . man!"

"Oh, Bobbie Sue," Vicki had said, fighting tears. "If he'd been a man, he'd still be here."

It stormed on Thanksgiving, reminding Vicki of the night she had first seen Antonio. But then, it seemed that everything reminded her of Antonio.

Bobbie Sue had invited Vicki to have dinner at her house, but it was too painful to be around Bobbie Sue and Tom, to see how happy they were together.

Instead, Vicki spent the holiday with Mrs. Heath. The older woman listened intently as Vicki told her everything that had happened since she left Pear Blossom Creek.

"He's dead," Mrs. Heath exclaimed softly. "I can scarcely believe it. Do you know what this means? It means I don't have to be afraid anymore. I can sit outside at night and watch the fireflies. Bless you, child!"

Time passed. Days turned to weeks. Christmas came and Vicki went to visit her mother and her sister for a few days, but she was glad to get back home, glad to get back to work.

She accepted a date with Arnie for New Year's Eve and they went to a party at Bobbie Sue's house. She tried to have a good time. She danced with Arnie and laughed at his jokes; she even let him take her outside, where they stood in the shadows and necked like a couple of teenagers, but her heart wasn't in it. His kisses, while pleasant, didn't make her heart pound or send her blood racing.

With a sigh, he let her go. "I keep hoping I can light

some sparks between us," he said glumly. "But I guess the fire's just on my side."

"I'm sorry, Arnie, really I am, but . . ."

"It's that guy, isn't it? That stranger that was hanging around for a while?"

She nodded, afraid to mention Antonio's name for fear she would burst into tears.

"Well, you can't blame a guy for tryin' one more time," Arnie said with a wistful smile. "But if you've got it bad for the guy, why didn't you let him know?"

"I did, but we had a few problems we couldn't work out."

"I'm sorry, Vicki. If there's anything I can do to help . . . ?"

"Thanks, Arnie."

The blaring of horns and a few distant gunshots announced the arrival of the new year.

Arnie held out his arms and waited, letting the decision be hers. She hesitated only a moment, then moved into his embrace and let him kiss her. There were no bells, no skyrockets. It was just a friendly kiss. A few minutes later, she pleaded a headache and asked Arnie to take her home.

After getting ready for bed and making sure all the doors and windows were locked, she sat in front of her bedroom window and stared into the darkness, wondering where Antonio was. Had he spent the evening at the castle with Lady Kathryn? Or had he spent it with another woman? Had he kissed her at midnight and wished her a happy new year?

She let the tears come then because it was too painful to hold them back any longer. Later, lying in bed feeling sorry for herself, she resolved to put Antonio Battista out of her mind once and for all.

And it worked, too, until she woke up the next morning.

Trying to forget Antonio was like trying to give up chocolate. No matter how good her intentions were, sooner or later she had to give in. The longest she had ever gone without chocolate was a day and a half. The longest she managed to go without thinking of Antonio was an hour and a half, while she took a nap. And then, even though she wasn't consciously thinking of him, he was there, in her dreams, his dark eyes filled with a yearning that matched her own. In her dreams, she could be with him. Never before had she had dreams that were so realistic. She could taste him and touch him, hear his voice, inhale his heady masculine scent. He beckoned to her and she obeyed, surrendering her body to his touch, fulfilling his every desire as he fulfilled hers. She went to bed earlier each night, eager to be in the arms of her phantom lover, to hear his voice whispering that he loved her.

It was pathetic, she thought as she went to bed that night, that her dreams were happier and more fulfilling than her current reality. But if she couldn't have Antonio in the flesh, she would settle for whatever she could get.

Antonio lay on his back in the bed she had slept in, her pillow beneath his head. Her scent filled his nostrils; her image was constantly in his mind. Try as he might, there was no escaping her.

Soon after he had returned to the castle, he had gone in search of female companionship. The girl, Steffie, had been about Victoria's age, but that was where the similarity ended. Steffie had lived a hard life. The knowledge was there, in her eyes, in the harsh lines around her eyes and mouth, in her cynical expression when she told him what it would cost him to have her spend the night.

He had taken her to an expensive hotel, fully intending to bed her and hopefully ease his ache for Victoria. But nothing had happened. He had looked at her and felt nothing but disgust, not for her, but for himself. He had slipped her an extra fifty, told her to stay and enjoy the room, and left her there.

Now, he closed his eyes, courting sleep. He was a vampire, a creature who was alive only during the hours of darkness, yet these nights he sought sleep at the time when he was usually the most active. Sleep. He stalked it relentlessly, needing it as he needed blood to survive. In sleep, he could walk in her dreams. He could hold her and love her as he so longed to do. In her dreams, she did not resist him. In dreams, she was his, only his, eager for his touch, for his kisses. In sleep, her inhibitions were few and easily overcome. It was wrong, and he knew it, but he could no more resist invading her dreams than he could resist the need to quench his unholy thirst. He had let her go. Surely, he deserved some kind of reward for such an unselfish act. If he could not have her in the flesh, he would settle for whatever he could get.

February came, and with it, a flurry of activity. There was a wedding shower for Bobbie Sue and wedding rehearsals and suddenly it was Valentine's Day. Vicki had been surprised to learn that Bobbie Sue and Duncan had decided to be married at night so Ramsey and his wife could attend. But maybe it wasn't so surprising at that. After all, Duncan and Ramsey had been best friends for years before Ramsey was turned.

Vicki cried as she watched Bobbie Sue and Tom kiss after they had exchanged their vows. She wept because she was truly happy for her best friend. She wept because she was green with envy for the happiness she saw in Bobbie Sue's eyes. She wept because she missed Antonio. Her heart ached for him, constantly yearning for something she could never have. She knew he had left her because he thought it was the right thing to do, because he didn't want to deprive her of the chance to live a normal life, have children and grandchildren. But what good was a normal life if she couldn't share it with the man she loved?

After the wedding, she met Edward Ramsey's wife. Kelly Ramsey was lovely. Tall and slender, she had long, wavy black hair and brown eyes. Vicki also met Grigori Chiavari and his wife, Marisa. She wondered what the other guests would think if they knew there were vampires in their midst.

Later, standing quietly beside Bobbie Sue while Duncan and his vampire friends reminisced, Vicki studied the vampires. If she hadn't known differently, she would never have guessed that Duncan's friends were vampires and yet . . . Vicki studied Edward and Kelly and Grigori and Marisa. There was something about them, something elusive that they shared with Antonio. After a time, she realized it was the allure of the vampire, that innate charisma that allowed the Undead to seduce their prey so easily.

Grigori Chiavari reminded her a great deal of Antonio. They were both handsome and charming, with smiles that few women could resist. They had the same rugged athletic build, the same long black hair, though Antonio's eyes were dark blue and Grigori's were black.

Marisa Chiavari was petite, with shoulder-length dark brown hair and green eyes. She and Grigori looked good together, she small and feminine, he the epitome of male perfection. Grigori never missed a chance to touch his wife. It was obvious that he adored her, as she adored him.

Jealousy streaked through Vicki when she saw the way Grigori and Marisa looked at each other.

Only when like marries like. The words repeated themselves in Vicki's mind as the night wore on.

Grigori had brought Marisa across.

Ramsey had brought Kelly across.

Vicki frowned. Why couldn't Antonio bring her across? Deep inside, hadn't she always known that was the only answer? Why hadn't Antonio suggested it? Why hadn't she?

Because, like it or not, a small part of her was repulsed by the mere idea of becoming what he was.

It was a truth she didn't want to acknowledge, but the truth nevertheless.

She studied the vampire couples during the rest of the evening, wondering if it would be rude to take Kelly and Marisa aside and ask them the hundreds of questions running through her mind. Did they miss being mortal? Were they ever sorry they had accepted the Dark Gift? Would they do it again? Did they ever miss the daylight world? Did they miss eating and drinking, walks in the park, bright summer days, watching the beauty of a sunset, the promise of a sunrise? Did they regret giving up the chance to have children? If given the chance, would they return to mortality?

On the outside, Kelly and Marisa seemed perfectly happy with their vampire state and hopelessly in love with their husbands.

Vicki blew out a sigh. Did she love Antonio enough to take the step Marisa and Kelly had taken to be with the men they loved?

It was a thought that preyed on Vicki's mind long after the reception was over.

Did she want to be a vampire? Did she want to give up the sun and drink blood to survive? Did she want to give up all hope of having a family?

Did she want to spend the rest of her life without Antonio?

No!

Day after day, she weighed the pros and cons. And every night when she lay in bed, alone and lonely, she asked herself if she was making the right decision, a decision that, once made, could not be unmade. It wasn't like a bad haircut that would eventually grow out. It wasn't like picking out the wrong shade of lipstick or the wrong pair of shoes. This was a life-altering event. If she wasn't happy with the fit, she couldn't take it back.

In the eight days it took her to make up her mind, Vicki bought a disposable camera and had Bobbie Sue take her picture from every possible angle so that she wouldn't forget what she looked like when looking in a mirror was no longer possible. She had her eyebrows tattooed so that she would never have to mess with applying eyebrow pencil again. She indulged her passion for chocolate. She had always tanned quickly and she spent hours sunbathing in the nude until she was a nice golden shade of brown, all over. She got up early to watch the sun rise. She stopped in at the Curl and Dye for a trim and got a manicure and a pedicure while she was at it. She went to lunch with Bobbie Sue a couple of times, called her mother and her sister and told them she was going on a long vacation and not to worry if they didn't hear from her for a while.

She spent time with Mrs. Heath. The woman was amazing, Vicki thought. Now that she was no longer afraid to leave the house after dark, Mrs. Heath had become quite a gadabout. She played bingo at the church on Monday night, went to the monthly midnight sidewalk sales and the late movie, and sat out in her garden in the evening.

After eight days and nights of "should I or shouldn't I," Vickie called Gus and quit her job. She withdrew her savings from the bank. She called the utility companies and turned off the gas, water, electricity, and the phone. She didn't tell Bobbie Sue where she was going for fear that her friend might talk her out of it.

She closed up her house and then, without a backward glance, she hopped into her car and went in search of her vampire.

Chapter 38

Antonio prowled the empty rooms and lonely halls of the castle like a caged beast. He had done what was best for Victoria, that was the important thing. No matter that he felt as though his heart had been torn from his chest, or that he had given up his best reason for existing. He loved her with his whole being and because he loved her, he had let her go. In time, he would forget her.

He laughed harshly, humorlessly. Time. If there was one thing he had in abundance, it was time. And never had it passed so slowly. Every day without Victoria seemed like an eternity. He took no pleasure in rising, or in feeding. He had growled at Lady Kathryn so often she had gone into hiding, leaving him more alone than ever.

Alone and in darkness. Strange, he thought, he had lived for centuries cloaked in the shadows of the night, but he had never realized how dark his life was until the light of Victoria's love was no longer there to illuminate his heart and soul.

Victoria. Her scent filled every room in the castle. Her memory filled his every waking thought. He started to go after her a hundred times, but he always turned back. No matter how much he regretted letting her go, it was for the best.

He swore under his breath. Whose best? Not his! Never his.

Did she ever think of him?

Had she found someone else?

He slammed his fist against the wall. Pain vibrated up his arm. Blood oozed from his knuckles. He hit the wall again and again, breaking through paint, plaster and mortar.

He drew his arm back, ready to strike again, when he heard a knock at the front door.

Frowning, he glanced over his shoulder. Who would be coming to call at this hour of the night? He laughed humorlessly. Who would be coming to call on him at any hour?

He wrenched the door open, his angry words dying in his throat when he saw her standing there. He shook his head, unable to believe his eyes. He had dreamed of her, thought of her, yearned for her for so long, he was sure his lonely heart had conjured her image. An indrawn breath carried her scent to him.

Still unconvinced, he stroked her cheek. Soft feminine flesh, warm with life.

"Victoria?" She wore a pair of jeans that clung to her like a second skin, a black knit sweater, and a pair of fur-lined boots. Her hair fell over her shoulders in shimmering chestnut waves. In six hundred and twelve years, he had never seen anything more beautiful.

"Hello, Antonio."

"What are you doing here?" He drank in the sight of

her. What difference did it make why she was here? She was here, and that was all that mattered. He thanked a generous Fate for allowing him to see her one more time.

"Are you going to invite me in?"

He stepped back. "You need no invitation. You will always be welcome in my home."

She crossed the threshold, and he followed her into the parlor. His hungry gaze moved over her, every fiber of his being yearning toward her. "Is something wrong?"

She turned to face him. "That depends on you."

He shook his head. "I do not understand."

"Do you love me, Antonio?"

"You know that I do."

"Then you know that I love you, too."

"We have been through this before."

"I want to spend the rest of my life with you," she said, moving toward him.

He thought of a hundred reasons why he should send her away, but when he tried to put them into words, they no longer made sense.

"Will you share your life with me, Antonio?"

Unable to deny the urgings of his own heart any longer, he nodded. Right or wrong, he wanted her, all of her, for however long she was willing to put up with him and his unnatural lifestyle.

"I asked Ramsey to bring me across."

Her words slammed into him with the force of a stake through the heart. He stared at her, too stunned to speak. Opening his senses, he searched for some hint of supernatural power. To his relief, he found none.

Vicki shrugged. "He wouldn't do it."

"Why?" he asked incredulously. "Why on earth would you ask him to do such a thing?"

She looked at him as if he weren't too bright. "Because I want to be what you are, of course. Because it's the only way we can ever truly be together."

"He was right to refuse you," Antonio said. "A decision like that—"

"He said you should do it."

Antonio stared at her, not knowing whether to laugh or cry.

"Will you? Or will I have to search the world for a vampire who will bring me across?"

"You are determined to do this thing?"

"Yes. Very."

"My warrior woman." He drew her into his arms. "You must be sure, sweeting. Once it is done, it cannot be undone."

"I'm sure. I've thought about it for weeks and weeks." She looked up at him, frowning. "You do know how to do it, don't you?"

"Yes, I know how, though I have never made another vampire."

"Good."

"There is no hurry. When you are ready, let me know."

"I'm ready now. I want to share your life, all of it. I don't want to waste a minute."

"You will not age. Are you sure this is the age you wish to be from now on?"

She thought about that. She was twenty-two, old enough to know what she wanted. She could wait a year or two or five and still be young, but what if something happened to her while she was waiting? She was in good health now, but could get deathly ill or hit by a truck or, heaven forbid, become the target of another madman with a penchant for redheads.

"I'm sure."

He swept her into his arms and carried her up the stairs to the bedroom. At his nod, a fire sprang to life in the hearth.

Gently, he placed her on the bed, then sat down beside her and drew her into his arms.

She looked up at him, her eyes wide. "Are you going to bite me now?"

"Yes, but there is more to it than that."

"Will it hurt?" she asked tremulously.

"No," he said, and then he explained how it was done, that he would take her blood and then she would take his. Her earthly body would die and when she awoke, she would be as he was, a creature of the night.

"Are you still sure this is what you want?" he asked.

"Yes."

"You must remove your crucifix."

Vicki wrapped her hand around the thick silver cross. She had worn it for almost as long as she could remember. How could she take it off?

He read the pain and confusion in her eyes. And waited.

"Will I still feel the same about everything when I'm a vampire?"

"That is up to you. You need not surrender your faith or your beliefs. There are priests and rabbis among the Undead. They are men who did not ask for the Dark Gift, but who have adjusted to it and manage to continue to live their religion, though slightly modified. Becoming a vampire is like mortal death. Whatever a man is in this life is what he takes with him into the next world. The same is true of becoming a vampire. A man who was a liar when he was alive will be a liar when he is turned, just as an honest man will remain an honest man when he becomes a vampire."

She thought that over for a moment and then she removed the cross and chain and wrapped it in a hanky she pulled from the pocket of her jeans. She held it tightly for a moment and then placed it in the back of the bottom dresser drawer. When she closed the drawer, she knew she had also closed a door on one chapter of her life. Tonight, a new chapter would begin.

She looked deep into Antonio's eyes, dark blue eyes filled with love and hope, and then she sat down beside him and kissed him.

With a low groan, he tightened his arms around her. He fell back on the bed, carrying her with him, his mouth working its familiar magic, carrying her to places she had never been before, making her forget everything but her need for this man in her life.

She felt the brush of his fangs against her neck, a sudden rush of heat followed by waves of intense pleasure. She knew a moment of fear as all the strength seemed to leave her body. The world grew dark, and she was falling, falling, her hold on life growing weaker as she fell into the darkness.

And then she heard Antonio's voice calling her back, telling her that he loved her, that she must fight to live. Must drink.

He pressed something warm to her mouth and she drank, drank his life and his memories.

"Sleep now, my sweetest one." His hand stroked her brow. "When you awake tomorrow, I will show you the world as you have never seen it before. Sleep . . ."

Filled with an aching tenderness, Antonio gazed at the woman in his arms. He had not prayed since he was turned, but he prayed now, prayed fervently that he had not made a terrible mistake, that she would not hate him for doing what she had asked.

He wiped the blood from her mouth. Though he had never slept in this bed, he knew Victoria would not want to awake in a coffin; indeed, he had a feeling he would be taking his rest in a bed from now on.

After removing her shoes, he tucked her under the covers, fully clothed, and then he went through the castle, making certain all the wards were in place. They would sleep here tonight; tomorrow, he would move the bed to a more secure location. But tonight . . . Tonight, for the first time in his preternatural life, he would take his rest beside a woman he loved.

Tonight, he thought as he stretched out beside her. Tonight, and for all his tomorrows.

She didn't want to wake up. She felt warm and secure and at peace for the first time in her life. Sighing, she turned onto her side, remembering the dream she'd had the night before. It was very like the dreams she'd had before, the ones with the golden goblet, only this time she had been the one to drink the contents, and in doing so, she had become a vampire. One of the Undead. A creature of the night.

Eyes still closed, she frowned. Had it been a dream? It had seemed so real. Fully awake now, she realized that she was vividly aware of the texture and smell of the cotton pillowcase beneath her cheek. She knew the sun had set. She knew it was raining.

She knew she wasn't alone in the bed.

"Good evening, my sweet one."

"Antonio." She rolled over and he was there. Propped up on one elbow, he was watching her, his expression oddly vulnerable. "What happened?"

"You do not remember?"

"No . . ." She looked past Antonio, only then realizing that not only could she see him clearly, but she could also see everything else in the room with perfect clarity even though the room was dark. "You did it, didn't you? You made me a . . ." She stared at him. "A vampire."

He nodded, his expression closed to her. "Do you hate me now?"

"Hate you?" Sitting up, she looked at her hands, her arms. She threw back the covers and wiggled her toes. "I don't feel any different, and yet . . ."

Everything was different. She felt as if she had been reborn, as if she could run forever and never get tired. As if she could fly to the moon and back again.

She looked back at Antonio. He was sitting up now, and she noticed he wasn't wearing a shirt, only a pair of black trousers. She couldn't stop looking at him. Had his lips always been that sensual, his shoulders so broad, his arms so muscular? He looked incredibly sexy, with his sleep-tousled hair and deep blue eyes, eyes that watched her, unblinking, waiting for her to answer his question. Hate him? Not if she lived a thousand years, she thought. And she just might!

"Victoria?"

She heard the rough edge of worry in his voice, saw it in the taut set of his shoulders.

"Talk to me," he said. "Tell me what you are feeling, what you are thinking. Have I made a mistake? Have you changed your mind?"

"That depends."

"On what?"

"Are you going to marry me, Mr. Battista? I mean, I'm dying to . . ." She laughed softly. "Wrong choice of words. I mean I'm really anxious for us to make love, but I promised my mother I'd wait until I got married, and I'd hate to break a promise to my mother. So," she asked breathlessly, "are you going to marry me?"

He laughed then. It came rumbling up from deep

within him, a sound filled with joy and relief and love as he bounded off the bed, pulled her into his arms, and twirled her around the room.

"I will marry you, Victoria Lynn Cavendish, any night you wish."

Chapter 39

Though he had said he would marry her any night she wished, Antonio decided plans for the wedding would have to wait until Victoria grew more accustomed to her new way of life. Because he didn't want her to experience any discomfort, particularly that first night, he took her hunting before her preternatural hunger grew unbearable. If he had his way, she would never know pain or hunger or deprivation of any kind. She had willingly given up her life to be with him, and he intended to make sure that she would never have cause to regret it.

Vicki had expected to be reluctant to hunt for prey, repulsed by the act of taking blood from another, but such was not the case. Antonio told her how to summon prey, and she felt a surge of pride as she called a young man to her and took him into her arms. She soothed his fears, was careful not to hurt him.

Feeding seemed like the most natural thing in the world. Perhaps because Antonio had insisted she feed before the hunger had time to become painful, she wasn't tempted to take too much. She wiped her memory from the young man's mind and sent him on his way, then looked up at Antonio, smiling.

He smiled back. What an amazing man he was. He had taught her so many things, helped her find her way in her new life. And he loved her, without question or doubt. It was a wondrous thing indeed to be loved by Antonio. She shared every part of his life, knew him in ways she would never know anyone else.

"My warrior woman," he said proudly. "I think you were born to be a vampire. I have never seen anyone take to it so easily, or so readily."

She basked in his praise, in the love in his eyes, the beauty of the night that surrounded them. Never before had she noticed how many stars there were in the sky, or heard the myriad sounds of the night that ordinary mortals never heard—the beating of a moth's wings, the way the earth spoke to the trees, the sound of dew sliding down a blade of grass.

Hand in hand, she walked beside Antonio as they turned and headed for home. They could have returned to the castle with a thought, but Vicki liked to walk. She reveled in her newfound strength. Energy flowed through her, making her feel once again as if she could soar through the heavens or run for miles and miles.

"It is wonderful, is it not?" Antonio asked, smiling down at her.

"Yes!" Letting go of his hand, she twirled round and round in a circle, then threw back her head and laughed. "No wonder you love being what you are."

He caught her in his arms and whirled her around. "It is you I love, my sweet one, now more than ever."

"I want to go everywhere! See everything! Can we?"

"Whatever you wish."

"Can we afford it? I only have a few hundred dollars to my name."

"I have more than enough."

"Handsome *and* rich," she said with a grin. "Who could ask for more?"

They walked in silence for a moment, and then she frowned. "Where will we get married?"

"Anywhere you wish."

"Can we be married in a church?"

"If you like."

"I thought vampires couldn't go inside churches."

"Some are more difficult to enter than others."

She thought of her church in Pear Blossom Creek, the crosses, the holy water, the priest. She was sure Antonio would not be comfortable there. But she still wanted to be married in a church.

She frowned, thinking they should have gotten married before Antonio brought her across. She couldn't invite her mother now, or any of her friends. How could she explain it when she and Antonio didn't eat any of the wedding cake, or drink any of the champagne when people toasted them and wished them well? Her mother would expect to be there to help her dress. How could she explain her lack of a reflection in the mirror or excuse her absence during the day?

Well, there was no help for it. She would simply tell her mother that she and Antonio had eloped, and they would be married in a small nondenominational church. Perhaps they could ask Ramsey and Kelly to stand up with them . . . And what about Bobbie Sue? How could she get married without her best friend at her side?

In a rush, she told Antonio of all her concerns.

"Do not worry," he said, drawing her into his arms. "It will all work out."

And it did.

Vicki found a small church with a minister who was willing to marry them after dark. There would be no need to explain to Bobbie Sue or Duncan why the wedding had to be at night. Both knew that Antonio was one of the Undead. Vicki's only concern was finding a way to tell her best friend that she, too, was now a vampire.

The next night, she drove into town and called Bobbie Sue.

"Girl, where are you?" Bobbie Sue exclaimed. "I can't believe you left town and didn't say a word."

"I'm sorry. I'm with Antonio."

"Well, I guessed that! But you might have told me you were leaving," Bobbie Sue said with an exaggerated sigh of exasperation.

"I know. I should have let you know, but I was afraid you'd try and talk me out of going."

"Well, you're right about that. Call me crazy, but I just don't think running around with a vampire is a good idea. When are you coming home?"

"I am home."

"You are? When did you get back?"

"I mean Antonio's home."

"I see." Disapproval was evident in those two brief words.

"It's not like that. We're getting married."

"Married! Oh, Vicki, do you think that's wise?"

"Please be happy for me, Bobbie. You're the only one I can share this with."

"But, hon, he's . . . I mean, well, I just don't see how you can make it work unless . . ."

"Unless what?"

"Never mind," Bobbie Sue said quickly. "The idea is too awful."

"I'm sorry you feel that way."

There was a long silence on the other end of the phone. Vicki could almost see the wheels turning inside her friend's head.

"Bobbie?"

"You're not thinking of letting him . . . Oh, geez, Vicki, tell me you're not thinking of becoming what he is!"

"No, I'm not thinking about it."

"Oh, thank goodness, I was afraid you were going to—"

"I already did it."

Another long silence, this one filled with disbelief and disapproval. Then, "You mean that now you're a— Oh, Vickie, I don't know what to say."

"Say you'll be my matron of honor."

"You know I will, hon, but . . ."

Vicki's hand tightened around the receiver. "But what?"

"Well, how are we going to shop for dresses with you there and me here?"

"We aren't. Just buy something you love that you can wear again. It's going to be very informal."

"Oh, well, all right. When's the big day . . . er, night?"

"We haven't set a date yet. I'll let you know."

Bobbie Sue giggled. "Imagine, both of us getting married so close together. Who'd have thought? Duncan wants to have children right away. He says he's waited so long to get married, he doesn't want to wait to have kids."

"That's wonderful," Vicki said, forcing a smile into her voice. There would be no children for her and Antonio. It was her only regret.

"What's your mother going to say when she finds out you're marrying a vampire?"

"Are you kidding? I'm not going to tell her, or Karen, either."

"Won't they think it's a little odd that you're getting married at night and the bride and groom don't eat or drink anything at the reception?"

"They won't be there. I'm going to call and tell Karen and my mom that we're eloping."

"Oh, well, that's a good idea, I guess. It'll sure save a lot of explanations." Another pause. "Can I ask you something? You don't have to answer if you don't want to."

"You want to know what it's like."

"Yes."

"It's wonderful, Bobbie, you can't imagine what it's like. Everything is . . . How can I explain it? It's like living your whole life in black and white and then tumbling over the rainbow to the land of Oz where everything is in glorious Technicolor."

"If you say so," Bobbie Sue muttered dubiously. "Did he make you drink his blood?"

"No, he didn't make me."

"But you did?"

Vicki sighed. She could hear the revulsion in Bobbie Sue's voice. Not that she could blame her. Not too long ago, she had felt the same way.

"Oh, Vicki . . . " Bobbie Sue wailed.

"Bobbie, you love Duncan. Wouldn't you do anything you had to do to be with him?"

"Well, sure, but come on, Vickie, turning into a vampire for the man you love isn't like giving up smoking because he has to, or cooking low-fat foods cause he's on a diet. I mean, this is forever."

"Edward Ramsey is going to walk me down the aisle," Vicki said, changing the subject. "Antonio wants to know if Duncan will be his best man."

Bobbie Sue laughed at that, laughed until she cried.

Vicki couldn't blame her, not really. It was going to be an odd assemblage—a vampire bride and groom, a vampire hunter turned vampire giving the bride away, a vampire hunter standing up with the groom, vampires for guests. Bobbie Sue, Tom, and the minister would be the only mortals present.

Vicki was certain there would never be another wedding quite like it.

"I'll tell Tom," Bobbie Sue said, sniffing back her tears. "Have you bought a dress yet?"

"I ordered one through a mail-order catalog. Wait until you see it. I sure hope it fits."

"Why didn't you go to a bridal shop and . . . Oh, never mind. Mirrors. I forgot."

"Yeah," Vicki said. "I'm thinking we should have gotten married before, well, you know."

"Why didn't you?"

"I didn't want to wait, and to tell you the truth, I didn't think of it at the time."

"You really have the hots for him, don't you? Where are the two of you going to live?"

"I don't know yet. He's got houses everywhere."

"Must be nice. I guess Duncan and I will be moving soon. He's going to work for that vampire school in Los Angeles, remember the one I told you about? Can you imagine me in L.A.?"

"Maybe I can talk Antonio into buying a house out there. We could be neighbors."

"I'd like that. Listen, I've got to go. I'm gonna be late for work."

"All right. Tell Gus and everyone hello for me. I'll let you know the date and time of the wedding as soon as I know."

"Okay. Bye, hon."

"Bye."

Vicki was feeling more than a little depressed when she returned to the castle. She sat in the car for a few minutes, thinking about her conversation with Bobbie, rehearsing what she would say to her mother.

Antonio met her at the door. One look at her face and he knew something was wrong.

Vicki blew out a sigh when he asked her what it was. "Nothing, really. Well, it's Bobbie Sue. I told her I was a vampire now . . ."

"And she does not approve?"

"No, she thinks it's awful." Blinking back her tears, she looked up at Antonio. "She's my best friend. I wanted her to understand."

He wiped her tears away with his fingertips. "Did you really expect her to approve?"

"No, I guess not, but . . . How have you stood it for so long?"

"How would you feel if the situation were reversed and Bobbie Sue told you she was a vampire?"

Vicki grinned at him through her tears. "I would have felt just like Bobbie Sue. Horrified and betrayed. Do you think she'll still be my friend, once she gets over the shock? I mean, she said she'd stand up with me at the wedding, but what if she decides she doesn't want to be around me anymore after that? What if she looks at me differently? I don't think I could stand that."

"If she is truly your friend, it will not make a difference."

Resting her head on his chest, Vicki wrapped her arms around him. "I love you."

"As I love you." He kissed the top of her head. "For now and always."

* * *

At last, the date was set and the night of the wedding was upon them. Vicki arrived at the church in her wedding dress, her one regret being that she couldn't see how she looked. And then she brightened. So, she wouldn't have any wedding pictures, but that didn't mean she and Antonio couldn't have their portrait painted. An old-fashioned wedding portrait, Vicki thought, like the one of her great-grandparents, with her sitting in a white wicker chair and Antonio standing behind her looking properly solemn, one hand resting on her shoulder. The thought cheered her immensely. She might even have a second one painted for her mother.

"You look lovely," Bobbie Sue said, coming forward to give her a hug.

"Do I?"

Bobbie Sue nodded. She wore a tea-length dark blue silk dress with a square neckline and long sleeves, and carried a bouquet of wildflowers. "Are you nervous?"

"Not a bit." Vicki picked up her own bouquet. It was made of baby's breath and blood-red roses. She knew brides usually carried white flowers, but red seemed more fitting for this occasion. Besides, red roses had always been her favorite.

"It's time," Edward said, joining them. "Are you ready?"

Vicki nodded and Edward offered her his arm. "Here we go, then."

The pianist began playing. A moment later, Bobbie Sue was walking down the aisle toward the altar.

Vicki took a deep breath. Bobbie Sue had said she looked lovely, but she didn't truly believe it until she walked down the aisle on Edward Ramsey's arm and saw the way Antonio's eyes lit up when he saw her. In that instant, Antonio became her mirror and she knew that she looked beautiful, would always look beautiful in his eyes.

The church was alight with dozens and dozens of tall white tapers. Ferns and white daisies decorated the altar.

Duncan had agreed to act as Antonio's best man and he looked quite handsome in his tux. Kelly Ramsey, Marisa, and Grigori were their only guests.

Vicki listened intently to the words the minister spoke, smiling faintly when he got to the part where he pronounced them man and wife "so long as you both shall live." Barring unforeseen accidents, death would never part them.

The minister smiled benignly, then nodded at Antonio. "You may kiss your bride."

Vicki looked into Antonio's eyes as he drew her into his arms. "I shall love you forever and beyond," he murmured, and then he lowered his head and claimed his first kiss as her husband.

And Vicki knew, in the deepest parts of her heart and soul and mind, that she had made the right decision. The only decision.

Bobbie Sue hugged Vicki. "I wish you all the happiness in the world," she whispered. "And no matter what happens, you'll always be my best friend."

Vicki nodded, her eyes filling with quick, happy tears.

Marisa took Vicki's hands in hers and gave them a squeeze. "You look radiant," she said. "I hope you'll be as happy with Antonio as I am with Grigori."

"Thank you."

"If you ever have any questions about your new lifestyle that you can't ask Antonio," Marisa said with a wink, "just call me."

"I will."

"That goes for me, too," Kelly said, giving Vicki a hug. "We women have to stick together."

Grigori came forward to wish Vicki well, shook hands with Antonio, and then Grigori and Marisa took their leave.

Duncan kissed her cheek, then whispered, "Are you sure about all this?"

"A little late to be asking that question, don't you think?" Vickie asked with a smile. "But yes, I'm sure."

Duncan nodded. First Marisa, then Edward and Kelly, and now Vicki had joined the ranks of the Undead. He grunted softly. Maybe he should look into it. The thought that he was even considering it brought him up short. Still, they all looked very happy together. He looked at Bobbie Sue. Maybe they should talk about it one of these days.

"Come, wife," Antonio said, taking her by the hand. "The hour grows late."

They bade good-bye to Duncan and Bobbie Sue and then Antonio whisked them back to the castle where Lady Kathryn was waiting for them.

She beamed as they entered the parlor. "I knew it!" she said, flitting around the room. "I knew you were perfect for him the first time I saw you. And now we can all be together."

"We can be together later," Antonio said, sweeping Vicki into his arms. "Tonight, my bride and I wish to be alone."

"Of course you do." Still beaming with pleasure, Lady Kathryn sailed from the room, the sound of her merry laughter trailing behind her.

Vicki locked her arms around her husband's neck. "Well," she said impishly. "Here we are, all alone. Just you and me. So . . . " She kissed his cheek. "What would you like to do now?"

Carrying her up the stairs, he told her, in whispered words that made her blush, just what he wanted to do, and how he wanted to do it.

Inside the bedroom, he put her down, letting her body slide ever so slowly down the length of his until she was standing on her own two feet.

"Oh, Antonio, look!"

Reluctantly drawing his attention from his bride's numerous charms, he glanced around the room. White candles lit the room with a warm golden glow. The air was fragrant with the scent of hundreds of flower petals that were spread on the bedspread and over the floor.

"It looks like Lady Kathryn was busy in our absence," he remarked.

"She's a dear old soul," Vicki said. "I'm glad she's here."

"I have a feeling the two of you are going to conspire against me every chance you get," Antonio remarked with mock despair.

"Well, maybe once in a while," she said brightly, "but . . ."

"Victoria."

She looked up at him, everything else forgotten as he whispered her name.

"I never believed this day would come," he said. "I never believed you would truly be mine."

"Oh, Antonio, I think I've always been yours." She cupped his face in her hands and kissed him tenderly. "Yours," she murmured. "Now and always. And don't you forget it!" she warned with a saucy grin. "If I ever catch you even *looking* at another woman . . ."

He laughed as he pulled her back into his arms. "It will never happen, my sweet."

"Well, it better not."

Antonio shook his head in disbelief. "We have not yet been married for an hour and already you are jealous of a woman who does not exist."

"You're right, I'm just being silly."

His hands skimmed over her body, lightly, possessively. Reaching around behind her, he began to unfasten the back of her gown, inch by slow inch. She shivered with anticipation when his fingers brushed her skin. With a whisper of silk against silk, her dress slid over her hips to pool around her ankles, leaving her standing there clad in nothing but her underwear.

Antonio whistled softly. She wore a white bra and bikini panties that were little more than wisps of lace, white silk stockings, white satin heels, and nothing more. She was beyond beautiful, her body supple and slender with delectable curves and valleys he was eager to explore. Her skin was smooth and unblemished, begging his touch.

She blushed under his heated gaze and then, surprising him once again, she began to undress him, her fingers trembling as she removed his coat and shirt, unfastened his belt and his zipper. He stepped out of his trousers. She pulled his shorts down and he kicked them aside.

Vicki waggled her eyebrows at him. "Hubba hubba."

"Hubba hubba?" He shook his head in wry amusement.

"You're very sexy, you know." He should have looked silly standing there in nothing but a pair of black leather boots and an erection. But he didn't. He looked altogether gorgeous.

"Indeed?" Sitting on the edge of the bed, he pulled off his boots and socks.

Feeling suddenly brazen, Vicki kicked off her high heels, then removed her bra and panties and flung them aside. She peeled her stockings off slowly, one at a time, and tossed them aside as well. And then, hips swaying provocatively, she moved toward Antonio, coming to rest in the vee between his thighs.

She leaned against him. He circled her waist with his hands and then fell back on the bed, drawing her with him, so that they lay together, heart to heart and heat to heat.

Knowing that it was his bride's first time, Antonio tried to be gentle, tried not to rush her, but she was as ardent as he, her hands exploring his body as eagerly as his hands explored hers, learning each line and curve, the texture of flesh and form, the way the softness of her body complemented the roughness of his.

With a low groan, he rolled over until she lay beneath him, her eyes glowing with hunger and desire. He kissed her deeply, savoring the taste of her, the silky texture of her lips. His tongue slid across her lower lip and when she opened for him, his tongue dueled with hers in a mating dance as old as time. Her legs tangled with his, her foot running suggestively up and down his calf while her hands moved restlessly over his back and shoulders.

Reining in his own need, he caressed her until she writhed with impatience. Only then did he possess her, his body melding with hers, two halves of one whole now forged together, two hearts beating as one.

He felt her teeth nip at his neck, moaned with pleasure as heat flowed through him. Because they had shared blood, their union was explosive, a shared moment that went beyond anything mortal lovers ever knew. He knew what she was feeling, what she wanted, what she needed at the same instant she did. He saw the wonder of it in her eyes as she shared in his pleasure. She turned her head, giving him access to her neck when she saw his fangs. When he tasted her, their joining was complete. A moment later, she shuddered beneath him, moaning with pleasure as her body convulsed. His release came seconds later.

Sated and feeling complete for the first time in centuries, he rolled onto his side, carrying Victoria with him. He wrapped one arm around her waist, holding her body to his while his other hand stroked her hair.

If he'd had any doubts about what his bride was feeling, they vanished when she looked at him, her smile that of a woman who knew she had pleased the man she loved, a woman who had been well and truly pleasured in return.

"Is it always like that?" she asked. "If it is, I'm sorry I waited so long."

Antonio laughed softly. "Believe me, my sweet, for us, it will only get better."

"Really?" She raked her nails down his broad chest. It had never occurred to her than a man could be beautiful, but he was, from head to foot and all the good places in between. She loved looking at him, touching him. Loved the way his muscles rippled at her touch. "I'm not sure I could survive anything better."

"Ah, but you will."

He rained kisses along the length of her neck, his breath hot against her skin, his touch awaking her desire. It surprised her that she could want him again so soon. She remembered reading in some magazine that it took a while for a man to be ready for lovemaking again. But as she caressed Antonio, she realized he was more than ready.

Grinning in anticipation, she wrapped her arms around him.

Later, lying exhausted in his embrace, she closed her eyes. Antonio had been right, she thought as sleep claimed her. It did get better.

Epilogue

A year later

Vicki strolled alone under a blanket of stars, her thoughts erratic. Being a vampire was far different from anything she had imagined. She had expected to miss so many things—cheeseburgers and fries and chocolate chip cookies, coffee and malts and soft drinks, taking long walks in the morning, sitting on the front porch watching the sun go down, having lunch with Bobbie Sue, eating popcorn at the movies.

But the truth was, she didn't really miss mortal food and drink. In the beginning, she had missed the sunlight, but she had quickly discovered that the moon's light was equally beautiful. She and Bobbie Sue remained the best of friends. They saw each other often, though long lunches were out of the question.

Antonio had been right, Vicki thought with a grin. She had been born to be a vampire. She loved staying up late at night. She loved the fact that she no longer had to work. Best of all, she loved Antonio, because he was willing to let her explore her new lifestyle. If she felt the need to be alone, he understood, because there were nights when he, too, needed time alone. But those times were few.

Vickie hadn't thought that she and Antonio would have any social life to speak of. All the books and movies implied that vampires were solitary creatures who did little more than drink their victims dry and sleep in coffins. And while she knew that wasn't true, she hadn't expected to have vampire friends. To her surprise, Antonio, Grigori, and Ramsey had become friends, which worked out well, because Marisa, Kelly, and Vicki had also become good friends. The six of them got together several times a week to watch movies or play cards. Sometimes the men got together to watch football while the women went to the mall to shop. At other times, they all got together to play croquet in the moonlight. That was another good thing about being a vampire, Vicki thought. Traveling long distances wasn't a problem. Even though they all lived in different parts of the country, they were able to get together whenever they wished.

Vicki had to laugh sometimes when they were all gathered together doing something as human as playing canasta. Who would have thought that vampires did anything so mundane?

She had talked Antonio into getting a telephone. It made getting in touch with the others so much easier, plus it meant they could have a computer.

Vicki had only one real regret, and that was that she and Antonio couldn't have children. She didn't know how she was ever going to accept that part, especially now, when Bobbie Sue was pregnant with twin girls. Still, Vicki was happy for Bobbie Sue and Tom and contented herself with the fact that she was going to be a godmother to Bobbie Sue's children. If she couldn't have a child of her own, Vicki thought, then being a godmother was the next best thing. She would be part of the twins' lives. She would be able to buy the girls presents on holidays and birthdays, and watch them grow.

Vicki's steps slowed when she heard Antonio coming up behind her. No mere mortal would have heard him, she thought with a smug smile.

Coming up beside her, he slipped his arm around her waist and pulled her close. "Are you tired of walking yet, my sweet?"

"Not really. It's so beautiful out here. Was there something you wanted me for?"

"Several somethings," he replied with a wicked grin. "Shall I whisper them in your ear?"

"Oh, I don't know," she said with an exaggerated sigh. "Why don't you just show me instead?"

"Even better."

Swinging her into his arms, Antonio carried her swiftly into the castle and up the stairs, his nostrils filling with the fragrant scent of her skin and her hair. He would have been able to find her in the dark, he thought, even without the benefit of his vampire senses.

He carried her into the bedroom and nudged the door closed with his heel. He undressed her slowly, marveling anew that she was his, would always be his.

He made love to her for hours, worshipping her with every touch, every breath.

As always, dawn's early light came all too soon. They showered together, then returned to bed. He hadn't slept in his coffin since Victoria was turned. Though she had taken to every other aspect of vampire life with enthusiasm, she had refused to sleep in a coffin of her own, or share his. But he didn't mind. Sleeping beside her in bed was infinitely better. Her beloved face was the last thing he saw before the Dark Sleep carried him into oblivion, the first thing he saw when he awoke. And should they wish to make love on waking, they were already in bed. What man could ask for more?

Slipping his arm around her, Antonio drew Victoria close to his side. "Rest well," he murmured, brushing a kiss over her cheek.

"As always, with you beside me."

Vicki snuggled against him, her head resting on his shoulder, her arm draped across his waist.

With a sigh of utter contentment, Victoria Lynn Battista closed her eyes.

The future stretched before her, endless nights of discovery to be shared before sunrise with the man she adored.